The
Tax Inspector

The
Tax Inspector

PETER CAREY

ALFRED A. KNOPF   NEW YORK

1992

THIS IS A BORZOI BOOK
PUBLISHED BY ALFRED A. KNOPF, INC.

Copyright © 1991 by Peter Carey

Originally published in Great Britain by Faber and
Faber Ltd., London, in 1991.

Grateful acknowledgement is made to Warner/
Chappell Music, Inc., for permission to reprint an
excerpt from 'Beds Are Burning' by Robert Hirst,
James Moginie, and Peter Garrett. Copyright © 1987
by Sprint Music Pty. Ltd. All rights reserved.
Used by permission.

Library of Congress Cataloging in Publication Data

Carey, Peter.
The tax inspector / Peter Carey. — 1st American ed.
p.   cm.
ISBN 0-679-40434-1
I. Title.
PR9619.3. C36T39   1991
823—dc20   91-52727
                                                  CIP

Manufactured in the United States of America
First American Trade Edition

A signed first edition of this book
has been privately printed by The Franklin Library

For Alison

Monday

1

In the morning Cathy McPherson put three soft-boiled eggs outside Benny Catchprice's door and in the afternoon she fired him from the Spare Parts Department. That's who she was – his father's sister. They were both the same – big ones for kissing and cuddling, but you could not predict them. You could not rely on them for anything important. They had great soft lips and they had a family smell, like almost-rancid butter which came from deep in their skin, from the thick shafts of their wiry hair; they smelt of this, from within them, but also of things they had touched or swallowed – motor oil, radiator hoses, Lifesavers, different sorts of alcohol – beer, Benedictine, altar wine on Sundays. She was the one who stroked his ear with her small guitar-calloused fingers and whispered, 'I love you little Ben-Ben,' but she was still a Catchprice and it was not a contradiction that she fired him.

Cathy was married to Howie who had a pencil-line moustache, a ducktail, and a secret rash which stopped in a clean line at his collar and the cuffs of his shirt. He had the ducktail because he was a Rock-a-Billy throwback: Sleepy La Beef, Charlie Feathers, Mickey Gilley, all the losers of Rock 'n' Roll, they were his heroes. He had this rash because he hated Catchprice Motors but no one ever said that. Cathy and Howie sat behind the counter of the Spare Parts Department as if they were Shire engineers or pharmacists. They had a Waiting Room. They set it up with ferns and pots and pans so it smelled of damp and chemical fertilizer and rotting sawdust. In the places on the wall where any normal car business had charts of K.L.G. spark plugs and colour calendars from Turtle Wax, they had the photograph of Cathy shaking hands with Cowboy Jack Clement, the framed letter from Ernest Tubb, the photograph of the band on stage at the Tamworth Festival: Craig on bass guitar, Kevin on drums, Steve Putzel on piano, and Cathy herself out front with a bright red Fender and huge, snake-skin boots she got mail order from *Music City News*. The band was called Big Mack. If they had paid as much attention to Catchprice Motors as they paid to it, there would have been no crisis ever.

Until the Friday afternoon they fired him, Benny worked on the long bench which ran at right angles to the front counter where Cath and Howie sat like Tweedledum and Tweedledee. Behind him were the deep rows of grey metal bins, above his head was the steel mesh floor of the body panel racks. In front of him was a sweaty white brick wall and a single turquoise G.E. fan which swung back and forth but which was never pointed the right way at the right time.

He was sixteen years old. He had unwashed brown hair which curled up behind his ears and fell lankly over his left eye. He had slender arms and a collar-bone which formed a deep well between his neck and shoulder. He worked with a Marlboro in his mouth, a Walkman on his head, a Judas Priest T-shirt with vents cut out and the sleeves slashed so you could see the small shiny scar on his upper right arm. There was a blue mark around the scar like ink on blotting paper – he had tried to make a tattoo around it but the scratches got seriously infected and whatever words were written there were lost. He had a dark blurry fuzz on his sweaty lip, and bright blue cat's eyes full of things he could not tell you.

Those eyes were like gas jets in a rust-flaked pipe. They informed everything you felt about him, that he might, at any second, be ringed with heat – a peacock, something creepy.

Benny rode the length of the counter on a six-wheeled brown swivel chair, from computer to microfiche, from black phone to green phone. He slid, sashayed, did 360° turns, kicking the concrete floor with his size ten Doc Martens combat boots. He had long legs. He was fast and almost perfect. He ordered in parts ex-stock, entered the inventory for monthly delivery and daily delivery and special runs. He made phone quotations to ten different panel shops, to Steve-oh, Stumpy, Mr Fish. He was expert and familiar with them and they gave him a respect he could never get in Catchprice Motors which benefited most from his professionalism.

He hunted by phone and by computer for – to give a for instance – a Jackaroo brake calliper which General Motors at Dandenong said was a definite N/A and est. 12 weeks ex-Japan. It was hot and sweaty back there, with no air but the fan, and dust falling from the steel mesh floor above his head. It was also stressful, no one said it wasn't, and he was good at most of it, but she fired him.

He was shocked and humiliated, but she was the one doing the crying. She offered him a job in the front office – serving petrol! Serving petrol! Her chin was crumpled and her wide nose was creased. You could smell the butter in her hair and the Benedictine on her breath.

She knew what being fired meant to him. They had sat together at her kitchen table at three and four in the morning, he smoking dope, she drinking Benedictine and Coke, while her old man was snoring in the bedroom. She was the forty-five-year-old who was still planning her escape. Not him. He wanted this life. It was all he ever wanted.

But now she was saying he was 'not sufficiently involved'. He was too stunned to say anything back, not even a threat. But when she was back at the front counter, he thought he understood – she imagined he made mistakes because he listened to comedy tapes on the Walkman. She saw him laughing and thought he was not serious.

The truth was: he wore the Walkman to block out the dumb things she and Howie said. They were so loud and confident. They went on and on in some kind of croaking harmony – her bar-smoke voice and his bass mumble. They were like two old birds who had been in one shitty cage all their lives.

He liked his aunt. She was more his mate than his aunt, but her ignorance could be embarrassing. She was frightened of bankruptcy and her fear destroyed what little judgement she had. He turned up the volume on 'Derek and Clive Live' and laughed at the lobsters up Jayne Mansfield's arse. Cathy and Howie were killing the business one dumb little bit at a time and Benny could not bear to listen to them do it.

He did not deny his own mistakes, but they were truly minor in comparison. Every part he dealt with had at least seven digits. What anyone else would call a Camira engine mount was a 5434432 to Benny. These digits jumped places, transposed themselves, leap-frogged. They were like mercury in his fingers as he tried to keep them still: 6's rolled over, 2's and 5's leap-frogged and 4's turned into 7's. Benny's wrists were covered in numbers. Numbers stretched along his long fingers like tattoos, across his palms like knitting, but he still made errors.

He was asked to put in an order for three dozen 2965736 electrical connectors. The next day the truck turned up with thirty-six

2695736 Bedford bumper bars, all non-returnable. He put in an express order for a body shell of a 92029932S Commodore Station Wagon but he typed 92029933S instead so they delivered a sedan body and an invoice for $3,985.00.

These were serious mistakes. They saw him laughing at 'Derek and Clive Live' and thought he did not care. The opposite was true: every mistake made him hot with shame. It was his business. He was the one who was going to have to rescue Catchprice Motors from the mess they had made and carry it into the twenty-first century. He was the one who was going to find the cash to pay for their old people's home, who would buy them their little pastel blue tellies to put beside their beds. He would care for them the way they never cared for him – even Mort, his father – he would shame them.

So when he was fired from Spare Parts by his sole protector he was not only humiliated in front of the mechanics – who hated him for his mistakes and went out at night to the pub to celebrate – he was also pushed into a crisis, and the light in his eyes looked to be blown right out. He was dog shit. He had no other plan for life. He was a car dealer.

Of course the Catchprices were all car dealers, or they were known in Franklin as car dealers, but Benny was alone in wishing to describe himself that way. The others accepted the label even while they dreamed of losing it. They were Catchprices, *temporarily* G.M. dealers from Franklin near Sydney in the State of New South Wales.

The family had been in Franklin when it had been a country town with a population of 3,000 people and limited commercial potential. Then it was twenty miles from Sydney and in the bush. Now it was twenty miles from Sydney and almost in the city and there was no Sydney Road any more – there was the F4 instead, and when it left Franklin it passed through two miles of deserted farm land and then the suburbs started.

Franklin was no longer a town. It was a region. The population was 160,000 and they had bulldozed the old Shire Hall to make municipal offices six storeys high. Benny could tell you the value of the rates the Shire collected each year: $26 million. There was drug addiction and unemployment it is true, but there were airline pilots and dentists out along the Gorge. They came tooling down the F4 in Porsches and Volvos.

All of this should have been good for business, but Catchprice

Motors, a collection of soiled and flaking white stucco buildings with barley-sugar columns and arched windows, had somehow got itself isolated from the action. It was stranded out on the north end of Loftus Street opposite the abandoned boot-maker's and bakery. Loftus Street fed the stream of the F4, but the commercial centre had shifted to a mall half a mile to the south and there were now many people, newcomers to the area, to whom the name Catchprice had no meaning at all. They did not know there was a G.M. dealership tucked away between A.S.P. Building Supplies and the Franklin District Ambulance Centre.

There was a sign, of course, which said CATCHPRICE MOTORS and most of the Catchprices lived right behind it. Gran Catchprice's windows looked out through the holes in the letters 'A' and 'P'. Her grown-up son, Benny's father, lived in a red-brick bungalow which fitted itself against the back wall of the workshop like a shelf fungus against a eucalyptus trunk and her married daughter, Cathy, had taken over the old place above the lube bay.

The Catchprices clustered around the quartz-gravel heart of the business. Time-switched neon lights lay at their centre. The odours of sump oil and gasoline sometimes penetrated as far as their linen closets. They were in debt to the General Motors Acceptance Corporation for $567,000.

That Sunday night following Benny's dismissal, two members of the family kept him company. They sat above the showroom where the late Albert ('Cacka') Catchprice had sold his first 1946 Dodge to Jack Iggulden. In those days the rooms above the showroom had been Cacka's offices, but now they were his widow's home. The glass display case which had once displayed bottled snakes and sporting trophies now held Frieda Catchprice's famous collection of bride dolls. There were eighty-nine of them. They were all frizzy, frilly, with red lips and big eyes. They occupied the entire back wall of her living-room.

Granny Catchprice was eighty-six years old. She liked to smoke Salem cigarettes. When she put one in her mouth, her lower lip stretched out towards it like a horse will put out its lip towards a lump of sugar. She was not especially self-critical, but she knew how she looked when she did this – an old tough thing. She was not a tough thing. She made jokes about her leaking roof but she was frightened there was no money to fix it. She made jokes, also, about the state of the bride dolls behind the glass display case. She liked to say, 'Us girls are getting on,' but the truth was she could not even look at the dolls, their condition upset her so. She would walk into the room and look up towards the neon tubes, or down towards the white-flecked carpet. She ducked, dodged, avoided. She always sat at the one place at her dining table, with her back hard against the case of dolls. The glass on the case was smeared. Sometimes it became all clouded up with condensation and the dolls had streaks of mould and mildew which, at a distance, looked like facial hair.

When she sat with her back to the dolls on Sunday night she had to face her youngest grandson. She would have preferred not to see how his spine was curved over and how his animated eyes had gone quite dead. He was not bright, had never been bright, could still not spell 'vehicle' or 'chassis' but he had a shining will she had always thought was like her own. She did not necessarily like him, but he was like a stringy weed that could get slashed and trampled on and only come back stronger because of it. Of all the things she had ever expected of him, this was the last – that he should allow himself to be destroyed.

She gave him a big white-dentured smile. 'Well,' she told him. 'The worst accidents happen at sea.'

He did not seem to hear her.

She looked across at his brother for support. She had dragged that one out here all the way from the Hare Krishna temple in Kings Cross but now he was here she could see that he was more frightened by his brother's collapse than she was. His name was Johnny but now he was a Hare Krishna he would not answer to it. He was Vishnabarnu – Vish – he looked at her and gave a little shrug. He had his grandfather's big knobbly chin and wide nose, and when he shrugged he squinched up his eyes just like Cacka used to do and she thought he would be no use to anyone.

He had the same neck as his grandfather as well, and those sloping strong shoulders and the huge calves which knotted and unknotted when he walked. He would be no real use, but she liked to have him near her and she had to stop herself reaching out to touch his saffron kurta with her nicotine-stained fingers. He was so clean – she could smell washed cotton, soap, shaving cream.

'It's not worth being upset about,' Vish was telling Benny. 'It's a dream. Think of it as a dream.'

Benny looked at Vish and blinked. It was the first thing to actually engage his attention.

'That's right,' Vish said, speaking in the way you coax a baby's arms into its sleeves, or a nervous horse into its bridle. 'That's right.'

Benny opened his mouth wide – ah.

Vish leaned across the table on his elbows, squinting and frowning. He peered right into the darkness of Benny's open mouth. Then he turned to his grandmother who was in her big chair with her back to the dolls' case.

'Gran,' he said. 'I think you're wanted in the kitchen.'

She went meekly. It was not characteristic of her.

2

The rain was so bad that summer that the plastic-painted walls of the ashram developed water bubbles which ballooned like condoms. You had to puncture them with a pin and catch the water in a cup. The quilts which the devotees threw on top of the rusty-hinged wardrobes at four each morning became sticky with damp and sour with mildew. The walls of the staircase they flip-flopped down on their way to chant *japa* at the temple were marbled with pink mould, but Ghopal's, the restaurant owned by I.S.K.O.N. (the International Society of Krishna Consciousness), was in a new building with a good damp course and all through that wet summer it stayed dry and cool. The devotees kept the tables and floors as clean as their dhotis.

Govinda-dasa oversaw them. He had been a devotee since the early years when Prabhupada was still alive and nothing that had happened since his death had shaken him, not the corruption of the Australian guru whose name he would never pronounce, not the expulsion of Jayatirtha who was accused of taking drugs and sleeping with female devotees, not the murders at the temple in California. He was now forty-one. He had a sharp, intelligent face with dark, combative eyes and small, white, slightly crooked teeth. He said 'deities' not 'deetes'. He was educated and ironic, a slight, olive-skinned man with a scholarly stoop.

Govinda-dasa was not an easy man to work for. He was too often disappointed or irritated with the human material that was given him. He was kind and generous but these qualities lay like milk-skin on the surface of his impatience, wrinkling and shivering at the smallest disturbance. He could not believe that young men whose only concern in life was the service of Krishna could be so complacent.

He found spots on tables which had seemed perfectly clean before his eyes had rested on them. He liked the *Bhagavad Gita* and *The Science of Self-Realization* to be placed on the table in a certain way which was at once casual and exact. He liked the glass jars on each table to hold nasturtiums and daises which the young *brahmacharis* had to go and beg from the women who cared for the temple decorations. They did not like the women having power over them.

Govinda-dasa had such a passion for bleach that you could smell it still amid the ghee and cardamom and turmeric at ten o'clock on a busy night. He made it so strong that Vishnabarnu wore rubber gloves to stop the rash on his thick, farmer's arms. Vishnabarnu did not mind the bleach. Being inside Ghopal's was the opposite of Catchprice Motors – it was like being inside an egg. The Formica tables shone like pearly shells under neon light.

It was Govinda-dasa who took Gran Catchprice's call the night after the day when Benny got fired. He recognized the old woman's voice. She was an *attachment*. All devotees vowed to shed attachments. He put his hand over the receiver and looked at Vishnabarnu, who was arranging sprouts and orange slices on a plate of dhal. There was, even in that simple activity, such kindness evident in his big square face. You really did gain something just from looking at him.

He had such a big body, wide across the shoulders and chest, but his voice was high and raspy and his eyes lacked confidence. Now the phone call had produced a deep frown mark just to the right of his wide nose. He placed the dish of dhal and salad on the bench. He picked up a cloth and slowly wiped his big hands which were covered with nicks and cuts and stained yellow with turmeric. Then he picked up the plate and carried it to table no. 2.

Then he came back to the call.

'Who is it?' he asked.

'Don't dissemble,' said Govinda-dasa. There was no other devotee he could have used the word to, no one who would have understood it.

Vishnabarnu picked up the towel and gazed at his stained hands. For a moment it seemed as if he might actually refuse the call, but then he looked up at Govinda-dasa, grinned self-consciously, and held out his hand for the receiver.

'Hi-ya Gran,' he said.

The lightness of his tone was outrageous, as if he had never made a vow to anyone. Govinda-dasa's nostrils pinched. He leaned against the counter, folding and unfolding the urgent order for table no. 7, straining to hear both sides of the conversation.

Vish turned his back. His Grandma said: 'Benny needs you here at home.'

'Can't do that, Gran.'

'It's not good,' she said.

In the privacy of the shadowed wall, Vish smiled and frowned at once. There had been so many 'not good' things that had happened to Vish and Benny. Their grandmother had never seemed to notice any of them before.

'How is it not good?'

'Can't say right now,' she said.

Above the phone was an image of a half man, half lion – Krishna's fourth incarnation, Lord Nara Sinha – ripping the guts from a man in his lap.

Vish humped his body around the phone. 'I'm needed here,' he said.

'This is your home,' she said. 'You're needed here too.'

Vish looked at Govinda-dasa. Then he turned back to the wall and rested his forehead against it. When you were a *brahmachari*, living in an ashram, it was hard to imagine that Catchprice Motors still existed. It was hard to remember the currents of anger and fear which made life normal there.

He tried to think what could be so bad that Granny Catchprice would actually notice. Probably something not very bad at all. 'O.K.,' he said at last. 'Put him on.'

'He can't talk,' she said. 'He's lost his voice. They fired him from Spare Parts.'

The inside world of the temple was calm and beautiful. It had marble floors and eggshell calm. When they said you knew God through chanting his name, they were not being poetic.

'Did you hear me?' she said.

'Yes.'

There was a long silence on the phone while Vishnabarnu felt the cool dry wall against his cheek.

'I'm not talking to my father, if that's what you want.'

'You don't have to talk to your father.'

Vish shut his eyes and sighed. 'I'll try for the 9.35,' he said at last. 'I'm going to have to borrow some money.'

He turned to see that Govinda-dasa was holding out ten dollars between thumb and double-jointed finger.

'Table 7 is in a hurry,' Vish said.

'Is this how you serve Krishna?' Govida-dasa asked, pushing the money at Vishnabarnu like it was a lump of carrion.

One sharp tooth rested on his lower lip and he looked straight into Vish's eyes until Vish had to look down.

'You have no reason to feel superior to Janardan,' Govinda-dasa said.

Vishnabarnu respected Govinda-dasa more than anyone else except his guru, but now he felt impatient and disrespectful. He was shocked to recognize his feelings.

'If Janardan puts on a wig and smokes grass and talks about sex-pleasure, he's no more wedded to Maya than you are.'

'I know, Govinda-dasa.'

'But you don't know, or you wouldn't act like this. What is the greatest fear of any intelligent human being?'

Vishnabarnu closed his eyes. 'To spend their life as a lower animal.' He had fifteen minutes to make the train. 'Govinda-dasa, I have to go.'

'Will your attachment to your family bring you closer to God?'

This meant that you did not move closer to God by associating with Bad Karma. You associated with God by abandoning attachments, by chanting his name, by eating *prasadum*. Through good association you became a better person and took on His qualities of Compassion, Cleanliness, Austerity and Truthfulness.

Vish removed the damp note from between Govinda-dasa's fingers.

'I'm sorry,' he said. He looked briefly into Govinda-dasa's

blazing eyes and then walked out on to the landing and down the stairs towards the street.

In the dark shelter of the doorway he paused. He looked out through the rain at the traffic and the hooker in the red bunny suit standing in the white light of the BMW showroom across the street. He looked back up the white-walled stairway towards the restaurant. He looked out into the dark-bright street. He did not want to go to Catchprice Motors. He did not want to go through this silent anger with his father or walk back into that spongy mess of bad things that was his childhood.

He took the four steps down on to the street and chanted God's name once each step. And then he ran. He pounded through the rain-puddled streets – Darlinghurst Road, Oxford Street, Taylor Square – splashing his robes. He ran strongly, but without grace. His shaven head rolled from side to side and he bunched his forearms up near his broad chest like parcels he didn't want to get wet. He came down the dark part of the hill at Campbell Street and emerged on to the bright stage of Elizabeth Street like a bundle of rags and legs. His braided pigtail of remaining hair, his Sikha, glistened with drops of rain like sequins.

He ran against the Don't Walk sign: a mess of yellow illuminated by three sets of headlights. At the ticket counter he slipped and fell. He grazed his knees.

He burst into the carriage on the 9.35. His heart was banging in his ears. His breath worked his throat like a rat-tail file.

He collapsed in his seat opposite a man in shorts and a woman in a tight red dress. They did not see him. The man's hairy leg was between the woman's resisting knees and he was kissing her while he massaged her big backside.

Vish was coming home.

3

Granny Catchprice had her tastes formed up on the Dorrigo Plateau of Central New South Wales – she liked plenty of fat on her lamb chops and she liked them cut thick, two inches was not too much for her. She liked them cooked black on the outside and pink inside and when she grilled them in her narrow galley up above the car yard the fat spurted and flared and ignited in long liquid spills which left a sooty spoor on the glossy walls of her kitchen and a fatty smell which impregnated the bride dolls in the display case and the flock velvet upholstery on the chairs in the room where Vish sat opposite his expressionless brother. He knew whatever had gone wrong with Benny was his fault. This was something which was always understood between them – that Vish had abandoned his little brother too easily.

It was eleven o'clock on Sunday night and the griller was cold and the chop fat lay thick and white as candle wax in the bottom of the grill pan in the kitchen sink. Granny Catchprice was on her knees, her head deep in the kitchen cupboard, trying to find the implements for making cocktails. She was busying herself, just as she had busied herself through Cacka's emphysema. Then she had run ahead of her feelings with brooms and dusters. Now she was going to make her grandson's aerated brandy crusters but first she had to find the Semak Vitamiser in among the pressure cooker and the automatic egg poacher and all the aluminium saucepans she had cast aside when Benny told her that aluminium drove you crazy in old age.

People were used to thinking of Granny Catchprice as a tall woman although she was no more than five foot six and now, kneeling on the kitchen floor in a blue Crimplene pant suit which emphasized the slimness of her shoulders and the losses of mastectomy, she looked small and frail, too frail to be kneeling on a hard floor. The bright neon light revealed the eggshell scalp beneath her grey hair. Her lower lip protruded in her concentration and she frowned into the darkness of the cupboard.

'Drat,' she said. She pulled saucepans from the cupboard and dropped them on to the torn vinyl floor in order to make her search less complicated. She forgot Vish did not drink alcohol and he was too engrossed in his fearful diagnosis of his brother's condition to pay any attention to what she was doing.

The word *Schizophrenia* had come into his mind when he looked into Benny's ulcerated mouth and now he was wondering how he could find out what Schizophrenia really was. A saucepan clattered. His grandmother's red setter yelped and skittered across the slippery kitchen floor.

Benny winked at him.

Vish narrowed his eyes.

Benny pursed his lips mischievously and looked over his high bony shoulder towards the kitchen, then back at his older brother.

'Bah-bah-bah,' he said. 'Bah-Barbara-ann.'

Vish did not normally even think profanity. But when this quoted line from their father's favourite song told him that Benny's lost voice, his curved spine, his dead eyes, his whole emotional collapse had been an act, he thought *fuck*. He felt angry enough to break something, but as he watched his grinning brother take a pack of Marlboros from the rolled-up sleeve of his T-shirt, all he actually did was squinch up his eyes a little.

Benny lit a cigarette and placed the pack carefully in front of him on the table. He rolled his T-shirt up high to where you could see the first mark life had made on him – a pale ghost of a scar like a blue-ringed smallpox vaccination. He leaned back and, having checked his Grandma again, put his long legs and combat boots on the table and tilted back on the chair.

'No, seriously . . .' he said.

'Seriously!'

For a moment it looked as if Benny was going to mimic his brother's outraged squeak, but then he seemed to change his mind. 'No, seriously,' he said, 'I've got something great for you.'

There was a long silence.

'An opportunity,' said Benny.

Vish was breathing through his nose and shaking his head very slowly. He brought his hands up on the table and rubbed at the cuts on his knuckles. 'Do you know what it takes for me to come out here? Do you know what it costs me?' His eyes were so squinched up they were almost shut, with the result that his face appeared simultaneously puzzled and fatigued.

'I got *fired* from my own business,' Benny reminded him. 'I need you more than ever in my life. Isn't that enough of a reason to come?'

For a Hare Krishna the answer was no. Vish did not have the stamina to explain that again, nor did he want to hear what the 'opportunity' was.

'Sure,' he said.

Benny leaned across the dining-table to pat him on his shaven head. 'I wanted my brother . . . he's here. I needed a cocktail . . . she's making it. Relax . . . calm down. You going to have a brandy cruster? A little Sense Grat-if-ication? Put a wig on.'

Benny's eyes were like their father's – the same store-house of energy. Humour and malice lay twisted together in the black centre of the pupil. 'Put on your wig,' he said. 'God won't see you if you have a wig on.'

'Don't be ignorant.'

'Fuck yourself,' Benny hissed.

Vish had a hold of his younger brother's grimy little wrist before Benny knew what was happening. Benny was a sparrow. He had light, fine bones like chicken wings. He yelped, but he was not being held hard enough to really hurt him.

'Please let me go,' he said. 'You shouldn't have called me that. You know you shouldn't call me that.'

'You shouldn't have said what you said.'

'About the wig?'

Vish tightened his grip.

'Let me go,' Benny said. He bowed his head until the burning end of his cigarette was half an inch from Vish's hand. He never could stand being held down. His chin quivered. The cigarette shook. 'Let me go or I'll burn your fucking hand.'

'I came here to *see* you,' Vish said, but he let go.

'Oh sure,' Benny said. 'You thought I'd flipped out, right?'

'I was worried about you.'

'Sure,' said Benny. 'You've been worrying about me for years. Thanks. Your worry has really helped my life a lot.'

'You want me here or not, Ben? Just say.'

Benny was messing with the butts in the yellow glass ashtray, pulling the skin off the cigarette and shredding the filter. 'I'm not joining the Krishnas,' he said. 'Forget it.'

'Listen Ben, you give this up, I'll give up the temple. I'll get a straight job. We'll get a place together. We'll get jobs.'

'Get it into your head,' Benny said. 'We don't need to get jobs. We've got jobs. We've got our own business. This is what you've got to understand.'

'They fired you.'

'They think they fired me.' Benny had these eyes. When he smiled like this, the eyes looked scary – they danced, they dared you, they did not trust you. The eyes pushed you away and made you enemy. 'They can't fire me,' he said.

'Cathy fired you. That's why I'm here. She fired you and you went down in a heap.'

Benny took out a fresh Marlboro and lit it. 'The situation keeps changing,' he said.

Vish groaned.

'No, look,' Benny said. 'Think about it. This is the best thing that could have happened.'

'Then why am I here? Why did I get this call from Gran?'

'Just listen to me. Think about what I'm saying. Cathy fired me, but she's a dead duck. She's got an unemployed carpenter for a drummer and a lead guitarist with a fucked-up marriage and they've actually got a record on the Country charts. They're charting! Nothing's going to stop these guys going on the road. This is *it* for them. What I'm saying is, they're entitled – it's their name too and if she wants to keep it, she'll have to leave the business and go on the road with them. She fired me but she doesn't count.'

'Benny, I don't know what you're talking about.'

'Then listen to me. She always thought she was Big Mack, right? She thought the Mack was hers because McPherson is her name, but Mickey Wright got a lawyer and the lawyer says the name is for the whole band. She's *got* to go on tour with them or they'll go and tour without her. She's got to go. She's out of here. She doesn't count. You leave the Krishnas, fine,' Benny said. 'But you stay here with me. We can run this show together. I can go through the details for you any time you like.'

'Did you work this out before Gran phoned me?'

'They feed you at the temple,' Benny said. 'I know – you've got no worries, well you've got no worries here. I'll guarantee a living. Don't shake your fucking head at me. You can make two hundred grand a year in this dump, really. You can walk on fucking water if you want. We can set this town on fire.'

The dog came and pushed his nose up between Benny's legs. Benny kicked him away and he went back to the kitchen, slipping and scratching across the floor to where Gran Catchprice was hunched over her defective Semak Vitamiser.

'This is our inheritance,' Benny said. 'I'm not walking away from that and neither are you.'

Vish shook his head and rearranged his yellow robe. In the

kitchen his grandmother was turning the single switch of the blender on and off, on and off.

'Did you talk to Him?'

'Who's Him?'

'You know who I mean . . . our father.'

'He's irrelevant.'

'Oh yes? Really?'

'His only relevance is these.' He held up a bottle of pills – Serepax prescribed for Mr Mort Catchprice.

'Benny, Benny. I thought you quit that.'

'Benny, Benny, I'm not selling them. I'm trading them.'

'For what?'

'Personal transformation,' Benny said.

Vish sighed. 'Benny, he's not going to let you do any of this. What do you think you're going to do?'

'Tonight,' Benny rattled the Serepax and pushed them down into the grubby depths of his jeans pocket, 'I'm swapping these with Bridget Plodder for a haircut. Tomorrow, I'm personally moving some of that stock off the floor.'

'You're selling *cars*?' Benny was coated with dirt. He had grimy wrists, dull hair, this film across his skin, but there was, once again, this luminous intensity in his eyes. 'You don't even have a driving licence.'

'He can't stop me,' Benny said. 'I've turned the tables. I've got him over a barrel.'

'Stay away from him, Ben.'

'Vish, you don't even know who I am. I've changed.'

'You're sixteen. He can do what he likes with you.'

'I've *changed*.'

For the second time that evening, Benny opened his mouth wide for Vish and pushed his face forward. Vish looked into his brother's mouth. Whatever it was he was meant to see in there, he couldn't see it.

4

At three-thirty on Monday morning Vish performed his ablutions, chanted *japa*, and made *prasadum* – a stack of lentil pancakes which he laid in front of the guru's picture before beginning to eat.

Monday

At five-thirty Granny Catchprice had her Maxwell House standing up at the kitchen sink. She politely ate some of the cold pancakes her grandson offered her.

At six-thirty the pair of them, she in an aqua-coloured, quilted dressing-gown, he in his yellow dhoti and kurta, opened the heavy Cyclone gates to the car yard and locked the Yale padlock back on its bolt.

Just after the seven o'clock news there was a short, heavy thunderstorm.

At seven-thirty Mort Catchprice, unaware that his elder son had spent the night in his grandmother's apartment, gingerly nursed a newly registered vehicle through the yellow puddles of the service road and out on to the wet highway which was already heavy with city-bound traffic.

At eight-fifteen Cathy and Howie came down from their apartment and crossed the gravel to unlock first the showroom and then the Spare Parts Department. She wore her snake-skin boots. He wore pointy-toed suede shoes. He walked with the weight on his heels to keep the toes from spoiling in the wet.

At eight-twenty the air compressor thumped into life.

At eight-thirty-three a high racketing noise cut across the yard from the workshop – an air-driven power wrench spun the wheel nuts off the right-hand rear wheel of an HQ Holden.

At eight-thirty-five Benny Catchprice rose from the cellar one step at a time, feeling the actual weight of himself in his own calf muscles as he came up the steep stairs without touching the grimy handrail. He rose up through the cracked, oil-stained, concrete floor of the old lube bay and stood in the thick syrupy air, breathing through his mouth, blinking at the light, his stomach full of butterflies.

He was transformed.

His rat-tailed hair was now a pure or poisonous white, cut spiky short, but – above the little shell-flat ears – swept upwards with clear sculpted brush strokes, like atrophied angel wings. The eyes, which had always alarmed teachers and social workers and were probably responsible, more than any other factor, for his being prescribed Ritalin when eight years old, were so much at home in their new colouring that no one would think to mention them – no longer contradictory, they seemed merely nervous as they flicked from one side of the car yard to the other, from the long side wall of the workshop to the high louvred windows of his grandmother's kitchen.

His brow seemed broader and his round chin more perfectly defined, although this may have been the result of nothing more than Phisohex, soap, petroleum jelly, all of which had helped produce his present cleanliness.

His lips, however, were the most remarkable aspect of his new look. What was clear here now in the reflected quartz-gravel light underneath the cobwebbed rafters had not been clear yesterday: they were almost embarrassingly sensual.

Benny was fully aware of this, and he carried with him a sense of his new power together with an equally new shyness. He was waiting to be looked at. He lined up the toes of his shoes with the crumbling concrete shore of the old lube bay floor. He knew he was on the very edge of his life and he balked, hesitating before the moment when he would change for ever.

The old lube was directly beneath the cobwebbed underfloor of Cathy and Howie's apartment, at the back end of the car yard farthest from the big sliding Cyclone gates. He looked out at the glittering white gravel of his inheritance.

The Camiras and Commodores were laid out like fish on a bed of crushed ice. They were metallic blue and grey. There was a dust silver Statesman fitted with black upholstery. On the left-hand side near the front office was a Commodore S.S. with spunky alloy wheels in the shape of a spinning sun. The G.M. cars were angled towards the road, like arrows which suggested but did not quite point towards the creature the family seemed so frightened of – the Audi Quattro 90 with leather trim. A $75,000 motor car they had traded from a bankrupt estate.

The compressor cut off, revealing the high whine of a drill press which had been going all the time. In a moment one of the mechanics would look out over his bench top and see him. Benny could imagine himself from their point of view. They would see the suit, the hair, and they would whistle. They would think he was effeminate and stupid, and maybe he was stupid, in a way. But in other ways he was not stupid at all. He had redevelopment plans for that workshop, and he knew exactly how to finance it.

When Vish had abandoned him five years ago, had run off to leave him unprotected, he had drawn Vish on his cellar wall, being

fucked by a donkey with a dunce's hat. He had drawn his father
tied to a chair. He had drawn a black eagle but it would not go black
enough. That was a long time ago, on the day he had moved into
the cellar. He did not draw these dumb things any more. The
donkey and dunce's cap were now covered with a dense knitted
blanket of red and blue handwriting. Among these words, one set
repeated.

I cannot be what I am.

He was stupid, maybe, but he would not continue to be what he
was, and when Cathy fired him he had already spent $400 on a
Finance and Insurance course at the Zebra Motor Inn and he had
passed it – no problems with the numbers.

He had also spent $495 on the 'Self-Actualization' cassettes, $300
on the suit, $150 on sundries and, as for where the money came
from, that was no one's business and totally untraceable. So when
his father began by saying, no way was he going to sell cars, all he
did was ask himself 'How do I attain the thing that I desire?'

Then he followed the instructions of the 'Self-Actualization' cassettes, descending the imaginary coloured stairways to the mental
image on the imaginary Sony Trinitron which showed the object of
his desire. His father was finally irrelevant.

The rain which had been falling all summer began to fall again.
Summer used not to be like this. This was all the summer he had
inherited. The raindrops were soft and fat. They made three large
polka dots on the padded shoulders of his 80 per cent silk suit. He
would not run. It was not in his new character to run. He walked
out across the crunching gravel. His legs felt a little odd to him – as
if he had just risen from his sick-bed. Rain ricocheted off the
metallic roofs and bonnets of the Holdens and flecked his shining
cheekbones with glittering beads of water. He passed beside the
Audi 90. It was jet black. Very sexy. He could see himself reflected
in it, held in it. When he came in the door of the Front Office he was
blushing crimson.

This was where Cathy thought he was going to sell petrol. The
Front Office was at the front of the left-hand arm of the 'U' which
made up Catchprice Motors. There were a couple of old Esso
pumps out front and sometimes the apprentice would bring a car
around to get a litre or two for a road test, but petrol was cheaper –
and cleaner – at a regular service station. The underground petrol

tanks at Catchprice Motors had been there nearly forty years. They were rusting on the inside, and the outside was under pressure from the water table. The petrol tanks Grandpa Catchprice had installed were now rising like whales and the concrete on the forecourt cracked a little more each summer. You would have to be mentally deficient to stand on the forecourt at Catchprice Motors.

When Benny took up his station in the Front Office, the two old Esso petrol pumps were in the very centre of the big glass window in front of him. Behind his back was a white door with a grubby smudged area around its rattly metal handle. Across the road, through the giant trunks of camphor laurels which he was going to cut down the minute Cathy was on the road, he could see the abandoned boot-maker's and bakery.

Benny stood in the centre of the office with his legs apart and his hands folded behind his back. His skin smelt of soap. Rain sat on his cheekbones. In an ideal world, his brother would be beside him, might be beside him yet.

He was going to sell his first car.

When the rain stopped again, Benny planned to move out into the yard. He wanted them to *see* him. He wanted to see himself in the mirror of their faces.

It was still raining when the first 'prospect' appeared. A woman in a white Mitsubishi Colt pulled up under the trees on the other side of the petrol pumps. The rain was heavy now, far too heavy to walk out into, and Benny did not see the red 'Z' plates which would have told him the Colt was a government car.

He was the first member of the Catchprice family to see the Tax Inspector. He did not know there was anything to be frightened of. He adjusted his shirt cuffs. All he thought was: watch me.

5

The Tax Inspector parked the Colt on a small island of weeds which was more closely associated with the Building Supplies Store than with Catchprice Motors. This was an old Taxation Office courtesy which Maria Takis, alone of all the auditors in her section, continued to observe – you did not humiliate your clients by parking a Taxation Officer car right on their doorstep, not even in the rain.

A wall beside a pot-holed laneway bore flaking signwriting with arrows pointing towards SERVICE DEPT and SPARE PARTS DEPT but there was no mention of an OFFICE or ALL ENQUIRIES. Rainwater spilled over the blocked guttering and ran down the wall, rippling across the signs, and flooded back across the cracked concrete forecourt towards the car yard itself.

Maria Takis walked carefully through the shallow edges of the puddle in the direction of the petrol pumps. Behind the petrol pumps she found an oddly beautiful boy standing like a mannequin in an empty neon-lit office.

He came to the doorway to give her directions. When she thanked him, he reached his hand out through the open door so he could shake her hand.

As she walked through the rain across the car yard towards the old wooden fire escape he had pointed out, she could feel the skin of his hand still lying like a shadow on her own. Had she not been eight months pregnant she might have thought about this differently, but she felt so full of baby, of fluid, such a net of bulging veins and distended skin (she would have drawn herself, had you asked her, like an orange with twig legs) she did not expect to be the object of anybody's sexual attentions.

In any case: she had more serious things to think about.

She could hear shouting, even here at the bottom of the storm-bright fire escape, above the din of the rain which fell like gravel on the iron roofs of Catchprice Motors and cascaded over the gutter and splashed her shoes. The rain cooled her legs. It made patterns on her support stockings, as cool as diamond necklaces.

The treads of the stairs were veined with moss and the walls needed painting. The door she knocked on was hollow, ply-wood, with its outer layer peeling away like an old field mushroom. The Tax Inspector knocked reluctantly. She was accustomed to adversaries with marble foyers and Miele dishwashers. She was used to skilful duels involving millions of dollars. To be sent to this decaying door in Franklin was not only humiliating, but also upsetting on another level – after twelve years with the Taxation Office she was being turned into something as hateful as a parking cop.

No one heard her knock. They were shouting at each other. She knocked again, more loudly.

Maria Takis was thirty-four years old. She had black, tangled hair and a very dark olive-skinned face which her mother always said was 'Turkish' (i.e. not like her mother) and which Maria began, in her teenage years, to accentuate perversely with gold rings and embroidered blouses so that even now, coming to a door as a tax auditor, she had that look that her mother was so upset by.

'Pop po, fenese san tsingana.' ('You look like a gypsy.')

There was nothing gypsy about the briefcase in her hand – it was standard Taxation Office – two gold combination locks with three numbers on each side, two large pockets, two small pockets, three pen-holders on the inside lid, a Tandy solar- and battery-powered 8-inch calculator, three pads of lined writing paper, six public service Biros, and a wad of account analysis forms with columns for the date, the cheque number, the cheque particulars and columns to denote capital, business, or personal. She had a book of receipt forms for any documents she removed from the premises, a standard issue Collins No. 181 day-a-page diary, a tube of handcream, a jar of calcium tablets, two packets of thirst Lifesavers, and her father's electricity bill.

Her identification warrant was in her handbag and she was already removing it as she waited for the door to open. It was a black plastic folder with the Australian Taxation Office crest in gold on the front and her photograph and authorization on the inside. In the photograph she looked as if she had been crying, as if she had somehow been forced to pose for it, but this was her job. She had chosen it freely.

'Yes?'

A plump woman in a chamois leather cowgirl suit stood behind the flyscreen door. Her hips and thighs pushed against her skirt and the chamois rucked and gathered across her stomach. Her bare upper arms fought with the sleeve holes of the waistcoat top. Everything about her body and her clothes spoke of tension. Her plump face reinforced the impression, but it did so as if she was someone sweet-tempered just woken from her sleep, irritable, yes, frowning, sure, but with a creamy complexion and pale, well-shaped, sensuous lips, and a natural calm that would return after her first cup of coffee. She had dense, natural straw-blonde hair set in a soft curl, and small intelligent eyes which stared out at Maria from behind the flyscreen door.

Maria wondered if this was Mrs F. Catchprice. The abrupt way she opened the door and took Maria's I.D. told her this was unlikely to be the taxpayer's accountant.

'I'm Maria Takis . . .' She was interrupted by an old woman's voice which came out of the darkness behind the flyscreen.

'Is that Mortimer?'

'It's not Mort,' said the big woman, shifting her gaze from the I.D. to Maria's belly. She said it wearily, too quietly for anyone but Maria to hear.

'Mortimer come in.' The voice was distressed. 'Let Mortimer come in. I need him here.'

Rain drummed on the iron roof, spilled out of gutters, splashed out on to the landing around Maria's feet. There was a noise like furniture falling over. The woman in cowboy boots turned her head and shouted back into the room behind her: 'It's not Mortimer . . . It . . . is . . . *not* Mort.' She turned back to Maria and blew out some air and raised her eyebrows. 'Sorry,' she said. She scrutinized the I.D. card again. When she had read the front she opened it up and read the authorization. When she looked up her face had changed.

'Look,' she said, coming out into the rain, and partly closing the door behind her. Maria held out her umbrella.

'Jack,' the old woman called.

'Look, Mrs Catchprice is very sick.'

'Jack . . .'

'I'm Cathy McPherson. I'm her daughter.'

'Jack, Mort, help me.'

Cathy McPherson turned and flung the door wide open. Maria had a view of a dog's bowl, of a 2-metre-high stack of yellowing newspapers.

'It's not Jack,' shrieked Cathy McPherson. 'Look, look. Can you see? You stupid old woman. It's the bloody Tax Department.'

Maria could smell something sweet and alcoholic on Cathy McPherson's breath. She could see the texture of her skin, which was not as good as it had looked through the flyscreen. She thought: if I was forty-five and I could afford boots like those, I'd be saving money for a facelift.

'This is ugly,' Cathy McPherson said. 'I know it's ugly. I'm sorry. You really have to talk to her?'

'I have an appointment with her for ten o'clock.'

'You'll need someone to interpret,' Cathy McPherson said. 'If this involves me, I want to be there. Does it involve me?'

'I really do need to talk to her. She is the public officer.'

'She's senile. Jack hasn't lived here for twenty years.'

Maria released the catch on her umbrella. 'None the less she's the public officer.'

'She pisses in her bed.'

Maria collapsed her umbrella and stood in front of Cathy McPherson with the rain falling on her head.

'Suit yourself,' Cathy McPherson opened the door. Maria followed her into a little annexe no bigger than a toilet. Dry dog food and Kitty Litter crunched beneath their feet. The air was spongy, wet with unpleasant smells.

The door to the left led to a galley kitchen with hot-pink Laminex cupboards. There was a flagon of wine sitting on top of a washing machine. There were louvred windows with a view of the car yard. Ahead was the sitting-room. They reached it through a full length glass door with yellowed Venetian blinds. For a moment all Maria could see were rows of dolls in lacy dresses. They were ranked in spotlit shelves along one end of the room.

'Who is it?' Granny Catchprice asked from a position mid-way between Maria and the dolls.

'My name is Maria Takis. I'm from the Taxation Office.'

'And you're going to have a baby,' said Mrs Catchprice. 'How wonderful.'

Maria could see her now. She was at least eighty years old. She was frail and petite. She had chemical white hair pulled back tightly from a broad forehead which was mottled brown. Her eyes were watery, perhaps from distress, but perhaps they were watery anyway. She had a small but very determined jaw, a wide mouth and very white, bright (false) teeth which gave her face the liveliness her eyes could not. But it was not just the teeth – it was the way she leaned, strained forward, the degree of simple attention she brought to the visitor, and in this her white, bright teeth were merely the leading edge, the clear indicator of the degree of her interest. She did not look in the least senile. She was flat-chested and neatly dressed in a paisley blouse with a large opal pendant clasped to the high neck. It was impossible to believe she had ever given birth to the woman in the cowgirl suit.

There was a very blond young man in a slightly higher chair beside her. Maria held out her hand, imagining that this was her accountant. This seemed to confuse him – Australian men did not normally shake hands with women – but he took what was offered him.

'Dr Taylor will give you his chair,' said Mrs Catchprice.

Not the accountant. The doctor. He looked at his watch and sighed, but he did give up his chair and Maria took it more gratefully than she might have imagined.

Mrs Catchprice put her hand on Maria's forearm. 'I'd never have a man for a doctor,' she said. 'Unless there was no choice, which is often the case.'

'I was hoping your accountant would be here.'

'Let me ask you this,' Granny Catchprice said. 'Do I *look* sick?'

Cathy McPherson groaned. A young male laughed softly from somewhere in the deep shadows beside the bride dolls.

'No,' said Maria, 'but I'm not a doctor.'

'What are you?' said Mrs Catchprice.

'I'm with the Taxation Office. We have an appointment today at ten.' Maria passed Mrs Catchprice her I.D. Mrs Catchprice looked at it carefully and then gave it back.

'Well that's an *interesting* job. You must be very highly qualified.'

'I have a degree.'

'In what?' Mrs Catchprice leaned forward. 'You have a lovely face. What is your name again?'

'Maria Takis.'

'Italian?'

'My mother and father came from Greece.'

'And slaved their fingers to the bone, I bet.'

'Mrs Takis,' the doctor said. 'I'm sorry to interrupt you, but I was conducting an examination.'

'Oh,' said Mrs Catchprice, 'you can go now, Doctor.' She patted Maria's hand. 'We women stick together. Most of us,' said Mrs Catchprice. 'Not all of us.'

Cathy McPherson took two fast steps towards her mother with her hand raised as if to slap her.

'See!' said Mrs Catchprice.

Maria saw: Cathy McPherson, her hand arrested in mid-air, her face red and her eyes far too small to hold such a load of guilt and self-righteousness.

'See,' said Mrs Catchprice. She turned to Maria. 'My housekeeping has deteriorated, so they want to commit me. Not Jack – the others. If Jack knew he'd be here to stop them.'

'No one's committing you,' Cathy McPherson said.

'That's right,' Mrs Catchprice said. 'You can't. You thought you could, but you can't. They can't do it with one doctor,' she patted Maria's wrist. 'They need two doctors. I am correct, am I not? But you don't know – why would you? You're from Taxation.'

'Yes.'

'Well you can't see me if I'm committed.' Mrs Catchprice folded her fine-boned, liver-spotted hands in her lap and smiled around the room. 'Q.E.D.,' she said.

'The situation,' said Dr Taylor, with the blunt blond certainties that come from being born 'a real aussie' in Dee Why, New South Wales. 'The situation . . .' He wrote two more words on the form and underlined a third.

'Put a magazine under that,' said Mrs Catchprice. 'I don't want to read my death warrant gouged into the cedar table.'

A Hare Krishna emerged from the gloom with some newspaper which he slid under the doctor's papers.

'The situation,' said the doctor, 'is that you are incapable of looking after yourself.'

'This is my *home*,' said Mrs Catchprice, and began to cry. She clung on to Maria's arm. 'I own this business.'

Cathy sighed loudly, 'No you don't, Frieda,' she said. 'You are a shareholder just like me.'

'I will not be locked up,' said Mrs Catchprice. She dug her hands into Maria's arm and looked her in the face.

Maria patted the old woman's shoulder. She had joined the Taxation Office for bigger, grander, truer things than this. She knew already what she would find if she audited this business: little bits of crookedness, amateurish, easily found. The unpaid tax and the fines would then bankrupt the business.

The kindest thing she could do for this old woman would be to let her be committed. Two doctors attesting to the informant's senility might be enough to persuade Sally Ho to stop this investigation. Sally could then use her ASO 7 status to find something equally humiliating for Maria to do, and this particular business could be left to limp along and support this old woman in her old age.

But Mrs Catchprice was digging her (very sharp) nails into Maria's forearm and her face was folding in on itself, and her shoulders were rounding, and an unbearable sound was emerging from her lips.

'Oh don't,' Maria whispered to the old woman. 'Oh don't, please, don't.'

The Hare Krishna knelt on Mrs Catchprice's other side. He had great thick arms. He smelt of carrots and patchouli oil.

'What will happen to you when you're too old to be productive?' he asked the doctor. His voice was high and breathless, trembling with emotion.

'For Christ's sake,' Cathy McPherson said. 'For Christ's sake, just keep out of this, Johnny.'

'Christ?' the boy said. 'Would Christ want this?'

Cathy McPherson groaned. She closed her eyes and patted the air with the palms of her hands. 'I can't handle this . . .'

'Krishna wouldn't want this.'

'Johnny, please, this is very hard for me.'

'In the Vedic age the old people were the most respected.'

'Fuck you.' Cathy McPherson slapped the Hare Krishna across his naked head. The Hare Krishna did not move except to squeeze shut his eyes.

'Stop it,' said Maria. She struggled to her feet.

'I think *you* should stop it,' the doctor said, pointing a pen at Maria. 'I think you should just make your appointment for another time, Mrs . . .'

'Ms,' Maria told the doctor.

The doctor rolled his eyes and went back to his form.

'Ms Takis,' said Maria, who had determined that Mrs Catchprice would not be committed, not today at least. 'Perhaps you did not hear where I am from.'

'You are a little Hitler from the Tax Department.'

'Then you are a Jew,' said Maria.

'I am a *what*?' said the doctor, rising from his seat, so affronted that Maria burst out laughing. The Hare Krishna had begun chanting softly.

'Oh dear,' she laughed. 'Oh dear, I really *have* offended you.'

The doctor's face was now burning. Freckles showed in the red.

'What exactly do you mean by that?'

'I meant no offence to Jews.'

'But I am not a Jew, obviously.'

'Oh, obviously,' she smiled.

'Hare Krishna, Hare Krishna.'

'Shush darling,' said Mrs Catchprice, who was straining towards the doctor so that she might miss none of this.

'I meant that if I were a doctor with a good practice I would be very careful of attracting the attention of the Taxation Officer.'

'Hell and Tommy,' exclaimed Mrs Catchprice and blew her nose loudly.

'I have an accountant.'

Mrs Catchprice snorted.

'I bet you do,' said Maria. 'Do you know how many accountants were investigated by the Taxation Office last year?'

'Hare Krishna, Hare Krishna.'

'I'll report you for this,' said Cathy McPherson to Maria Takis.

'And what will you "report" me for?'

'For interfering in our family, for threatening our doctor.'

'Mrs McPherson . . .'

'Ms,' hissed Cathy McPherson.

Maria shrugged. 'Report me,' she said. If Sally Ho ever heard what Maria had just done, she would be not just reprimanded – she would be drummed out. 'They'll be pleased to talk to you, believe me.'

The doctor was packing his bag. He slowly put away his papers and clipped his case shut.

'I'll phone you later, Mrs McPherson.'

'Would you like one of my dolls?' Mrs Catchprice asked Maria. 'Choose any one you like.'

'No, no,' Maria said. 'I couldn't break up the collection . . .'

'Jonathon,' said Mrs Catchprice imperiously, 'Jonathon, fetch this young lady a doll.'

'Could I have a word with you?' Cathy McPherson said.

'Of course,' said Maria, but Mrs Catchprice's nails were suddenly digging into her arm again.

Cathy McPherson obviously wished to talk to her away from her mother, and Maria would have liked to have complied with her wishes but Mrs Catchprice's nails made it impossible.

Maria did not feel comfortable with what she had just done. She did not think it right that she should interfere in another family's life. She had been a bully, had misused her power. The child in her belly was made with a man whose great and simple vision it was that tax should be an agent for equity and care, and if this man was imperfect in many respects, even if he was a shit, that was not the issue, merely a source of pain.

Cathy McPherson stood before her with her damaged cream complexion and her cowboy boots. Maria would have liked to speak to her, but Mrs Catchprice had her by the arm.

'Not here,' said Cathy McPherson.

Mrs Catchprice's nails released their pressure. Jonathon had placed a Japanese doll on her lap.

'It's a doll bride,' said Mrs Catchprice, 'Bernie Phillips brought it back from Japan. Do you know Bernie Phillips?'

'This is my *mother*,' said Cathy McPherson, her eyes welling up with tears. 'Do you have the time to look after her? Are you going to come back and wash her sheets and cook her meals?'

'No one needs to look after me,' said Mrs Catchprice. 'You are the one who needs looking after, Cathleen, and you've never been any different.'

'Mother, I am forty-five years old. The cars I sell pay for everything you spend.'

'I don't eat any more,' Mrs Catchprice said to Maria. 'I just pick at things. I like party pies. Do you like party pies?'

'I've got a whole band about to walk out on me and steal my name because I'm trying to care for you,' Cathy said. 'You want me to go on the road? You really want me to leave you to starve?'

'Bernie Phillips brought it back from Japan,' said Mrs Catchprice, placing the doll in Maria's hand. 'Now isn't that something.'

'Fuck you,' screamed Cathy McPherson. 'I hope you die.'

There was silence in the room for a moment. The noise came from outside – the rain on the tin roof, Cathy McPherson running down the fire escape in her white cowboy boots.

6

When she was twenty, after she had run away from both her marriage and her mother, Maria Takis went back to the island of Letkos to the house she was born in and stayed for six weeks with her mother's uncle, Petros, a stern-looking old man who bicycled ten miles along the dirt road to Agios Constantinos for no other reason than to buy his great-niece an expensive tin of Nescafé which he believed would please her more than the gritty little thimblefuls of *metries kafe* he made on his single gas burner.

Petros was the worldly one. He had worked on ships to New York and Shanghai, Cape Town and Rio and to have questioned or refused the Nescafé would have been somehow to undercut who he was. Maria had not come all this way to make her life fit the expectations of others, but just the same she could no more tell him she hated Nescafé than she could confess that she was already married and separated.

Instead she said, 'It is too hot today,' and held the handles of his bicycle as if this might prevent him buying it.

'It is always hot,' he said. He had to wrench the bicycle away from her and his dark eyebrows pressed down on eyes that suddenly revealed a glittering temper.

'No, no,' she said. 'It is hotter than it used to be.'

That made him laugh. He mounted his bicycle and rattled down the chalky road towards the square still laughing out loud and when her parents' friends and relations came to meet her he would tell them, 'When Maria lived here the summers used to be cooler.'

Everyone in Letkos found this very funny and Maria found them very irritating.

'I didn't remember the heat,' Maria said, too many times. 'Only the air. We left in the autumn and arrived in Sydney in the summer.' She told them about how hot it had been walking the streets of Newtown looking for work with her mother – like hell, like a heat so hot and poisonous you could not breathe – but she could see their eyes glaze over as they stopped listening to her. It was not their way of thinking about Australia and they did not want to hear. Australians were all rich, all drank Nescafé. That was why Nikkos refused to apologize for the state of her parents' house. He was meant to look after it but he had stolen the furniture and let the goats eat the pomegranate tree and he could not see that this would matter to Maria or her family. But she had grown up mourning for this beautiful little house which Nikkos had filled with goat shit. It was the place her mother meant when she said, 'Let's go home,' whispering to her husband in bed in a shared house in Sydney where you could hear the people in the next room doing everything.

On the ground floor of the house in Letkos her mother had cooked preserves, fried eggplant, keftethes – the room was always sweet with spices and oil. In the house which Nikkos had wrecked they kept almonds and walnuts and dry rustling bundles of beans. Maria had sat on the wooden doorstep in a great parallelogram of sunshine, eating pomegranate from the tree in the garden.

The first house in Sydney was a painful contrast. They rented a room from a friend of an uncle in Agios Constantinos. His name was Dimitri Papandreou. He smelt of sweat and old rags and was stingy. He used newspaper instead of toilet paper. He turned off the hot water when he left the house each morning. He had a secret tap no one else could find, not even Helen, who was smaller than Maria, and who was sent climbing under the floor boards to search for it. Dimitri Papandreou's wife worked at Glo-weave. The family therefore expected Maria's mother to look after all of the Papandreous. Dimitri Papandreou would cook lentils or beans and keep them in an aluminium pot in the fridge for weeks. It was his way of criticizing Maria's mother.

'Let's go home,' Maria's mother said whenever she imagined they were alone, but she never had a chance – fifteen men from the village had come to Australia and they were all working on the production line at the British Motor Corporation in Zetland. They were like men in a team.

Helen would ask their father if they could go home, but Maria was less principled. She sat on his lap and he stroked her hair.

'O Pateras son ine trellos,' ('Your father is crazy') her mother would say as she and Maria and Helen looked for work in the merciless heat (so endlessly hot, inescapably hot) of the Newtown streets. She had no English and Maria would walk with her to interpret and to help push Helen's stroller.

'What does that sign say?'

'Just a room to let.'

'It looks like a factory.'

'No, Mama.'

'It's a factory,' she said half-heartedly. 'No, Helen, no, no wee-wee yet. He's crazy. His life was better. He had a house – better oil, better fruit. Look what we had to carry out here – oil, ouzo – in our bags – he asks me to carry oil to him. Now he sends me out here to be humiliated.'

'Please, Mama, don't.'

'Don't don't.' Her mother's eyes were more and more shrunken, like *throubes*, shrunken in on themselves around the small hard pip. 'Don't you say "don't" to me. You think he is happy? Listen to them all when they sit around. What are they talking about?'

They came to the house. They sat in a circle in the kitchen. They were all from Agios Constantinos. They said, remember the year this happened. Remember the time that happened. They never talked about Australia.

'What is better here?' her mother asked. 'Help her. Help her. She has to wee-wee.' She was ashamed to have Helen pee in the street and turned her back even as she said, 'Help her.'

'The future,' Maria said, holding her little sister suspended over a gutter between two parked cars.

'That's what he says, but you never wanted to go. You were only four and you didn't want to go.'

'I know, Mama,' Maria said bustling her sister back into the stroller.

'You lost the use of your legs.'

'I know, I know.'

'He went to Athens for his immigration tests and when he came back and we told you we were going to Australia, you lost the use of your legs. The doctor had to come all the way to Agios Constantinos in an ambulance.'

Her father always said there was no ambulance.

'An ambulance,' her mother said. 'He couldn't find anything the matter.'

'I know.'

'You can't remember. Do you remember your father held out the *loukoumia* to you and you ran to get them. It was a trick to make you walk but if he hadn't offered you sweets you wouldn't have walked – you didn't want to go. We had a house. For what did we come? So

I can walk the streets and be a beggar for work? Did you ever see anyone in Agios Constantinos do their wee-wee in the street?'

The newspapers, of course, had their columns of employment ads, but the Letkos women could not read the letters of the alien alphabet. The newspapers were closed to them. They walked. They worked an area – Enmore, Alexandria, Surry Hills – going from factory to factory, following up the rumours their relations brought to the house. It was all piece-work, and her mother hated piece-work. Childhood friends competed against each other to see who would get the bonus, who would get fired.

Once a week they called on Switch-Electrics Pty Ltd in Camperdown. The women would converge on the footpath, swelling out around the Mercedes-Benzes which were never booked for parking on the footpath, pushing towards the door marked OFFICE. They would be there from seven in the morning. At eight o'clock the son would emerge. He had three folds of fat on his neck above his shirt collar. He had thick arms covered in pale hair. He had three pens in his shirt pocket.

He would point his thick finger into the crowd and say, 'You, you.'

He was like God. He did not have to explain his choices.

'You and you.'

One time he might choose you and another time he might not.

'No more. Vamoose.'

The woman would beg in Greek, in Italian, in Spanish, in Catalan. They would do anything – kneel, weep – it was acting, but sincere at the same time.

The man with the pens in his shirt pocket would flap his arms at them as though they were hens.

'Piss off. Go home.'

Sometimes the man's mother would come out. She was nearly sixty but she dressed like a film star with tight belts and high heels. She had bright yellow blonde hair and pink arms and red lips and dark glasses. She would come out of a side door carrying a mop bucket filled with water. She would swing it back and then hurl it towards the women, who were already running backwards and tripping over themselves, spilling back through the white Mercedes-Benzes into the path of the timber trucks from the yard next door. As the trucks blasted their horns and as the women screamed, a fat tongue of grey water would splat on to the foot-path and the son and daughter would stand in the doorway, laughing.

Maria's mother lost 85 per cent of her hearing in one ear in a Surry Hills sweat-shop where she made national brand-name shirts. She would say, this machine is deafening me. The owner was Greek, from Salonika. He would say, if you don't like it, leave.

Later she worked at Polaroid, polishing lenses. Then she got arthritis in her fingers and could not do it any more.

It was not a coincidence that, after the Tax Office began checking the returns of Mercedes-Benz owners, Maria was one of the two auditors who sat in the office of Switch-Electrics Pty Ltd opposite this same man with the fat neck and the three pens in his shirt pocket. He was now sixty years old. When he squeezed behind the wheel of his car, air came out of his nose and mouth like out of a puffball. He was a sad and stupid man, and his business was riddled with corruption and evasions which cost him nearly one million dollars in fines and back taxes.

Maria was not above feelings of revenge on behalf of all those women he had humiliated. She was pleased to get him, pleased to make him pay, and when he wept at the table she felt only a vague, distanced pity for him. She looked at him and thought: I must tell Mama.

Her mother was battling with cancer in the George V Hospital at Missenden Road in Camperdown and Maria brought flowers and Greek magazines and gossip that would cheer her up. It was for this reason – certainly not for her own pleasure – that she finally revealed what she had previously thought she could never reveal – her pregnancy.

The approaching death had changed Maria, had made her softer with her mother, more tolerant, less angry. She sat with her for ten, twelve hours at a stretch. She bathed her to spare her the humili-ation of being washed by strangers. She fed her honey and water in a teaspoon. She watched her sleep. Death had changed the rules between them. The love she felt for her mother seemed, at last, without reserve.

As it turned out, the emotions Maria Takis felt were hers, not her mother's. She had hoped that the idea of a birth might somehow make the death less bleak. She had imagined that they had moved, at last, to a place which was beyond the customs and morality of Agios Constantinos. But death was not making her mother's centre soft and when Maria said she was going to have a baby, the eyes that looked back at her were made of steely grey stuff, ball-bearings, pips of compressed matter. Her mother was a village woman, standing in a dusty street. She did not lack confidence. Fear had not shifted her.

'We'll kill you,' she said.

It was a hard death and the story of Switch-Electrics Pty Ltd never did get told.

7

'Yes, but do we have milk?' Mrs Catchprice used her walking stick to flick a magazine out of her path. 'It's very clever,' she told Maria. She hit the magazine so hard the pages tore. 'The roof leaks right into the kitchen sink. It washes my dishes for me.'

'Mrs Catchprice,' Maria smiled. 'It's nearly eleven.'

'Are you hungry?'

'I really need to start our meeting.'

'You sit down,' Mrs Catchprice said.

'There are questions I have to ask you, or your accountant.'

'Vish will get you a glass of milk.'

Mrs Catchprice struck the magazine again. Vish crossed from the kitchen to the plastic and paper confusion of the annexe, holding out a carton of milk at arm's length. He gently lowered the milk carton into a green plastic bag.

'You take my chair,' Mrs Catchprice told Maria. 'It's too low for me.' She pushed the magazine with the rubber tip of her stick and slid it underneath a bookcase.

'Gran, the milk was off.'

'Be a dear,' said Mrs Catchprice. 'Go and see Cathy. They've got milk in Spare Parts for the staff teas.'

'I can't ask Cathy. Cathy won't give me milk.'

'You don't understand Cathy,' said Mrs Catchprice. She pulled free a dining chair, turned it on one leg so it faced away from the bride dolls, and then sat down on it hard. 'Ask her for milk,' she said. 'She won't kill you.'

Maria thought: she 'plonks' herself down. She is pretty, but not graceful. She is full of sharp, abrupt movements which you can admire for their energy, their decisiveness.

She looked to see what the Hare Krishna was going to do about his orders. He had already gone.

'Bad milk!' said Mrs Catchprice. 'I've got old.'

'We all get old,' Maria said, but really she was being polite. She had an audit to begin. She wanted to make it fast and clean – a one-day job if possible.

'One minute you're a young girl falling in love and the next you look at your hand and it's like this.' She held it up. It was old and blotched, almost transparent in places.

Maria looked at the hand. It was papery dry. She thought of bits of broken china underneath a house.

'I can see it like you see it,' Mrs Catchprice said. 'I can see an old woman's hand. It has nothing to do with me. I think I'll have brandy in my milk. Did he take an umbrella?'

'I guess so.'

'I know he looks peculiar but he's very kind. He looks like such a dreadful bully, don't you think?' She leaned forward, frowning.

Maria had worked in the Tax Office twelve years and had never begun an audit in such a homey atmosphere. She opened her briefcase, removed a pad and laid it on her lap. 'He's got a nice smile,' she said.

'Yes, he has.' Mrs Catchprice fitted a Salem into her mouth and lit it without taking her eyes off Maria Takis's face. 'The Catchprices all have kissing lips. Actually,' she said, as if the thought was new to her, 'he's the spitting image of my late husband. Did you meet his younger brother, Benny? Vish's been looking after Benny since he could stand. They told you about their mother?'

'I haven't talked to anyone,' Maria said. 'I thought my colleague had talked to you to set up this interview. I . . .'

'Did you talk to Jack? Jack Catchprice, my youngest son.' She nodded to a colour photograph hanging on the wall beside the doorway to the kitchen. It was of a good-looking man in an expensive suit shaking hands with the Premier of the State of New South Wales. 'Jack's the property developer. He tells everyone about his funny family. He tells people at lunch – Benny's mother tried to shoot her little boy.'

Maria closed the pad.

'It's no secret,' Mrs Catchprice said. 'Benny's mother tried to shoot him. What sort of mother is that? Nice, pretty-looking girl and then, bang, bang, shoots her little boy in the arm. Benny was three years old. I'm not making it up. Shot him, with a rifle.'

'Why?'

'Why? God knows. Who would ever know a thing like that?'

'What was she charged with?'

'Oh no,' Mrs Catchprice said. 'We wouldn't report it. What would be the point? She went away, that's what matters. We wouldn't want the family put through a court case as well. Everyone in Franklin gossips about it anyway. They all know the story – on the Sunday Sophie Catchprice was confirmed an Anglican, on the Monday she did this . . . thing. *Confirmed*,' said Mrs Catchprice, responding to the confusion on Maria's face. 'You're a Christian aren't you? Your mother still goes to church I bet? Is she a Catholic?'

The Tax Inspector's mother was dead, but she said, 'Greek Orthodox.'

'How fascinating,' said Mrs Catchprice. 'How lovely.'

It was not the last time Maria would wonder if Mrs Catchprice was sincere and yet she could not dismiss this enthusiastic brightness as false. Mrs Catchprice might really find it fascinating – she brought her Salem to her lips, inhaled and released the smoke untidily. 'I always told them here in Franklin,' she said, 'that if they went in with the Presbyterians I'd switch over to the Catholics. We never had a Greek Orthodox. I never thought about Greeks. But now I suppose we have. We have all types here now. The Greek Orthodox is like the Catholic I think, is it not?'

'The service is very beautiful.'

'Oh I *do* like this,' said Mrs Catchprice. 'It's so *lovely* you are here. Has Johnny gone for the milk?'

'Mrs Catchprice, do you know why I'm here?'

'You mean, am I really ga-ga?' said Mrs Catchprice, butting her Salem out in an ugly yellow Venetian glass ashtray.

'No,' Maria said, 'I did not mean that at all.'

'You are a Tax Inspector?'

'Yes. And I'll need an office to begin doing my audit.'

'They're up to something, all right.'

Maria cocked her head, not understanding.

'You met her?' Mrs Catchprice said.

'Your daughter?'

'And her husband. I don't like him but I've only got myself to blame for the fact she even met him.'

'And you feel they are up to something?'

'There's something fishy going on there. You'll see in a moment. They'll have to give you access to the books. They won't let me look but they can't stop you. I think you'll find the tax all paid,' said Mrs Catchprice, folding her hands in her lap. 'We've always paid our tax. It's not the tax I'm worried about.'

Maria felt tired.

'People always expect car dealers to be crooks, but you try buying a car from a classified ad and you'll see where the crooks are. When my husband was alive, we always worked in with the law. We always supported the police. We always gave them presents at Christmas. A bottle of sparkling burgundy for the sergeant and beer for the constables. I would wrap up the bottles for him. He'd take them down to the police. They thought he was the ant's pants.'

'Mrs Catchprice,' Maria said, patting the old woman's hand to ease the sharp point she was making, 'you weren't *bribing* the police?'

'It was a small town. We always supported the police.'

'And now you're supporting the Taxation Office.'

'I wonder where that boy is with the milk.'

'Mrs Catchprice. Are you Mrs F. Catchprice?'

'Frieda,' said Mrs Catchprice. 'I've got the same name as the woman who was involved with D. H. Lawrence. She was a nasty piece of work.'

'There's no other Mrs F. Catchprice in your family?'

'One's enough,' she laughed. 'You ask the kids.'

'So you are the public officer and also the one with the anomalies to report?'

'Me? Oh no, I don't think so.' Mrs Catchprice folded her arms across her chest and shook her head.

'You didn't telephone the Taxation Office to say you were worried that your business had filed a false tax return?'

'You should talk to Cath and Howie. They're the ones with all the tricks up their sleeves. All this talk about being a professional musician is just bluff. She's an amateur. She couldn't make a living at it. No, no – what they want is to set up a motor business of their own, in competition to us. That's their plan – you mark my words. But when you look at the books, you take my word, you're going to find some hanky-panky. I won't lay charges, but they're going to have to pay it back.'

'Mrs Catchprice, you do understand – I'm a *tax* auditor. I'm here to investigate tax, nothing else. You phoned the Taxation Office. Your call is on record.'

Mrs Catchprice looked alarmed.

'They recorded me? Is that what you say?'

'They recorded your name.'

Mrs Catchprice was looking at Maria, but it was a moment before Maria saw that there were tears flooding down her ruined cheeks.

'The terrible thing is,' said Mrs Catchprice, 'the terrible thing is that I just can't remember.'

8

At twelve o'clock Mort Catchprice returned from the coast with a Volvo trade-in and saw Benny standing in front of the Audi Quattro. He did not recognize him. He knew his son intimately, of course, had held his little body, bathed it, cleaned it, cared for it from the year his wife had run away. He had seen his body change like a subject in slow-motion photography, seen its arms thicken and its shoulders broaden, its hooded little penis grow longer and wider, its toenails change texture and thickness, insect bites appear and fade, cuts open like flowers and close up with scabs the colour of dead rose petals. He knew what his son was like – a teenager with pimples, razor rash, pubic hair – someone who treated his skin as if he wished to make himself repulsive – left it smeared with dirt, ingrained with the residue of sumps and gearboxes. He had rank-smelling hair and lurid T-shirts in whose murky painted images his father could see only violence and danger.

What Mort saw as he drove slowly down the lane-way to the workshop, was not his son but a salesman, hired without his knowledge, against his wishes, a slick car salesman like Jack, neater than Jack, someone they could not, in any case, afford to pay.

He was mad already when he drove in beneath the open roller doors into the large grey steel-trussed space that was the workshop. He parked the Volvo on a vacant Tecalemit two-poster hoist.

He moved an oxy gas stand and began to push a battered yellow jack back against the wall when Arthur Dermott came shuffling over from his work bench rubbing his hands with a rag and grinning under his wire-framed spectacles.

'They tell you?' he asked, reaching for the crumpled pack of Camels in his back pocket.

Mort felt hot around the neck. *He saw the salesman. He knows I'm weak.*

'They tell me what?'

'Tax office is raiding you,' Arthur said, lighting the cigarette with satisfaction.

He saw the salesman.

'What?'

'Tax Office is raiding you. The way we heard, it was serious. The boys are a bit stirred up, job-security-wise.'

'Bullshit, Arthur. Who told you that?'

Arthur nodded towards Spare Parts. 'Howie come and took Jesse off the fuel pumps to carry all the books up to your Mum's apartment. They're doing their raid up there.'

'All right, Arthur, how about the Camira?'

'A Welsh plug and some coolant.'

'You road test it?'

'It's an R.T., yep.'

'O.K., now you can pre-delivery the blue Commodore.'

'I thought I was going to do the brakes on the Big Mack truck?'

'Forget the fucking Big Mack truck, just do what the fuck I tell you.'

It was true what Granny Catchprice said – the Catchprices had kissy lips. Mort had the best set of all of them. And although he was a wide and burly man, spilling with body hair, and with a rough, wide nose which had been broken twice on the football field, it was the lips which were remarkable not just for their fullness but also – in that bed of blue-black stubble – their delicacy.

Yet had you seen him emerge from under the roller doors of the workshop you would have seen a fighter, not a kisser. He came up the concrete lane-way beside the Spare Parts Department like a front row forward, occupying the centre of the road. He wore a clean white boiler suit, cut short at the arms and open for two or three press studs so the hairy mat of his wide chest was visible. He walked with a roll to his shoulders and his lips had gone thin and his eyes were looking at nothing they could see.

He knew there was no way he could have been told about the Tax Inspector, but he was still mad about not being told. When he passed the fern-filled window of Spare Parts he was giving them a chance to tell him, but they did not tap on the window or come out to tell him.

Also: they had hired a salesman without consultation.

In any case, fuck them, they made him angry almost every day of his life. Now he was going to piss the salesman off. He did not want to fight. He was sick of fight, sick of his body being a mass of stretching ropes. All he wanted was to be someone with a Garage, not a Service Station, not a Dealership, not a Franchise, but a Garage with deep, wide, oil stains on the floor and a stack of forty-four-gallon drums along his back fence, a Garage in a country town. There was one in the paper this week, at Blainey – $42,000, vendor finance. Blainey would be good enough. You could be the guy who drives the school bus, delivers the kerosene and fuel oil, cuts the rust spots out of the school teacher's old car, fixes the butcher's brakes with used parts, is handy with a lathe, is a good shot, a good bloke, a scout master, the coach of the football team, someone who, when looking for a screw or bolt, upturns a drum full of old saved screws and bolts on to the workshop floor and can find – there it is – a ⅜-inch Whitworth thread with a Phillips head.

Instead he had one kid lost to a cult, the other with severe learning difficulties and the belief he was a genius. He had a $567,000 debt to GMAC and a tax audit which, maybe, who knows, would put the lot of them in jail.

He stepped around the puddle on the end of the lane-way and crossed by the petrol pumps. There, twenty metres ahead of him, standing in front of the Audi Quattro, was the striking blond-haired young man in a glistening grey suit, the salesman. He was flexing his knees, holding his yellow-covered guide to auction prices behind his back. When he turned and looked him straight in the eye, Mort felt a sexual shiver which made him speak more harshly than he had planned.

'Get your arse out of here,' he said.

'You promised,' the salesman said, but he turned and walked away, swinging his shoulders and wiggling his butt like a frigging tom cat. My God, it was an embarrassment, the way he moved.

'And don't come back,' he said. Even as he said it he recognized his son. He wanted to cry out, to protest. He felt the blood rise hot in his neck and take possession of his face. He stood in his overalls in the middle of the yard, bright red.

His phone was ringing – loud as a fire bell. He walked towards it, shaking his head. In any other business of this size, one where the sales director was not wasting half her time trying to be a Country singer, there would be a service manager to answer the phone and soothe the customers. There would also be a workshop manager to co-ordinate the work flow, and a foreman to diagnose the major problems, work on the difficult jobs, do the final road tests and then tick them off on the spread sheet. Mort did all of these jobs. So even while he worried what the hell he would do about his embarrassing son, he also knew that three Commodores on the spread sheet were in for a fuel pump recall. General Motors graded this job as 4.2 which meant they would pay Catchprice Motors for forty-two minutes' labour, but they made no allowance for the time it took to drain the tank. He tried to cover himself by using Jesse, the first-year apprentice, but each recall still cost the business fifty dollars. That was Howie's calculation. He had said to Howie: 'What you want me to do about it?'

Howie said: 'Just help us keep Benny out of Spare Parts, Mort. Benny loses us more in a day than you could in a week.'

Mort walked into the Spare Parts Department to ask Cathy would she hold his calls for half an hour so he could help out on the fuel pumps. She should be standing in the showroom, but she never would. She had a handwritten sign there, saying please come over to Spare Parts and now she was on the phone making a parts order, doing Benny's job in fact, probably fucking up as well.

Howie was on the phone too. He was meant to look like Elvis's original drummer, D. J. Fontana. This was bullshit. He looked like what he would have been if Granny Catchprice had never hired him – a country butcher. He had a tattoo on his forearm and a ducktail haircut, always four weeks too long. He had his pointy shoes up on the desk, and the phone wedged underneath his chin. He had smoke curling round his hair, and clinging to his face. He stank of it.

'Listen, Barry, no: *I* went in there personally and asked them for it. They haven't got the record in stock. It's not even on their damn computer.' He paused. 'I know.' He paused again and nodded to Mort to sit down. He lived his life surrounded by radiator hoses and shock absorbers but he acted like he was in show business. It was pathetic. He wore *suits*, probably the only spare parts manager in Australia to do it. The suits all came mail order – with extra long jackets and padded shoulders.

'We *were* number eight. That was two days ago. If you can't keep the record in the shops, we're dead meat.'

He took his feet off the desk but only to flick ash off his trousers.

'I'm sympathetic, of course I am.' He was a slime. He was dark-haired and pale-skinned and he closed his heavy-lidded eyes when he spoke to you. That made you think he was shy, but he was a slime. Before he came into their lives, Cathy never fought with anyone.

When Howie put the phone down, Mort said: 'They tell me the Tax Department is upstairs with Mum.' He was pleased with how he said it – calm, not shaky.

'It's an audit,' Howie said. He had the desk covered with papers. Mort saw the record company logo – nothing to do with Catchprice Motors.

'So what's that mean?' Mort asked. 'An audit?'

Howie opened his drawer and pulled out a pink and black pamphlet. He stood up and brought it over to the counter. Mort took it from him. It was titled *Desk Audits & You.* 'They tell me Benny's gone blond.'

'What's it mean?' Mort tapped the brochure on the counter.

'It means ooh-la-la,' Howie said.

'What's it mean?' Mort could feel himself blushing. 'Are we in the shit or aren't we?'

'Mort, you're blushing,' Howie said.

He could not walk out. He had to stay there, enduring whatever it was that Howie knew, or thought he knew, about his son.

9

You did not need to like a car to sell it. A car was a pipe, a pump for sucking money from the 'Prospect' before you maximized it. You did not need to feel nothing, but Benny loved that fucking Audi. It looked so polite. It had its suit on, its hair cut, but it could take you to hell with your dick hard, and it would be no big deal to sell it. It could sell itself to anyone who liked to drive.

Of course seventy-five grand was a lot of money. So what? There were plenty of different ways to skin the cat, cut that cake, parcel it, package it, make it affordable for the 'Prospect' and profitable to the business, and he – dumb Benny – knew these ways.

He had, right now, the missing spare key in his pocket and the first 'prospect' who came his way, he was going to demo it, licence or no licence. This would surprise the Catchprice family, who were so worried about scratching it they would not even let him *wash* it. What would they do when he handed them the paper work – the sale made, the finance pre-approved by ESANDA? What would they say? *No please, don't sell the Audi, Benny? No please, you're only sixteen and we'd rather pay four hundred bucks a week?* They had dropped their bundle. Lost it. They had a jet black Audi Quattro sitting in the star position in the yard and instead of thanking God for giving them such a beautiful opportunity, they blamed each other for having it and worried that the floor plan payments were going to send them broke.

He could see Bozzer Mazoni across the road checking for change in the public phone box which held up the boot-maker's collapsed veranda. Bozzer had orange, red and yellow hair, a huge star ear-ring, maroon boots with black straps and a fence chain wrapped around his ankle. He looked across and saw Benny standing there. Benny raised his hand in a formal wave. Bozzer squinted and ducked his brilliant head. You could see him thinking *fucking yuppy*. He did not have a clue who Benny was.

Then the woman from the 7-Eleven came out of the drive-way with her Commodore. She knew Benny, too, from the time she tried to get him and Squeaker Davis done for shop-lifting in fourth year. As she came along the service road, she slowed down, and Benny waved at her. She frowned, and waved back, but you could see it – he was transformed – she had no more idea who he was than Bozzer had.

He waited for Vish, but Vish would not come down from Gran's flat. He was hiding, praying like a spider in a web. He was scared of that fucking car yard, but if he would only look out of the window, he would see – Benny had the *power*, Vish could have it too. They could stop being nerds. They could be millionaires, together.

Benny could feel this power, physically, in his body, in his finger tips. He was so full of light, of Voodoo. He could feel it itching on the inside of his veins. If he opened his mouth it would just pour out of him. He straightened his hard penis so it lay flat against his stomach. He felt so incredible, waxed all over, free of body hair, full of clean-skinned possibility, that he did not even know what to think about what he thought.

But nothing would stay constant. The power ebbed and flowed as it had all morning while the rain had kept him locked in the front office. You looked at the feeling, it went. You thought about the plan, you got scared. When he heard his father's feet on the gravel the hair on the nape of his neck bristled and he wanted to put his hand across his navel and hold it. It was so hard to keep his hand behind his back. His body was already doing all the things it did when it was scared. It was sweating at the hands, and the arsehole. The heart was squittering in its cage. He made himself turn and look his father in the eye.

'Get your arse out of here,' his father said. He had what the boys used to call 'the look' – bright blue peas, crazy lasers. If you were a dog you would back away.

Benny lost it.

'Get out of here,' Mort said, 'before I throw you out.'

Benny walked back to the front office, and shut the door. When his father walked back down the lane-way to the workshop, Benny sat behind the grey metal desk and shut his eyes, trying to get his power back. He did the exercises he had learned from 'Visualizing, Actualizing'. He exhaled very slowly and he laid his pretty, long-fingered hands flat on the desk.

He could see his own reflection in the glass in front of him and once again he was astonished by himself. *I look incredible.* He had moved so far beyond the point where Spare Parts could be an issue in his life.

He wondered how he looked to someone who had never seen him before, someone walking past the petrol pumps on the way to A.S.P. Building Supplies. He imagined himself seen framed by the arched windows and barley-sugar columns. He thought he would look religious or scientific. He was pleased to think he was a most unusual-looking person to be in the office of a car dealership.

He unlocked his desk drawer and removed a magazine. The viewer would have no idea what this religious or scientific person was looking at. It was unimaginable. When Benny had first looked at it, he had felt a numbness, a dizziness, like a new piece of music that he must somehow own or name. It was shiny and thrilling, as if something that had always been a part of him was now being revealed.

It was a women being fucked up the arse. She had short blonde hair. She had a thin waist and a plump arse that was as smooth and round as something in a dream.

Whoever looked in the window would not know this. They would not know how clean he felt, so clean that he could feel the thin, shiny scar-skin on his arm as it brushed his poplin shirt. He smelt of Pears shampoo. He had no hair on his arms, his legs, not even the crack of his arse.

The woman's legs were bound with woven metal straps. They looked like battery straps from a fifties Holden, but where the terminal points would be, they disappeared into some fabric – it was unclear how they were attached.

The woman was held at the shoulders and arms. She was held at the top of the calves and the ankles. The base was made of moulded fibreglass. It was more or less in the shape of a shallow 'n', not a hard thing to make, really easy. You could do it in your back yard, your cellar. The end result was that her arse stuck up in the air and she could not move. She could not fucking *move*.

You could not see the man's face, just his torso and cock. There was a pic of him putting Vaseline on his cock. They showed it close and it was good quality printing – you could feel the coolness of grease on the knob.

Benny thought: this is not nothing.

It was now sunny. Steam lay along the borders of Loftus Street. The traffic continued between these hedges of steam, unaware of the lives inside Catchprice Motors.

Benny thought: they could not imagine me.

When he heard a boot scrape on the concrete floor of the Spare Parts bays, he slipped the magazine into the drawer and locked it. He turned in his chair (only his tumescent lips could have betrayed him) and as he turned he saw Jesse.

Jesse was only five foot five inches tall. He was fifteen years old and had a freckled, scrunched-up little face, but he was fast and graceful. He was the wicket-keeper in the Franklin XI. He was Mort's little mate. He had carrot-coloured, springy straight hair. He got his job because Benny failed his apprenticeship, and he thought – they all thought, Cathy, Howie, Granny Catchprice, the men, the cleaners – they all thought it was because Benny was dumb. They thought they were above him.

Jesse had been fitting new fuel pumps to the recalled Commodores. He had been standing in the pit, soaking himself in petrol. He feinted a light punch to Benny's shoulder and then tried to grab his nuts with his grease-black hands.

Benny jumped back from the greasy hands as if they were 240 live. He stood in front of the window. He put his legs astride and held his Aloe-Vera'd hands behind his back and looked Jesse in the eye.

Benny was older. Benny's family were Jesse's employers. Benny was taller. None of this counted. The first thing Jesse said, he tried to put Benny down.

'You reckon you're a salesman, that it?'

Benny smiled. 'You got no future, Jesse.'

This was new territory for both of them. Jesse blinked three times, quickly, before he spoke. 'You got fired, not me.'

'Fired?' Benny said. 'Do I look like I am fucking fired?'

It was then he saw Mort coming back up the lane-way from the workshop, swinging his arms. Jesse said something but Benny did not hear him. He folded his arms behind his back and stood right in his father's path. The heavy aluminium door swung and hit his shoe, but Mort did not even look at him. He walked straight to the bookshelf behind the desk where young Jesse was looking through the dusty spares catalogues for old Fords and Chevrolets. He did not ask Jesse what he was doing there and why the fuck he was not getting the fuel pumps changed. He put his big hand on the apprentice's shoulder. It fitted round it like a 'U' bolt. 'How's tricks, titch?' he said, and stood beside him, right against him, looking at the old Chevrolet catalogue.

'Stephen Wall done another oil seal,' Jesse said.

Mort was red and blotchy on his neck. He didn't seem to hear what Jesse said. When he looked up at Benny his eyes were frightened and angry and his trunk was already twisting towards the door. 'Who in the fuck do you think *you* are?' he said.

Benny looked at his father with his mouth open.

Mort walked out the back door, into the Spare Parts bays.

He came back in a second later.

'You look like a poof,' he said and banged out of the office and into the yard.

Benny felt like crying. He wanted to tie his father up and pour water over his face until he said he was sorry. He felt like a snail with its shell taken off. He was pink and slimy and glistening. Even the air hurt him. He felt like dying. It was not just his father. It was everything. He could feel depression come down on him like mould, like bad milk, like the damp twisted dirty sheets in the cellar. He wanted to go to the cellar and lock the door.

'If anyone's a poof,' he said to Jesse, 'it's him.'

But Jesse was so dumb. He looked at Benny and grinned. 'That'll be the day,' he said.

'You're a fucking baby,' Benny said.

'You got mousse on your hair?'

'No I haven't.'

Jesse considered this a moment. 'You look pretty weird, you know that? You looked better before. How do you get it to stand up like that if you don't use mousse?'

'Gel.'

'You're going to do that every day now? It must take you an hour to get ready to come to work to sell petrol.'

'Listen, little bubby,' Benny said, 'you're going to remember me, I'm going to be famous and you're going to remember that all you could do was worry about my fucking hair.' He knew already he would be sorry he had said that. Jesse would tell the others and they'd fart and hee-haw like about Bozzer and his bullshit story of his father who was meant to be a yuppy with a 7 Series BMW.

But if he had to be sorry, he was fucked anyway. *I cannot be what I am.* In the corner of his eye he saw something. He turned. It was

Maria Takis, walking slowly back to her car. She waved at him. Benny liked her face. He liked her wide, soft mouth particularly. He waved back, smiling.

'Christ,' he said, 'that's all woman.'

'That's all woman,' Jesse mimicked. 'You're a poof, Benny, admit you're a poof.'

Benny heard himself say: 'She's mine.' He meant it too. He committed himself to it as he said it.

He watched the Tax Inspector getting into her car. He had a very nice feeling about her. He had had a nice feeling about her this morning, the way she spoke, the way she looked at him. He took an Aloe-Vera facelette and wiped his cheeks.

Jesse said: 'You want to fuck a whale?'

Benny looked at Jesse and saw that he was very young, and very short. He had soft, fair, fluffy hair in a line from his ears down to his chin. Benny felt his power come back. He felt it itch inside his skin.

He said, 'When you're grown up you'll like their bellies like that.'

'You don't like girls, Benny.'

'Their tits get big,' Benny said. 'Their nipples too. They like you to drink their milk while you fuck them.' He was smiling while he spoke. He felt his skin stretch. His face was full of teeth.

Jesse frowned.

Benny thought: you dwarf. He thought: I am going to rise up from the cellar and stand in the fucking sky.

'She's from the Tax Department,' Jesse said. 'I had to carry all the ledgers and that up to your Granny's flat for her. She's going to go through your old man like a dose of salts.'

This was the first time that Benny had heard about the Tax Department. He was travelling too fast to notice it. 'I don't care where she's from.' He looked down at Jesse and smiled as he checked his tie. 'I am going to fuck her.'

Jesse was going to say something. He opened his mouth but then he just made a little breathy laugh through his nose and teeth.

Finally he said, 'You?'

'Yes.' Benny's chest and shoulders felt good inside his suit. His posture was good. He was suffused with a feeling of warmth.

'We can realize our dreams,' he told Jesse.

Jesse blushed bright red.

'Also,' Benny said. He held up a single, pink-nailed forefinger and waited.

'Also what?'

'Also I am selling five vehicles a week, starting now.'

Benny smiled. Then he picked up the 'Petrol Sales' invoice book and went to read the meters on the pumps.

10

Mrs Catchprice sat in her apartment above the car yard in Franklin, and was angry about what happened in Dorrigo nearly sixty-five years before.

Her grandson chanted. It did her no particular good, although she liked the company. He chanted on and on and on, and she smiled and nodded, watching him, but she was Frieda McClusky and she was eighteen years old and she would never have the flower farm she had been promised.

In Franklin she narrowed her cloudy eyes and lit a Salem cigarette.

In Dorrigo she lost her temper. She emptied her mother's 'Tonic' across the veranda. She threw a potato through the kitchen window and watched it bounce out into the debris of the storm. She would never have a flower farm in Dorrigo. Then she would have her flower farm somewhere else.

She walked out down the long straight drive. She was eighteen. She had curly fair hair which fell across her cheek and had to be shaken back every ten yards or so.

I was pretty.

She was tall and slender and there was a slight strictness in her walk, a precision not quite in keeping with the muddy circumstances. The drive ran straight down the middle of their ten-acre block. The gutters on each side of it were now little creeks running high with yellow water from the storm. Occasional lightning continued to strike the distant transmitter at Mount Moomball, but the thunder now arrived a whole fifty seconds later. It was six o'clock in the evening. Steam was already beginning to rise from the warm earth.

There was a dense forest of dead, ring-barked trees on either side of the slippery, yellow-mud road. They were rain-wet, green-white. They were as still as coral, fossils, bones. There was a beauty in them, but Frieda McClusky did not care to see it.

There were three trees fallen across the road. She had to pick her way between the thickets of their fallen branches. She was fastidious in the way she touched the twigs. She kept her back straight and her pretty face contorted – her chin tucked into her neck, her nose wrinkled, her eyes screwed up. When a branch caught in her coat, she brushed and panicked against the restriction as though it were a spider's web.

She wore a pleated tartan skirt and a white cotton blouse with a Peter Pan collar. On her feet she had black Wellingtons. She carried a tartan umbrella, a small hat-case, a navy blue waterproof overcoat, and – for her own protection – a stick of AN 60 gelignite which had been purchased four and a half years ago in order to blow these dead trees from the earth.

In a year when no one had ever heard the term 'hobby farm', the McCluskys had sold their family home in Melbourne and moved here to Dorrigo a thousand miles away. There was, of course, no airport in Dorrigo, but there was no railway either. From the point of view of Glenferrie Road, Malvern, Victoria, it was like going to Africa.

Frieda's father was fifty-eight years old. He had energy in the beginning. He had blue poplin work-shirts and moleskin trousers which went slowly white. He set out to ring-bark every large tree on the ten-acre block. When the trees were dead he was going to blast their roots out of the earth with gelignite. The ten acres he chose were surrounded by giant trees, by dramatic ravines, escarpments, waterfalls. It was as romantic a landscape as something in a book of old engravings. Within his own land he planned rolling lawns, formal borders, roses, carnations, dahlias, hollyhocks, pansies, and a small ornamental lake.

He had notebooks, rulers, pens in different colours. He had plans headed 'Dorrigo Springs Guest-house' which he drew to scale. He listed his children on a page marked 'Personnel'. Daniel McClusky – vegetable gardener. Graham McClusky – carpenter, mechanic. Frieda McClusky – flower gardener. It did not seem crazy at the time. He wrote a letter to the Technical Correspondence School so he might 'qualify in the use of handling of explosives to a standard acceptable to the chief Inspector of Explosives of New South Wales'. He bought Frieda *Large Scale Plantings* by A. C. Reade. She learned to push the soil auger hard enough to take samples from the land. She parcelled up each sample in separate brown paper bags and sent them by train to C.S.I.R.O.

Frieda's mother was not listed as 'Personnel', but the move had a positive effect upon her temper. She bought a horse and wore jodhpurs which made her skittish and showed off her good legs and her small waist. She brushed Frieda's hair at night, and stopped going to bed straight after dinner. She was less critical of Frieda's appearance. Sometimes she walked down the drive-way with her husband, hand in hand. You could see them pointing out the future to each other. Frieda watched them and felt a great weight removed from her.

Frieda loved the feel of the soil between her fingers, the smell of earth at night in deep, damp gullies, chicken and horse manure, rich reeking blood and bone from the Dorrigo abattoirs. She liked the smell of rotting grass as it slowly became earth. She liked to dig her garden fork down deep and see the pink-grey bodies of worms, lying still and silent, hiding from the air.

She was stupid enough to be grateful for the life she was given. She did not see what her brothers saw – that they were stuck with mad people. They did not have the decency to share their thoughts with her. They left an envelope propped against the ugly little butter dish Aunt Mae had given them. The letter said they could not have expressed their feelings because 'we would have been talked out of it'. They said they were now men and had to choose their own lives and would write later. They left their shirts and sweaters folded neatly in their drawers.

Marcia McClusky blamed her husband, although, typically, she never did say this clearly. By noon on the day they opened the envelope, Stan and Marcia McClusky had stopped speaking to each other. By the following evening Marcia was sleeping in the boys' room. The next morning neither of them got up.

It was grief of course, but grief does not stay grief for ever. It changes, and in this case it also must have changed, although into what is by no means certain. It could not be grief, it was something drier and harder than grief, a knot, a lump. They lay all day, cocooned in their beds in their own rooms, like grubs locked out of metamorphosis. They read second-hand romances and detective novels – three, sometimes four a day – while the ring-barked trees outside slowly died and grew white and were left to crash and fall around the house in storms.

Frieda worked cheerfully around her parents, cooking, cleaning, dusting, as if she could, by the sheer force of her goodwill, effect their recovery. She carried the vision for them. Not a guest-house any more. She pared it down to the thing she had been promised – the flowers. She would have a flower farm. For three years – an impossible time in retrospect – she ran to and fro, trying to make them cheerful again. She paid for the *Horticulturalist* from housekeeping. She began a correspondence with the Horticultural Society. She grew flowers – Gerberas particularly – and exhibited them at local shows.

Only in the midst of the violent storms of summer did she express her anger. With giant trees crashing in the night, she hated her parents for putting her in terror of her life. In the clear white flash of lightning, she said things so extreme that their remembrance, at morning, was shameful to her.

But when the giant red cedar finally hit the house it was afternoon, and there was no sleep to take the edge off her rage or make her forget the extremity of her terror.

The cedar wiped out the south-west corner of the veranda and pushed its way into the kitchen. The noise was so great that her parents actually rose from their beds, both at the same time.

The sky to the east was still black. But the sun came from the west and as they came out on to the shattered veranda it shone upon them. They stood staring at the receding storm and squinted as the unexpected sunlight took them from the side. In the light of the sun they looked spoiled and sickly, like things left too long in the bath. Frieda saw the toes sticking from the slippers, the string where the dressing cord should be, the yellow, dog-eared pages of a musty Carter Brown in her father's hand, and felt all her unpermitted anger well up in her. She opened her mouth to release some word bigger than a pumpkin. She could do nothing but hold her hands apart and shake her head. They put their hands across their brows to shade their eyes from glare.

She fetched her mother's tonic and poured it away in front of her.

She took the bread and butter pudding from the oven and threw it off the edge of the veranda.

'Maggots,' she said. 'You nearly killed me.'

No one said anything, but by the time she reached the front gate her mother was on the phone to the police.

Percy Donaldson was the Sergeant. He was half-shickered when he got the call and he dropped the car keys down between the slats on the veranda and had to take his son's bicycle to get Frieda back. Mrs McClusky, who had seen her daughter walk up towards the Ebor Road, hadn't troubled to tell him that the runaway had a stick of AN 60 and a bag of detonators in a little lilac whats-oh hanging round her neck.

He found her up at the beginning of the gravel road where the town's macadam stopped. It was dark by then, although not pitch black. She waved the gelly at him: 'You grab me and you're minced meat.' He could see her pale face in the light of his bicycle lantern. 'I've got the detonators,' she said in a trembling voice. 'I know what to do with them.'

'Whoa,' he said. 'Easy girl.' He peered into the poor, pale yellow nimbus of light which was all the flat battery was able to bring to bear on the girl. She sure was pretty.

'It's real,' she said. 'I'm Stan McClusky's daughter.'

'I know who you are, Frieda.'

'Good,' she said.

She did not even have the detonators wrapped up. They clinked next to each other in their little bag next to her breast.

'You want to wrap them things up,' he said. 'They'll blow your little titties off.'

It was because of that remark she refused to speak to him all night. And it was all night they were to spend together – because she would not return with him, and he would not leave her alone, and so they walked together over the pot-holed road – Percy hearing those damned detonators clinking round her neck while they walked for ten hours with their stomachs rumbling – neither of them had eaten before they left – until at piccaninny dawn they were on the outskirts of Wollombi. Fifty-two miles. Ten hours. Over five miles an hour!

As they walked on to the mile-long stretch of macadam which was Wollombi, Frieda burst into tears. Her face was caked with dust and the tears made smudgy mud and she bowed her head and howled. Percy felt sorry for her. He lent her his handkerchief and watched helplessly as her pretty little shoulders shook. The milkman was stopped a little up the road. He was ladling milk from his bucket, but staring at the policeman and the crying girl.

'You've got guts,' Percy said, motioning the milkman to piss off. 'I'll say that for you.'

He guessed she was frightened of what trouble she had got herself into, which was true, but he had no idea how empowered she was. Under the mud of her despair and misery ran this hard bedrock of certainty – the fact that gelignite was as light as a feather. Until that day she had thought it was a thing for men.

She and Percy got a lift with a fellow who was a traveller in Manchester and Millinery. His car was filled with samples but they wrapped the bicycle in hessian bags and strapped it to the roof with twine. They travelled home together in the dickey seat, silently, but companionably, like soldiers who have fought beside each other in the same trench. The only charges ever laid were against her father for not keeping his gelignite locked up.

Everyone in Dorrigo heard the story, of course, Freddy Sparks the butcher knew it, told it to people who had already heard it. But he never did connect it with the sweet cloying smell that rose from Frieda Catchprice's handbag when she opened it to pay the bill. The source of the smell was nothing to look at – like a cheap sausage, or some cold porridge wrapped in brown paper. It was a stick of AN 60 gelignite.

This was the year Frieda did her mines exams and got a permit herself. No one wanted to let her have it – her parents least of all – but she wanted to make a flower farm and they were too frightened to say no.

11

She was carrying gelignite in her white leather clutch-bag when she first danced with 'Cacka' Catchprice. He arrived in August as official scorer for the touring Franklin 'Magpies'.

All that time I was pretty and did not know it.

This thought could still make her rheumy eyes water – she had been brought up to think herself so goddam plain, such a collection of faults – wide mouth, small bosom, thin legs – which would all be clear for all the world to snicker at if she did not listen to her mother's advice about her shoes, her skirt, her lipstick colour.

I could have married anyone I damn well pleased.

When she walked into town in gum boots, holding gelignite in her clutch-bag, her dancing shoes in a paper bag, she had decided to get married, to anyone, she did not care – anything would be better than staying in that house another year – but when she opened the wire gate in the fence around the C.W.A. rooms, she almost lost her resolve and her legs went weak and rubbery and she really thought she was going to faint.

She saw men in blazers leaning against the ugly concrete veranda posts. There was a string of coloured lights in a necklace under-neath the veranda guttering. Under the wash of blue and red there were girls she recognized, people she had 'dealt with' in the shops who were now powerful and pretty in scallops of peach organza. They did not try to speak to her. The smell of beer came out to meet her, as alien as sweat, hair oil, pipe tobacco. She had to make herself continue up the path in her gum boots.

Inside it was no better. She sat beneath the crepe paper streamers, on a chair in a corner by the tea urn, and removed her muddy gum boots. She kept her head down, convinced that every-one was looking at her. When she saw that the gum boots were too big to fit in her paper bag, she did not know what to do with them.

If it had not been for the gum boots Cacka might never have spoken to her. If she had come in with shiny black high heels, he would almost certainly have found her beyond his reach. But he came from a red clay farm where you had to wear gum boots to go to take a shit at night. His mother wore gum boots to get from the back door to the hire car which took them to their father's funeral.

'Tell you what,' he said. 'I'm going to put these out the back. You tell me when you want them. I'll get them for you.'

'You're most kind,' she said.

'How about a dance when I get back?'

'Oh,' she said.

'I know I'm not an oil painting.'

'Thank you,' she said. 'That would be lovely.'

He had this bulk, this thick neck and sloping shoulders, so all his strength seemed centred in his chest, which occasionally touched her breasts when he danced with her, formally, apologetically. He held her as if she were somehow fragile, and she let herself be held this way. She had spent three years being 'strong' and now she was so tensed and wound up that when, by the fifth dance, she allowed herself to give her weight to him, she could not give a part of it, but laid the full load on his shoulders which she dampened with a tear or two.

His nose had a big bump in it just beneath the eye, and his left ear was slightly squashed and the skin around his left eye was blue and yellow, but he was also very gentle, and it was not that opportunistic gentleness the roughest man will adopt around a woman – it was written permanently on his lips which were soft and well-shaped and formed little cooing words she felt like warm oil-drops in her ears. This was a man whose secret passion was the Opera, who had the complete HMV recording of *Die Zauberflöte* hidden beneath his bed – eight 78 rpm records with a cast most of whose names he could not pronounce – Tiana Lemnitz, Erna Berger, Helge Rosvaenge, Gerhard Hüsch, and the Berlin Philharmonic conducted by Sir Thomas Beecham.

Die Zauberflöte, however, meant nothing to Frieda. She was thirsty for what was practical, and when she drew him out she was the daughter of a man with little coloured pens and pretty pencils and paper plans on flimsy sheets of tracing paper. She loved to hear him talk about post-hole digging, barbed wire, white ants, concrete fencing posts, poultry sheds.

'You really want to hear this stuff?' he asked.

'Oh yes,' she said.

'Truly?'

'Truly and really.'

And when the band played 'Begin the Beguine' she held him tightly and sang the words softly in his ear. It was that which put the little wet spot on his Jockey shorts – that voice she did not even know she had. He told his mate, Billy Johnston, with whom he shared a room at the Dorrigo Court House Hotel, 'I didn't even kiss her, mate. I didn't even touch her. She's got these little tits, you know. I think I love her.'

At ten o'clock in the morning on the day after the dance, he came to call on her. She met him in her gum boots – halfway up the muddy drive – and told him she was going to have a flower farm there. She was going to blast those trees herself if no one would do it for her.

She said this almost angrily, for she had to say it and she expected that saying it would drive him from her, but Cacka was too shocked to laugh – he thought he never saw a sadder bit of country in his life.

'If it's flowers you want,' he said, 'I could show you land more suitable.'

All her life she would accuse him of lying about this, but even she knew this was not quite fair. Cacka withheld things and had secrets but he rarely told an outright lie. This land did exist, forty-five minutes from the central markets just the way he said it did. He was happy and in love. He really saw the land. He really saw Gerberas on it. It was the opposite of lying.

What he omitted was that it was part of a deceased estate and held up for probate.

It was ten years before Frieda and Albert Catchprice finally got possession of that land, and then she was the one who showed him how he could put a motor business on it. The only thing she had ever wanted was a flower farm, but what she got instead was the smell of rubber radiator hoses, fan belts, oil, grease, petrol vapour, cash flows, overdrafts and customers whose bills ran 90, 120 days past due. It was this she could not stand – she did it to herself.

12

It was the day they had tried to put her in a nursing home, but it would be the same on any other day – when Mrs Catchprice went to lock the big Cyclone gates of Catchprice Motors, she would look up at Cathy and Howie's apartment window. The look would say: just try and stop me.

At six o'clock exactly – in two minutes' time – Howie would look through the Venetian blinds and see her apartment door open, like a tricky clock in a Victorian arcade. First, the old woman would put her nose out and sniff the air. Then she would look down at the cars. Then she would come out on to the landing and stare at the window where she thought her enemy was waiting for her to die.

She thought it was Howie who conspired to commit her. She needed no proof. It was obvious. He was fiddling with the books, renting other premises, preparing to set up as a Honda dealer, in opposition.

He was plotting, certainly, continually, every moment of the day, but what he was plotting to do was to have a life like Ernest Tubb, The Gold Chain Troubadour. He was plotting to have his wife run away with him.

It was only Cathy who kept him locked inside those Cyclone gates. She had an entire band trying to drag her out on to the road. She had 'Drunk as a Lord' with a *bullet* on the Country charts. She had fans who wrote to her. She had a life to go to, but she was a Catchprice, and she was tangled in all that mad Catchprice shit that had her shouting at her mother while she fed her, at war with her brother while she fretted about his loneliness, firing her nephew while she went running to his cellar door, knocking and crying and leaving presents for him – she bought him *dope*, for Chrissakes, *dope*, in a pub, to cheer him up. You would not want to know about that kid's life, his brother either. They were like institution kids with old men's eyes in their young faces, but she loved them, unconditionally, with an intensity that she tried to hide even from her husband. Howie could not trust those boys, either of them, but he had learned not to speak against them in his wife's presence.

Indeed, Howie had become as calculating and secretive as Granny Catchprice thought he was, but he did not covet Catchprice money or the Catchprice Goodwill Factor and he did not want to set up in competition to the family firm. His 'happy thought' was of long tendrils of vines snaking through brick walls of Catchprice Motors, collapsed fire escapes, high walls covered by bearded mosses and flaking lichens, rusting Cyclone fence collapsing under a load of Lantana and wild passionfruit. He was not counting on Granny Catchprice's death to free him – he judged it would be too long in coming.

Mrs Catchprice had the only authorized keys to the Cyclone gates, and she would not give them up. Every morning at half-past six she opened them, and every night she locked them up again. They were not light or easy. You could see her lean her brittle little shoulders into the hard steel and guess what it might take her to get those big galvanized rollers moving. But she would not give up those keys to anyone. If you wanted to get a car out of the yard outside the 'hours' you were meant to go up the fire escape and ask her, please, if it was not too much trouble.

Granny did not have guests and neither did Mort. When they shut the gates at night it was as if they were severing connection with 'The General Public' until the morning.

It was only Howie and Cathy who were 'social'. Their guests had to drive down the workshop lane-way and park outside the entrance to the Spare Parts Department. They then honked once or twice and Howie went down to let them in. This was never any problem with musicians. But Howie was sometimes embarrassed to have their visitors first approach their apartment along a steel-shelved avenue stacked with leaf springs and shock absorbers.

At six o'clock, on the dot, Gran Catchprice came out on to her landing. She not only looked across at him, she bowed, and gave a mocking little curtsy.

'You old chook,' he said. He frowned and fitted a cigarette into the corner of his smile.

Cathy came in from the kitchen with two cans of Resch's Pilsener. She was wearing a gingham skirt which showed off her strong, well-shaped legs, and white socks and black shoes like a school kid. She gave him one can and sat on the rickety ping-pong table.

It was two and a half hours before their meeting with the band but already she had that high nervous look she had in the fifteen minutes before she did a show. He loved that look. You could not say she was beautiful, but he sat night after night in bars for a hundred miles around Franklin and watched men change their opinion of her as she sang.

She had a good band, but it was nothing special. She had a good voice, but there were better. It was her words, and it was her feelings. She could turn the shit of her life into jewels. She had plump arms and maybe a little too much weight under the chin and her belly pushed out against her clothes, but she was sexy. You had to say, whatever problems she had in bed, she was a sexy woman. You could watch men see it in her, but never straightaway.

'Big night,' he said. He stood up so she could take the bar stool and he sat instead on the ping-pong table.

'Sure,' she said. She was bright and tight, could barely talk. Tonight she was going to have her meeting with the band and with the lawyer. She drank her beer. He leaned across to rub her neck, but you could not touch her neck or shoulders unless she had been drinking.

'Don't, hon.' She took his hand and held it. Something had happened with the neck and shoulders. Sentimental Cacka had dragged her out of bed at two in the morning to sing 'Batti, batti' from *Don Giovanni* to his visitors. It happened then, he guessed. She never said exactly, but he saw it exactly, in his mind's eye. You could see the shadows of it. You could draw a map from them.

'What you think?' she said.

'About what?'

'Will I do it?'

'You've got to decide,' he said. 'I can't tell you what to do.'

'I'm just hurt, I guess. I'm pissed off with them for talking to a lawyer.'

'Sure,' he said. 'I know.' He patted her thigh sympathetically – he was the one who had persuaded Craig and Steve Putzel that they could pull Cathy out on the road if they did what he said. He was the one who found them this so-called Entertainment Lawyer. He had manoeuvred them all to this point where they were an inch away from having the lives they wanted, all of them. He brushed some ash off his suede shoe. He buttoned his suit jacket and unbuttoned it.

'Big night,' he said again. Through the Venetian blinds he could see Mort walking down the fire escape from this mother's apartment. This time next year, all this was going to seem like a bad dream.

Cathy saw Mort too. 'They've been talking about the doctor,' she said. 'You can bet on it. He's been telling her it was all my idea, the coward.'

Howie always thought Mort was a dangerous man, but he doubted he would be dishonest in the way Cathy imagined. He watched Mort as he bent over the whitewashed sign Howie had written on the windscreen of the red Toyota truck. He scratched at it with his fingernail.

'He doesn't like my sign,' he said.

Cathy lifted the Venetian blind a fraction so it pinged.

Mrs Catchprice had walked back from the gates and joined her son. She also scratched at the whitewash with one of her keys.

'You know he thinks "As-new" is sleazy,' Cathy said. 'You must have known they'd wipe it off.'

'Ah,' said Howie, 'who cares.'

That surprised her. She looked at him with her head on one side and then, silently, drew aside his jacket, undid a shirt button, and looked at the colour of his rash.

She said: 'You really think I'm going to take the leap, don't you?'

He wasn't counting on anything until it happened. She had been this close four years before, and once again, two years before that. Each time Granny Catchprice pulled her strings. You would not believe the tricks the old woman could pull to keep her workhorse working.

'If we're done for tax I can't go on the road. You know that. I can't just desert them.'

'Yes you can,' he said. He did up his shirt button. 'This time you've got to.'

'Yes,' she said. 'I've got to.'

She had that tightness in her bones, a flushed luminous look, as if she was about to do a show. He watched her drain her beer.

'You look beautiful,' he said.

'This time I'm going to do it.'

'When you look like that I want to fuck you.' He came and held her from behind and began to kiss her neck. She accepted his kisses. They lay on her skin like unresolved puzzles.

'He's coming up here,' she said.

She meant Mort. He could see why she said it. Mort was walking across the yard this way, but he was probably on his way to hammer and yell at Benny's cellar door. Mort's house shared a hot water service with their apartment, but Mort had not visited them for nine years.

'He's coming *here*,' she said. 'This is it. It's starting.'

She had such amazing skin – very white and soft.

'Don't!' She broke free from his hands, suddenly irritated.

'It's nothing,' he said. 'It'll be about the nursing home.'

'They're going to try and make me stay.'

'Cathy, Cathy . . . they don't even believe you're leaving them.'

'She's sending him to say something to me.'

'Honey, calm down. Think. What could they say to you at this stage?'

Cathy's eyes began to water. 'She's so unfair.'

Howie stroked her neck. 'You're forty-six years old,' he said. 'You're entitled to your own life.'

'She makes him say it for her. He's going to say how much she needs me.' She put her hand on his sleeve. 'He's coming up the stairs.'

'Let me lock the door,' Howie said.

Mort had not visited their apartment since he argued with Howie about the ping-pong table eleven years ago.

'This is the living-room,' he said. 'There's no room for a ping-pong table.'

'With all respect,' Howie had answered, 'that's not your business.'

'Respect is something you wouldn't know about,' Mort said. 'It's the Family Home. You're turning it into a joke.'

Even allowing for the fact his father had just died, this was a crazy thing to say. Howie could not think of how to answer him.

'Respect!' Mort said.

Then he slammed his fist into the brick wall behind Howie's head. It came so close it grazed his ear.

'I'll lock the door,' Howie said, not moving.

Cathy poured some Benedictine into a tumbler. Then the door opened and she looked up and there was Mort and his lost wife, side by side. But it couldn't be Sophie. Sophie had left thirteen years ago.

13

It wasn't Sophie. It was Benny. He had made himself into the spitting image of the woman who had shot him. Whether he had meant to do it, or if it was an accident of bright white hair, the effect was most disturbing, to Cathy anyway.

All through the day the men from the workshop had come and gone with their grubby job cards, cracking their jokes about her nephew's 'look', but not one of them had said – how could they have known, they were all too young – how like his mother it made him seem. His hair was the same colour, the *exact* same colour, and it gave his features a luminous, fresh-steamed look. Sophie had grown her hair long in the end but at the beginning she had it short like this and now you could see he had the cheekbones. He was like his mother, but he had a damaged, dangerous look his mother never had. No matter what shit she put up with from the Catchprices she kept her surface as fresh and clean as a pair of freshly whitened tennis shoes right up to the day she shot her son.

Cathy said: 'Benny, you look nice.'

The person he made her think of was Elvis – not that he looked like Elvis, but he *felt* how Elvis must have felt when he walked into Sam Phillips's recording studio in Memphis – a shy boy, who maybe never played but in his bedroom, with the mirror. Sam Phillips must have seen his sexy lips, but the thing that struck him was how inferior Elvis felt, how *markedly* inferior. He said this in an interview on more than one occasion.

Benny had already phoned her once today to say he was going to 'hurt' her, and she knew he had a temper which you can only describe as violent, but she knew him with his little arms tight around her neck at three in the morning, and when she complimented him he blushed and lowered his eyes because he knew she meant it and would never lie to him.

It was only when Mort heard his son's name that he actually realized Benny had come up the stairs behind him.

'Oh, shit,' he said.

Cathy looked at Mort and wondered now if he even saw the similarity.

Benny raised his eyebrows at his father and shrugged apologetically. He put out his hand as if to take his sleeve or his hand, but the sleeves on Mort's overall were cut off and there was nothing to hold on to except a hand he would not take. Cathy would have taken his hand, but it was not offered her.

Benny had been in trouble with almost everything, lying, cheating, truancy, shop-lifting, selling bottled petrol for inhalation, trying to buy Camira parts from the little crooks who hung about in Franklin Mall; but now he just looked very young and frightened of being laughed at. He walked lightly on his feet, holding his back straight. You could hear his new shoes squeaking as he crossed the room to the yellow vinyl armchair which had once belonged to Cacka. When he sat and crossed his long legs, he revealed socks as long as a clergyman's – no skin showed. Benny folded his clean hands in his lap and looked directly at his father, blushing.

Mort's colour was also high and his lips had a loose embarrassed look. He shook his head and shut his eyes.

'Ignore your father,' Cathy said. 'You look wonderful, better than your uncle Jack.'

'Thanks Cath,' Mort said. He leaned against the window-sill opposite her and stared critically at the stupid ping-pong table. It was not properly joined in the middle. It was marked with stains from their 'Social Ambitions' – ring marks from glasses and bottles, sticky circles of Benedictine stuck with dust.

'You singing tonight?' he asked. 'You got a jig-jig?'

'Very funny,' she said. 'What do you want?'

Mort shook his head as if in disappointment at this hostility. He looked down at his boots a moment as if he was considering a riposte, but then he looked up, spoke in what was, for him, in the circumstances, a calm voice: 'Why does this Tax Inspector have her office in Mum's apartment?'

'You come up here to ask about that?' Cathy crossed her arms below her breasts and shook her head.

'Mort . . .' Howie said.

'I don't believe you,' Cathy said.

'Tough,' said Mort.

'The auditor needs a desk,' Howie said, 'that's all. She could have taken any vacant desk. She could have had your office.'

'You wouldn't want me near a Tax Inspector,' Mort said. 'You couldn't trust me not to give the game away.'

Cathy looked into his eyes and he held hers. He was her brother in a way that Jack had never been. She and Mort were the ones who had sung opera together, killed chooks, sold cars, but now she had no idea what he thought about anything.

'There is no game,' Cathy said.

'I wouldn't know.'

'No,' Cathy said. 'You wouldn't, but you'd better find out. If I was you I'd be finding out what makes this business tick pretty damn fast.'

'You going to try and run away again, Cathy?' Mort grinned. 'Did you get another letter from The Gold Chain Troubadour?'

There was silence which was broken by the sound of Benedictine being poured into Cathy's tumbler. Benny crossed his legs and laid his left palm softly on the back of the right hand.

'Look,' Mort said. 'What I came up here to say was that I've had a talk to Mum.'

Cathy poured herself some extra Benedictine, but then she didn't drink it.

'I talked with Mum and we both decided that if you want to sell the back paddock to cover us with any back taxes, we'll vote in favour. That's why I'm here, to tell you that.'

'Do you remember,' Howie said, smiling sideways at Cathy, 'that we wrote your mother in as head salesman?'

'Sure.'

'And we claimed tax deductions for what we said we paid her?'

'Sure, I remember that. We had Jack's smart-arse accountant. You all got excited about how you were going to keep the trade-ins off the books. But do you remember what I said then?'

'Tell me.'

'I said that I didn't want to do business like Jack. I said we've gone off the rails. We shouldn't be playing tricks with tax. We should be running the business by its original principles . . .'

'Mort,' Howie said. 'I'm trying to explain that if this audit goes through we are going to need *twenty* back paddocks to pay the bill.'

'And I'm trying to tell you, Mr Rock 'n' Roll,' said Mort, suddenly shouting and jabbing his finger at Howie, 'that this business will run itself just fine if we stop listening to crooks and stick to Cacka's philosophy.'

It was very quiet. Then there was a squeaking noise. The ping-pong table started to move in front of Benny's nose. It pushed towards him, then withdrew. It was Cathy pushing with her big thighs. She had a bright little smile on her face.

'Philosophy?' she said. Her mouth was small in her big face and she had two hot spots on her pale cheeks. 'What sort of philosophy would that be, Mort? Like Socrates? Like Mussolini? What sort of philosophy did you have in mind exactly?'

Mort said: 'He was one of the greats.' Benny looked down at the floor. He thought: don't, please don't.

'Mort,' Cathy said. 'Say he was a creep. Admit it. It's not your fault.'

'He was human, but he was one of the greats.'

'Look at us,' Cathy said. There was a bang as she slammed her glass down on the table. Benedictine spilled. (Howie went to the kitchen to get a Wettex. Benny despised him for doing it.) 'Look at us,' Cathy said, watching Howie wipe the table. 'We don't know how to be happy. Look out of the window. We're car dealers. That's all we do. You cannot be a *great* car dealer.'

'You can be a great *boot-maker*,' Mort said.

Benny agreed. He took a facelette of Aloe-Vera and wiped the back of his hands. He thought: *I* will be a great car dealer.

Cathy took the Wettex from Howie and folded it and placed it on the table. Howie picked it up and took it out to the kitchen.

'You want to talk about *great*,' Cathy said. 'Elvis was great.'

Mort laughed.

'Hank Williams was great, but Christ, Morty, even if you could be a *great* car dealer, you could not be great and bankrupt at the same time.'

'Spend some time with the books, Mort. I'd be happy to take you through them.'

'Listen,' Mort said. 'I don't like this business. I don't think you like it either, but we're stuck with it. If we want to save our arse, we should go back to Cacka's principles.'

'And what principles were you thinking of?' Howie asked.

'You remember Catchprice Motors, Cathy?' Mort asked his sister. 'We didn't wind our speedos back. We paid our taxes. We told the truth.'

'Why do you mime the words of the hymns in church?' Howie asked.

Mort looked at him, his mouth loose.

'I just meant to ask you,' Howie said. 'I wondered why you won't sing out loud. Barry Peterson asked me why someone with such a good voice wouldn't sing out loud. I wondered if this had something to do with Cacka's philosophy.'

'Shut up, Howie,' Cathy said.

'What I'm getting to,' Mort said, his neck now blazing red above his white overall collar, 'is Cacka paid his taxes. He'd have shut the doors if he couldn't pay his taxes.'

'Mort,' said Cathy, more gently than before, 'Franklin has changed.'

'If it's changed so much we have to be cheats, I'd rather run some little garage up at Woop-woop. I'd rather be on the dole.'

'You might get your wish,' Cathy said.

'How?' asked Benny.

They all looked at him. For a moment the only noise came from the rattling air-conditioner.

'What?' Cathy said, frowning at him.

'How will my father get his wish?'

'What this conversation is about, Benjamin, is that we are being investigated by the Taxation Department.'

'I know that.'

'And by the time they have finished with us, we'll have to sell the business to pay them back.'

'So, what are you going to do, Cathy?' Benny asked.

'Don't speak to your auntie like that.'

'No,' Benny insisted, 'what are you going to do to protect us? *What positive steps can be taken towards realizing our desires?*' He blushed and stood up. They were all staring at him. Not one of them had any idea of who he was and what it was he had quoted to them. Howie was smirking, but none of them had any plan appropriate to their situation. In their shiny suits and frills and oily overalls, they were creatures at the end of an epoch. The climate had changed and they were puzzled to find the familiar crops would no longer grow. He stood up. He was full of light. They saw him, but did not see him, for the best and most vital part of him was already walking down the path towards the actualization of his desires. *I am new. I am born now.* Even while they stared at him across the bottle-stained emptiness of the ping-pong table, he was descending the staircase, not the one that led to his physical actual cellar – not the metal staircase with its perforated treads, the oil-stained ladder with the banister he must not touch – but the other staircases which are described in seven audio cassettes, *Actualizations and Affirmations 1–14.*

He was descending the blue staircase (its treads shimmering like oil on water, its banisters clear, clean, stainless steel) and all they could think was that he had no right to wear a suit.

At the bottom of the blue staircase he found the yellow staircase.

At the bottom of the yellow staircase, the pink.

At the bottom of the pink, the ebony.

At the end of the ebony, the Golden Door.

Beyond the Golden Door was the Circular Room of Black Marble.

In the centre of the Circular Room of Black Marble he visualized a Sony Trinitron.

Benny turned on the Sony Trinitron and saw there the vivid picture of what it was he desired: all the books and ledgers of Catchprice Motors, wrapped in orange garbage bags and sealed with silver tape.

'Leave it to me,' he said out loud.

By then he was already walking across the crushed gravel of the car yard. His father was a yard ahead of him.

'What?' he said.

14

Maria's image of herself was made in all the years before 15 July, the day she finally discovered that she was pregnant. No matter what kicks the baby gave her, no matter how it squirmed and rolled and pushed and made her lumpy and off-centre, no matter how her legs ached, her back hurt, irrespective of the constipation, haemorrhoids and insomnia, the fine webs of spider veins and stretch marks that threatened to make her old and ugly overnight, she could still forget what her body had actually become. She could look in the mirrors as she entered the birth class and be surprised to see a short, big-bellied woman.

There were also other times when she knew exactly what she looked like and then she felt that she had been that way for ever, and then it was almost impossible to remember that it had only been on 15 July last year that she had discovered she was pregnant.

On 15 July she still had beer and wine in her refrigerator, no milk. She made her last cup of strong black coffee, not even bothering to taste it properly, and slipped into her quilted 'Afghan' skirt and embroidered black silk blouse not guessing that before five weeks had passed the $220 skirt would be unwearable.

Her period was late, but her period was often late, or early. She stopped in Darling Street, Balmain, and spent $15 on a pregnancy test kit and drove over the Harbour Bridge to Crows Nest where she was auditing a property developer. It wasn't until after lunch she found the pregnancy test kit in her handbag.

In the property developer's white bathroom she saw a slender phial of her urine turn a pretty violet colour.

She sat it on the window ledge and shook her head at it. Such was her capacity for denial that she assumed the kit was faulty and at three o'clock she spent another $15 on a second kit and got the same result.

She tried to phone her best friend at the Tax Office. Gia Katalanis had an office with a view and an answer machine on her desk. Maria left a message: 'Extraordinary news.'

As for Alistair, she put it off. She knew where he was, in an office two floors above Gia's. Even when she phoned him, on his direct line, at five o'clock, she did not know quite what she was going to say.

'I want to buy you dinner,' she told him, looking out of the property developer's spare office to where $80,000 yachts heeled over in the Nor'-easter.

'I can't,' he said.

She understood exactly what he meant – his wife.

'Oh, yes you can,' she said. She laughed, but it did not soften the effect – she had already crossed a line. 'It's something good,' she said. 'Not bad. It's worth it.'

She knew how false this was even when she said it – that what she was to present him with was something totally unacceptable, something that could not fit into the odd shapes they had made of their lives.

'I'm going to have to tell such dreadful lies,' he said.

'That's life,' she said.

But when she hung up she knew that was exactly what she did not want life to be. She dropped her half-finished can of Diet Coke into the rubbish bin. That night when she met Alistair at the Blue Moon Brasserie the first thing he noticed was that she had taken all the silver rings off her hands.

'What happened?' he asked as they sat down. It was her hands he was talking about.

But she was already telling him that she was pregnant and she would have the child.

She had rehearsed a more reasoned, gradual, diplomatic speech, but in the end the words came out gracelessly, sounding more angry than she thought she felt. 'You're going to have to choose,' she said. It was amazing. It was just like saying 'pass the bread' – only words, gone already, disappeared into that loud river of talk that bounced off the hard tiled floor of the Brasserie.

Alistair nodded as he nodded with men when arguing on

television, absorbing their points, holding his counsel, the picture of reasonableness. He was holding her newly naked hand, massaging her wrist, but he suddenly looked very far away and she was frightened by what she had begun.

He was almost fifty. He had a craggy, handsome face and curly grey hair. She had watched that face so closely for so many years she could no more describe him than she could, as a child, have described her mother or father. The shape of his face corresponded to some shape in her mind, a place to lie down and sleep and be safe.

'I don't care if we don't get married,' she said, although this was different from what she had planned to say. 'But you're going to have to choose.'

He sat looking at her, nodding his head. Without his face seeming to change, he began to cry.

She watched the frightening fat drops run down the creases of his tanned and ruined face. They dropped like blobs of jelly and splashed into his Cabernet Sauvignon.

'You wouldn't stop me seeing our child?'

'Of course not,' she said. 'You'll always be its father.' She saw her whole adult life dissolving as she spoke. She saw what she was embarked on. Alistair could not leave his drunk, unhappy wife. He was not sufficiently strong, or cruel, and she was suddenly, as the Blue Swimmer Crabs were placed in front of her, not at all sure she wanted a child. She was cut through with fear. It pierced her like an iceberg.

Alistair did not see this fear, that she should not have a baby, that she was not suited. She never let anyone but Gia see it, but it was almost always there, and it had been present all that Monday at Catchprice Motors. At the birth class that evening there was no avoiding it. They rubbed her nose in 'reality' and would not let her look away.

She sat on a bean bag, surrounded by couples, and watched the videotape called 'Belinda's Labour'.

After thirty minutes of film time – thirty hours of real time – the baby's head emerged. The husband's mouth was open, staring at it. The midwife's green-gloved hands delivered the baby. The wife saw the husband's face and could only have read it as a banner headline shouting GRIEF. The baby was blue. Its head flopped, as if it were broken or rotten. There was a silence as if something unexpectedly, horribly wrong had happened. It was like a home movie of an assassination.

But this videotape had been *selected* to show the birth class. There could be nothing 'unexpected' in this respect. This birth happened over and over, like the hellish mechanical creatures in Disneyland who are condemned to repeat the same action eighty times a day. Someone had planned to show them this record of thirty hours of pain.

In a moment, of course, the class would criticize the husband. He was not supporting his wife. He was looking at the distressed baby. At that second, he thought the child was dead.

But all Maria could think was: I don't want it.

She was angry and frightened, although none of the women in the room could have guessed these feelings. It was not, as they say, how she 'presented', which was strong and confident and often funny.

If Gia had been there, as she normally was, they would have stayed for herbal tea at the end. But Gia was not there, and although she could hardly be angry at Gia for this, it occurred to her now that Gia might, on the very night she went into labour, not be in her own bed when Maria rang for her.

Maria left the birth class without saying goodnight to anyone. The lifts were prone to jamming and there was a hand-written sign advising birth class members to use the stairs. The stairs were like Hong Kong: concrete, sweaty-smelling, guarded by heavy metal fire doors. Maria Takis clattered down them alone, like a victim in a movie.

Who will care for me?

The street was empty of people, lined with parked cars. There was a derelict man peeing in the middle of the vacant block which had once been the Crown Street Maternity Hospital. The destruction of this hospital felt both cruel and personal. She thought: I am becoming neurotic.

Her car was parked round the corner, not her car, the Tax Department's car. She should not be driving it for private use. Once she would have thought this an important principle. Now she did not give a damn. She looked in the back seat before she unlocked the car, and then she turned on the light and looked again. Mrs

Catchprice's Japanese Bride sat propped up against a Sister Brown Baby Bath.

'Dear God, please save me.'

15

The Blue Moon Brasserie was loud, full of clatter and shouting. Glasses broke, were swept up. The air was rich with olive oil and garlic. The Tax Inspector threaded her way through the chrome-legged chairs towards her table. She was wearing a red deco blouse and a black skirt with a red bandanna which sat above her bulging stomach. She wore a peasant print scarf around her head and silver bracelets and a necklace. In the privacy of her bedroom mirror, she had thought all of this looked fine, but now she saw how she was stared at, she felt she had made an error of judgement – she was a blimp with bangles.

The grey-aproned waiter was eighteen years old and had nicked himself shaving. He was new that day and had no idea that this pregnant woman's emotional life was deeply enmeshed with the place he worked at. He sat her in the corner, next to the table where she had told Alistair that she was having a baby. All around her there were couples, lovers, husbands, wives. They touched each other's sleeves, arms, hands, and were pleased with each other's company. It was a perfectly ordinary table – square, varnished, wooden, as devoid of obvious history as a hotel bed. Then it had seen the death of an affair. Now it celebrated a birthday. Maria craned her neck towards the blackboard menu but she was really watching that table – a man with a thick neck and pouched, melancholy eyes took a small gold-wrapped box from his wife – whose face Maria could not see – and passed it to his daughter. The daugher was sixteen or so, very pretty with long dark hair.

'Happy birthday, angel,' her father said. He gave her a kiss and a crumpled rag of a smile. He rubbed at the table surface, dragging bread crumbs into his cupped hand.

'I've been flirting with stockbrokers,' said Gia Katalanis, sitting down opposite Maria.

Gia was crisp and yellow in a linen suit. She dumped her files and briefcase on the floor and papers from the files spilled out towards the wall. She looked down at the papers, wrinkled her nose and shrugged.

'I've been flirting with stockbrokers,' she said again, leaning forward and taking Maria's hands. She was small and blonde with a dusting of golden hairs along her slim, tanned arms. She smelt of shampoo and red wine. She had straight hair she always cut in a neat fringe. She had fine features, a fine chin which clearly suggested both frailty and determination. 'Well they *think* they are stockbrokers,' she said, 'but they are used car dealers in their secret hearts. One of them is from Hale & Hennesey. We hit them for three-forty thou in back taxes, plus the fines, and I think he fell in love with me.' She laughed. 'Ask me is he cute.'

'Is he cute?'

'He's cute.'

A champagne cork popped at the next table and they both turned to watch the champagne being poured into the sixteen-year-old's birthday glass, then laughed at their own Pavlovian response to the cork pop.

'These days,' Maria said, 'when they drink champagne in movies, I always look at the label.'

'Me too,' Gia said. 'Exactly.' She lit a St Moritz and put lipstick on its gold filter tip. 'Heidsieck,' she said. 'Krug, Taittinger, Bollinger, Moët, Piper-Heidsieck . . .'

'Pol Roger . . .'

'Veuve Clicquot.'

'I used to think anything with bubbles was champagne,' Maria said. 'When I told my mother I had drunk champagne she said, "Po po anaxyi yineka" – no one will want to marry you now.'

'Your mother always said that.'

'She was right, poor Mama. This would kill her if she wasn't dead, really. Even my father. I visit him at night and I always ring first and say, "Papa I'm going to come over." I don't want to shame him with someone . . .'

'But, Maria, come on – the street knows . . .'

'The street knows? Don't be nice to me.'

'O.K., all Newtown.'

'Newtown? Mrs *Hellos* knows. She was in Balmain inspecting real estate. I always felt safe in Balmain . . .'

'Oh God, Mrs Hellos. I saw her in D.J.'s with that buck-toothed nephew.'

'Tassos.'

'Tassos, that's right. She said, poor Mr Takis, such a good man – first his wife, now his daughter. I said, but Mrs Hellos, Maria is not dead. No, said Mrs Hellos – so melodramatic, you know – no! So I said – Mrs Hellos, are you saying it is better that Maria is dead? I'm not saying nothing, said Mrs Hellos, I'm just thinking about Mr Takis and his kidneys.'

'Oh God, Mrs Hellos. Oh shit,' Maria said laughing. 'Dear Gia, you always make me laugh. The birth class was so miserable without you.'

Gia took Maria's hand. 'Did they show one of those horror tapes again?' Maria's skin was so moist and supple and her fingers so long that it made her own hands seem dry and neurotic.

'Uh-huh.' There was a veiled, weary look around her eyes.

'Are you mad at me?'

'Of course not. Really. Not even a tiny bit.'

'Oh Maria, I'm sorry. Did you have a shitty day as well?'

'Well, I wasn't flirting with stockbrokers.'

'But I thought they finally sent you out to catch some rats?'

'They sent me to Franklin. Can you believe that?'

'*Franklin*. My God. Who's in Franklin?'

'No one's in Franklin. It was some shitty little G.M. dealer.'

'Maria, you've got to just tell them "no".'

'That's what they want. They're going to keep giving me these insulting little audits until I blow up. I'm like the emperor's wife. They have to kill me too.'

'The emperor's ex-wife.'

'I cooked dinners for the creeps when Alistair was director. They came to my house and drank *my* Heemskerk Cabernet. They were meant to be my friends. Billy Huxtable, Sally Ho. It was Sally who sent me to Franklin. I said, "What if I go into labour in Franklin?" She said, "There are very good medical facilities." What a bitch! Plus, the clients – really – they were mice! They looked like they were Social Welfare clients, not ours. They were trying to commit her – this is an old woman, eighty-six – to a mental home when I arrived. Her children were trying to lock her up, and she seemed more sane than they did. If I hadn't arrived she'd be locked up right now.'

'Good for you, Maria.'

'Well, maybe – I'm investigating her, and I'm sitting here, talking about champagne, surrounded by people drinking vintage Bollinger.'

'Well, let's go somewhere else. I don't like all this either.'

Maria chose not to hear that. 'It makes me feel sleazy,' she said.

'What? The clients or the restaurant?'

'Both, together. The juxtaposition.'

'Maria, you're not sleazy. You're the least sleazy person I know.'

'I'm going to pull this investigation. I can stop it.'

'You can't stop it, and you're being really dumb. Listen, my dear, you are the least sleazy person I know. You never spend more than twenty bucks here. You've got a village mentality. Remember when you told me Alex was wealthy . . . He had a new 1976 Holden and went to Surfers Paradise for his holidays. You know what you said to me . . . You said, "Typical Athens Greek." And you wouldn't go out with him.'

'I was a little prig,' Maria said. 'All I'm thinking is how I can cancel the investigation.'

'So you're going to break into the computer, right?' When she was anxious Gia had a tendency to shout.

'Shush,' said Maria. 'I think that is what I am going to do. Yes.'

'You don't know how to.'

'Shush, please, but yes I do. I'm not going to be made into a bully.'

Gia picked up Maria's bread roll and began to tear it up. 'O.K. Maria . . . O.K. . . . If you're really upset by crooks drinking vintage Bollinger, we'll just go somewhere else.'

Maria saw the stoop-shouldered man at the next table flinch as he heard himself labelled a crook. He looked up sharply.

Maria said, 'All the poor guy is doing is giving his daughter a birthday party.'

Gia leaned across the table and spoke in her idea of a whisper. 'That "poor guy" is Wally Fischer.'

'Oh.'

'Oh. That's right. Oh. We're going to get him. He's an inch away from jail. He can get away with dealing smack and organizing murder but he's not going to get away with tax. He didn't hear me.'

'I thought he was an accountant being sweet to his wife and

daughter,' Maria whispered. 'He heard us. He knows we're talking about him now.'

'This restaurant makes me sick,' Gia said. 'Let's go somewhere else.'

'No,' Maria said. 'I like it here.'

Gia started giggling.

'I do,' Maria said.

'I know you do.'

'When the baby's born I won't be able to afford to come here, but it's very cheap for the sort of place it is.'

'I know,' Gia said. 'You can get *focaccias* for $7.50 and wine for $3 a glass and once you sat next to Joan Collins, right over there.'

'Right,' Maria said. 'And you always give me the best scandal here.'

'I'm less interesting elsewhere?'

'There are artists and celebrities here. The atmosphere is good,' Maria said. 'It promotes gossip. It's the only corner of my life where gossip is acceptable. It stops me being a total prig.' She seemed to have abandoned her thoughts about breaking into her client's tax file. 'Also, I have a history here. Alistair and I used to sit there, it was our table.'

'Don't do this to yourself.'

'He's a part of me,' Maria said. 'Don't make me pretend he isn't.'

'Maria, he's a creep – he dumped you.'

'He didn't dump me. I dumped me. What did he do?'

'Even now, you can't see who he is.'

'I know who he is,' Maria said quietly. 'Please. Gia, allow me to know him a little better than you.'

'O.K.,' said Gia, grinning like a cat. 'So allow me to tell you where Paulo wants to kiss me.'

She was gifted with perfect recall. She recited a whole phone conversation with her 'love interest'. He wanted to kiss her armpit. He had said to her, 'Guess where I want to kiss you?' She had guessed everywhere but arm pit. She had shocked him with her guesses. This sort of talk was making Maria look alive and happy again. The headscarf showed off her beautiful face, her dark olive skin and white, perfect teeth. She could have any man she liked, even now, this pregnant.

Gia spoke very quietly, so quietly no one could have heard them, but they laughed so much they could hardly see. Through her tear-streamed vision Maria saw Wally Fischer speaking to Tom, one of the owners of the Brasserie.

Tom was a small, solemn man of thirty who had made himself look forty with a belly and a pair of round, wire-framed glasses. He leaned across the table and put a hand on the back of their chairs.

'Gia, Maria, I'm sorry . . . would you mind, you know, a little *cleaner*.'

'All we're doing is laughing,' Gia said. 'It's not as if we're murdering anyone.'

The words fell into the silence like stones into an aquarium. Maria could see Gia's eyes widening as she heard what she had said. She looked at Maria and made a grimace, and up to Tom and shrugged, and across to Wally Fischer who had heard this very clearly – his thick neck was beginning to puff up and turn a deep plum colour.

Gia was pale. She sat with her palms flat on the table. She looked helplessly in Wally Fischer's direction and smiled.

'Hey,' she said. Her voice was so loud and scratchy, Maria knew she was very frightened. 'I'm sorry, really.'

Wally Fischer moved his chair back and stood up. You could feel his physical strength. He had bright, shining, freshly shaven cheeks and you could smell his talcum.

'One,' he said to Maria, 'I don't like my daughter having to listen to smut.' He turned to Gia: 'Number two: I like even less for her to hear people say untrue and insulting things about her father.'

'All I . . .' Gia began.

'Sssh,' said Wally Fischer. He was no longer plum-coloured. He was quite pale except for the red in his thick lips. 'You've done enough hurt for one night.' He blinked his heavy-lidded eyes once, and turned to take his daugher by the arm.

'Sheet,' said Gia as they walked out of the door. She leaned across to the abandoned table and retrieved the Bollinger from the bucket.

'Gia, don't.' Maria looked down, ashamed.

Gia was pale and nervous, but she was already holding her trophy high and pouring Wally Fischer's Bollinger into her empty water glass. 'Have some. Don't be such a goody-goody.' Maria looked up to see Wally Fischer looking in the window from the street. He made a pistol with his finger and pointed it at Gia. Gia did not see him but she looked pale and sick anyway, and there seemed no point in making her more distressed. 'Have some,' she said to Maria.

Maria took the champagne, not to drink, as an act of solidarity. It frothed up and spilled on to the wooden table. Gia drank without waiting for the froth to settle. Her hand shook.

'You all right?' Maria asked.

'Yeah, I'm O.K. But I don't want to come here any more.'

Maria took her hand. Gia shut it into a fist, self-conscious about her bitten nails.

'We don't have to come here,' said Maria.

'It stinks,' Gia said. 'I can smell the dirty money at the door.' Gia pushed away the champagne. 'I don't even like the taste of this.'

'It isn't the restaurant that's the problem. It's us.'

'For instance?'

'We keep doing things we don't believe in. I didn't join the department to be an anal authoritarian. I'm not going to bankrupt these poor people out at Franklin.' Maria soaked up the spilled champagne with a paper napkin. 'I'm going to pull their file,' she said.

'Maria, what's happened to you?'

'Nothing's happened.'

'You've had a character transplant.' Gia took back the champagne and drank it.

Maria smiled. 'Sorry to disappoint you.'

'A complete character transplant.'

'Goody two-shoes?' Maria asked, her eyebrows arched.

'That was a long time ago I said that . . .'

'Fourteen years . . .'

'I was angry with you. You made me feel bad about cheating on my car mileage. But there are people in the department who would drop dead if they thought you were going to pull a file.'

'And you?'

'I think it's very therapeutic, Maria. I think it's exactly what you should do.' Gia reached over and emptied the last of Wally Fischer's champagne into her glass. 'You know the computer codes? That's the important thing. You'll need old Maxy's access code.'

Maria smiled.

'And you need a corrupt ASO 7 to open doors for you at night?'

'Just lend me the keys.'

'You're kidding,' said Gia, draining the champagne and standing a little unsteadily. 'You think I'd miss this?'

'It's an offence under the Crimes Act.'

'Come on,' Gia said, making scribbling Amex signs at Tom. 'Don't be so melodramatic. All we're going to do is work late at the office.'

16

Sarkis Alaverdian was depressed and unemployed, and when he came to sit on his back step, he saw Mrs Catchprice standing at the bottom of the back yard, below the culvert under the Sydney Road. He saw a still, pink figure, like a ghost. It just stood there, looking back at him.

Sarkis stood directly under the light of the back porch. He was not tall, but he was broad. He had a weight-lifter's build, although when he walked he did not walk like a gym-ape, but lightly, more like a tennis-player. He had not had a pay cheque in ten weeks but he wore, even at home, at night, a black rayon shirt with featured mother-of-pearl buttons on the collar points. He wore grey cotton trousers shot with a slight iridescence, and soft grey slip-ons from the Gucci shop. He had curly black hair, not tight, not short, but tidy just the same. He had a broad strong nose, and a small tuft of hair, a little squiff on his lower lip.

He was twenty years old and he had been forced to come and stand out here while his mother made love with the Ariel Taxi driver. He was ashamed, not ashamed of his mother, but ashamed on her behalf, not that she would make love, not exactly, although a little bit. He had known something like this would happen when they moved from Chatswood. When she wanted to be away from Armenians, he had both sympathized with her and suspected her. He had readied himself for it and prepared himself so he would behave correctly, but he could not have imagined this taxi-driver. It was the taxi-driver who made him feel ashamed.

The taxi-driver was 'out of area'. He was not even meant to drive in Franklin, but he came down here and cruised around, mostly up at Emerald and Sapphire where the women were abandoned and lonely and often just getting used to the idea that they would now be poor for ever. Before Sarkis lost his job, he had been in this particular taxi a number of times. He had once taken it from Cabramatta Leagues Club to Franklin. The taxi-driver did not recognize Sarkis, but Sarkis recognized him.

Sarkis liked women. He liked their skin, their smells, and he liked the things they talked about. When you are a hairdresser you talk with women all day long. At apprentice school they will call this 'chatter', but ultimately it is more important than finger-waving or working on plastic models with wobbly heads, both of which are things that are very important in apprentice school but don't exist in salon life. If you have talent and you can chatter, you will end up being a Mr Simon or Mr Claude, i.e. you will own your own salon and you can have the pleasure of hiring and firing the ones who topped the class at tech.

The tragedy was that it was chatter that ruined him. He had put Mrs Gladd in the No. 2 cubicle with her dryer on extra low. This was at half-past four. He did this so he could talk with this little blonde – Leone – who had almost perfect hair – naturally blonde, and so dense and strong you could do almost anything you liked with it. He was giving her his 'Sculptured' look. It was a dumb word, but reassuring. It was a tangled, curled sort of look, that looked like you just got out of bed until you noticed just how 'deliberate' it was. He talked her into it because it was going to suit her, but also because it was the sort of job you could pick and fuss over, and he was picking and fussing while he talk-talk-talked and he knew how nice it felt to have someone doing this, all these little pick-pick-cut-snips to your hair, and he had checked Mrs Gladd at ten to five and then gone back to pick-pick-cut-snip. Leone was getting this honey glaze around her eyes. He talked to her about skiing. He worked out she went with her girlfriend. He talked on and on. When he asked her to the Foresters for a drink he was holding up the mirror for her and she just nodded.

She was beautiful.

'Yes,' she said, 'I'd love to.'

He had made her incredible, like a film star, and he had (*fuck it*) forgotten, completely, that Mrs Gladd was still under the slow dryer. He went off to the Foresters and locked her in. The cleaners found her at half-past ten – pissed off beyond belief.

Mrs Gladd got it in her head she had been 'traumatized'. She got herself on television with Mike Willesee and they took a film crew round to Mr Simon's one Friday morning at ten o'clock. Sarkis held his coat up so they could not see his face on camera, but the show made him famous anyway and once Mr Simon had fired him live on camera he could not find another salon to employ him, not even as a washer.

That was why he had to stand in the back garden. Everyone he knew was in Chatswood or Willoughby. He no longer had a car to drive there in. When he heard the mattress squeaking, he could not even take a stroll around Franklin – it was not safe at night.

Sarkis knew this taxi-driver did not like women. He made the boys laugh, saying things like, 'If they didn't have cunts you wouldn't talk to them'. His mother did not know this. She was still celebrating her independence from the Armenian community. She was wearing short skirts and smoking in the street. Ready-snap Peas had closed their doors and she had lost her job as well, but it still seemed, to Sarkis, that she was having a good time. She had come all the way to Franklin because she had convinced herself that there were no Armenians here. But the first people they met were Tahleen and Raffi who ran the corner store in Campbell Street. The first thing they did was offer to drive Sarkis and his mother to the Armenian Church on Sundays. Sarkis thought it wouldn't hurt – if only from the employment point of view. But he could not budge his mother. She said: thank you. She thought: no way, José. From there on she walked an extra mile to buy her ciggies from another shop.

His mother's feeling about the Armenian community made her judgement bad. She might have hated them, but she was one of them. When she met someone who was not Armenian, she got herself into a drama. No way she was going to serve *Gargandak*. She was reinventing herself as Australian. But if not *Gargandak*, what cakes were right? She did not know what to call the people, even. But she was so happy she did not care. The taxi-driver was a Yugoslav. She called him 'Doll'. She was thawing out the Sara Lee Cherry Cheese Cake. She opened all her miniature bottles of liquor. She called the taxi-driver Doll even though he was lean and balding, with a slight stoop and nicotine stains on his fingers. The only thing like a doll was his eyes, which were very blue. They were doll eyes only in colour. They stared at you. No matter how you might smile, he never smiled back. Even when Sarkis's mother offered the tiny bottles of Gilbey's gin and Bond 7 whisky which she had kept from the time they had shared a house in Willoughby with Anna from East-West Airlines, even when she laughed, and showed him how to do the twist, he never once smiled.

For a while Sarkis sat at the kitchen table and cut out more fabric for ties. The fabric he was cutting was 100 per cent French silk. It was dark green with hard-edge motifs in silver and black. He concentrated hard on the cutting because the fabric was beautiful, because it had been expensive, and because he was angry and did not want to see what was happening on the other side of the servery door where the taxi-driver was adjusting his pants. It made him ill to think of that thing being put inside his mother.

The taxi-driver smelled of unwashed sweat. His mother did not know shit about men. She took the taxi-driver to show him her wedding pictures. They were in the bedroom. He could hear her light young voice – she was still only thirty-six – as it named the members of the wedding party. The names were of Armenians who had once lived in the suburbs of Teheran. She talked about them as if they were certainly alive.

Tomorrow she would tell Sarkis all the good things she had found out about the taxi-driver – he was kind, he supported his sick father or he was a bad dancer but had read her palm 'sensitively'. She would not learn that the taxi-driver cruised the Franklin streets which were named after jewels putting his dick wherever there was isolation and desperation. He could have AIDS. His mother did not even think of this possibility. Instead she opened up her minia-tures. She showed him wedding pictures. She pointed out Sarkis's father to the taxi-driver. She said how handsome he was, like Paul McCartney.

Earlier, in the living-room, she told the taxi-driver he looked like George Harrison. This made the taxi-driver smile. It was extra-ordinary to see. It was impossible to know why he smiled, whether from pleasure or because he could see how ridiculous it was.

Sarkis put down his scissors and folded the fabric. Then he went out to sit on the back steps which were farthest from the bedroom and where the noise of the trucks on the Sydney road drowned out the various noises of the night. Sarkis was normally optimistic. He could lose three jobs and not be beaten. He could be angry and irritable, but he always had a way forward. He was a member of a race which could not be destroyed. He had energy, intelligence, resilience, enthusiasm.

But tonight he was oppressed by his circumstances: he could not get a job, a girl friend or even a sewing machine. He could not even telephone his friends in Chatswood.

It was in this mental state that he saw Mrs Catchprice standing at the bottom of the yard. He thought it might be someone from the Commonwealth Employment Service come to take his dole away because they were already paying benefits to his mother.

'Hey,' he said.

The figure waved, a tinkly little wave from the wrist. Did not look like the C.E.S.

'Who's that?' He picked up a Sidchrome spanner for protection.

'I'm a ghost.'

Sarkis felt prickly on the neck. Then a match flared and he saw an old woman with a cigarette stuck to her pouting lower lip. She had a big black leather handbag in the crook of her arm, a pink floral dress and a transparent plastic raincoat. 'We had a poultry farm for twenty years,' she said. He could smell the meat-fat smell then, from that far away, the Aussie smell, as distinctive as their back yard clothes-lines with their frivolous flags of T-shirts, board shorts and frilly underwear, so different from Armenian washing which was big and practical – sheets, rugs, blankets, grey work trousers and cotton twill shirts.

'You're not a very good ghost,' he told her. He stood, and stepped down into the yard.

'I'm damned near old enough,' said Mrs Catchprice, dropping the lit match on to the sodden ground where it sizzled and went out. 'I'll be eighty-six in March. You might find it hard to imagine, but we had two thousand birds and this was just the bottom of the property. There was a little natural pond here and a stand of Gymea lilies. I was going to have a flower farm, but there was better money in poultry then, so it ended up being poultry. You had some here yourself, I think . . . last week?'

'The Health Department made us kill them.'

'You're better off without them. There is nothing nice about poultry. The smell of plucked feathers makes me nauseous now. Who washed the chook-poo off the eggs? Your mother I suppose. I always washed the eggs. I sat at the kitchen table with a bucket and a bowl. You never forget the smell of it on your fingers.'

'I've found your cigarettes here,' said Sarkis. 'You smoke Salem. You just take a few drags and throw them away. Do you come from the nursing home?'

'I'm Mrs Catchprice.'

'Where do you live?'

'Are you local?' asked Mrs Catchprice, coming forward to peer at the good-looking young man by the light of the kitchen window. 'You must know Catchprice Motors.'

He did. He had bought a fuel pump there once from a woman in a cowgirl suit. 'And that's where you live?'

'And where needs be I must wearily return,' said Mrs Catchprice, throwing her Salem in among the Hydrangeas. 'Don't you find the nights are sad?'

'I'll walk you to your car,' said Sarkis.

'Car!' said Mrs Catchprice, straightening her back and tilting her chin. 'Car. I have no car. I walk.'

Walk? Sarkis was young and strong, but he would never walk at night alone in Franklin. There were homeless kids wandering around with beer cans full of petrol. They saw fiery worms and faces spewing blood. They did not know what they were doing.

'I think I'll walk with you a bit of the way,' Sarkis said.

'How lovely,' said Mrs Catchprice. 'I didn't catch your name?'

'Sarkis Alaverdian.' He was scared. He slipped the Sidchrome spanner into his back pocket. He thought: her family should be ashamed.

17

Mrs Catchprice did not stand in Sarkis's back yard in order to employ him. Yet if she had set out that night with no other purpose than to rescue a life from the asbestos sheet houses in the real estate development she had once planned, this would have been consistent with her character.

In the days when Catchprice Motors had sold combine harvesters and baling twine, she had taken boys from the Armvale Homes, girls in trouble with the police. She had given them positions of trust, placed a shoplifter in charge of petty cash, for instance. She was erratic – loud in her trust on the one hand but vigilant and even suspicious on the other. She was ready to ascribe to her protégés schemes and deceptions too complex and Machiavellian for anyone but her to conceive of, and yet she could manage, in the same breath, to think of them as 'good kids'. She was sentimental and often patronizing (she spoke loudly of her beneficiaries in their presence) and what is amazing is not that a few of them never forgave her for it, but that most of them were so grateful for her patronage that they did not even notice.

Mrs Catchprice was their lucky break. Some of them even loved her. And Howie, who had been one, could – despite the complications of his Catchprice-weary heart – still say, 'You old chook,' and smile. The first time he ever saw a T-bone steak was at Mrs Catchprice's table. The first time he took a shit where you could lock the door was in that apartment which was now his home. He was an orphan from Armvale Boys' Farm. He was given Mort's Hornby 'OO' train set when Mrs Catchprice decided Mort had grown out of it. That was her style. She gave away Cathy's teddy bear without asking her, not to Howie, to someone else.

Even now, when she no longer had either an executive position or a majority shareholding, it did not take a lot to tip Frieda Catchprice into charity, and when she stood in Sarkis's backyard on that red loam earth which should have been her flower farm but which had supported instead two thousand laying hens in twenty-three separate electrically heated sheds, charity was the emollient she automatically applied to the sadness she felt. She reached for it, almost without thinking, much as she always pecked at her honey and Saltata crackers in the hope that one more smear of Leatherwood honey might finally remove that metallic taste in her stomach which she secretly and wrongly believed was caused by cancer.

She was a ghost. She told him she was a ghost as a joke, but she meant all her jokes. This is how it was with ghosts – you stood in one life, but you could see another. You were in one world, but not part of it. You visited your past mistakes and tried to undo them. You held your babies to your breasts and suckled them. You sponged them through their fevered nights. You petted them and wept, knowing you were doing something wrong that would result in them growing up without properly loving you.

Sarkis's backyard was a corner of the second piece of land she had wanted to grow flowers on. It had been within her grasp but what had she done? First she had turned it into a poultry farm, and then she had turned it into a housing development. These things had made her 'Mrs Catchprice' but she had wanted neither of them. It was Cacka who wanted them. He aspired to poultry farming like other people dreamed of a beach house or an imported Chevrolet Bel-aire. No one aspired to poultry farms. It was something poor battlers did in the rough scrub outside town, a desperate part-time occupation. It was never clear how the passion for it entered Cacka's head, but if you went to live at his family's orange-primed bungalow out at Donvale and listened to the never-ending argument, you would get an education in egg marketing, and one of the first things Frieda learned (after discovering which was Old Mrs Catchprice's seat) was that the Egg Marketing Board were a pack of little Hitlers who wanted you to pay them fourpence a dozen and wouldn't let you sell direct to shops without a special permit.

She also learned, pretty damn smart, that Cacka's mother had no time for chooks.

'I hope you ain't an Oprey singer,' she said to Frieda. 'I told him already, we won't have Oprey or the chooks.'

Her boys thought this was very funny, everyone except for Cacka who sat beside his fiancée at the kitchen table, blushing bright red.

Poultry was one of the few species of livestock Old Mrs Catchprice had no time for, and even at sixty-five she was plotting new ways to make a living from her fifty acres and her three strong boys. She had Romney Marsh, some Border Cross, ten Jerseys with some odd scars where you might expect a brand to be, poll Herefords, and half-a-dozen sows she thought Frieda might like to take an interest in. She had the resprayed Ferguson tractor Hughie brought home one night without explaining. She had Cacka and the youngest brother, Billie, advertised in the *Gazette* as fencing contractors. Also, the family had a few acres given over to wheat and had traded cases of apples with de Kok's grocery until there were complaints about their codlin-moth infestation.

The Catchprices were in the habit of listening to the Country Hour each day at lunch. They came in across the treeless, car-littered Home Paddock to the bungalow and sat around the electric-blue Laminex table brushing the flies off their serious faces, drinking black tea – they had no midday meal – and listening to the market prices delivered in a proper English accent.

It didn't matter what the prices were – they were always broke. That was Cacka's point to them, and he never let up no matter how they spoke to him. He was not thick-skinned, but he was persistent. When he wanted something he talked about it in that 'cooing' way, talk and talk, on and on, rubbing his big dirt-dry hands together and smiling sadly and looking at you with his brown eyes, talking on and on until you would give him anything he wanted. He sat at the table in that depressing bright-orange weatherboard bungalow propped on its 'temporary' concrete blocks in the middle of the barren paddock and he folded his arms across his big chest and tilted back on a battered chrome chair and talked on and on about the future in a way that would have seemed almost insane were it not for the fact that he had been smart enough to have Frieda McClusky there to listen to him.

And while it is true that Frieda did not want chooks any more than the old lady did, she loved him, and loved him in a more tender and protective way than she would have imagined possible. She could not bear to see him want a thing like that and just not have it. All her instinct warned her about poultry, even then, before she heard of battery farming. But she had needs even stronger than her instincts and she pressed her little breasts against his big back each night and put her arms around him and squeezed her thigh up in around his furry backside and knew that it was up to her to get him his chook farm.

She would spend all her life going over these events, thinking of how it might have been otherwise. She thought it self-deceiving to give herself too much credit for love. What she remembered was how much she had wanted to escape that musty confinement of one more family, that sour, closed smell like a mouse nest in a bush-hut wall. She gave this prominence in her memory, and it was true, of course, but she was wrong to discount the effects of love.

Also, she wanted Cacka to admire her, and sometimes she made this need for admiration the only reason she had sacrificed the perfect flower farm to wire netting and chook shit and the Egg Marketing Board of New South Wales.

Also: there was gelignite. She had a passion to let it off with her mother-in-law watching. She wanted to split wood and shatter earth and frighten her and make her go away.

Also: to hurt herself, to fill herself brimful of blame and rage. She wanted to make the damned earth bleed. *See. See. See what you made me go and do.*

It was old Huey Dawson who showed her the land – eight o'clock in the morning and all the dew so heavy they were drenched just walking through it: grass, Watsonias, wild roses drifted there from God knows where, stands of spotted gums with pale, pale green trunks so slippery they would make you cry. It was five acres cut off from the bottom of old Doctor Andes's property and it had never seen a cow on it. There were tiny bush orchids and native grasses with seeds like yellow tear drops – it had probably been that way for ever. It was lot 5, folio 14534 being parcel 54 of the parish of Franklin. It had vendor finance of 5 per cent and no deposit and she had to take Cacka to it (along the straight, soft, sandy road where the overgrown acacias brushed the edges of the ute and made him anxious about the powdery duco) and when he resisted because he was actually frightened of the financial commitment and was ready to run back to the bungalow and listen to stock prices on the radio, she showed him how he could make a good business on this piece of land: three acres for chooks, one acre for the lucerne, maize and oats. She had the idea – it was original, she read it nowhere – of building the brick building where they cooled down the hens in heat waves. She did not mean to insist that she was smarter than he was, but when she saw his scheme about to flounder, she panicked. It must happen, it had to happen, she would not let him fail.

It was the beginning of a pattern – every time she helped him get something he wanted, a poultry farm, a car dealership, she drove him further from her. She was the one who talked him into that damn poultry farm when it was the last thing on earth she wanted.

This was the site of Catchprice Poultry – Cacka and Frieda Catchprice were to be the first ones west of Sydney with battery farming. And although she entered into the business as a full partner with her husband she had no idea what battery farming was and had not appreciated the consequences.

Now she knew. Men can do this sort of thing and not think about it. They can cut the chickens' beaks, and amputate their legs if necessary. They can walk out into the shed every day for ten years and see and smell those rows of caged birds and not think about it any more than how nicely the eggs roll into the conveyor belt and how clean they are. Nothing wrong with this – Frieda did not feel censorious about men's ability to disconnect their feelings. She thought it useful. God had planned it so one half of humanity could kill the food, the other half could nurture the young.

But what she was too young to know, what she learned later, was that it was damned silly for a woman to do men's work, by which she meant work that entailed a denial of female feelings – killing people in war, working in slaughter houses, putting chooks in rows in cages. This was something men can do and it will have no harmful effects for them.

But it sends a woman's chemicals into conflict. This was how she got breast cancer – that poultry farm. She never told anyone this, but shocked Cacka and the doctor on the eve of her mastectomy by saying, 'Take them both off.'

She could see the idiots thought she was unnatural, that she had got so used to ordering Cacka around that she now wanted to be a man. Did they think she *wanted* to lose breasts? To spend the rest of her life with these huge scars like plastic sandwich wrapper?

Cacka could be weepy and sentimental about her breasts, but Frieda Catchprice was an animal caught in a trap, eating through its own limbs. She was poisoned and wanted to be free from the parts that would kill her. And sure enough, there was a second mastectomy – the one they so confidently told her she didn't need to have – another five years later.

When Frieda Catchprice stood in Sarkis Alaverdian's back yard, she ran over and over all these events, looking for a crack in the story, a place where she might have acted differently and have come to a different place. She worked up and down the events, like a fly trying to find its way through glass to air.

The trucks thundered over the Sydney Road overpass above the 60 × 120-ft blocks which had been sold thirty years before as Catchprice Heights. The streets were named Albert, Frieda, Cathleen, Mortimer, Jack. It was the Catchprice Estate that Sarkis Alaverdian was now a prisoner of. And it was now Mrs Catchprice, walking with him back to Catchprice Motors, who determined to set him free.

'Do you have a suit?' she asked.

Monday

18

It was only after they had escaped from Vernon Street (where the twelve-year-olds were ripping the insignia off a Saab Turbo) that Mrs Catchprice offered Sarkis a job as a salesman. Sarkis had seen the twelve-year-olds too late to avoid them and he did not wish to turn round or even cross the street because it was like running, like blood in the water, and he had no choice but to continue walking. Three of them were sitting on a white-railed garden fence. Two were perched on the Saab's hood. The space they left to walk through was bordered by the bright white stones of their naked kneecaps.

The Saab's alarm started. Sarkis took Mrs Catchprice's bird-wing arm, and Mrs Catchprice, who must have seen what was happening, just kept on talking. She was telling him stories about the disadvantaged people she had employed at Catchprice Motors.

'But I am boring you,' she said.

He was frightened, not bored. He guided the old woman under the dark umbrella of mould-sweet street trees, between the gauntlet of twelve-year-old knees – stolen commando boots, lighter-fluid breath. Even in the midst of it, he could not hurry her. He felt the bones through the wrapping of her plastic coat. Old women needed extra calcium. He had his own mother on 800 mg a day, and she was young. Without calcium they became hunch-backed and fragile. And although Mrs Catchprice was not hunch-backed, she had that dried, neglected feeling in his hand, like shoes no one has bothered to oil. She was someone's grandmother, or mother – they should treasure her. She should eat with them, sleep in their house. They should listen to her papery breathing in the night and it should give them a sense of completeness they would never have without her. If not for her, they would not exist.

Sarkis could press 140 kg. He could split a shirt by flexing his deltoids, but the twelve-year-olds were like dogs in a pack. Their breath stank like service stations and their nails scratched. They were feral animals. He was scared of them, even now, twenty metres past the Saab. There was a dull thudding noise. They were running over the roof of the Saab and jumping on its hood and if the owners were smart they would stay in their house and wait for the cops to come. A breeze brought a flower scent he could not name. A rock bounced off a low paling fence and rolled along the

93

footpath past his feet. The car alarm stopped for a moment and everything was suddenly very quiet.

He steered her off the street, and on to a rough clay path across the burnt-out Kmart lot. This was maybe dumb. How could he tell? He hoped that the buskers from Victoria had not come back to live in the concrete pipes. He could see the pipes glistening nastily in the centre of the site. He could smell them from here: piss like a subway tunnel. She stumbled and gripped his arm. It was then she asked: 'Do you have a suit?'

Maybe she said other things and he missed it. He was worrying about her bones, the buskers.

'Yes,' he said.

'Well, you'd better come to the garage at eight-thirty tomorrow morning and we'll see how we go.' Sarkis was thinking how could he tell her to shut up, not to talk so loud. The piss-smelling pipes might hide Nasties, people without a human heart. They might beat you because they thought you had money, or a job, or a handsome face you did not deserve.

She held out her hand. He shook it. Just a little thing – a Chinese dish – bones and rice paper.

'It's a deal?' she asked.

What?

'Yes,' he said.

They passed the concrete pipes and no one tried to hurt them, although Sarkis muddied his slip-ons and his socks. *Did we shake hands about what I thought we shook hands about?*

They came out on to Loftus Street. Sarkis saw the Esso sign illuminated in the sky above Catchprice Motors. *Am I employed?*

'Do you walk at night very often?' he said, but his mind was trying to figure out a way to check on what had happened to him.

'Always,' said Mrs Catchprice.

'Actually,' said Sarkis, 'it's very dangerous.' They had come to a bench which the Franklin Council had bolted to a concrete block beneath the collapsing veranda of an old store. Mrs Catchprice sat down on the seat and began looking for a cigarette in her handbag.

'Really very dangerous,' Sarkis said. He sat beside her, with his arms resting on his knees. He peered across the road, through the trees, at Catchprice Motors.

'You don't want your new employer bumped off, eh?' said Mrs

Catchprice, and flashed her big white teeth at him.

He could have kissed her wrinkled-up old face.

'If these louts give me trouble,' she said, 'I'll blow them up.' She opened her handbag wide and held up what Sarkis thought at first was a piece of salami. He took it from her. It was about fifteen centimetres long and very sticky.

'Gelignite. You know what that is? Smell your fingers.'

Sarkis sniffed. It was musty and aromatic, like amyl nitrate.

'Nitroglycerine,' she said.

The street lights were an orange-yellow and made everything look like a colour negative. You had to think about the most ordinary things to work out what they really were and even when they had been pigeon-holed and labelled, read and understood, they kept some of their spooky double-self. So when Mrs Catchprice said, 'I'm a lot more dangerous than they are,' she had orange lips and a yellow face and copper hair, and she was very scary looking.

'You know how to let it off?'

'Oh yes,' Mrs Catchprice said. 'I know how to "let it off" just fine.' Her teeth were huge and gold in her orange mouth. She was standing in Loftus Street, but she was walking through the grass, trees and wild roses while the Catchprice boys were standing with their hands on their hips and their great dusty legs were sticking out of their little blue shorts. She walked from stump to stump in her straw hat and summer dress with her crimping pliers and her gelly in an old Gladstone bag. She used a torch battery to do the detonators. She beefed up the gelly with some 'Nitron' fertilizer which sure did lift the stumps out of the soil and made Cacka wince and squinch up his face and push his great dusty hands across his battered ears.

Broken earth was like any fresh killed thing – a rabbit, a fish – alive with colour. When you fractured it, the smell poured out, like from a peeled orange, and the hedgerows were made from long pale blue trunks and giant yellow flowers with the bees still feeding off them.

Mrs Catchprice held up the handbag by her forefinger and let it swing there. 'You know how old this gelignite is?' she asked Sarkis. 'You can see it's old by how it sweats. When it's like this you can let it off just by throwing it.'

Sarkis's previous employer had pierced nipples with metal rings in them. He showed Sarkis the photo. He had a metal stud which went through the end of his penis. Sarkis did not ask what the metal rings were for. He smiled and nodded. Likewise with this gelignite – smile. Later he would tell her that the twelve-year-olds were too stupid and doped-up to even understand what a stick of gelignite was. Now he would get her home. He would make her a cup of tea. After work one day he would even cut her frail, old, over-treated hair. It had lost its elasticity but you could still do something with hair like that. He could give her oil with hot towels. She would enjoy that. It was more personal than a steaming machine.

'So,' she said, taking back her stick of gelignite and putting it in her handbag where Sarkis could see a great number of crumpled twenty-dollar bills. 'You were out of work, and now you have a chance again.'

'Thank you,' Sarkis said.

'This is lovely,' said Mrs Catchprice. 'This is what I always liked best about having a business. I liked giving young people a chance.'

'I won't disappoint you,' Sarkis said. 'You won't be sorry.'

'This is lovely,' Mrs Catchprice said. 'This is such a nice town, even now.'

'I'm Armenian,' said Sarkis. 'We are famous for being salesmen.'

'Armenian?' said Mrs Catchprice brightly. 'How fascinating. Have you lived in Franklin long?'

'Six months.'

It was this answer that seemed to make Mrs Catchprice step out on to the road, straight in front of an on-coming car. Sarkis grabbed for her but she was gone. She was bright pink and silver in the car's headlights and it was only when it stopped that Sarkis realized it was a taxi and she had hailed it. She did not seem capable. She seemed too old and frail to be capable of making sudden movements and yet that was what particularly distinguished her – she leaped, jolted, slammed, and – right now, she jumped into the taxi and banged the door hard behind her.

'Come on,' she called as she wound down the window. 'Don't dawdle.'

When Sarkis entered the back seat of the cab, Mrs Catchprice was telling the driver: 'You cannot call yourself a taxi-driver and not know about the Wool Wash. You wait,' she said to Sarkis. 'You'll like this.'

Sarkis recognized the driver – whatever he had done with his mother had not taken very long. The driver sat there with his meter on, staring into the rear vision mirror. He did nothing to acknowledge that he knew who Sarkis was. Mrs Catchprice continued to talk about the Wool Wash. Sarkis could not listen. He looked at the back of the man's little shoulders and pink shell ears. He looked at the fleck of dandruff sticking to the stringy hair below his bald spot.

'If you don't know where the Wool Wash is,' Mrs Catchpole said loudly, tapping the driver on the shoulder, 'it might be polite to turn off your meter while you find out.'

The taxi-driver flinched from the touch and spoke into the mirror. 'Please,' he said. 'In my taxi, control your mouth.'

'It is my eyes you should worry about, not my mouth,' said Mrs Catchprice, fiddling with her handbag. 'I have a cataract on one eye,' she said, producing a crumpled pack of Salems, 'but I can still see your name is Pavlovic and you are plying for trade out of area.'

Pavlovic's shoulders stiffened. Then he turned the meter off. 'Wullwas?' he asked.

'W-o-o-l W-a-s-h.'

When the driver could not find the Wool Wash in his street directory, Mrs Catchprice took it from him.

'Everyone knows the Wool Wash,' she told her new employee. 'It is the most lovely part of Franklin.' But it was not listed in the driver's street directory. Mrs Catchprice stared at the map page, looking at the bend in the river where she thought the Wool Wash was.

'I never heard of it,' said Pavlovic.

'I never heard of it either,' said Sarkis.

To the taxi-driver she said: 'Just head south. I'll direct you,' but she was stricken with that horrible feeling that sometimes came to her on her night-time walks. It was as if all her past had been paved over and she could not reach it, as if she was a snake whose nest had been blocked while she was out and could only go backwards and forwards in front of the place where the hole had been, finding only cold hard concrete where she had expected life.

19

While Maria sat in the Blue Moon Brasserie, discussing Catchprice Motors, Benny Catchprice was playing Tape 7 of *Actualizations and Affirmations*. Tape 7 was not to be played unless or until you experienced 'Blockage'.

'You are not transformed,' Tape 7 now said to Benny. 'So whose fault do you think that is?'

Benny had come back from work feeling powerful and confident and he had undressed to do the mirror exercise and then suddenly – zap – he lost it. As he faced himself in the mirror he felt 'the fear'. It was hard to stand straight. He put his hand across his navel. His balls went tight in his newly hairless scrotum and he sweated around his arsehole. Five minutes ago he felt fantastic to be so clean and smooth, like a fucking statue. It had been just a blast to look at himself in the mirror and see his power. Then suddenly the thing that made him feel great – how he looked – marble white skin, wide shoulders, slim waist – made him feel like shit.

He turned to Tape 7 and pressed the 'Play' button.

'You paid us $495,' Tape 7 said, 'so if you're cheating, who are you cheating? Can't be us, we've got our money. If you're cheating, you're cheating yourself.'

'Fuck you,' Benny said and pushed at the cassette player with his foot. There was a grease mark on the foot, dust on his hands as well. That was the old Benny – he drew dirt on to himself like iron filings on to a magnet. Snot, sleep, grease, blackheads, he made neglect so much a part of him that no one, not even Mort Catchprice, wished to touch him and everything he made contact with became tarnished, mildewy, mouldy, ruined in some way. Something that had been shining clear silver in its polythene-wrapped box became 'used' the minute Benny touched it. Even his Christmas presents had been unpleasant to receive – rammed shut at the corners and torn and gummed up with glue and sticky tape so they felt like an oil-skinned table on which jam has been spilled and not properly cleaned.

'You're so used to cheating,' the tape said.

'Shut up.'

'What story do you tell yourself? Nobody loves you? You're too stupid? These are just stories you use to cheat yourself.'

'What do you fucking know?'

'That's why you're the way you are. You have no authenticity. You are unable to separate the bullshit you tell yourself from the truth. You've paid your $495 so now you can see – you either do the job properly or you see how you cheat yourself.'

The step he had omitted was no big deal. It was embarrassing, but he would do it if it was important – he had to fold his clothes carefully in separate parcels and then float them down the river. 'This does not mean flush them down the toilet,' the tape said. 'And if you are asking, is it O.K. if I put them in the sea, it is not. It means a river, not the sea, not a lake, not a drain. If you have any doubts as to whether it is a river or not, you can assume you're trying to cheat yourself out of your life and it is not a river.'

To wrap a shoe in black paper and tie it with gold ribbon seemed like an easy thing to do when you heard it on the tape. Benny swept nails and pins and cake crumbs from the bench with the flat of his hand and wiped the surface with a 'Fiery Avenger' T-shirt.

'You are going to wrap your old clothes to do honour to yourself. If you cannot do honour to your past, how are you going to do honour to your future? Each one of these parcels is you and I want you to dress it like you are dressing it for the funeral of a King or Queen.'

It sounded easy. It sounded inspiring, until you tried it and all of your old self kept soaking out of you, crumpling the paper, tangling the ribbon. When it was done, and wrapped, he saw the parcel had no 'Integrity'. It was a lumpy shitty thing. This was why the transformation could not be complete.

Slowly he unwrapped the shoes on the table and then he tried to flatten the paper with his hands. The paper would not go flat. It was Benny-ised.

'Shut up,' he told the tape. 'I'm going to fucking *iron* them.'

He dressed in his suit again. He took his time dressing properly, and when he remembered that he had not cleaned the smudge on his foot, he unlaced his shoes, took off his trousers, rubbed off the smudge with a wet washer, and dressed once more. Then he walked up the stairs.

He knew Granny Catchprice was out walking and he knew that Vish was up there in her apartment, skulking, waiting like some kind of missionary. He had been up there all day long, hiding. If you asked him why he was hiding he would deny it, but Benny knew he was hiding, from Mort, from Benny, from the cars themselves. He had been cooking curry and now he was standing in front of the bride doll cabinet doing stuff in front of the picture of his guru. There was a bowl of yellow food beside the picture and there was a sprig of jasmine in a Vegemite jar. Vish believed the picture could taste the food with its eyes.

Benny said: 'Whatcher doing?'

Vish turned and saw him.

'Hi,' he said. He looked wide awake, alert, without that dumb, blissed-out look he normally got from chanting.

'You should have come and seen me,' said Benny, and patted the wings of his platinum hair flat on the side of his head. 'History is being made round here.' *I look like her.*

'I'm pleased you came,' Vish said. He was pleased too. He walked towards Benny as if he was going to hug him, but then he stopped, a foot in front of him, grinning. He made no acknowledgement that his brother had undergone a total transformation.

'You should have come down.' Benny said. 'I was expecting you.'

'I didn't want to hassle you.' Vish smiled. It was impossible to know what he was thinking.

'You shoulda dropped in, you know.' Benny said. He was standing in front of his brother in a $300 suit and his brother was saying nothing about it. He had never owned a suit before, neither of them had. 'I've been thinking about you all day. About all that stuff we talked about . . .'

'Now we can talk,' Vish nodded to the dining-table and pulled out a chair.

'I was just hanging out down in the cellar after work,' Benny said. 'You should have come down.'

Vish sat down and patted the chair beside him.

'I've *changed*,' Benny said. 'For Chrissakes, look at me.'

Vish looked up and squinted his eyes at Benny. 'Your appearance?'

'Oh Vish,' Benny said, grabbing his brother by his meaty upper arm. 'Don't be a pain in the arse. Come on, come and help me iron some stuff. Will you do that? Remember when you used to iron my school shirts? Come down to the cellar and help me iron my shirts.'

'You want me to come to your cellar?'

Benny sighed.

'It's just that you never wanted me to be there before.'

'There's stuff I want you to see,' Benny said, patting his brother softly on the cheek. 'You'll never understand if you don't come.'

20

'Welcome to the Bunker,' Benny said.

It was worse than anything Vish could have imagined. The air was as thick as a laundry. The concrete floor was half an inch deep in water. It was criss-crossed with planks supported by broken housebricks. A brown-striped couch stood against one end, its legs on bricks. The bricks were wrapped in green plastic garbage bags. Electric flex was everywhere, wrapped in Glad Wrap and bits of plastic bag with torn ends like rag; it crossed the planks and ran through the water. Two electric radiators stood on a chipped green chest of drawers, facing not into the room but towards the walls where you could see the red glow of two bars reflected in what Vish, at first, thought was wet floral wallpaper. It was not wallpaper. It was handwriting, red, blue, green, black, webs of it, layer on layer. In the corner to the left of the door was a white fibreglass object, like a melted surfboard in the shape of a shallow 'n'.

'What's that?'

'Wigwam for a goose's bridle.' Benny pushed him towards the striped couch which stood against the end wall.

The melted surfboard had straps on it like safety belts.

'Sit down, come on.'

Vish looked at the couch he was being offered. 'I came to iron for you,' he said, stepping gingerly away from the couch and looking for a clean flat surface to place the iron on.

'What's the matter?' Pride and blame jostled each other in Benny's voice. He jutted his round smooth chin a little and checked his tie. 'You don't want to look at me? Am I ugly?'

'Benny, you can't stay here. You deserve better than this.'

'You're my brother, right? You're the guy who came up on the train to see me because I was in the shit? That's you?'

'I won't let you stay here.'

'We're family, right?'

'Yes, we're family. That's what we're going to talk about.'

'Then don't patronize me, O.K.? I know I deserve better than this. I'm not going to live here for ever. I'm going to buy a double block at Franklin Heights. There's some great places up there now. They got tennis courts and everything. Vish, we could do so fucking *well*.'

Vish put the steam-iron down on the work bench. 'I won't let you live like this . . .'

'You're scared of money. I understand. Don't worry. I'll look after the money.' Benny smoothed a green garbage bag on the regency couch and sat on it. 'I've changed, just like you changed once. I've made a tranformation.'

Vish looked up at Benny and was about to say something before he changed his mind.

'What?' Benny prompted.

'It's not the time.'

'Say it – it's O.K. You think I can't handle money?'

'No one can change.'

'You can fucking *see* I changed. You're not the only one who's spiritual.'

'You dyed your hair.'

'Is that all you can fucking see . . .'

'You cleaned your face. You got a suit. You know what that makes me feel? It just makes me feel depressed. Even if you had plastic surgery, you couldn't change. I couldn't either. We're both going to be the same thing for all eternity. Even when we die and get born again, even if we get reborn a dog . . . we're the same thing. Everything has a Sanatana Dharma,' Vish said. 'It means Eternal Occupation. It doesn't matter what form we take, this is like our essence – it stays the same.'

Benny sighed and crossed his legs. 'The way I see it,' he said at last, 'is that there are white ants breeding underneath their feet, but they can't see it.'

Vish nodded, waiting to see how this connected.

'They think they're on a rock,' Benny said. 'Howie, Cathy, Mort. They think they're on a rock, but they're on ice. They don't know what's beneath them. Down here,' he gestured at the walls – blue, red, green, words written over each other so they looked like ancient blotting paper. 'Down here I make the future, our future.

I've prepared myself for a completely new life. For you too. We can do this thing together.'

'What about Mort?'

'No, no, I won't hurt him. I'll look after him. I'll look after all of them. Go ahead,' Benny said, seeing Vish trying to read the writing on the wall. 'Please . . . you're my brother, partner . . . It's not a secret from you.'

Vish could read: 'Let a virgin girl weave a white wool carpet . . .' Some foreign names: 'Kushiel, Lahatiel, Zagzagel . . .'

'There's nothing to be frightened of. I'm going to run this business effectively, that's all. I'm transforming myself,' Benny said. 'By various methods, not just that.'

'Into what?'

Benny grinned. He nodded his head and looked self-conscious. 'I can show you a new layout for the whole place. A proper workshop, a modern showroom. If we put all the insurance work through British Union, we can finance it all through them.'

'Into what?' Vish insisted with his forehead all creased and his eyes squinting at his brother. 'Into what are you transforming yourself?'

'Many things.'

'For instance.'

'Angel.'

'Angel?'

'I have changed myself into an angel.'

Vish was suddenly back in that odd dreamy world you enter when you hear someone has died, or you see someone shot in the street in front of you. He heard himself say: 'What sort of angel?'

Benny hesitated. 'There's angels for all of us,' he said, standing up and brushing at his trousers. 'Like you found out at the temple, right? Angels they never told us about in Sunday School.' He smiled and folded his hands behind his back like a salesman on the lot and Vish, seeing the clear confidence in his eyes, thought, once again, that his brother was mentally unwell.

'Benny,' Vish said, 'you've got to get out of here. Whatever's bad, this place only makes it worse.'

'You ask me, then you don't want to listen to my answers. I already told you. I'm going to buy a block at Franklin Heights.'

'It stinks in here. I won't let you live like this.'

'Let's be honest. It's because of you I'm here. You put me here, Vish. And that's why you're here now.'

'Oh no. Let's be clear about this. I took you to the ashram. I would have got you in.'

'I was a runaway minor. They shat themselves when they knew that.'

'I would have got you in. You ran away before they had a chance.'

'Bullshit, Vish, you kissed their arses. Where else could I come except down here? You think I was going to stay with Old Kissy Lips alone? Is that how you were looking after me?'

Vish bowed his head.

'Hey,' Benny said.

Vish had his eyes squinched up tight.

'Come on,' Benny said.

Vish felt his brother's arm around his shoulder.

'I'm not mad at you,' Benny said. 'I was never mad at you. We each got out of home, in different ways. All I want is you fucking listen to me, eh?' He paused, and smiled. 'O.K.?'

'O.K.' said Vish, also smiling, 'Fair enough.'

'Ask me what angel I am.' He pushed his brother in the ribs, 'Go on.'

'What angel are you?'

'Fallen angel,' Benny said, 'Angel of Plagues, Angel of Ice, Angel of Lightning.'

Vish shook his head.

'Hey, it's not for you to say yes or no. You think I made this up?' Benny held up a book – *A Dictionary of Angels*. 'This is not bullshit. Look up Krishna. He's there, and all his atvars.'

'Avatars.'

'Atavars, yes. If I'm wrong, you're wrong too.' He opened the front of the book and let Vish read the inscription: 'I cannot be what I am – A.V.'

'Who is A.V.?' Vish asked. 'You've become an angel? Is that it? You've become an angel from this book?'

The truth was that Benny did not know. He had made himself into an angel, and he came out looking like his mother. But he was not his mother, he was an angel. The angels were his creation. By writing their names he made them come true.

He made Saboeth with a dragon's face and the power of destruction. He made Adonein, a mischievous angel with the face of a monkey. They were his masters. They were his victims. He smoked dope and took their power. He broke their spines and crushed them as he tore them out of books. He played Judas Priest with the volume turned up full. He had a real blue tattoo wing which ran from his right shoulder blade to his round, white, muscled buttock. The angels had feet with five toes and toenails and heavy white callouses round their heels.

'You've become an angel?' Vish asked.

'Hey,' said Benny, 'relax . . . I was just kidding you.'

'Really?'

'I was just scaring you. We don't need to do anything extreme.'

21

When Benny was three years old, his mother was only twenty-three. Her name was Sophie Catchprice. She had bell-bottomed jeans and long blonde hair like Mary in Peter Paul and Mary. She had bare feet and chipped red nail-polish on her toenails. She stood at the door of her bedroom one Saturday afternoon and saw her husband sucking her younger son's penis.

There was a Demolition Derby in progress in the paddock behind the house. The car engines were screaming, hitting that high dangerous pitch that tells you they are way past the red line, and you could smell the methyl benzine racing fuel right here in the bedroom. Sun poured through the lace curtains with the rucked hems. All around her were signs of her incompetence: the bed unmade; the curtains still stained; an F.J. generator-coil on the dressing table; Mort's .22 still leaning in the corner next to the broken standard lamp. She had told him for two years – pick up that rifle.

She saw her husband, the father of her children, with his hand inside his unzipped trousers. Neither Mort nor Benny knew she was there. She was a fly on the wall, a speck, a nothing. She felt like her own dream – where she scratched her stomach and found her innards – her life – green and slippery and falling through her fingers. She picked up the rifle. What else was she to do?

'Give him to me,' she said. But she could not look at Benny. She was frightened of what she would see. He was three years old. He had a white Disney T-shirt with Minnie kissing Mickey: SMACK it said. Johnny had one the same, but Johnny was safe with his Grandma in Spare Parts.

'You evil slime,' she said.

'Hey come on,' Mort said. His trousers were undone, but Benny was not reaching for his mother. He clung tight to his father's neck. Sophie felt like her chest was full of puke.

She had to do something. She heard the shell 'snick' into the firing chamber as if someone else put it there. She was not even angry, or if she was angry then the anger was covered with something rumpled and dirty and she could not recognize it. What she felt was sourer and sadder than anger, more serious than anger. Her fingers felt heavy, and spongy. She looked at Benny. His little eyes seemed alien and poisoned. He balanced on his father's hip staring back at her.

'Come to Mummy,' she said.

But Benny was looking at the rifle. He shook his head.

'Give him to me,' she said to Mort, 'and I won't hurt you, I swear.'

'Put that rifle down,' he said. 'You don't know how to use it.'

Sure, she knew how to. She could not see what else to do but what she did. But even as she did it, as she took one action after the other, she expected something would happen that would stop her travelling all the way to the logical conclusion. She walked a little closer to Mort, frowning and then there was nothing left to do but fire. Even as she did it, she thought she lacked the courage.

She fired from less than a metre. The bullet missed her husband and caused a red flower to blossom on the arm of her son's Mickey Mouse T-shirt.

It was Sophie who called out, not Benny. Benny looked as if he'd fallen playing – his lip pouted and his big eyes swelled with tears.

Sophie held out a hand towards him, but Mort crouched on the floor, holding his corduroy trousers together, shielding the wounded child with his big body. Benny clung to his father. He had his arms around his neck. Blood was smeared all round Mort's ears and collar.

Sophie reached out towards her son but he flinched from her.

'Go *way*,' he screamed. He was three years old, alive with rage towards her. She could not bear to be the focus of it. 'Go way.'

The windows were filthy. The sunlight illuminated the small balls of fluff which drifted across the uncarpeted floor. Their child's blood was a bright, bright red, like newly opened paint. It flooded the chest of Benny's shirt. Sophie felt soaked with shame. It was unendurable.

'What did you do that for?' Mort was crying, stroking Benny's head.

She felt the first flicker of doubt.

'You know what you were doing, slime.'

'Tell me,' Mort screamed. 'Tell me what we've done.'

She brought another shell into the chamber, but everything she thought so definitely was now dissolving in the acid of her chronic uncertainty. What she had seen was already like a thing she might have feared or dreamed or even, yes, imagined.

'I was kissing his tummy,' he said. He had blood on his fingers. He was streaking blood through his son's fair hair.

'Kissing!'

'I was fucking *kissing* him,' he said. 'For Chrissake, Sophie. Why do you want to kill our little boy?'

She looked at his big swollen lips and his bright blaming eyes and saw the way the terrified child held him around the neck, and she believed him.

It was like you pour water on a fire that is burning you. Sophie just put the barrel of the rifle in her mouth and fired. She messed that up as well. The bullet passed beside her spinal column, and out through the back of her neck.

She ran from the house, across the car yard. She waited for a wall, a barrier, but nothing stopped her flight. Her father-in-law was selling a Ford Customline to a man in a leather jacket. He held up his hand and waved to her. She ran down Loftus Street, splashing blood behind her. She had not planned to leave, not leave her little boys, not leave by train, but she was at the railway station and she had twenty dollars in her slacks and she had done a crime and she bought a ticket and boarded the 6.25 train to Sydney which was just departing from the platform next to the booth. She was dripping blood and nearly fainting but no one looked at her particularly. No one tried to stop her. She just kept on going. She just kept on going on and on, and as the train pulled out she could see the Demolition Derby in the back paddock behind Catchprice Motors.

22

When his little brother was being bashed up by Matty Evans behind the boys' lavatories, Vish came running into the school yard from the hole in the fence next to the milk factory. He had a housebrick. He was not yet Vish – he was still John. He was nine years old. He was bigger than Benny but he still had to carry the brick in both hands. He pushed his way through the circle of yelling boys and threw the brick, point blank. It hit Matty Evans on the side of the head and he dropped so fast and lay so still that the little kids started crying, thinking he was dead. There was a dark red pool of blood glistening on the hot asphalt playground, and teachers were yelling and making everyone stand in line even though it was the magpie season and two kids were swooped just standing there. Johnny Catchprice vomited up his sandwiches, just as the ambulance arrived. It drove straight into the school yard and left deep ruts in the grass in front of 'Paddles' Rogers's rose garden.

Matty Evans got six stitches and they clipped his hair like he was a dog with mange. Paddles paddled Johnny Catchprice for every one of those stitches. Johnny's hand puffed up so much he had to be excused from English Composition and this was why Mort put on his suit and came up to the school to talk to Paddles during the double Algebra on Thursday afternoon.

Everyone thought he had come to threaten law suits, but Mort was not shocked by either the crime or the punishment. What panicked Mort was that he maybe had a 'disturbed child' on his hands, that a whiff of his home life could be detected in the open air. He put on his grey suit and went up to school, not to sue, but to plug the leak somehow. He was not sure how he would do it, not even when he opened his mouth.

Paddles was a little bald-headed man with a swagger and a hairy chest which grew up under his shirt collar. He felt himself an inch away from litigation and so he was chatty and pleasant and over-eager. He looked across at Johnny and winked.

Johnny laid his bandaged hand on his lap and looked out of the window at the ruts the ambulance had left on the green lawn.

'No matter who bullied whom,' Mort said, 'I never saw him do anything like this in all his life. And when I say all his life, I mean, all his life. I don't know if you know it, but his mother left us when he was five . . .'

'Noo-na,' said Paddles sympathetically. He was confused about what Mort Catchprice was up to. This gave him an odd 'hanging-on-every-word' look.

'She just pissed off.'

Johnny shut his eyes.

'At that time I couldn't cook, I couldn't sew, and I wasn't seeing my kids as much as I should have. I was coaching the Under-fifteens in the football and the cricket. I was setting up the panel shop. But suddenly there were all these fucking bureaucrats – pardon my French – wanted to take my boys away, because I was a man.'

'Isn't that typical,' said Paddles. 'Sure. I can imagine . . .'

'You can imagine,' Mort said. 'You can imagine I soon found out how to cook and how to sew. I was there for them in the morning and I was there for them at night, so when I say Johnny doesn't do this sort of thing,' Mort kicked Johnny underneath the desk, 'hitting a boy with a *brick*. When I say this is not him, I know what I'm talking about. You understand me?'

'Yes,' Paddles said. 'Sure. Hell, yes.' The minute he said yes he thought he had made a legal mistake.

'Good,' Mort said, kicking Johnny again. 'So you understand why I'm upset – I work for years of my life to give you a sweet, gentle kid, you give me back a kid who hits another kid with a brick.'

It was only then that Johnny got the joke – his dad was *lying*.

'It's not in his character. I hope you agree?'

Paddles thought he could see Mort assembling evidence for court. 'Without prejudice?' He saw the kid trying to hide his grin. 'Look,' he said. 'It will never happen again.' He meant the strapping.

Mort meant brick-throwing. 'That's your decision,' he said, 'totally, but if I hear of any more behaviour like this, you're the man I'll be holding responsible.'

Johnny and his father walked out of the school, making odd little noises up behind their noses, holding their laughter in like you keep water in a garden hose with your thumb. They walked out across the lawn, biting their lips and creasing their eyes.

They left a screech of rubber on Vernon Street that stayed there for two months. Mort was wailing with laughter, banging the wheel. Thump, thump, thump with the fat heel of his hand, and his lips now all big and loose with pleasure at the lie he had told. He grabbed Johnny's thigh – a horse bite – and squeezed him till he yelped, and then Johnny laughed too, not at the lie, but at their shared experience, their complicity.

'Not in his character!'

It was 100 per cent his character. That was the joke – this mild, sweet-faced boy could attack his father with a tyre lever.

'You little bastard,' his father said, admiringly it seemed.

They were like each other, twins, they had the same chin, the same ears, the same temper too.

He knew that when the time came, he would never be able to explain about his father – how you could want to crush him like an insect, how he was also almost perfect.

He'd drive them to wherever the Balmain Tigers were playing – 40, 60 K's – no wuckers. He played Rock 'n' Roll really loud – AC/DC, Judas Priest. He was the one who bought the Midnight Oil tape.

How can we sleep when our beds are burning
How can we sleep while our world is turning

He sang the words out loud. He was as good as Peter Garrett – he could have been a Rock 'n' Roller. They ate potato crisps, hot dogs, twisties, minties, pies. At the game he did not abandon them for the bar. He was their mate. They argued and farted all the way home to Franklin. He cooked pancakes and served them up with butter and sugar and fresh-squeezed lemon juice.

He was a good father. He got up at six each morning so he could cook them a proper breakfast. He brushed their hair. He fussed over their clothes. He gave them expensive fizzy vitamins and did not over-cook the vegetables.

He was affectionate. He was never shy to kiss them on the cheek or hold them. He liked to kiss. He had soft kissing lips. And it was the lips which were the trouble, the lips that showed when things were going bad again.

Johnny looked like his Dad. Naturally this was not so interesting for their Dad to look at. Benny looked like the other person, the one they were not allowed to ask about and the bad nights always began with their father staring at Benny and looking sad. Then he would cuddle in to him and stroke his hair and kiss him on the neck. He was not ashamed of it. He said: 'You see those other fathers, too scared to even touch their kids. They're just terrified of natural feelings.' He kissed them both, often, like you saw mothers kissing babies. Kissing their necks and backs.

Once he started kissing Benny's neck, he would not stay soulful and doggy-eyed for long. Johnny could watch the mood-change coming like wind across a paddock full of wheat. His dad's eyes would turn snaky. He'd start to talk sarcastic, spiky. He would laugh and say mean things about the shape of Johnny's head or how fat his legs were. He did not mean them really – nasty and nice were all the same to him when his mood changed. He had only one objective: to get Johnny to leave the room so he could be alone with Benny.

Johnny slammed the door to counterfeit his exit from the house. He sat outside the blessed circle of affection, outside the blue centre of the flame, safer but more lonely, excluded but responsible. He became the ugly one. He became a peek, a sneak. He watched his father stroke Benny's hair, waited for the moment when the mustard velvet cushion would be placed across his brother's lap. It was then he would come in throwing darts or pillows.

Sometimes Benny just looked at him with wet open lips and a smile on his face, sometimes he needed him bad. Sometimes Mort and Benny both shouted at him, told him to piss off out of there.

The day they saw Paddles it was still seven whole years away from the night when he would smash his father's bedroom window with a cast-iron casserole and cut him with the Stay-sharp knife.

He was not Vish yet.

He was still Johnny and when Mort said, 'Come on, killer, I'll buy you a quarter pounder,' he looked at the big face and in spite of everything, was still proud to be just like his Daddy.

23

At ten-fifteen on Monday night, while Maria and Gia drove from the Blue Moon Brasserie towards the Taxation Office, Cathy stood at her open refrigerator door wondering what she could be bothered cooking; Mrs Catchprice walked along Vernon Street, Franklin, and offered to employ Sarkis Alaverdian; Vishnabarnu finished ironing Benny's wrapping paper and began to iron his jeans.

'I'm going to get you out of here,' he said.

'You never did listen to anyone but yourself, Vish.' Benny straightened the orange plastic sheet beneath his suit and adjusted his socks once again. 'I'm asking you to be my partner.'

'I'll take you out of here,' Vish smiled. 'If I have to pick you up and carry you out.'

'Only problem,' Benny lit a Marlboro and blew a long thin line towards his brother, 'I *want* to be here. You want to help me, stay here with me.'

Vish put the iron on its end and folded the jeans one more time.

'You're a stubborn fucker, aren't you?' Benny said.

Vish looked up and smiled.

'We know the truth though,' Benny blew a fat and formless cloud of smoke. 'You've got the business and the personal mixed up. The problem is you were always jealous.'

'Oh really? Of what?'

'Of me and Him.'

'Benny, you hated him. You used to cry in your *sleep*. We were plotting to poison him with heart tablets.'

'You were jealous of us. That's why you went crazy. It wasn't the business. If you want him to retire, we can do that. We can look after him. We can get him out of here.'

'This is nothing to do with Mort.'

'You smashed the window. You stabbed him. You have to admit you've got a problem with him, not with the business.'

'I was protecting you.'

'You want to protect me – be my partner.'

Vish had that red-brown colour in his cheeks. His neck and shoulders were set so tight – if you touched him he would feel like rock.

'Benny, I'm not coming back. O.K.? Never, ever.'

Benny laughed but he felt the sadness, like snot, running down his throat. He did not say anything. He could not think of anything to say.

Vish folded the jeans and laid them carefully beside the bottled brown snakes Benny had rescued from his Grandpa's personal effects. He took the AC/DC T-shirt and smoothed it against his broad chest. 'You should have washed them first,' he said.

'I'm never going to wear them again,' Benny said.

He waited for Vish to ask him why. But Vish was a Catchprice – he was never going to ask. He just kept on ironing, with his big square face all wrinkled up against the steam.

After a while, Benny said: 'Aren't you even curious?'

Vish jabbed at the T-shirt with the point of the iron.

Benny asked: 'Do you think I look like her?'

'Like who?'

'Like who?' Benny mimicked the high scratchy voice. He pulled the photograph out of the silky pocket of his suit and pushed it at his brother. Vish took it and held it up to the light.

'Oh, yeah.' He looked up at Benny but made no comment on his dazzling similarity.

Benny took the photo back. He put it in his pocket.

Vish said: 'Remember the night you saw her?' He folded the T-shirt arms over so they made a 45° angle with the shoulder, then he pressed them flat. He was grinning.

'You saw her too,' Benny smiled as well. 'Who else would stand like that at the front gate at two in the morning.'

'It could have been anyone.' Vish folded the T-shirt so its trunk was exactly in half. When the hot iron hit it, the shirt gave off a smell like Bathurst – oil, maybe some methyl benzine.

'It must have been her,' Benny said. 'Anyone gets shot with an air rifle – if they're innocent they call the cops.'

Vish smiled.

'Admit it – you think about her too.'

'All I try to think about is Krishna.'

'Bullshit, Johnny. What total bullshit.' Benny said. 'You should learn to ask questions, it's amazing what you find out. Did you know how long it took you to get born? Ask me.'

'You don't know.'

'Ten hours. You know how long it took me? It took me thirty hours. You don't believe me, ask Cathy. The second baby should be faster but I was lying back to front. They cut our mother open to get me out. It fucked up all her stomach muscles. She got a stomach like an old woman when she was twenty, all wrinkled like a prune.'

'And that's why she shot you? Come on, Benny. Give up. Get on with your life.'

'Hey,' Benny rose from the couch, his finger pointing. 'Forget all this shit you tell yourself about me. Forget all the bullshit stories you carry in your head.' He straightened his trouser legs and ran his palms along his jacket sleeves. 'What did I tell you?'

'When?'

'Any time.' He held his palms out. The gesture made no sense. 'Ever. I told you we could do this thing together. I told you I was changed. Angel. Look.' He walked carefully along the plank to reach his brother. Then he opened his mouth for his brother to look in.

What he meant was: light. I have light pouring out of me.

'Benny you need help.'

'You don't believe me,' Benny hit his forehead with his palm. 'You jerk-off – you're walking away from two hundred thou a year. You don't know what you're doing. You don't know where you are. Where are you?' Benny helped him. He pointed. He pointed to the walls, the writing. He invited him to look, to read, to under-stand all this – the very centre of his life – but all Vish did was shrug and unplug the iron. He stood the iron end up on the bench beside the clothes and the snakes. Right behind him was the fibreglass 'thing' in the shape of a flattened 'n'.

'Where are you?' Benny asked. 'Answer me that.'

'I'm in your cellar, Benny.'

'No,' said Benny. 'You are inside my fucking head and I have got the key.'

All around Vishnabarnu were the names of angels. They hung over him like a woven web, a net, like a map of the human brain drawn across the walls and ceilings of the world. He knew himself a long way from God.

24

Benny greased the Monaro out of the back paddock with its lights off. He was not licensed, and the car was not meant to be driven on the road, but his father was watching a video in his bedroom and he took the Monaro out on the far side, on to the little gravel lane which ran right beside the railway tracks.

There was a path direct to the Wool Wash, and for a moment he had toyed with the idea of walking there. The path led out through the hole in the paling fence at the back of Mort's house.

This was the path they had walked with old Cacka down to see the frogmouth owl, the path they walked together each day to go swimming down at the Wool Wash. The path went (more or less) straight across the back paddock, crossed the railway line, curved round the Council depot where a huge Cyclone fence protected nothing more than a pile of blue gravel and two battered yellow forty-four-gallon drums, cut round the edge of the brickworks clay pit and then went straight across those little hills which had once been known as 'Thistle Paddocks' but were now a housing estate known as Franklin Heights. The path then ran beside the eroded drive-way to the 105-room house, down into the dry bush gullies, and then out on to the escarpment where a path was hacked into the cliff wall like something in a comic strip. The path led finally to the clear waters of the Wool Wash pool.

The truth was: it was not like that any more. The path was fucked. It was cut like a worm by a garden spade – new yellow fences, subdivisions, prohibitions, walls, new dogs, shitty owners with psychotic ideas about their territorial rights, frightened lonely women who would press the panic button on their Tandy burglar alarms at the sight of a stranger climbing over their fence.

Once it had been the best thing in Benny's life. Now it was just an imaginary line cutting through suburbia. Once he had been able to sit above the Wool Wash for hours on hot still days in summer doing Buddha grass and feeling the wind bend the trees and show the silver colour in the Casuarinas and watching the old eels making their sand-nest in the river. When everything was so bad he thought he had to die, his mind went there, to the Wool Wash, and when Tape 7 said find a river, there was only one river.

He considered the path but it was not a serious option. When his brother went off to bed, he carried his gift-wrapped clothes and his sawn-off shot gun down to the Monaro. Fifteen minutes later he came down the S's to the Wool Wash with the tacho needle almost on the red line. He put the nose too close into the corner on the second last bend and he nearly lost it in the fucking gravel. He changed down even as he knew he shouldn't. The tail kicked out. Fuck it. He flicked the wheels into line and and saved it. He cut a clean line across the next curve and came down into the car park at 150Ks but he was prickling hot with shame. It was such a shitty gear change.

He did two slow circuits with his quartzes on, blasting a pure white light through the cloud of clay dust his arrival had created. His four headlight beams cut like knives through the dust, illuminating the bullet-scarred, yellow garbage bins, the POLLUTED WATER signs, and twisted galvanized pipe boom gates (NO 4-WHEEL DRIVE ACCESS).

He had a 1:3 ratio first gear and he just walked the Monaro like a dog on a leash, torqued it round the perimeter of the parking area, checking to make sure there was no one here to mock what he was going to do.

The Franklin Redevelopment Region now had a hundred thousand school kids. The banks of the Wool Wash were littered with beer cans and condoms and paper cups. Petrol-heads came here to do one dusty spin-turn before screaming up through the S's for the race back to the skid pan at the Industrial Estate. Stolen cars were abandoned here, virginities were lost, although not his. At weekends you could buy speed and crack by the gas barbecues. It was the sort of place you might find someone with their face shot away and bits of brain hanging on the bushes.

Benny drove round the edge of a metal boom gate. It bottomed out on some grass tussocks, and then he just slid it – you could feel the grass brushing along the floor beneath his feet – out of sight behind some ti-tree scrub.

When he had shut off the engine and the lights, he tucked the shot gun underneath his seat. Then he carefully removed his suit trousers and his shirt. He folded them loosely and placed them on the lambswool seat cover. He put on a T-shirt and a pair of swimming trunks and then he put on his shoes as a protection against AIDS.

Even though it was warm, the rain clouds made the night dark and his flash light was weak and yellow. He walked warily out across the empty car park to the river, carrying the ironed clothes in a red Grace Bros plastic shopping bag. The bank just here was flat and wide and treeless. When he got to where the round boulders started, he took off his good leather shoes and placed them in the shopping bag.

Benny failed every science subject he ever took, but he knew this water in Deep Creek now contained lead, dioxin and methyl mercury from the paper factory on Lantana Road. It was surprisingly cold on his feet. He could feel the poisons clinging like invisible odour-free oil slicks. They rode through the water like spiders' webs, air through air, sticking to everything they touched. Benny moved quickly, but carefully.

He heard the sound of the approaching car when it was up on the turn off from Long Gully Road. It was a Holden. He recognized the distinctive sound of the water pump, that high hiss in the night. He hesitated, wondering whether he should go back to the car and wait but he did not want to have to walk into the poisons twice.

There was a light wind, a cool wash of air that pushed up the river like a wave and the big Casuarinas on the shore bent and made a soft whooshing noise. No matter what had changed, it still smelt like the Wool Wash – moss, rotting leaves, something like blackcurrants that was not blackcurrants, and the slightly muddy tannin smell of the water which you could once drink, puddles full, from Cacka's old slouch hat.

The first package was the sneakers. He had them in a shoebox now, wrapped in ironed black paper and tied with a gold ribbon. He pushed the package out into the current, following it for a metre or two with the weak beam of his torch until it was lost.

He whispered: 'When my past is dead, I am as free as air.'

Then he squatted and pushed out the blue parcel which contained his T-shirt. It was flat and neat like a twelve-inch L.P. For a moment it seemed to mould itself like a Kraft cheese slice on to a rock, but then it was picked up and although it was lost to sight Benny thought he could hear the sound of its paper skin brushing over the shallow rapids downstream.

He said: 'When my past is cleared, there is only blue sky.'

The Holden was coming through the S bends above the river. He could see its lights as they cut out into the air. The car was burning oil and the lights cut back and shone white in the smoke of its own exhaust.

He hurriedly launched the gold parcel, throwing it a little carelessly so that it landed thin edge in and sank a little before it surfaced.

He spoke quickly: 'My past is gone and I am new – born again – my future will be wrapped with gold.'

He stepped off the rock. He tried to put a shoe on, but he could not get his foot into it. The leather stuck on his wet skin. He leaned over to fix it. Then his ankle twisted and he stumbled. The Holden was through the last bend. Benny picked up the shoe and ran barefoot. Death was everywhere, but no way was anyone going to see him doing rituals in his underwear. The earth was alive with organisms which wished to make a host of his blood. He felt cuts, nicks, toxins, viruses. The car – a fucking taxi! – was driving right down to the water's edge. He fled the beam of its lights and ran to his car. He got in, locked the doors, sat the shot gun across his lap.

The taxi did not stay long. As soon as it began its ascent through the S's he dressed, and backed the Monaro out into the centre of the car park. When he turned to head back to Franklin, he saw, in the halogen-white glare of the headlights – Granny Catchprice. Her legs were apart. Her left hand was shading her eyes.

25

'You pay me now,' Pavlovic said. 'Or I leave you here, dead-set. You walk all the way back to Franklin, wouldn't worry me.' He leaned back, opened the door on Mrs Catchprice's side, and smiled.

Sarkis was smiling too. He had that hot burning sensation down the back of his throat. He sat on the edge of the back seat of the taxi with his broad white hands on his knees. He was baring his teeth and narrowing his eyes – 'smiling' – but Pavlovic wasn't even aware of him. He was turned almost completely round in his seat with his hawk nose pointed at Mrs Catchprice.

'Might give you nicer manners,' he said.

'You'll be paid later,' said Mrs Catchprice. 'I don't carry cash on me.'

'You pay me now,' said Pavlovic.

'You heard her,' Sarkis said, but he was the one no one seemed to hear.

'Or you get out of my cab. That simple,' he smiled again. His mouth was prissy and pinched as if he could smell something nasty on his upper lip.

Sarkis did not want to have a brawl in these trousers and this shirt but he could feel anger like curry in his throat. His eyes were narrowed almost to slits in his incredulous, smiling face. Pavlovic was so *thin*. Sarkis smoothed the $199 grey moire trousers against his muscled thighs. He looked at Mrs Catchprice to see what it was she wanted him to do.

Mrs Catchprice, it seemed, needed nothing from him. Whatever Pavlovic said to her did not matter. Indeed she was concerned with her cigarette lighter, which had fallen down the back of the seat. 'I did not come to the Wool Wash to sit in the car. Ah,' she held up her Ronson. 'I cannot bear it when I see people sitting in their car to look at the scenery.'

Pavlovic sighed loudly and Sarkis – he couldn't help himself – slapped him on the side of the head, fast, sharp.

'You stop that,' Mrs Catchprice said. 'Right now.'

Sarkis opened his mouth to protest.

'I don't hire louts,' said Mrs Catchprice.

Pavlovic said something too but Sarkis did not hear what it was. Pavlovic was holding a clenched fist in the air and Sarkis kept an eye on it, but all his real attention was on Mrs Catchprice – what did she want him to do?

'Maybe you should pay him,' he said.

Mrs Catchprice 'acted' her response. She smiled a large 'nice' smile that made her white teeth look as big as an old Buick grille. 'I always pay my suppliers when they have *completed* the job.'

'I could have the police here,' Pavlovic smirked and rubbed his bright red ear. 'Or I could leave you here. I like both ideas.'

Sarkis did not actually have a police record, but he had experience of the police in Chatswood. To Mrs Catchprice, he said: 'Maybe you should look in your handbag.'

Mrs Catchprice's smile became even bigger. 'You must not equate age with stupidity,' she said. 'You'd have to be senile to walk around at night with money in your bag.'

She made him ashamed he had suggested such a cowardly course but he had seen the twenty-dollar notes very clearly in the jumble under the street lights before they caught the taxi. He did not wish to insult or anger her, but he tapped her very playfully on the back of the hand. 'I think I may have seen some there.'

Mrs Catchprice looked at him briefly, frowned, and addressed herself to the balding, hawk-nosed driver. 'What will the police think,' she asked, 'of a taxi-driver operating outside the correct area?'

'They do not give a fuck. Excuse my language, but if you were nice, I would care. You are not nice, so I could not give a fuck. The police got no bloody interest in what area I'm in. Most of the young constables don't even know what an area is. But I tell you this – they got plenty of interest in assault, and they got plenty of interest in robbery. That's their business.'

'Maybe you should check your handbag,' said Sarkis.

'I can see I'm going to have to train you,' said Mrs Catchprice. 'When I say I have no money it is because I have no money.' To the taxi-driver she said: 'You wait.' Then she slid out of the door and disappeared into the night.

The taxi-driver leaned back and shut the door. Mrs Catchprice appeared in the headlights of the car walking towards the river. Then – so suddenly it whipped Sarkis's head forwards and backwards – Pavlovic reversed, made a U-turn, and before his passenger could do anything he was bouncing up the pot-holed track with the red electric figures on the meter showing $28.50.

They were half way through the first S bend when Sarkis leant forward and hooked his forearm round the taxi-driver's long thin neck. He pulled it back so hard he could feel the jaw bone grating against his ulna. All he said was: 'Turn back.' The driver's stubble was rubbing against his forearm. He hated to think of this against his mother.

'Road,' Pavlovic gasped. 'Too narrow.'

'O.K.'

'Can't breathe.'

'Shut up.'

'Breathe.'

Sarkis released his arm a little. The taxi-driver screamed. He screamed so loud he made the taxi like a nightmare, a mad place: 'You a dead man, Jack.' Sarkis could feel the wet on his arm. Not sweat. Pavlovic was crying. 'I hit my panic button, they get you, cunt. They get you in the cells, they fuck you with their baton, you wait.' The car slowed and slowed until it was juddering and kangaroo-hopping up the road. As the car leaped and jerked, Pavlovic was flailing around with his arm, trying to grab first Sarkis's ear or eye but also – the panic button. Sarkis grabbed Pavlovic's hand and held it. He held it easy, but he was now scared, as scared as Pavlovic. Pavlovic was crying but it was not simple scared-crying, it was mad-crying too.

'You pull up here,' Sarkis said.

'You get twenty years for this. You're dead.'

'She gets murdered or something,' Sarkis said. '*She*'s dead.' The car shuddered and stalled.

'You,' yelled the taxi-driver, his face glowing green in the light of his instruments, but he didn't finish the sentence.

'What you think I'm going to do to you?' Sarkis asked. 'Did I hurt you?'

'Just pay me,' Pavlovic said, glaring at him from streaming eyes.

'O.K.,' Sarkis said, relieved. 'You go back and get her, I'll pay you.'

'O.K. You take your arm away now.'

Sarkis unhooked his arm from under the driver's chin.

'O.K.,' said Pavlovic, blowing his nose. 'You got money on you?'

'At home.'

'Then I'll take you home for the money, then we come back here and get her.' He was hunched over the wheel. He did not need to tell Sarkis he had his finger an inch away from the panic button.

'We get her first.'

'You want me press this fucking button?'

That button was enough to get Sarkis put in jail. Pavlovic used it like a pistol. First he forced him to abandon Mrs Catchprice. Then he drove him to his house where his mother had $52 hidden under the lino in the sitting-room.

While Sarkis stole his mother's money, Pavlovic sat in the cab with the engine running. He stayed hunched over the wheel, his finger on that button.

'Come on,' Sarkis said when he got back in the cab. 'I've got the money.'

'Hold it up. Hold the notes.'

Sarkis showed him – five tens, one two.

Pavlovic twisted his neck to see the money. He had to keep his finger on that button. Even when he backed out of the drive-way he had to sit twisted sideways in his seat, and he drove back to the Wool Wash one handed, all the way, in silence.

When the meter showed $52 they were almost there, on the main road up above the Wool Wash Picnic Area. Pavlovic stopped the car.

'You pay me,' he said, 'or I hit this fucking button now. I charge you with fucking assault, at least. You understand me.'

'Relax,' said Sarkis. 'No one's going to hurt you.'

'Shut up, Jack. Just pay me.'

'I need a lift back. O.K. Can you hear me? I'll pay you more money when we get back.'

'Give me the fucking money or you're a dead man.'

'You don't want to make more money?' Sarkis held out the $52 and Pavlovic snatched the notes. 'I need a lift back,' Sarkis said. 'I'll pay you.'

'Not in this cab, Jack.'

'Just calm down, relax a little.'

'Get out,' screamed Pavlovic.

Sarkis shrugged and got out of the car.

Pavlovic locked the car doors.

'Listen,' Sarkis began, but the taxi was already driving away, leaving him to stand in pitch darkness.

It was now five minutes to eleven o'clock on Monday night. Mrs Catchprice was already back in Franklin, walking back across the gravel towards her apartment.

26

The Australian Tax Office was in Hunter Street. The glassed, marble-columned foyer remained brightly lit and unlocked and, apart from video cameras and an hourly M.S.S. patrol, the security for the building depended on deceptively ordinary blue plastic Security Access Keys which were granted only to ASO 7's and above. This was why Gia now had a key and Maria did not.

In the six months she had had the key, Gia had never used it. It sat in its original envelope in the bottom of her handbag, together with its crumpled instruction sheet. Now, standing before the blank eyes of video cameras which were connected to she knew not what, Gia read the instructions to Maria.

'O.K. Hold the key firmly between thumb and forefinger. Ensure blade is unobstructed.'

'We should have read this in the car,' Maria said. 'I can't see where the shitty thing goes.' She jabbed the key at the button.

'First you've got to step into the elevator, Señora.' Gia took Maria's arm. 'Then you put it in the Security/Air-conditioning slot.'

A red light came on. A buzzer sounded. Maria started.

'Calm down,' Gia said. 'No one's going to shoot you. All we're doing is working late.'

The lift ascended and the liquid display panel above the door wished someone called Alex a happy birthday. Maria seemed pale and unhappy. Gia took her arm and squeezed it.

'Relax,' she said.

'You know,' Maria said, 'that's exactly the wrong thing to say to me. If you're dealing with an agitated person, a maniac, you never say "relax". Relax means what you feel is not important to me. I read that in the *Sydney Morning Herald* yesterday.' She took Gia's hand and held it: 'You're very brave to come with me. Thank you.'

'I think this is going to be very therapeutic,' Gia said. 'I only wish Alistair could see you do it.'

'This is nothing to do with Alistair . . .'

Gia thought: Sure! It was the first real sign she'd seen that Maria would let herself be angry with him.

The door opened on to the rat-maze partitioned world of the eighteenth floor which now housed the file clerks and section heads and auditors who concerned themselves with returns from small businesses like Catchprice Motors.

When Alistair's star had been in the ascendant they had all worked here – although not on small businesses. During those years, no one on the eighteenth floor would have wasted their genius on Catchprice Motors.

They went to big-game fishing conventions in Port Stephens and photographed the people with the big boats and then investigated them to see if their income correlated with their assets. They spotted Rolls-Royces on the way to work and, on that chance encounter, began investigations that brought millions into the public purse. It is true that they were occasionally obsessive (Sally Ho started fifteen investigations on people with stone lion statues in their gardens) but mostly they were not vindictive. They investigated major corporations, multi-nationals with transfer pricing arrangements and off-shore tax havens. They went hunting for Slutzkin schemes, Currans, and sham charities. This is the work for which Alistair recruited Maria Takis and her best friend Gia Katalanis.

It had not been a rat-maze then. Alistair had had all the

partitioning ripped out. There had been no careful grading of offices and desks but a clamorous paddock of excitable men and women who lived and breathed taxation. They worked long hours and drank too much red wine and smoked too many cigarettes and had affairs or ruined their marriages or did both at the same time. More than half of them came from within the Taxation Office but many – those with new degrees like Gia and Maria – came from outside it, and thereby leap-frogged several positions on the promotion ladder without sensing that the old Taxation Office was a resilient and unforgiving organism. Had they realized what enemies they were making it is unlikely they would have acted any differently – they were not cautious people. They were sometimes intolerant, always impatient, but they were also idealists and all of them were proud of their work and they were not reluctant to identify themselves at dinner parties as Tax Officers.

It was Alistair who created this climate, and for a long time everyone in the Taxation Office – even those who later revealed themselves to be his enemies – must have been grateful to him. It was something to be able to reveal your profession carelessly.

It was Alistair who said, on national television, that being a Tax Officer was the most pleasant work imaginable, like turning a tap to bring water to parched country. It felt wonderful to bring money flowing out of multi-national reservoirs into child-care centres and hospitals and social services. He grinned when he said it and his creased-up handsome face creased up some more and he cupped his hands as if cool river water were flowing over his big, farmer's fingers and it was hard to watch him and not smile yourself. This was one half of Alistair's great genius – that he was good on television. He sold taxation as a public good.

The Taxation Office had never had a television star before, so it was not surprising that Alistair would be envied and resented because of it nor – when the political forces against him succeeded – that he would be treated spitefully in defeat. What was less expected was that the bureaucracy would punish his lover almost as severely, more severely in one way, for Alistair's office, although much smaller and no longer in the power corner, was at least properly carpeted and had all of its shelving and wiring correctly installed.

'Oh, the *bastards*,' said Gia when she stood at the doorway of

Maria's office. 'The unmitigated petty little bastards.'

There was still wiring running across the floor from the computer to the black skirting board which was meant to hide it. There were no shelves. There were books and papers stacked on the floor. The only filing cabinet was grey and it was littered with sawdust, aluminium off-cuts, a hammer and a chisel.

'They fixed the modem,' Maria said. 'Gia, I don't care. I'm never here.'

Gia picked up a tradesman's dustpan and began to sweep the floor.

'It's not the point,' she said. She picked up metal shavings and a little block of hardwood and dropped them in the pan. 'What I can't believe is that anyone would hate you. It's not as if you were arrogant. It's not as if you were ever anything but lovely to everyone. Whatever fix Alistair is in, it's nothing to do with you.'

'It's to do with all of us,' Maria said. 'We should all be ashamed that he should be treated the way he is.'

Gia did not comment. She thought the great man of principle was a coward and a creep. He spent his days behind his ASO 9 desk in a poky little office across the hall. He now had nothing to do, except administer a division which no longer existed. All he was doing was reading nineteenth-century novels and waiting for his $500,000 superannuation while Maria and her child faced a hostile future you could optimistically call uncertain.

'Does he talk to you now?' Gia began to sweep the little coloured pieces of electrician's cable into the dustpan.

'He never didn't talk to me,' Maria said, 'and don't start that.' She wanted to leave the office and get on with it.

'Is he nice to you?' Gia asked, sweeping stubbornly.

'Gia, I don't just want to stand here. Let's just do it, quickly. Please.'

'You think I want to hang around here?' Gia emptied the dustpan into the wastebin and started going round the book shelves wiping the dust off with a Kleenex tissue. 'Is he paying for anything?'

'This baby is my mistake, not his. If you want to be mad at someone, be mad at me. Now I need to get into Max Hoskins's office.'

'Sure.'

'You said you could unlock the doors.'

'Only the front door, only the lift to the floor.'

'O.K.'

Maria picked up the hammer from the top of the filing cabinet and walked off down the hall. By the time Gia found her she had fitted the claw beneath Max Hoskins's door and was levering upwards. 'Kick it,' she said.

'No,' said Gia, out of breath. 'We can't do this.'

'You hold the hammer. Push it down.'

Gia sighed and held the hammer and Maria slammed her shoulder hard against the door.

'Careful. I don't want you to go into labour.'

'Again.'

This time the door ripped open.

'This is break and entry,' Gia said, rubbing at the splintered wood at the base of the door. 'This is not some prank. This is like a violation . . . If you want to punish Alistair, you should do something to hurt him, not you. You need this job.'

'*This is nothing to do with Alistair*. I'm just damned if I'm going to let the department make me into someone I'm not. Gia . . . please . . . I need to get at Max's terminal and then we'll go back to the Brasserie and I'll buy you a glass of champagne. If you want to wait for me there, that's fine, really.'

'Just hurry, O.K.'

Gia watched from the doorway as Maria took out Max Hoskins's day book and flipped it open. He had a standard ASO 7 office with a green-topped desk, a leather-bound desk diary, a view to the north, two visitor's chairs. Only a tortoiseshell comb left on top of the computer terminal was non-standard and it had an unpleasant personal appearance like something found on the bedside table of someone who had died.

'I got stuck with him,' Maria said, 'at that barbecue at Sally Ho's place. He complained to me about all the terrible problems of running a department. You know, the way they changed his access code each week and he could never remember it. You know what he does? He writes it down. He writes his access number in his day book, back to front or something.'

Maria flipped on the computer terminal and punched the numbers into it.

The terminal stayed closed.

'Well,' Gia said, 'I guess that's it.'

'You go,' Maria said. 'I'll get it. It'll be these digits plus one, or the entire sequence back to front.'

Gia could see the reflection of the screen on the polished wall behind Maria's back. She could see the flashing panel on the screen which read *Access Denied*.

'It can't be too hard,' Maria said. 'He's so dull.'

'Dull but *exceptionally* secretive. Come on, please. Don't do this to me, Maria. We can go to jail for this. You don't even care who these Catchprices are. I mean, what's the principle? I don't get it.'

'We'd both be a lot happier if you went back to doing what you believed in. I'm subtracting 1 from each digit.'

'Maria, damn you, don't torture me – I'm your *friend*.'

'I'm subtracting 2.'

'Don't do a poker machine on me,' wailed Gia. 'I'll never forgive you for that club in Gosford. Two hours with the creep breathing over your shoulder.'

'We're in.'

Maria rose from the keyboard with her hands held high above her head. 'See! See! *Access Records. Add New Records. Edit Records.* We're in. We can edit.'

Maria was the worst typist in the world. This was why Gia made herself walk into the office. She only sat at the keyboard because she wanted to get out quickly. She called up *Edit Records*. 'How do you spell it?'

'C-a-t-c-h-p-r-i-c-e.'

'File number?'

'Left it in the car. Call them all up. There. That one. Catchprice Motors.'

The last two entries were a record of Mrs Catchprice's call alerting the department to irregularities and a File Active designation dated for this morning when Maria had left to begin her audit in Franklin.

Gia went through the file deletion procedure. She took it to the penultimate step where the screen was flashing *Delete Record Y/N*.

'They'll see the broken door,' Gia said.

'If there's no file, there's no job. Hit it.'

Maria leaned across Gia and hit the Y key herself. The screen lost all its type. It turned solid green. A single cursor began to flash and the terminal began to emit a loud, high-pitched buzz.

'Run,' said Gia.

Maria did not argue. She ran as well as she could run with the weight of her pregnancy. The air was dull and hot and the corridors were heavy with a dull, plastic smell like the inside of a new electrical appliance. Gia tried to go down the stairs. ('They'll get us. Jam the elevator.') Maria pulled her into the lift. 'I don't want to use my key,' said Gia, her little chin set hard and her eyes wide.

'Use it,' said Maria, panting. 'The keys can't be coded.'

'Are you sure?'

'Of course not.'

The lift doors opened. The foyer was empty. Gia walked briskly from the building with her head down. Maria waddled just behind her, red in the face and out of breath. Did they imagine themselves being filmed? Yes, they did. They walked up the hill in Hunter Street to the car. They did not say a word. They drove back to the Brasserie and parked behind Gia's car.

'We're in a lot of trouble,' Gia said.

'No we're not,' Maria insisted. 'We're not in any trouble at all.'

'You're going to tell me why, aren't you?' Gia blew her nose.

'Yes,' Maria grinned. 'I am.'

It was midnight. It was summer. The windows were down. You could smell jasmine among the exhaust fumes of the Darlinghurst bus. Maria wondered what she was going to say next.

27

Maria's father was angry at the street she lived in. He spat at it and scuffed at its paspalum weeds with his half-laced boots. He hit the stone retaining wall outside Elizabeth Hindmath's with his aluminium stick and lost the rubber stopper off the end. The rubber stopper rolled down the street, bouncing off the cobblestones, and finally lost itself in the morning-glory tangle opposite Maria's cottage.

'See, see,' George Takis cried triumphantly, pointing his stick. 'See.'

He meant the street was too steep for a woman with a baby.

'Forty-five degrees,' he said, 'at least.'

It was nothing like forty-five degrees, but she did not contradict him. She did not point out that the streets of Letkos were far steeper and rougher than this one where she now lived in Sydney, that she herself had been pushed in an ancient German pram up streets steeper and rougher than the one that caused her father this upset – it was not the street he was upset with – it was the pregnancy. If he had articulated his anger honestly, he would have lost her. He was newly widowed and already had one daughter who would not speak to him, so he was angry with the street instead. It was too narrow, too steep. The drainage was bad and the cobbles were slippery. If she needed an ambulance they could never get it down there.

'You live here, you need good brakes. What sort of brakes it got?' He meant the pram. He wiped some dry white spittle from the corner of his lips and looked at her accusingly, his dark eyebrows pressed down hard upon his black eyes.

'I don't have one,' she said. She did not want to think about the pram. She did not want to think about what life was going to be like.

He sighed.

'I work,' she said. 'Remember.'

'You're not going to know what's hit you, you know that? You don't know what will happen to you. You get in trouble, you just stay in trouble. Always. Forever.'

'Shut up, Ba-ba.'

'You come home from the hospital, how are you going to buy a pram then? You need to have everything bought beforehand.'

'Who told you that? Mrs Hellos?'

'No one,' he said, hitting at the Williamsons' overgrown jasmine with his stick. 'I talk to no one.' He paused. 'I was reading the magazines at the barber's.'

'About babies, Ba-Ba? In a barber's shop magazine?'

'I bought it,' he said, fiddling with the button on his braces.

'Ba-Ba, this doesn't help me. Really. I know I must seem terrible to you, but it doesn't help.'

'Maria, come with me, I'll buy you a nice one. Come on. I'll buy it for you.' She could not really be angry with him. She did not need to be told how her pregnancy hurt him and excited him, how he struggled with it, how he loved her. They went shopping for a pram at Leichhardt Market Town and he got angry about prices instead, and afterwards she cooked him the noodles and keftethes which his wife had made for him three times a week for forty years, and afterwards, when it was dark, Maria drove him home to his house in Newtown, slipping into Greek territory like a spy in a midget submarine.

At midnight on the night she had failed to delete the Catchprice file from the computer, Maria felt George Takis's anger at the street might have some basis outside of his own shame. She parked her car up on Darling Street and then began the long walk down the steep lane.

She was tired already. She was heavy and sore and this was a street for a single woman with a flat stomach and healthy back. It was a street you walked down arm in arm with a lover, stumbling, laughing after too much wine, your vagina moist and warm and your legs smooth from waxing. This was so unsexy, and difficult. So endless.

She walked past the fallen stone wall at Elizabeth Hindmath's house. The rocks had tumbled out on to the street just as George Takis had said they would. The path was slippery with moss and lichen and Maria stepped very carefully. There was a movement in her womb like a great bubble rising and rolling – but not breaking – and it made her exclaim softly and put her hand on her rising stomach.

Sometimes at night she would lie on her back and watch the baby move around her stomach, watch its ripples, and guess its limbs, and although she would always try to do this fondly, with wonder, she would often end up in tears. She knew her fondness was a fake.

The moon was full and the air was heavy with honeysuckle and jasmine. Someone was playing Country music in a house down the street. There was a smell of oil in the air – at least she thought it was oil – which seemed to come from the container ships at the bottom of the hill.

She did not realize that the Country music was coming from her house until she was right outside it. Then she saw the small red light – the ghetto blaster – in the centre of her own front steps. The hair stood on her neck.

'Don't you recognize a tax-payer when you see one?' a male voice said.

Maria walked straight on.

Every Tax Inspector knows these stories: the mad 'client', whose business you have destroyed, who seeks you out and beats you or puts dog shit in your letter box. She kept on walking with her breath held hard in her throat. The cassette player turned off with a heavy thunk.

A woman called: 'We didn't think you'd be out so late. Being pregnant.'

Maria stopped a little distance off and stared into the shadow of her own veranda. She could see the axe she had left leaning against the stack of firewood.

'Are you going to ask us in?' the woman said. Her voice sounded thin, stretched tight between apology and belligerence.

'Maybe,' Maria said, 'we could all meet for a cup of coffee in the morning.'

There was a light on at number 95, but it was twenty metres away down hill and the lane was so slippery with moss it would be dangerous to run.

'We've got to work tomorrow.' It was a teenage boy. She could see his hair – shining white as a knife in the night. 'We've got customers to attend to.'

A cowboy boot shifted out of the shadow into the white spill from the street light.

'Mrs McPherson?' she asked.

The boy with the blond hair stood and walked down off the concrete steps.

'Benjamin Catchprice,' he said, extending his hand. 'We've been waiting two hours.'

'Fuck you.'

'Woooo,' said Benny, dancing back, grinning, fanning his hands, 'language.'

'You scared me shitless, you little creep,' Maria said. 'Who gave you my address? What right do you think you have to come here in the middle of the night?'

'We're sorry about that,' said Cathy McPherson. She was holding a goddam guitar – standing like a giantess blocking the access to the veranda, holding a guitar, wearing a cowgirl suit, her great strong legs apart as if it was her house, not Maria's. 'Really, we're sorry. We really didn't mean to frighten you. It wasn't the middle of the night when we got here.'

'Mrs McPherson,' said Maria. 'Don't you realize how prejudicial it is for you to be here?'

Cathy McPherson stepped down off the step. 'I'd be obliged,' she said, 'if I could use your toilet.'

28

Cathy was in this ridiculous position because she had done what *Benny* had said. She could not stand being told what to do by anyone, and she was here because *Benny* told her to be there – little frightened, crying Benny whom she used to take into bed and soothe to sleep – Benny who ground his teeth – Benny who wet his bed – Benny who did so badly at school she had to take him to Special Needs to have his I.Q. tested.

Now the alcohol had worn off and she was following the Tax Inspector into her house holding her guitar. She knew right away this woman had no personal connection with Benny. He had dreamed it. He had manufactured it inside his head.

Benny came behind her carrying his cassette player. He was smiling, not *at* anything or *for* anything, but smiling like an evangelist on television. He had been like this already when he had appeared in front of her. That was at ten o'clock and she had had a row with Howie about all the songs he had copyrighted 'Big Mack', and she had been sitting up drinking Scotch and Coke by herself because she was upset – about her mother, about the tax audit, about the ownership of songs she had written but now might not own, about the shambles she had made of her life – and Benny crept up the stairs – she had The Judds' version of 'Mr Pain' playing really loud – and gave her such a fright. He just appeared in the kitchen in front of her and spoke. She nearly shat herself.

He said, 'What are you doing to control your destiny?'

As if he read her mind.

He stood before her in his fancy suit and folded his hands in front of his crotch. The hands were even more amazing than the suit. She could not help staring at them – so white and clean like they had been peeled of history.

His hair shone like polyester in the neon light and when he spoke, it was in a language not his own – his mother's perhaps (although who could remember after all this time how Sophie spoke?). In any case, it was not the language of a problem child, not someone whose I.Q. you worry about.

He said: 'I can take you to talk to the Tax Inspector.'

Normally she would have poured him a drink and tried to talk him out of it, whatever the latest 'it' was. But she was dazzled, no other word for the experience. She turned off The Judds.

He said: 'Her name is Takis. There are only three in the phone book and I've ruled out the other two. She's not back yet because I've been ringing her every twenty minutes to check.' He wiped some perspiration from his lip with a handkerchief with a small gold brand-name still stuck in the corner.

She had sipped some more of her Scotch. Howie always said the Coke killed the Scotch but she could taste it. 'Ben, what's happened to you?'

'Getting fired was the best thing ever happened to me,' he said. She started to say sorry – and she was sorry – it was the worst thing she'd ever had to do – but he held up his hand to stop her. 'I've come to repay the favour,' he said.

She pushed out a chair for him but he would not sit. He grasped the back of the chair with his hands and rocked it back and forth.

'You can see I've changed?'

'You could have been your Mum,' she said.

He nodded his head and smiled at her. His eyes held hers. They were as clear as things washed in river water. 'We all possess great power,' he said. Jesus Christ – he gave her goose-bumps.

'Get your guitar,' he said. Not 'please' or 'would you mind', just 'get your guitar'.

Later she told Howie: 'It was like your dog stood up and talked to you. If the dog said get your guitar, you would. Just to see what happened next.' She lied about dog. She did not think dog at all. What she was thinking of was that holy picture where the angel appears to Mary. Only later she said dog.

She sneaked into the bedroom where Howie was asleep, straight up and down on his back – taught himself to do it in a narrow bed. She got down the Gibson. She brought it back into the kitchen and he was trying to unplug the ghetto blaster from over the sink. He had all the power cords tangled – toaster, kettle, blender.

'Benny, I don't know this is smart,' she said.

'What's smart? Waiting here so you get busted?' He pulled the ghetto blaster cord clear of the mess and wound it round his wrist.

'Spending the rest of your life stuck here paying off the tax bill? You want to stay here till you die?'

She saw it. She felt it. Some tight band clamped around her stomach.

'The Tax Inspector *likes* me,' he said. 'That's the key to everything.'

'You talked to her?'

'It's personal. We're going to call on her in a personal capacity. Come on Cathy – she's kind. She's a very kind person.'

'She sure doesn't feel kind about me.'

'You have the power,' Benny insisted. 'I'll introduce you properly. She is going to see who you are. We are going to show her your life.'

'My life?'

'Our lives have power,' he said. 'You're an artist. What was it Ernest Tubb wrote to you?'

'Oh, Ernest Tubb . . .'

'You have the talent to . . .?

'The *ability* to change the rhythms of the human heart.'

'Right. Ability. Plus: she's pregnant. She's full of milk.'

'Benny,' Cathy smiled, 'there's no milk till there's a baby.'

'O.K.,' Benny said impatiently. 'Forget that bit. Once she understands the consequences of her actions, she'll go easy on you. Sing her a song. Show her who you are. You've got to sell her. You've got to demonstrate what's at stake here. Come with me,' he said.

And she did.

But now the alcohol had worn off and she felt sour and dehydrated and she just wanted to apologize. She stood on one side of the Tax Inspector's neat white kitchen, filled with shame. Maria Takis was holding a shining metal kettle. Cathy admired 'nice things' although she did not own many and the obvious quality of the kettle, its good taste, its refinement, the sort of shop it must have come from, all this somehow made the intrusion worse. Cathy felt coarse and vulgar. She had not even washed her hair before she left.

'Ms Takis,' she said, although she hated to hear herself say 'Ms'. 'I think I've made a big mistake. I'm sorry. But I was really horrible to you this morning and it's been on my mind and I just wanted to say how sorry I was. I know you've got your job to do.'

She said she was sorry. She made herself small. But there was no relief. All it did was make the woman look at her as if she was a frigging ant.

29

Cathy McPherson came back from the bathroom smelling of Elizabeth Arden and whisky. She wore her chamois leather cowgirl suit with high-heeled boots with spurs. Her waistcoat cut into her big fleshy arms. She stood in the kitchen doorway with her huge guitar and her little white hands and sent confusing signals with her eyes.

The guitar was a big instrument – too big to take visiting, but presumably too valuable to leave in a parked car. Cathy McPherson leaned against the doorway, on the hallway side, fiddling with the little mother-of-pearl guitar picks which were wedged in beside the tuning pegs like ticks on a cattle dog's ear.

If this had been an investigation Maria had wanted to pursue, this would have been the turning point. Someone was about to divulge some information or to try to cut a deal, but Maria did not want more information about the Catchprices. She wanted them out of her house, out of her life and if this was a confession, she did not want to hear it.

She said: 'You didn't need to drive all this way to say sorry.'

'But we didn't come to say we were *sorry*.' It was the boy again, back from wherever he had been in her house. He slid around the edge of the guitar and stood with his back to the refrigerator. His hair looked as hard and white as spun polymer.

'Would you mind staying right here?' she said. She shifted her kettle on to the hottest and fastest of her gas jets. When she looked up, his eyes were on hers.

'Mrs McPherson is going to sing to you,' he said.

Maria looked at the woman.

'I'm really a singer,' she said. Her face was burning red.

The boy came into the kitchen and plugged the ghetto blaster into the power point next to the kettle.

'We're people, not numbers,' he said. He would not take his eyes off her eyes. She thought: this is the sort of thing that happens in Muslim countries – these dangerous doe-eyed boys with their heads filled with images of western whores in negligees. She looked away from him to his aunt.

'So you would like to sing to me in the hope it will affect your tax assessment?'

Cathy McPherson had the good grace to look embarrassed, but her nephew buttoned the jacket of his suit without taking his eyes away from Maria's. 'We think you're human,' he said in that nasal accent as sharp and cold as metal. He moistened his lips and smiled. For Chrissakes – he was coming on to her. 'We want to talk to you like humans.'

'O.K.,' said Maria. 'I'm going to make one cup of tea, then you're going to sing, and then you're going to get out of here because I've really had enough for one day.'

'Fair enough,' he said. 'We're going to present two songs.'

'You can have one.'

'One is fine,' Benny unbuttoned his suit coat. 'You can have recorded or live.'

'I don't care what it is. Just do it.'

'You'd like live?'

'Sure, live.'

'O.K., that will be live, then.'

He was one of those people whose personal space was too large, who could be too close to you when you were a metre from them.

She waited for the kettle to boil, staring at it like she might have stared at the floor numbers in an elevator. When the kettle boiled she gave them tea bags of English Breakfast tea but, for herself, an infuser filled with the foul-tasting Raspberry Leaf which Gia's naturopath said would strengthen the uterine muscles and promote a quick labour.

The Catchprices jiggled their tea bags in silence and dropped them into the kitchen tidy she held open for them and then she shepherded them into the living-room.

Maria sat down on the rocking chair her father had bought for her and put her feet up on the foot stool. She began to see the comic aspect of her 'information' and began to observe details of the Catchprices' dress in order to tell the story properly to Gia.

'Is this going to be too loud?' she asked.

'If you're worried about noise,' Benny said, 'we can play you the demo tape.'

'It's just acoustic.' Cathy was trying to fit her bottom on the window-ledge opposite. She strummed a few chords, stopped, started again, and then stood up. 'Ms Takis,' she said, 'it would be more polite if I sang sitting down, but I'm damned if I can get myself comfortable.'

'Fine,' Maria said.

'Thank you.' Cathy tapped her boot three times. The floor shook. It was an old wooden Balmain cottage which was badly built even in 1849.

'You were a married man I know,' she sang. The voice got Maria in the belly. It was raw, almost croaky, and way too loud for this street, this time of the morning.

> *I shouldn't have begun.*

Cathy McPherson changed physically. She became taller, straighter. The athletic armature of her body revealed itself and she rocked and rolled and showed a sexual confidence which was previously unimaginable. There was something happening in those belligerent little eyes which made her as soft as a cat rubbing itself against your leg.

> *You told me you'd always love your wife*
> *I shouldn't have begun.*

Thirty seconds ago she was big and blowzy like a farmer's wife, or someone with fat burns on their sallow skin, working in a fish 'n' chip shop at two o'clock in the morning. Her arms were still plump. Her belly still pressed against her leather skirt, but now you could not look at her without believing that this was someone who made love passionately – she was a sexual animal.

> *But it was late at night and I was lonely*
> *I didn't know I'd fall in love*
> *and now you've gone and left me baby*
> *with a freeway through my heart.*

She occupied Maria's living-room like a compressor unit or some yellow-cased engine so loud and powerful that it demanded you accommodate yourself to it. This was what Maria did not like about it – she felt bullied on the one hand and seduced on the other. Also:

the subject matter was discomforting. It seemed too close for coincidence.

> *Trucks are running*
> *through the freeway in my heart*
> *Twisting sheets*
> *All this noise and pain*
> *Ten retreads hissing*
> *through the driving rain.*

Just as the second verse was about to start, the singer saw Maria's face and stopped.

Maria said: 'Thank you.'

Cathy shrugged.

Maria said: 'How do you think this could affect my work?'

Cathy opened her mouth, then shut it, frowned, rubbed her bedraggled hair. 'This doesn't make a pinch of difference to anything does it?'

'No, it can't.'

'Fine.'

'What the hell could I do?' said Maria, angrily. 'What sort of corrupt person do you want me to be? Are you going to try to bribe me now?'

'I'm sorry.' And Cathy was sorry; at the same time she was angry. She was sorry she had placed herself in such a foolish position.

'If I cared more for Country music I could say something intelligent about your song.'

'You don't like Country music?'

'Not a lot, no.'

'I think you do,' Cathy said. 'But you're like your sort of person.'

Maria did not ask what her sort of person was.

'You are moved by it. Allow me to know that. Allow me to judge what an audience is feeling. I saw you: you were moved by it. What did you tell yourself about it? *Oh I mustn't be moved. This is masochistic?* Women like you always say "masochistic" when they feel things.'

'O.K., I was moved.'

'You're saying that but what you're trying to *tell* me is that you weren't moved at all.' Cathy said, sitting down. She sat on the edge of the sofa where Alistair and Maria used to make love. He used to kneel on the carpet there and she put her legs around his neck and opened up to him full of juice – she would get so wet all her thighs would be shining in the firelight and now there was a damn Catchprice sitting there holding a Gibson by the neck and another one watching and they were like burglars in her life.

'It doesn't matter,' Cathy said. 'I'm a real banana to be here but I'll tell you something for your future reference – Country music is about those places people like you drive past and patronize. You come to Franklin and you've decided, before you even get off the F4, that we are all retards and losers – unemployed, unemployable. Then you find we have an art gallery and some of us actually read books and you are *very impressed*. What you've just been listening to is poetry, but all you could hear was, oh, Country & Western. What I like about Country music is that it never patronizes anyone, not even single mothers.'

'We're not numbers,' Benny said.

Cathy looked up at Benny as if she had forgotten he was there. She sighed, but said nothing. She needed something stronger than a cup of tea.

'We're people,' said Benny.

Cathy looked at him again. He was not wilted or defeated. He was standing upright in the corner. Good for you, she thought. 'You go ahead with this audit of yours,' she told the Tax Inspector, 'and I'll be stuck in that shit-heap for the rest of my damn life just keeping them all alive. You go ahead, I'll never get to sing except in pubs within a 100-kilometre radius. I should have just walked out when I had the business healthy. "Guilt-free". That's a song I wrote. "Guilt-free", but if we get in strife with the tax, then I'm lumbered with the responsibility of a mother who hates me and a brother who refuses to sell a motor car because he wants to punish his Daddy for being a creep.'

'Don't,' Maria said. 'It doesn't help.'

'I'm going to lose my band and my damn name,' said Cathy, her lower lip quivering.

Maria stood up. She hoped the woman would not cry. 'Catchprice Motors is in the computer with an "active" designation,' she said gently. 'Even if I wanted to, I couldn't take it out.'

'I believe you,' Cathy stood up. 'Come on, Benny. Enough's enough.'

Now they were really going, Maria let herself look at the boy again. He caught her eye and did up his suit jacket and smiled. He did have an extraordinary face. If you saw it in a magazine you would pause to admire it – its mixture of innocence and decadence was very sexy – in a magazine.

'I'll see you around,' he said.

'You'll see her in the morning,' said his aunt. 'Which is now.'

'Yes, which is now,' Maria stood.

She shepherded the singer along the corridor to the front door. In a moment they would be gone. The boy was behind her. Maria was so convinced that he was about to put a guiding hand on the small of her back that she put her own hand there to push it off.

At the front door, Cathy McPherson turned, and stopped. She was solid, immovable. She looked at Maria with her little blue eyes which somehow connected to the heart that had written the words of that song. Not 'small' eyes or 'mean' eyes, but certainly demanding and needful of something she could not have expressed. Her breath smelt of alcohol. She said: 'When I was thirty-two I was ready to go out on the road. I mean, I wasn't a baby any more. Then my father died, and my mother sort of made it impossible for me to leave.'

Maria could feel the boy behind. She could feel him like a shadow that lay across her back. She was too tired to listen to this confession but the eyes demanded that she must. They monitored her response.

'I can't tell you how my mother did it, but she made me stay. I was the one who was going to save the business. And I did save it and then my mother decided I was getting too big for my boots and she turned on me, and I would have gone then, except I could not walk away and see it crash. I'm a real fool, Ms Takis, a prize number one specimen fool. If you fine us, I'll be stuck there. I won't be able to leave them.'

It would have seemed false to be her comforter and her tormentor as well. So even when she began to cry all Maria did was offer her a Kleenex and pat her alien shoulder. She wanted her to leave the house. She took the guitar from her and together the three of them walked up Datchett Street.

At Darling Street she shook hands first with Cathy McPherson and then she turned to the boy. He said: 'You can't just abandon us, you know.'

Cathy said: 'Come on, Benny.'

'No, she understands me. She's got a heart. She understands what I'm saying.'

'I'm sorry,' Cathy McPherson said. She grabbed his arm, and pulled him up the street. Maria could hear them hissing at each other as she walked back to her front door.

Tuesday

30

At Catchprice Motors they called a potential customer a 'Prospect', and as the big black cumulus clouds rolled in from the west and the first thunder of the day made itself heard above the pot-hole thump of the Fast-Mix Concrete trucks heading north towards the F4, Benny hooked a live one. It was a Tuesday, the second day of Benny's new life.

He found the Prospect there at eight-thirty, crunching around in the gravel beside the Audi Quattro. Benny made no sudden movements, but when the Prospect found the Quattro's door was locked, Benny was able to come forward and unlock it for him.

'Thank you,' the Prospect said.

'No worries,' Benny said, holding the black-trimmed door open and releasing a heady perfume of paint and leather. The driver's seat made a small expensive squeak as it took the Prospect's weight. The white paper carpet-protector rumpled beneath grey slip-ons whose little gold chains made Benny take them for Guccis. The guy folded his hands in his lap and asked to be given 'the selling points'. Benny had not slept all night – he had been working on one more angle in his campaign to seduce the Tax Inspector – but now all of his gritty-eyed tiredness went away and the fibreglass splinters in his arms stopped itching and he squatted on the gravel beside the open door and talked about the Quattro for five minutes without lying once. He watched the Prospect as he spoke. He waited for signs of boredom, some indication that he should shift the venue, alter the approach, but the guy was treating this like information he just had to have. After twenty minutes, Benny's knees were hurting and he had run out of stuff to say.

Then the Prospect got out of the Quattro. Then he and Benny stood side by side and looked at it together. The Prospect was five foot six, maybe five foot seven – shorter than Benny, but broader in the shoulders. He played sport, you could see it in the way he balanced on the balls of his feet. He had a broad nose, almost like a boxer's, but you could not call him ugly. He was good-looking,

in fact. He had a dark velvet suit and a small tuft of black hair –
you could not call it a beard – sitting underneath his lower lip.
He was twenty-two, maybe twenty-five years old, and he had
Guccis on his feet and he was looking up at Benny – what a wood
duck!

'So,' he said. 'When do we do the test drive?'

'Hey,' said Benny, 'don't panic.' The truth was: he was
unlicensed. They would kill him if they saw him demo this unit.
He was going to do it none the less, but gentlee gentlee catchee
monkey – he had to wait for Mort who was sitting in a
Commodore by the front office. He was hunched over in the seat
reading out the engine functions on the computerized diagnostic
device – the Compu-tech.

'The thing you've got to appreciate about an Audi,' Benny said,
'is nothing is rushed. They rush to make all this G.M. shit, but not
an Audi.'

'I have something for you,' the Prospect said.

Benny did not notice what he had. He was watching Mort
unplug the Tech II and put it in his back pocket.

The Prospect was occupied with a separate matter – with-
drawing a sleek silver envelope from his inside jacket pocket.

'Here,' he said.

He held it out to Benny.

Benny took the envelope. *What do you want?*

The Prospect smiled. Benny was spooked by his black eyes.

'You have good taste in ties,' the Prospect said. 'I'm sure you
will like this one.'

The envelope held a black and silver and green tie.

Benny felt a tingling at the back of his neck.

'Silk,' said Sarkis.

Benny looked up at the eyes and then down at the tie.

'I'll buy it,' he said. He had a boner. He did not want a boner.
He did not want a gift or come in his mouth, but the man's eyes
were like a sore tooth he could not keep from touching.

'No, it's a sample,' said Sarkis. 'I made it.'

Benny smiled at the Prospect. He wet his lips and smiled.

'You make ties?' he asked.

'There are no good ties in Australia,' said Sarkis, who was as
impressed with Benny's haircut as Benny had been with Sarkis's

shoes. You needed to be making big money to maintain a cut like that. 'There's a big market waiting for these ties. What I need is the capital to do it in a bigger way. Here . . . have it . . . It's a gift.'

The man held the packet out with one hand. The other hand he kept behind his back. He flexed his knees and looked out at the street trees with their pretty red-dotted lichen-encrusted leaves and their hairy, mossy trunks. They were side by side. Benny could feel the space between them.

'A present? Just for nothing?'

'For good luck,' said Sarkis, 'on my first day here.'

'First *day*?'

'I'm sorry . . .' Sarkis said, suddenly confused.

'First day? Come on, what are you saying to me. What are you proposing?'

'Working here,' said Sarkis. 'I'm sorry. I was hired to work here. She said someone would come and fill me in.'

'Got it,' said Benny. He felt a pain in his stomach. He watched his father nurse the Commodore slowly out along the brown-puddled service road. All the fibreglass splinters in his arms began to itch. 'Who hired you? Mrs McPherson?'

'The owner hired me,' said Sarkis. 'The old lady.'

This was exactly how Howie got into Catchprice Motors and it made Benny get a freezing feeling behind his eyes. 'Oh shit,' he laughed. 'You got hired by *Grandma*.' He tapped his forehead and rolled his eyes.

'She's got the keys,' Sarkis said. 'I saw her.'

'She's got the keys because she's got the keys – she doesn't own the business.'

'She told me that she did.'

'Well she doesn't. It's owned by my auntie and my Dad and me. Not even my uncle Jack has got shares. He's a property developer in town, but he doesn't work here so he can't have shares. Even my brother,' Benny said, 'could have had a future here . . .'

Then he saw the Tax Inspector's Colt making a right-hand turn across the traffic to come into Catchprice Motors.

'I've got to tell you,' Sarkis said, 'I never sold cars before.'

Benny groaned.

'So if you can help me . . .' Sarkis rubbed his fingers together, indicating money passing hands.

'What do you mean?'

'You help me, I'll split my commission.'

'We don't have commissions,' Benny said. 'This is a family business.' But he was mollified by the offer. 'This is a fucking minefield,' he said. 'It's a snake-pit. They all hate each other. None of them can sell a car. If you work here, you'd have to work for me.'

'Sure,' said Sarkis. 'Sure, O.K.'

'We've got a lot of stock to move,' Benny explained. 'We've got a fucking enormous tax bill.' He looked at Sarkis. 'What makes you think you can sell cars . . . what's your name?'

'Sarkis.' He hesitated. 'They call me Sam,' he told this kid. He hated how it sounded. The kid must be seven years younger and he was saying, 'Call me Sam'.

'Sam? Listen Sam. The first thing you've got to know is that the car is not the issue. The car is only the excuse. It's the F&I you make the money from. No one understands that. The kings of this business are the F&I men. There's no one in Catchprice Motors knows an F&I man from their arsehole. Someone says to my old man, "I need insurance", he picks up the fucking phone and dials the fucking insurance company for them and it costs us thirty cents and makes us nothing. You want to work here, you got to go away for five days and learn about F&I . . .'

'Sorry . . . what's F&I?'

'I've been telling you,' said Benny. 'Finance and Insurance. F&I. You stay here now, all this week, but next Monday you get on an F&I course. You learn how to use the computer, how to do the paper work. You don't need to know shit about cars. You don't need to know the difference between an Audi Quattro and a washing machine. A week from now you'll know how to sell them comprehensive insurance, disability cover, extended warranty. If that's impossible . . .'

'I'm Armenian,' said Sarkis. 'We're the best salesmen in the world.'

'Yeah, well don't go round giving people silk ties. You get people mad with you. Forget it now. Listen to me – I've got a hundred bucks and I want to buy a car from you, how are you going to do it? I mean, I come in here with a blue mohawk and a leopard-skin vest and a ring through my nose and when I've finished jerking off all I can get together is a hundred bucks . . .'

'You can't afford a car, sorry . . .'

'You know as much as the directors of this business.' Benny could see Cathy standing at the top of Grandma Catchprice's landing. She was waving her arms around and waving at Benny and Sarkis. 'You want to sell a car, you've got to understand finance, O.K. Listen to me,' Benny said, 'not her. You've got a hundred bucks, you want a nice car. I say to you, see that old F.J. Holden over there. I'll sell you that for a hundred bucks.'

'You call that a nice car?'

'No, I don't. Just be patient. O.K. You buy it from me for a hundred. O.K.?'

'O.K.' said Sarkis.

'O.K., now I buy it back from you at five hundred. Car hasn't even moved. What's happened?'

'You've lost money.'

'No, now you have five hundred bucks – you can afford to do business with me. You've got enough money for a deposit on a $3,500 car. I can finance it to you. I'll make good money on the sale, I'll keep on making money on the F&I. You understand me?'

'I think so,' said Sarkis.

'It takes time, don't worry,' Benny said. 'They think I'm dumb round here, I'll tell you now.' He could see Cathy lurching awkwardly down the stairs. 'But none of them appreciates this. You're getting it faster than they are. You can make two hundred grand a year in this dump, really. You believe me.'

'You want to know? I think it's a great opportunity.'

'You get this F&I under your belt, we can set this town on fire.' He turned to face Cathy who was weaving towards them. 'Just ignore this,' he told Sarkis. 'This doesn't count.'

31

Sarkis watched the chunky blonde woman in the gingham dress walk down the staircase. Her eyes were on him, he knew, and he was optimistic about the effect her presence would have on the conversation she was so obviously about to enter. At a certain distance – from the top of the fire escape to the bottom, and a metre or two onwards from there — she gave an impression of a bright blonde Kellogg's kind of normality and he hoped that she might, somehow, save him from this sleaze. But then she passed the point where there could be conjecture and he saw, even before he smelt her, that her face was puffy and her mascara was running. The smell was not the smell, as subtle as the aroma of Holy Communion, you get from a drink or two, but the deep, sour aura that comes from a long night of drinking, and it explained more readily than her high-heeled knee-high boots, the careful way she walked across the gravel.

'Who are you?' she asked Sarkis. She looked both hurt and hostile and Sarkis's strongest desire was to turn away from all this poison and walk to the sane, cloves-sweet environment of his home.

Instead he said something he had promised never to say again: 'Hi, I'm Sam Alaverdian.'

The 'Sam' did not make her like him any better. She sighed, and put her finger on the small crease at the top of her nose. 'So you're the latest candidate,' she said. 'Tell me, honey, what experience do you have?'

'He's Armenian.'

'What's that got to do with it, Benny?'

'They're the best salesmen in the world.'

'Oh shit, Benny, spare us, please. Tell me . . . what's an Armenian? Where's Armenia? You tell me.'

Obviously, Benny did not know. He stared at her as if he could vaporize her. His eyes got narrower and narrower and she stared right back at him. Sarkis did not want to work for either of them. They both stared at each other for a long time until finally, the woman shifted her ground. You could see her surrender in her shoulders before she spoke.

'I'm sorry,' she said. She put out her little white hand towards him and he stepped away from it.

'Don't give me shit about this,' he said. 'I'm saving you.'

The woman's face screwed up. She wiped her eyes and made a big black horizontal streak that went from the corner of her eye into her permed curly hair.

'I'm saving you,' Benny said again. He put out his hand to her and she took it and held it, and began to stroke the back of it. Sarkis was embarrassed but they were oblivious to him. 'I'm making it possible.'

'Honey, it was a nice try, but we can't stop the Tax Office. She's back.'

'I know she's back,' Benny said defensively. 'I *saw*. Maybe she just came to get her things . . . you won't know until you talk to her.'

'Forget it, Ben.'

'Try being positive, just for once.'

Cathy smiled and shook her head. 'Honey, you're *sixteen*.'

Sarkis did not want to interrupt. He waited until whatever process they were engaged in – Benny stroking her hand, she touching Benny's cheek – was completed. But when they brought their attention back to Sarkis, he said: 'I can sell.'

The Catchprices took their hands back from each other.

'What can you sell, Sam?'

'F&I,' Sarkis told her. From the corner of his eye he saw Benny smile. 'I'm an F&I man,' he said.

She frowned and scratched her hair. The hair was good and thick but dry and brittle from home perming. She took a Lifesaver packet from the pocket of her gingham dress, and bit off the top one.

'Please,' Benny said. 'I can use him.'

She squinted at Sarkis and frowned. 'We can't afford an F&I man.'

'You can't afford not to have one,' said Sarkis, wanting to be definite but having no idea how to be really definite, rushing her towards the idea of an F&I man while, at the same time, he dragged his own heels, anxious lest he be forced to talk any more about the alien subject.

'I'm very sorry, Sam, but my mother had no authority to hire you.'

'Don't worry about him. He's mine.'

'She made a verbal contract with me,' said Sarkis, remembering his father's argument with a builder when they first arrived in Northwood.

This made the woman stare at him very hard.

'Did she get the chance to tell you about her gelignite?'

'Yes.'

'You don't want to get involved with us, Sam.'

'I need a job.'

'How long you been living in Franklin?'

'Six months.'

'You better just forget it, Sam. You don't want this work. Please go away.'

'You're the one who should go away,' Benny said, very gently. 'You've got a reason to go away. We've got a reason to stay here.'

The woman looked at Benny and clenched her smudged eyes shut and opened her mouth and suffered a small convulsion or a shiver as if she might be about to weep. Then she turned and walked away across the gravel, holding out her hand to steady herself among the cars as she passed them.

32

In the gauzy rain-streaked light of Tuesday morning, Mort Catchprice became aware that there was an angel standing beside his bed. It had its back to him. It had broad shoulders and a narrow waist and on the cool white canvas of its back were wings of ball-point blue and crimson which seemed to lie like luminous silk across the skin.

In his dream he had been a river. It had been a rare and wonderful dream, to be water, to watch the light reflecting off his skin and so he came from sleep to meet the angel feeling unusually tranquil, and in the minute or so it took before he was really properly awake, he studied the wings and saw how they followed the form of the body, incorporating the collar bone, for instance, into what was clearly a tattooist's *trompe l'œil*, one which gave perfect attention to each individual feather, dissolving sensuously from crimson into blue, always quite clear, not at all ambiguous until the upper reaches of the marble-white buttocks where the feathers became very small and might be read as scales.

As he stirred and stretched, the angel turned towards him and was recognized. Then all the heavy weight of the past and present flooded back into his limbs.

He quickly saw that the tattooed wings were not the only thing his son had done to himself – he had also used a depilatory to remove any trace of body hair. His chest, his legs, his penis all had that shiny slippery look of a child just out of the bath.

It was the lack of hair that woke him properly. He understood its intention perfectly and as the blood engorged his own penis, he picked up the blue water jug beside his bed and threw it at the creature. The water spilled yet stayed suspended in mid-air like a great crystal tongue-lick – dripping diamonds suspended above the angel's dazzling white head.

The angel stepped, slowly, to one side and the jug hit the soft plaster wall and its handle penetrated the plasterboard. It did not bounce or break, but stuck there, like a trophy.

Benny gave his father a rather bruised and blaming smile. 'You're so predictable,' he said.

The crystal transformed itself into water and fell – splat – on to the floor. The alarm clock began to ring.

'Please,' Mort said. 'Please don't do this.' But even as he did say, 'please don't', the other cunning part of his brain was saying, please, yes, one more helping.

'Well sure,' Benny sat down in the rocking-chair beside the bed and began rubbing his hands along his long shiny thighs. 'We've got some dirty habits.'

His father sat up in bed with the sheet gathered around his hairy midriff. 'Not any more we don't.'

'You know I could have you put in jail,' Benny said. 'I wish I'd known that before. Did you see that on 'Hinch at Seven' last week? They take you to the Haversham clinic and they put you in a chair and they strap this thing around your dick and show you pictures of men doing it to little boys. You get a hard-on, you're done. They call you a rock spider and chuck away the key.'

Mort threw the alarm clock. He was not play-acting. It was a heavy silver clock from Bangkok Duty-Free and it hit the boy on the chest so hard it made him rock back in the chair. The confidence left his eyes and was replaced by a baleful, burning look.

'You shouldn't have done that,' he said. 'I'm going to have to do something if you hurt me.'

Mort was already sorry, sorry because he had been brutal, sorry because he was now even more vulnerable. He could see a large red half moon showing on the boy's chest. Anybody could examine it and see what he had done. 'I'm sorry.'

'Sorry isn't enough,' Benny said, rubbing at the mark. 'You're always sorry.'

Mort knew he had to get out of there before something bad happened. He slipped out of bed with his back to Benny. He bent down by the muslin curtains looking for his underpants.

'Christ,' said Benny. 'Look at the boner.'

Mort tripped and staggered with his toes caught in his underpants. 'God help me, shut up.'

Benny was standing, grinning. 'You can't say shut up to me now. I'm an angel. You like it?' He stood and turned and wiggled his butt a little.

'You'll never get them off,' Mort said. He did not ask how much the tattoos cost. 'Where did you get the money, are you thieving again?'

Benny said: 'It's the hair, isn't it? That's what you get off on.'

Mort was trying to find the shirt and trousers he had dropped on the floor at bedtime. They were tangled with a towel and dressing-gown.

'It's the hair got you stiff again? You stopped liking me when you got that stuff stuck between your teeth.'

Mort sat on the bed. 'I'm not listening to this shit. We're beyond all this now. We left it behind.'

'Oh, I'm a bad boy.' Benny made his eyes go wide. 'I made it up. It never happened.'

Mort zipped the trousers and pulled a T-shirt over his head. When his face emerged he felt all his weakness showing. 'What do you want?'

'Who was it who made me like this?'

'It's finished. We've got to get over it.'

'It's not over,' said Benny taking down his shirt from the coat hanger behind the door. 'It's never over. I think about it every day.'

'It's over for me. Benny, I've changed. I swear.'

'I've changed too,' Benny said. 'I'm an angel.'

'I'm not buying you a motor bike, forget it.'

'You don't listen. I didn't say Hell's Angel. I said, angel!'

'What the fuck does that mean?'

'Means I say to one man go and he goeth, say to another man come and he cometh.'

'That's the centurion.'

'I don't give a fuck what you call it,' said Benny.

'Don't talk to me like that.'

'I am talking to you like this. I want you to go to the Tax woman and show her your life.'

'Look,' said Mort. He sat down on the bed. 'My father did it to me. His father did it to him. You think I like being like this?'

'Just listen to me. Listen to what I say. She's a nice lady. Talk to her. That's all you've got to do. Tell her about Cacka's philosophy. Just make her responsible for you. She can't destroy us if she thinks we're decent people.'

'Benny, don't be simple.'

'Listen, I know who she is. I'm going out with her.'

'You're what?'

'I'm going *out* with her. Believe me. She's a human. She responds.'

He unbuttoned his slippery cool white shirt and returned it to the coat hanger. He hung the hanger behind the door again. He slipped off his underpants and ran his hands down his flawless hairless chest and between his thighs. 'You can't help yourself can you, Kissy? You're responding. You know I think you're shit, but you don't care.'

'I am shit,' Mort said.

'You are shit.' He hooked his finger into the top of Mort's underpants and tugged at the elastic. 'I went to her house last night. She's pregnant. Her tits are full of milk.' He let the elastic go and lay on the bed on his stomach. 'When I came back here I took the books off Granny's desk.' He rolled on his back, smiling. 'I wrapped them in a plastic bag and buried them.'

'You really think that's smart?' Mort said, but he had already stopped caring if it was smart or not.

'You want to argue with me, or you want to have some fun?'

'Benny, what's happened to you?'

'I'm an angel,' Benny said.

'What does that mean?' Mort put out a finger to feel the boy's smooth thigh.

'It means I am in control. It means everyone does what I say.'

33

He would 'show his life', sure, silly as this was. He would be a monkey for his son. You know what was weird? What was weird was he was finally an inch away from happiness.

Show his life? Bare his arse? Sure, but not like the little black-mailer imagined.

He would talk to her, sure he would. What's more: he was busting to do it. He had the day's job sheets spread out across his desk, but he could not concentrate on them. They had finally become irrelevant.

He knew nothing about tax. He could not even read the balance sheets he signed each year, but he knew enough, by Christ he did, to show his life to the Tax Inspector. He would embrace her. He would draw her towards him like a dagger, have her drive some official stake into the business, right into its rubbery, resisting heart.

Howie and Cathy were always full of blame, always had been. They could blame him for not selling. They could blame him for fuck-ups in the workshop. They presumably blamed him for Benny turning out a poof, and Johnny going to the cults, but they could not blame him for the tax investigation. They were the ones – Mr and Mrs Rock 'n' Roll – who played funny buggers with the tax.

Mort took three Codis tablets and stacked the work sheets in a pile and threw them in his filing cabinet. He came and stood in the cavernous doorway, pacing up and down just inside the drip line of the roof. When he saw the Tax Department's Mitsubishi Colt park at the end of the lane-way he put up his umbrella and walked right towards it. He filled his wide chest with air and came down the oil-stained concrete with a light-footed athlete's stride.

I'll show her my life.

The Tax Inspector was already erecting her umbrella, juggling with her papers and her case. When he saw her age, how pregnant she was, he laughed. The little bullshitter was going *out* with her?

This Tax Inspector was very, very pretty – a lovely soft wide mouth, and stern and handsome nose. He saw straightaway that she would want to walk quickly through the rain and that he was going to have to stop her. He was going to talk to her in front of the Front Office. This was what he had agreed with Benny.

You would think it would be humiliating, to be a prancing bear for your disturbed son. But actually, no. He was dancing on the edge of freedom.

'Mort Catchprice,' he said.

He had the workshop courtesy umbrella, big enough to take to the beach. He held it over her and her umbrella. She put her own umbrella down, but the rain was bouncing around their ankles. He guessed it was worse for the woman with stockings on.

Benny stood behind the glass with a strange-looking young man in a light-coloured suit. He grinned and pointed his finger at his father.

You want me to show her my life?

O.K., I touched you.

Not touched.

O.K., fucked, sucked. I made you stutter and wet your bed. Made you a liar too, quite likely. My skin responded. It's physiology. The male skin – you touch it, you get a response. Like jellyfish – you touch them, they fire out darts. The jellyfish cannot control it. There are men more sensitive than others. Is that unnatural? You hold their hand, they get a hard-on. Whose fault is that? When does that happen? If there is no reason then there is no God.

If there is a God I am not a monster.

In my great slimy shape, in my two great eyes, my dark slimy heart, I am not a monster. Was I the sort of creep who hangs round scout troops, molesting strangers?

'It must have occurred to you,' he said to the Tax Inspector, when he had introduced himself, 'that what you decide affects our whole life.'

She took a step away and put up her own umbrella again.

'Yes,' she said. 'All the time.'

Behind her back, he could see Benny winking and grinning. Benny could not hear a damn word he said.

'Does it look bad for us?' he asked.

'It looks nothing much yet,' she said. 'I'm sure you'll just be fine.'

'Oh no,' he said. 'It won't be fine.'

'Maybe you should let me discover that.'

'I don't need to. I can tell you,' he said. He was a little out of breath, but he felt great. 'Look at the salary claims for our sales manager. I'd look at that one closely.' There was thunder all around them now. The traffic on Loftus Street was driving with its headlights on. 'Plus the trade-ins. You're going to find the lack of trade-ins interesting.'

The Tax Inspector was shaking her head and frowning.

'Mr Catchprice, please . . . don't do this.'

Mort looked at Benny and saw that he was frowning too. He thought: maybe he can read my lips. He said: 'No one set out to be crooked. Not even Cathy.'

'Mr Catchprice, please.' She put out her hand as if to touch him and then something about him, some stiffness, stopped her. 'Please just relax.'

He laughed. It was a stupid laugh, a snort. He could not help it. She looked at him oddly.

'He wants me to show you our life,' he said.

The Tax Inspector frowned at him. She had such a pretty face. Benny was right – it was a kind face, but she would kill him with a rock if she could see his soul. Every time you turn on the television, someone is saying: child sexual *abuse*. But they don't see how Benny comes to me, crawling into my bed and rubbing my dick, threatening me with jail. Is this abuse?

'Maybe I should show you the true Catchprice life?' he said. He felt half dizzy.

I am the one trying to stop this stuff and he is crawling into bed and rubbing my dick and he will have a kid and do it to his kid, and he will be the monster and they'll want to kill him. Today he is the victim, tomorrow he is the monster. They do not let you be the two at once. They do not see: it is common because it is natural. No, I am not saying it is natural, but if it is so common how come it is not natural?

The rain was pouring down now. It was spilling across the front office guttering and running down the windows like a fish shop window.

Maria Takis looked at Mort Catchprice. He was staring her directly in the eyes and his own eyes were too alive, too excited for the context. His lips trembled a little. It occurred to her he was having a mental breakdown.

34

Cathy, at ten years old, you should have seen her – a prodigy. She'd never heard of Sleepy La Beef or Boogie or Rock-a-Billy. She listened to a Frankie Laine record once and laughed at it like everybody else. She knew *Don Giovanni, Isolde, Madame Butterfly*. Her teacher was Sister Stoughton at the Catholic School. There was no yodelling there. She sang 'Kyrie Eleison' at St John's at Christmas before an audience which included the Governor General. There was no 'Hound Dogs' or 'Blue Suede Shoes'. The nearest she came to that sort of thing was the jeans with rolled-up cuffs she wore to square dancing classes at the Mechanics' Institute. She did not like square dancing either, said it was like going fencing with a wireless turned up loud. She was nine years old when she said that.

But she was not spoiled, or precious. Frieda thought how lucky she was, to have this girl, not a silly girl, or a flighty girl, but a girl like her Mummy, a practical girl – pretty as all got out, with tangled curls like a blonde Shirley Temple. She did not have her mother's build. No one would ever tell her she had sparrow legs. They were sturdy, smooth-skinned. Frieda could not help touching them, feeling the solidity of them. She *was* her legs – sturdy and reliable.

At ten years old she was up before the alarm clock to make the wet mash for the chooks – wheat, pollard, bran mash and warm water, all mixed up in the same tub they took their baths in. Cathy always knew she was important in the family. She counted the eggs and helped clean them for market. Frieda encouraged her to see what she was achieving.

Mort at twelve was dreamy and difficult, had moods, would want to help one day and then not the next, wet his bed, got head lice ten times for Cathy's two. He was weepy and clingy one day and gruff and angry and would not even let you touch him the next. He was the one you could love best when he was asleep. You could not guess that he would be the one to care for her when she was old, that he would cook her stew to eat, make sure she had her rum and Coke, sit with her into the night playing cribbage.

Cathy and her Frieda had matching yellow gum boots and they would stomp around the chook yard together, before dawn. They used old kitchen forks to break the ice on the cement troughs so the hens could drink.

It was Cathy who discovered that the light they left on to keep away the foxes also made the hens lay more. She counted the eggs. She was a smart girl, not a difficult girl – you did not need to fear she was plotting some scheme against her family.

And when they moved to the car business in town it was no

different. At fourteen she knew how to record the day's petrol sales, enter the mechanics' cards on to the job cards, even reconcile the till.

Then Frieda gave Howie a job in Spare Parts, and it was as though she had brought a virus into their healthy lives. Cathy had never even heard of Rock-a-Billy. She did not know what it was. She only knew the very best sort of music, and suddenly there he was playing her this trash, and she was wearing tight skirts which did not suit her build and writing songs about things she could not possibly understand. She paid ten dollars a time to register them in the United States. Australia was not good enough. Everything Yankee was the bee's knees. She began to argue with everyone. She broke her father's heart and then she decided *she* was not happy. She decided it to win the contest. Something came into her eyes, some anger so deep you could not even hope to touch it.

Howie wore pink shirts and charcoal grey suits. He was always so meek-seeming, yes Ma-am, no Ma-am. He could fool you at first. He fooled Frieda. She defended him against Mort and Cacka – his bodgie hair cut, his 'brothel creeper' shoes. But they were right and she was wrong – Howie was really a nothing, a little throw-away with no loyalty to anyone.

But he got his way – he married Cathy and a month later he took her to inspect the old Ford Dealership and enquire about renting the premises. Frieda heard that for a fact, from Herbert Beckett down at Beckett's Real Estate – Cathy Catchprice was ready to go into competition against her own flesh and blood. Frieda never trusted the pair of them after that, never, ever.

When Cathy came up the stairs on Tuesday morning berating her for hiring a new salesman and accusing her of stealing the company books, Frieda Catchprice saw her daughter as you see into a lighted window from a speeding train, saw the pretty little girl helping her paint wood oil on the roosts, screwing her eyes up against the fumes.

Next thing she was a demon, some piece of wickedness with small blue eyes and teeth bared right up to the gum line.

'The Tax Office doesn't need the ledgers to lock you up in jail,' she said.

Frieda hugged her arms across her flat chest. She was wearing brown leather slippers and an aqua quilted dressing-gown. She had

a tough look on her face – her little jaw set, her lower lip protruding, but she was scared of what Cathy would do to her, and her
hand, when she brought the Salem to her lips, was trembling.

'I hired the salesman,' she said. 'That's my right, but if you think
I pinched the ledgers – you've got a fertile imagination.'

But the ledgers were gone and she would not invite Cathy into
her living-room to give her the pleasure of seeing this was so. So
they stayed all crushed in that little annexe – Frieda, Cathy, Vish –
like Leghorns in a wire cage for the train.

'You've got no right to hire an *ant*,' Cathy said, tossing her head
down towards where Sam the Armenian was making friends with
Benny. 'When Takis sees the books are gone she's going to go
through this business like a dose of salts.'

'*I'm* not the one who should be worried,' Frieda said.

'Mum, what are you imagining?'

Frieda knew she was at a disadvantage – age – the brain losing its
way, forgetting names, losing a thought sometimes in the middle of
its journey. She had looked at the ledgers herself and the truth was,
she could no longer follow them. She hid her weakness from her
daughter, cloaking herself in sarcasm.

'I can imagine you might find the prospect of an audit
frightening.'

'But you're the public officer,' Cathy said. 'You're the one who
goes to jail.'

Jail! Good God. She sucked on her Salem so hard that she had
nearly an inch of glowing tobacco on the end of the white paper.
'*I've* never cheated anyone.'

'Would you happen to recall the renovation we claimed on the
showroom?' Cathy said.

'I don't know what lies you've been telling.'

'Oh come on!'

Frieda could feel her chin begin to tremble. 'All they'll find when
they investigate is who is fiddling whom.'

'It wasn't the showroom. It was your new bathroom.'

'I asked Mrs Takis to keep an eye out for me. I'll be very
interested to hear what she finds out.'

'Please,' Vish said.

'You might think this Takis is cute,' Cathy said.

Frieda did not think Maria Takis was cute at all. She imagined she would turn out to be an officious bitch. That was why she took so much trouble to be nice to her.

Cathy said: 'She's a killer.'

'Good,' said Frieda. 'That's just what I want.' She jabbed out her cigarette into the plastic garbage can – it made a smell like an electrical fire. 'I want a killer.'

'You look at her eyes and nose – that'll tell you. She's one of those people who can't forgive anyone. Mummy,' Cathy said, 'she's going to destroy everything you spent your life making.'

The 'Mummy' took Frieda by surprise. Cathy was smart. She saw that. She saw how it affected her. She pushed her advantage. 'You might not be able to believe this, but I'm trying to help you.'

'It's true,' Vish said, nodding his head up and down. He was acting as though she was a horse he had to calm.

Cathy was the same. She held out her hand towards Frieda. She might have had a damn sugar lump in it, but Frieda whacked the hand away.

'Why did you do that?'

The answer was – because you think I'm simple. She did not say it. She was not entering into any arguments. You could lose an argument but it did not affect the truth. She folded her arms across her chest.

'There's something you think I did,' Cathy said. 'That's it isn't it?'

Frieda gave Cathy an icy smile.

'Why do we keep *hurting* each other?' Vish said. It was the scratchy broken voice that made his grandmother turn towards him. His mouth was loose, glistening wet and mortified. Tears were oozing from his squeezed-shut eyes, washing down his broad cheeks. 'All we ever do,' he bawled, 'is hurt each other.'

Cathy put her hand on his shoulder. 'Johnny,' she said, 'you're better staying in your ashram. You're happy there, you should just stay there.'

'He came to see me,' Frieda said. 'If you don't like it here, Cathy, why don't you go?'

'I want to go,' Cathy said. 'I want to go away and have my own life, but I have to help you first. I have to get it straight between us.'

'You've helped enough already,' Frieda said. 'Vish will help me back inside.'

As Cathy ran down the fire escape, Vish walked his grandmother back into the decaying darkness of the living-room. He sat her at the table and brought her ashtray and a glass of Diet Coke with Bundaberg rum in it. He blew his nose on a tight wet ball of Kleenex.

'You don't want to let Cathy upset you,' his grandmother said.

'Everybody is miserable here, Gran. There's no one who's happy.'

She brought the full focus of her attention to him and he had the feeling that she was, finally, 'seeing' him. 'You think we should all be Hare Krishnas?' she asked.

Vish hesitated. He looked at his grandmother's face and did not know what things he was permitted to say to it.

'You want me to say what I really think?'

She made an impatient gesture with her hand.

'Let the business go to hell,' he said.

He waited but he could read no more of her reaction than had he been staring out of a window at the night.

'It's making Benny very sick,' he said. 'If you let the business go . . . I know this will sound extreme . . . I really do think you'd save his life.'

'I never wanted this business,' she said. 'Did you know that? I wanted little babies, and a farm. I wanted to grow things.' She had a slight sing-song cadence in her voice. It was like the voice she used when praying out loud in church and he could not tell if what she was saying was true or merely sentimental. 'It was your grandfather who wanted the business. I never liked the smell of a motor business. He worshipped Nellie Melba and Henry Ford. They were the two for him, Nellie & Henry. I never liked the music, I admit it, and I never gave a damn about Henry Ford, but he was my husband, for better or for worse. It was Henry Ford this, and Henry Ford that, and now I look out of the windows and I see these cars, you know what I see?'

'It's a prison,' Vish said, then blushed.

'I was perfectly right not to like the smell. My nose had more sense than a hundred Henry Fords. They're pumping out poison,' she said. 'Our noses told us that, like they tell you if a fish is bad or fresh. Who ever liked the smell of exhaust smoke?'

'Benny.'

'Do you know we put concrete over perfectly good soil when we made this car yard? There's concrete underneath all the gravel in the car yard. Your grandfather liked concrete. He liked to hose it down. But there's good soil under there, and that's what upsets me. It's like a smothered baby.'

'Then let them have it,' Vish said, 'Let them take it . . .'

'I'd rather blow it up,' she said. 'With her and Howie in it.'

'No, no . . .'

'I mean it.'

'I meant the tax. If the Tax Department wants to fine us . . .'

'I didn't work all my life to let the Tax Department take everything I'd built up.'

The telephone began ringing in the kitchen.

'You've got to,' Vish said.

'I don't "got to" anything.' His Granny did not seem to hear the telephone. She looked at him in a way she had never looked at him before, more in the way she looked at Cathy, but never at Vish. It produced an equivalent change in him, a toughening of his stance, a stubbornness in the muscles of his thick neck that made his grandmother (so used to thinking of his gentleness, of seeing him chant, light his incense, say his Krishnas, bless his *prasadum*) see his physical bulk, his great muscled forearm, his squashed nose and the big fists he was now clenching stubbornly upon her dining-table.

Someone began knocking on the door.

35

The first thing Maria noticed was that the Catchprice Motors books were not on Mrs Catchprice's table where she had left them. There was an ashtray and a glass of some black liquid and when she sat down at the central dining chair on the long side and opened her briefcase she found the surface of the table unpleasantly sticky.

The Hare Krishna was called Fish. He plugged the telephone in beside the bride dolls' cabinet and Maria began to create the correct emotional distance between herself and her client who now sat down on a yellow vinyl chair some three metres away and arranged her ashtray and cigarettes on its stuffed arm.

Maria looked across the room, frowning. If pregnancy had not prevented her, she would have chosen this as the day to wear her black suit.

She had not been aware there was a call on the line until Fish handed her the telephone and said, without any other preamble, 'Your office.' So just as she was steeling herself to threaten Mrs Catchprice, she heard Gia's voice: 'I just had a death threat.'

When Maria heard 'death threat' she thought it meant a threat of dismissal because of their activities last night.

'What will they do?'

'What do you think they'll do? They're watching my house.'

'They're watching your *house*?'

'It was eight o'clock in the damn morning. In the morning. How could he find my name, by eight in the morning, let alone my number? How could he even know who I am?'

'Who is "he"?'

'Wally Fischer.'

Mrs Catchprice was holding her ashtray, a small replica of a Uniroyal tyre with a glass centre. She was craning her withered neck towards the conversation.

'He called you on the telephone?'

'Not him personally.'

'Gia, darling, please, tell me what happened.'

'The phone rang. I was still in bed. I picked it up. It was a man. He said: "This is Dial-a-Death, you insolent little slag." He said, "Which day would you like to meet your death? Today? We could just burn your car today. Then you could wait while we decided which day you were going to meet your death." '

'They're just scaring you,' said Maria, but her throat was dry. She had read about Dial-a-Death in a tabloid paper.

'You're not listening, Maria. They were watching the house.'

'They wouldn't dare. For God's sake, you're a Tax Officer.'

'He said, your slut friend has left. You are alone in the house. It was true: Janet had just left.'

'Have you called the police?'

'The police? Don't be naïve, Maria. You don't ring the police about Wally Fischer. He pays the police. He lives up the road from the Rose Bay police station. I've got to ring Wally Fischer. I've got to apologize.'

'Christ,' Maria said. 'I hate Sydney.'

'Maria, I called you for *help*.'

'I'm sorry.'

'I've got to go.'

The phone went dead. Maria closed her eyes.

'Everything all right?' said Mrs Catchprice.

'No,' said Maria. 'It's not.'

She sat for a moment trying to steady herself. She had failed her friend completely.

'I need those books,' she told Mrs Catchprice. 'I need them here right now.'

'I need them too,' said Mrs Catchprice. 'Are you all right?'

'I'll be a lot better when I have the books. Please,' she said. 'I want to wind up this job today.'

'How nice,' said Mrs Catchprice. 'I'm so pleased. There are so many important things I need to ask you.'

Maria heard herself saying, 'Mrs Catchprice, my best friend has just received a death threat.'

36

Jack Catchprice loved smart women, although to say he 'loved' them is to give the impression of hyperbole whereas it understates the matter. He had an obsession with smart women. He had a confusion of the senses, an imbalance in his judgement where smart women were concerned. Their intelligence aroused his sexual interest to a degree that his business associates, men admittedly, found comic as they watched him – slim, athletic, strikingly handsome, with a tanned, golfer's face and just-in-control curly blond hair, good enough looking to be a film star – go trotting off to Darcy's or Beppi's with some clumpy, big-arsed, fat-ankled woman whom he had just met at some seminar and on whom he was lavishing an amusing amount of puppy-dog attention. If he had been a whale he would have beached himself.

And indeed his sexual radar was somehow confused and his private life was always in chaos as he flip-flopped between these two most obvious types – the bimbos whom he treated badly, and the mostly unattractive geniuses whom he seemed to select from the ranks of those who would despise him – academics, socialists, leaders of consumer action groups.

It never occurred to him that it might be his own mother who had implanted this passion in him. The parallel was there for him to see if he wished to – in the privacy of the Catchprice home there was never any doubt about who the smart one was meant to be: not Cacka, that was for sure, no matter how many 'prospects' he shepherded across the gravel, cooing all the time into their ears. It was Frieda who read books and had opinions. She was the one who was the church-goer, the charity organiser, and – for one brief period – Shire Councillor. These things had more weight – even Cacka gave them more weight – than selling cars to dairy farmers, and yet it would have been repugnant for Jack to imagine that the women he fell in love with were in any way like his mother. He imagined he felt no affection for her, and whether this was true or not, there were betrayals he could not forgive her for. She had been the smart one, the one who read the front page of the papers, but she had let Cacka poison her children while she pretended it was not happening.

Jack had driven out from the city in an odd, agitated mood – bored, tense, but feeling the sadness that the various roads to Franklin – the F4, the old Route 81, or the earlier Franklin Road – had always brought with them. These roads, on top of each other, beside each other, followed almost exactly the same course. They made the spine of his life and he had driven up and down them for nearly forty years. It was an increasingly drab second-rate landscape – service stations, car yards, drive-in bottle shops and, now, three lanes each way. It was the path he had taken from childhood to adulthood and it always forced some review of his life on him. Its physical desolation, its lack of a single building or street, even one glimpsed in passing, that might suggest beauty or happiness, became like a mould into which his emotions were pressed and he would always arrive in Franklin feeling bleak and empty.

He would drive back to Sydney very fast, surrounded by the smell of genuine leather, with the Mozart clarinet concerto playing loudly. He left as if Catchprice Motors were a badly tended family grave and he were responsible for its neglect, its crumbling surfaces, its damp mouldy smell, its general decrepitude. And it was true – he was responsible. He had a gift – he could sell, and he had applied it to his own ends, not the family's. No one ever said a thing about this, but as Jack became richer, the family business sank deeper and deeper into the mud. They could see his betrayal in his expensive cars – which he did not buy from them – and his suits which cost as much as his brother made in a month.

When his mother called for help, he gave it, instantly, ostentatiously. She called him at nine-thirty on Tuesday morning, in the midst of her second meeting with the Tax Inspector. Even while she whispered into the telephone, Jack was mapping pencilled changes in his appointment book and by a quarter to ten he was on the road. He was meant to somehow 'send away this Tax woman' who his mother imagined was going to jail her.

It was impossible, of course. He could not do it. Indeed, driving out to Franklin was less useful than staying in his office and talking to some good professionals, but Jack was like a politician who must be seen at the site of a disaster – he felt he must be seen to care.

As for whether he did care or did not care he would have found it hard to know what was the honest answer. He thought his mother dangerous, manipulative, almost paranoid, but he was also the one who sent her the photograph of himself shaking hands with the Premier of the State. He would say he no longer felt affection for her, but he phoned her once or twice a week to tell her what building he had bought or sold and whom he had lunch with. If it was true he felt no affection for her, it was equally true that he craved her admiration.

He was her favourite. He knew it, and he carried a sense of the unjustness of his own favouritism. He thought Mort was more decent, and Cathy certainly more gifted but he was physically lighter, blond-haired, pretty – a McClusky, not a Catchprice.

The Jaguar had an intermittent fault in the electrics and was, because of this, missing under load. He came down to Franklin more slowly than usual – in forty-five minutes.

He saw the two salesmen standing under yellow umbrellas in the yard, but did not recognize the blond one as his nephew. He crossed the gravel, self-conscious in his Comme des Garçons suit. He climbed the fire escape which had rotted further since his previous visit.

In his mother's living-room, beneath the photograph of himself shaking hands with the Premier of the State, he met the Tax Inspector.

She was handsome beyond belief. She had a straight back, lovely legs, big black frightened hurt eyes, a chiselled proud nose, and a luxuriant tangle of curling jet-black hair. She was no more than five foot five and she had a great curved belly which he realized, with surprise, he would have loved to hold in both hands.

'You tell Jack,' his mother told the Tax Inspector. 'Jack will know what to do.'

The Tax Inspector told him about the death threat. She sat opposite him at the table. She was upset but she was articulate and considered in the way she assembled the information for him, telling him neither too much nor too little. This impressed him as much as anything else – he was impatient, he demanded that his executives say everything they had to say in documents of one page only.

He sat opposite her, frowning to hide his happiness. She was a jewel. Here, among the smell of dog pee and damp.

'O.K.,' he said, when she had finished. 'There are three ways to fix this. One: your friend does nothing. She'll get a few more calls and that will probably be that. The crappy part is she has to listen to this creep. It's upsetting.'

'It's terrorism,' said Maria, who was pleasantly surprised to find a Catchprice who was not angry and threatened and who seemed, more importantly, to be in control of his life. In the way he talked he reminded her of a good lawyer.

'Exactly,' he said. 'So we rule that out as an option. The second option would be to get some help. Someone – I could do it if she liked – would go and find out how to contact Wally Fischer. And then we could arrange for your friend to apologize. Maybe we could get away with a phone call.'

The Tax Inspector was drawing on the table with her finger.

'It sounds pretty bad, I know, but you can be sure it would work. She doesn't want to apologize?' Jack guessed.

'In a flash. I'm the one who thinks she shouldn't.'

'And she'll take your advice?'

'Let's see what the third option is.'

In fact Jack had no third option to offer her. He had been making it up as he went along. It was a bad habit to specify a number of points. It was a salesman's habit. Politicians did it too. You said: there are five points. It made you seem in control when you were winging it. People rarely remembered when you only got to four.

But this one demanded a third option and he had to find her one. If the friend wouldn't apologize, he would arrange to have someone telephone Wally Fischer and grovel on the friend's behalf, impersonate her even – why the hell not? He saw himself drifting into the fuzzy territory on the edge of honesty, but he could not see where else to go. He must fix this for her.

'I have some friends in the police,' he said. 'I can maybe arrange for one of them to have a quiet talk to Mr Fischer.' Actually this was better. He could talk to Moose Chanley in the Gaming Squad. Moose Chanley owed him one. If Moose couldn't make it sweet with Fischer, he would know someone with whom he had a working relationship. It was no big deal – networking – 98 per cent of property development was networking. He would need to have Moose phone the friend to tell her Dial-a-Death had been called off. Maybe it would be possible to get whichever of Fischer's thugs who was currently playing the role of Dial-a-Death to phone her and tell her it was off. *No, no, no. Take the simplest course.*

'Why did you pull that face?'

'I was thinking of Wally Fischer,' he said.

He had got himself off the main straight road and on to the boggy side-roads of lies and he had to get back on the hard surface again. This was a woman with a clear and simple sense of right and wrong. You could see this in the nose. It was a damn fine nose. It was chiselled, almost arrogant, but very certain. This was apparent when she rejected the thought of her friend's apology. She was a moralist. She had guts. She was one of those people whom Jack had always loved, people with such a clear sense of the moral imperatives that they would never find themselves in that grey land where 'almost right' fades into the rat-flesh-coloured zone of 'nearly wrong', people with a clear sight, sharp white with edges like diamonds, people whom Jack would always be in awe of, would follow a little way, more of a way than his profession or what might appear to be his 'character' would allow, people in whom he had always been disappointed and then relieved to discover small personal flaws, lacks, unhappinesses that proved to him that their moral rectitude had not been purchased without a certain human price – this one is lonely, that one impractical, this one poor, that one incapable of a happy sex life.

He could imagine none of these flaws in Maria, nor did he seek any. The only flaw he could see was that evidence which suggested there could be no intimate relationship between them, not that she was pregnant, but that because she was pregnant she was, although she wore no ring, married.

One step at a time.

He said: 'Let me make some phone calls.'

Once he had the death threats cancelled it was only a very small step to having her agree to have dinner with him. He knew this was an achievable goal.

37

Gino Massaro was a greengrocer from Lakemba. He had a large, hooked nose and little hands. He had soft, lined, yellowish-olive skin which was creased around his eyes and cheeks. In his own shop, he was a funny man. He spun like a bottom-heavy top with a black belt above his bulging stomach. He would shadow-box with the men (duck, weave, biff), have sweets for the children, flirt with the women ('How you goin' darling, when you going to marry me?') in a way his exquisite ugliness made quite permissible. In his shop he showed confidence, competence – hell – success. He had two kids at university. He spoke Italian, Australian, a little Egyptian. He had his name painted on the side of a new Red Toyota Hi-Lux ute – G. Massaro, Lakemba, Tare 1 tonne.

No one knew the Toyota was financed on four years at $620 per month. He also had a serious overdraft, and a weakening trade situation caused mainly by competition from the Lebanese – not one shop, three, and all the bastards related to each other – who were staying open until nine at night and all day Sunday as well. He also had a ten-year-old white Commodore with flaky paint and black carbon deposits above the exhaust pipe. On the Tuesday afternoon when he parked this vehicle in front of Catchprice Motors he had just spent $375 on the transmission and there was a folded piece of yellow paper on the passenger seat – a $935 quote for redoing the big end. He also carried – not on paper, in his head – four separate valuations for the Commodore from yards between here and Lakemba, every one of which told him that the car was not worth what he owed on it.

He parked on the service road, behind a yellow Cherry-picker crane. He touched the St Christopher on his dashboard, closed his eyes, and turned off the engine. Sometimes it worked, sometimes it didn't and today it didn't – the engine knocked and farted violently before it became still. Two salesmen in the yard stood watching him. Behind them was a red Holden Barina. He did not like the red or the flashy mag wheels. He did not like it that his son would say it was a woman's car, but it was the right price range.

He was not a fool. He knew he should prepare the Commodore, have it wax-polished, detailed, present it as well as if it were apples at five dollars a kilo. But who had time? Every second he was away from the shop he lost money. He picked the pieces of paper off the seat, and the ice-cream carton off the floor and thrust them into the side pocket.

Then he got out of the car, locked it, and walked into the car yard. With fruit he was a different man, not like this.

He was already on the gravel when he saw the face. He would have retraced his steps, but somehow he couldn't. The blond salesman was smiling at him in a weird kind of way, and Gino was smiling back.

Gino knew that his angelic smiling face was a lie, that he secretly and silently mocked his big nose, his fat arse, his car blowing too much smoke. But now he had come this far and he was somehow caught and caressed by the smile which made him feel that he did not care if he was despised and he had no will or even desire to turn back. It was the feeling you had with a whore. You knew it was not true, but you pretended it was. He thought: this kid with the yellow umbrella would rob me if I let him. But he could not turn back and so he walked across the gravel towards him. Lines of plastic bunting hung across the yard. They made a noise like wings flapping in a cage.

38

'I'll tell you what I'll do,' the one called Benny said. 'First thing, I'm going to give you five grand for your old car, smoke or no smoke.'

They were all sitting in the red Barina with the engine on and the air-conditioner running. The one called Benny was in the front seat, with his hand resting on Gino's headrest. The other one, Sam, was in the back. This one didn't say too much.

Gino sat with his hands on the wheel feeling the cool quiet air blasting on his face. He liked it in there. He liked the smell, the dark green digits glowing out of the black leather dark. He had that feeling, of surrender and luxury, like when you were in an expensive barber's shop. As long as they cut and snipped and combed he did not care what sort of haircut he was getting, only how it felt, like in that whore house in Surry Hills when he paid them to rub his toes afterwards – $100 an hour to have your toes rubbed. Those were the days – a crazy man.

'Five grand for the old one, smoke or no smoke, I don't care.'

Gino leaned down to undo the hood release – clunk – in order to hide his excitement.

'What do you say to that, Mr Massaro – from square one, you're out of trouble. Your credit rating is out of danger. You have an almost new car.'

It was true. He could pay out the loan on the Commodore. He stroked the hood release button, reading its embossed hieroglyphic symbol with the tip of his finger. 'O.K.,' he said. 'So where's the catch?'

'We've got a big tax bill to pay.'

Gino Massaro looked at the kid and grinned. 'Come on . . .' he said. 'I wasn't born yesterday.' He tried to get himself back into the sort of fellow he was in his shop. 'Come on,' he said, and boxed the kid's arm. 'Don't shit me.'

'Mr Massaro, if I tell you lies I'll go to hell for it.' He smiled. 'They'll torture me down there. They'll pull my toenails out for fucking ever.'

The kid made you smile. He could say this, maybe even mocking – who could say – but make you smile.

'Look over there,' the kid said.

There was a line of giant camphor laurels, their trunks covered with parasites, their leaves dotted red from lichen. In front of them, by a faded sign reading PARTS/WORKSHOP, a white Mitsubishi Colt with Z plates was parked on a patch of weeds. Gino had been audited. He knew the feeling.

'There's the Tax Department car, O.K.? I'll tell you what I'll do,' he smiled. 'I'll put in a word for you with the Tax Inspector . . .'

'Whoa, no get *away*,' Gino said. 'You keep those boys away from me.'

'But it's a girl,' Benny grinned. 'She's pretty too. She's very nice. You'd like her.'

'Let's stick to the car, O.K.,' he said. He got out of the car so he could think responsibly, but the air was muggy and unpleasantly heavy. He took out a handkerchief and wiped his forehead. He heard the two doors open and heard the salesmen walk across the gravel towards him. They lined up beside him and then the three of them stood in a line with their hands behind their back and stared at the Barina.

'Now I'm going to "load" you up,' Benny smiled pleasantly. 'Load up your trade in an effort to get your business.'

Gino smiled too, even as he thought he was being mocked. 'Loading up' was car dealer slang for whatever it was they were doing to him.

'I wasn't born yesterday,' he said. He punched Benny's shoulder again. This time the boy didn't like his suit touched. His brows came down hard against his eyes and he withdrew an inch, looking pointedly at Gino's hand. Gino took it away.

'We got to take enough shit from the Tax Department,' the boy said. 'We don't have to take shit from you. Come on Sam . . .' He turned to walk away.

'Christ,' Gino said. 'Don't be so sensitive.'

He looked up and saw the one called Sam shaking his head at him.

The one called Benny turned and said, 'Look, I'm trying to be straight with you, but this is losing us money and it really gives me the shits, excuse me – it makes me "sensitive" – when I am not believed. This is a family business, we're in a lot of trouble here and you're the one who'll benefit. That's O.K. with me, but it really pisses me off to be called a liar as well.'

The other salesman looked Gino straight in the eye and slowly shook his head.

'I didn't mean to offend you,' Gino said to the first boy, all the time puzzling about the other one shaking his head.

'I know you didn't,' Benny said. 'Forget it. It's over.'

'I've been audited myself. They're bastards.'

'You could drive it away,' Benny Catchprice said. 'We could do the paperwork in ten minutes and you could be on the road in fifteen. You don't have to ever touch your old car again.'

It was an attractive thought.

'So what do you want for this one?' Gino asked.

Benny said: 'Eleven. Do we have a deal?'

The second salesman made a cut-throat sign and rolled his eyes.

'So what do you say, Mr Massaro?'

The blond salesman was smiling at him in a weird kind of way, and Gino was smiling back. It was impossible not to. He had that quality – he was not a man, he was a boy, like an altar boy in Verona.

That was when Sarkis Alaverdian, who knew the car was valued at eight thousand, stood on Benny Catchprice's foot.

The altar boy's face changed, its brows contracted, its lips curled. Gino Massaro began to back away.

'That's very expensive,' he said.

'Don't go,' Benny said. 'I gave you a big trade-in. You only have to finance seven.'

'I'll tell you what I'm going to do,' Gino Massaro said. 'I'm going to think about it. I'll be back on Saturday morning with my wife.'

39

'I'm sorry,' Sarkis said. 'I guess I was nervous.'

Benny sucked in his breath. 'You arsehole,' he said. His jaw was drawn tight. His neck was all tendons and sinews. 'I am in control of my own life. I am in control of you as well.'

'Hey, come on – what sort of talk is that?'

'English,' said Benny, watching Gino Massaro drive away down the service road in a cloud of white smoke – his first damn sale – $3,000 clear profit plus the finance plus the insurance minus a drop of say five hundred on the shitty trade-in. 'English,' he said, as the Commodore entered Loftus Street. 'You better learn it. You better shave that hair off your lip you want to work here tomorrow.' He was kneeling, tenderly exploring the toe region of his shoe. 'What sort of fucking nut case are you? For Chrissakes I had him eating out of my fucking hand. I could have dumped the fucking Commodore at the auctions and got seven and a half for it, tomorrow, cash.'

'Look,' said Sarkis.

'Hey, don't "look" me,' the pretty boy said. '"Look" me and you're on your arse in the fucking street without a job. I had him. I had his little dago heart in the palm of my fucking hand.' He held out his hands. Sarkis saw them wet with viscera. He did not need this. He'd rather eat eggplant soup all summer.

'Goodbye,' he said. He held out his hand. 'Nice knowing you.'

The boy took his hand, and held it. 'What do you mean?'

'I mean, goodbye.'

Benny kept a hold of his hand, smiling.

A man in a XJ6 Jaguar was pulling up in front. The man had curly blond hair and a tanned face. He wore a beautiful grey silk suit. He walked across in front of Benny and Sarkis. Benny still had Sarkis by the hand.

'Hi-ya, Jack,' Benny said to the man.

'Hi-ya,' the man said. He walked on up the same fire escape Cathy MacPherson had come down.

'So,' Sarkis said, taking his hand back. 'I'm off.'

'Calm down, O.K.,' Benny said.

'Listen,' Sarkis said. 'I get more courtesy at the dole office.'

'Yeah, yeah,' Benny laughed. 'But the pay is not nearly so good. O.K., O.K., I know, I was excited. I'm sorry. O.K.?' He smiled. It was actually a nice smile. He touched Sarkis on the back. 'I was a creep, I'm sorry.'

'O.K.,' Sarkis said.

'It's my inexperience,' the boy said. 'I'm learning too.'

Sarkis thought: it is not fair. A person like this gets property and a business and all these cars and expensive suits and he doesn't have the first idea how to talk to people decently, and no matter what was old-fashioned and dumb about the Armenian School at Willoughby, at least there was this behind it – that you had some dignity about yourself and you spoke to others decently.

'Look,' the boy said. 'Let's take a break, O.K. Put our feet up, relax. What d'you say?'

Sarkis's mother thought he was arrogant and vain and this was why he had lost three jobs in a year. His father would have under-stood better. His father never bought a newspaper because the

Australians he worked with only read the sports pages and gave him the news section. When the horse races were on the radio his father would say: 'There go the donkeys.'

'O.K.,' said Sarkis, 'let's take a break.' He did not want a break. He wanted to sell every one of these cars they walked past. He was an Armenian. It was in his blood. Thousands of years of buying and selling.

He followed his boy-employer into the lube bay instead, and climbed down some metal stairs. In the dark he heard him fiddling with chains and keys and then they walked into something which stank like the inside of a rubbish bin and a laundry basket.

'Someone lives down here?' he asked, his voice dead flat.

'Sort of.'

Not sort of at all. The poor little sucker lived here. He had lived here a long time. He had new food, old food, bad-smelling clothes and oils and chemicals. The cellar would be enough to make you sorry for the boy, to wonder what drove him down here and why he could not live in a place with windows.

They were standing side by side now, shoulder to shoulder. There were cans of epoxy resin on a messy, muddled, low bench on which there were also school books, empty ice-cream containers, scrunched-up paper, ancient hurricane lamps with rusty metal bases, and several snakes, preserved in tea-coloured liquid in tall, wide-mouthed, screw-topped bottles like the ones in which Sarkis's mother still sometimes preserved lemons.

'You work with fibreglass?' he asked, responding partly to his own embarrassment but also to his sense of Benny Catchprice's prickly pride.

'My Grand-dad killed them,' Benny said. 'It was a different world, eh? Every one of them snakes was killed on a property where my Grand-dad sold a car.'

Sarkis nodded.

'We used to sell to farmers,' Benny said. 'That's why the business is like it is now. They were brought up to sell to farmers.' He picked up one of the bottles and handed it to Sarkis, who hefted its weight and gave it back. 'V. Jenkins,' Benny read from a small white label with spidery brown writing, 'F.J. Special sold September 1952.' He looked up at Sarkis as he put it down. 'The farmers were all flush with money. They would have all their cheques from the Milk

Board . . . never bothered to even put them in the bank. My Grand-dad would write out the order and they'd count out Milk Board cheques until they had enough to pay for it.'

'If you're going to work with fibreglass you should ventilate better.'

'S&L Unger,' Benny read from a second jar. 'Vauxhall Cresta 1956.'

'Tell me it's none of my business,' Sarkis said, 'but you'll poison yourself working with fibreglass down here.'

Benny put the bottle down, and Sarkis could see he had offended him.

Sarkis said. 'When I was your age I wouldn't have read the can either.'

Benny looked around the room a little, Sarkis too. The walls were covered in mould like orange crushed velvet. Benny pulled a blanket off what Sarkis had taken for a chair.

'You ever seen one of these?'

What it was was hard to say. It looked like a melted surfboard with buckles. The buckles were a little like the clips of skis. The whole thing was pale and white and a little lumpy. It was ugly, like something from a sex shop.

'What is it?'

'What do you think?'

Benny was grinning. He stood in front of Sarkis with his hands in his pockets. He looked excited, conspiratorial, uncertain – he was colouring above his collar.

'You want to try it out then?'

'What is it?'

'Try it out,' said Benny. He unfolded a sheet and flung it across the melted surfboard and then indicated with his open-palmed hand that the older man should 'try it out'.

'Give me your jacket.'

Sarkis was trying to make peace with Benny Catchprice, whose eyes were now bright and whose lower lip had seemed to grow swollen in anticipation. He gave up his jacket. Benny checked the label before he hung it, not on the new wooden hanger, but on a thin wire one. He suspended it from a water pipe above their heads where it partly blocked out the light.

Sarkis sat on the surfboard. It made no sense to him. It had a profile like an 'n' but flatter and it was not of even width.

'Wrong way,' said Benny. 'Face down.'

Sarkis hesitated.

'Come on, what's going to happen to you?'

What can happen?

Sarkis lay face down on the sheet. To get half comfortable you had to have your head down and your arse in the air.

'More up,' said Benny.

Sarkis squirmed upwards. The sheet was rumpled beneath him. He felt Benny adjusting something around his legs and then he felt a snap, and a pain. His legs were held, strapped by metal. His skin was pinched.

'Hey,' he said.

Benny got a strap to his right arm before Sarkis realized what was happening. He kept his left hand free but it did him no good. He was pinioned. Benny was giggling. He smelt of peppermint.

'Let me go,' said Sarkis Alaverdian. 'My pants are getting crushed.'

But Benny had him by the left hand, trying to pinion that one too. And all the time – this giggling, this weird luminous excitement on his face.

Benny was smooth and white, a stranger to the sports field and the gym, but he had two arms and he used them to slowly press Sarkis's stronger arm flat against the rubbery-looking epoxy. He snapped the clip around it with his teeth and chin.

He knelt for a moment, and brought his face close to Sarkis. 'Don't think you can walk out on me,' he said. His expression had changed completely. No smile – just small pink hot spots on his cheeks. His breath was cold and antiseptic.

Sarkis felt a prickle of fear run down his spine. 'O.K.,' he said. 'Very funny.'

Benny stood. 'Funny?' he said. 'You just stole my first sale. You cost me three thousand fucking dollars. Then you think you can walk away from me.'

Sarkis acted as normal as he could be with his backside in the air and his head full of blood. He tried to look his captor in the eye, but could not twist his neck enough. 'You admitted yourself, Benny,' (he was talking to the buckle of his belt) 'it was your fault too.'

'You don't get it, do you? Why did I say it was my fault? How could it have been my fault? Why do you think I'd say it was?'

'You were going to do this to me?'

'Sure.'

'You made this thing? What's it really for?'

'For this,' said Benny.

'O.K.' It hurt to twist his neck up, it hurt to leave his head down. 'Now let me go.'

'Let me go, let me go,' Benny mocked. He took a step away to a place where Sarkis could not even see his shoes. He was somewhere behind him, near his back. 'You don't know what you're asking – I gave you a family position. Do you appreciate that? I gave you my brother's position. You are some slime off the street. You are no one. I offer you a ground-floor position. You could make two hundred thou a *year*. And all you can do is fuck up my sale, and *then* you try and walk out on me.'

'Hey relax.'

'Oh no, you relax, mate. You relax a lot. You should have listened to my aunt,' Benny said. 'This is a serious business you have got yourself involved with.'

'What do you want me to do? Stay or go?'

Sarkis twisted his head sideways and this time, found him – the little spider was arranging a sheet of orange plastic on the sofa.

'Stay or go?' Benny laughed through his nose. 'You're going to have to be more clever than that.' He was fussing with the sheet of plastic – wiping it with a rag, smoothing it with his hand – so he could sit down without dirtying his suit. When he sat he made a crumpling noise.

'Stay or go,' he said. He arranged himself with his legs crossed and his manicured hands folded in his lap. He smiled at Sarkis just as he had smiled at Gino Massaro.

40

Vish knocked on the cellar door, not once, but many times. When he opened the door, still uninvited, Benny was sitting on the rumpled orange sheet on the couch and staring at him. He was the only neat thing in the middle of this stinking mess and he had laid himself out, so to speak, with his hands folded on his lap, as pale and perfect as a wax effigy.

He had changed the lighting since last night. He had altered the direction of those little reading lights which had originally been above the beds in the family home. He had rigged them up so they shone on the webs of handwriting on the distempered wall, on the green concrete ceiling, on anything but where you'd want a light to be. The room was criss-crossed with the shadows of electric wires.

Vish stepped forward on to an empty ice-cream container. He stumbled and put his hand down to stop him falling.

He put his hand on to a living thing. His heart whammed in his chest.

'Shit,' he said.

It was a human being, he saw that. He got such a fright he could hardly breathe. He had his hand on a man's buttocks.

The man was lying on his stomach and had to crane his neck so he could grimace up at the yellow-robed figure to whom he looked like a gypsy at a country show. He had a little wisp of beard under his lip and trousers made from some velvety material. He showed a lot of teeth, like someone about to be cut in half on stage.

'You left it too late,' Benny said. 'I found another brother.'

Vish held his kurta close to his chest and peered down at the poor fellow who had been pinioned in position like a butterfly. The man stretched up his head again and rolled his eyes at Vish. He had white dry stuff in a rim around the edges of his lips. Vish observed this and accepted it like he might have accepted the presence of a goat or a policeman.

'Anything you want to say to me,' Benny said, 'you can say to Sam. He's my brother.'

'Help me,' Sarkis said.

'He's only joking. No one needs you.'

'Please,' said Sarkis. 'My legs are hurting.'

'Is this what you call being an angel?' Vish said.

'Do I look like an angel?' Benny sneered. 'You think I'd live down here if I was a fucking angel? No, I'm not an angel – I'm an *attachment*. Isn't that it? Isn't that what they call me at the temple?'

Vish smiled and smoothed the air as if he was patting the roof of a sand castle. 'Even if they do say that . . .'

'No, you said that – your guru doesn't want you to have *attachments*. So now you're free.'

'Who is this bloke?'

'This is Sam. He's my brother. He's going to make two hundred grand a year. He's going to do an F&I course next week . . .'

'Don't hurt him,' Vish said. 'He hasn't done anything to you.'

'Don't side with him. That's fucking typical. You don't know what he's done to me.'

'You're an accessory,' Sarkis said to Vish, twisting his head upwards. 'Why don't you phone the cops, before you both get in a lot of trouble?'

'Listen to him,' said Benny. 'He's smart.'

'You want me to call the cops?'

'Don't ask me. Ask him. I'd like to know myself.'

'You want me to call the cops?' Vish asked the man. He came closer to him so he could see the dried white stuff around his mouth and his slightly yellow blood-shot eyes.

The man was quiet for a moment. It looked as though he was trying to swallow. 'Just let me go,' he said. 'I'm losing circulation.'

'See,' said Benny. 'I'm just calming him down. He got excited.'

'You're right,' Vish said. 'You're not an angel, you're an insect. You'll live and die an insect, a million times over. I'm sorry I ever listened to your stupid story. I'm really sorry I came back down here.'

Benny's lips opened and he went soft around the chin. He stood up, but he put out his hand towards his brother as if he meant to stroke his sleeve. He took the fabric between thumb and forefinger and held it. 'You give me dog shit to eat,' he said softly, 'I'll still grow wings. It's my nature. It's who I am. I'll tell you, Vishy, they burn us, they shoot us, they pour shit on us and lock us in boxes, but you cannot trap us in our pasts.'

Vish shook his head again.

'We could be lying around lighting our farts, or doing Ice or M.D.A.'

'Help me.'

'One more peep out of you and you're in deep shit,' said Benny. To his brother he said: 'I need you.' He held out his hand.

'I need you too,' said Vish. He took the hand and held it.

Benny looked at him and blinked.

'We're brothers,' Vish said. 'It is an attachment, but I've got it. I put you here, that's right. It's my responsibility. So now,' he grinned, putting his hand around his brother's neck, 'I'm going to get you out of here, tonight.' He made a move on Benny, trying to get a half-nelson on him, but Benny slipped out and started shouting and flailing with his bony hands. Vish stepped backwards and fell off the plank, twisting his leg and falling backwards into the pool of water. A glass fell and shattered. As Vish rose, his yellow robes clinging wet against his barrel chest, Benny came at him with the power cord from the toaster, twirling it like a propeller. The plug smashed a light globe, and bounced against the back of Vish's hand, and head. He retreated, holding his hand round an injured ear from which fat drops of blood fell, tracing a dripping line up the perforated metal steps to the world outside.

41

Maria waited for Gia in the Brasserie garden near the dripping ferns, sipping mint tea. There was an office love affair being conducted in the bar, and the waiters were eating at the long table by the kitchen, but apart from this the Brasserie was empty.

Maria had planned to tell Gia about Jack Catchprice but Gia was late, and by the time she had arrived, found a dry place to put her briefcase, and begun to deal with the Brasserie's celebrated cocktail menu, it was after six-thirty.

'What I am really looking for,' Gia said, 'is something very silly and alcoholic.'

'The Hula-Hula,' said Peter, taking his order pad out of his grey apron.

'Does it have an umbrella?' said Gia skittishly.

'Trust me. It's very kitsch. It's exactly what you're looking for.'

'But it tastes nice?'

'You want silly or you want nice?'

Gia considered.

'What's a Mai Tai again? I never had a Mai Tai.'

If you did not know her and saw her do this – run her newly painted fingernails down the cocktail list, fiddle with her gold choker chain – you would think she was vain and indulged, a political conservative from the Eastern suburbs. In fact she was a liberal who worried (excessively) about the waiters and their work and, in Peter's case, his music as well. In a town where 10 per cent was meant to be the norm, Gia tipped an arithmetically difficult 12.5 per cent.

'Have a glass of champagne,' Peter said. 'You love champagne.'

'Maybe I should. Should I, Maria? It would have a certain symmetry.'

'It would be bad luck,' Maria said. 'Have the Hula-Hula. Have anything. She has news to tell me,' she told Peter. 'She is withholding. She is driving me crazy.'

'She's the one who hoards her news,' Gia said. 'I'm normally the one who blurts it out. This is her own treatment. She has to wait for everything to be perfect.'

'If you want perfect, have the Hula-Hula,' said Peter. 'If you don't like it, I'll drink it for you.'

'I'll have the Hula-Hula then.'

'I'll have a fresh squeezed orange juice,' Maria said.

'It doesn't have coconut milk does it?'

'No,' said Peter. 'It's definitely Lo-Chol.'

'Good,' said Gia.

'Tell me,' said Maria. It was twenty minutes to seven.

Gia hunched down over the table. 'Well . . .' she said.

'Yes, yes.'

'Your fellow rang me first . . .'

'Jack . . .'

'Jack Catchprice. What he hoped was he could just get it stopped.'

'He couldn't?'

'I'm sure he could have but the cop he had in mind just had a major heart attack, but he was really amazing. He was very sweet to me. He got someone else, I don't know who it was, to talk to Fischer. This took like three hours. They were going back and forth until two-thirty.'

'Back and forth about what?'

'About calling it off. Anyway, at two-thirty this very prissy-sounding woman phoned me. I don't know who she was. Like a real bitch of a private secretary. She gives me two phone numbers. One of them was for his car phone. That's where I got him.'

'It makes my flesh creep.'

'It just rang, you know, like anyone's phone and then this man answered and then I asked was that Mr Fischer and he said who wants to know and then I said my name, and he said, yes, it was him, and I said, I believe you know who I am.'

'What did he say?'

'He said yes,' Gia shivered. 'It was so creepy and frightening. I can't tell you how frightening it was. It sounds like nothing . . .'

'No, no. I can imagine.'

'Maria, you *can't* imagine.'

Peter brought the drinks. Gia's cocktail was full of fruit and had curling blue and green glass straws sticking out of it. It looked like something in an art gallery whose level of irony you might puzzle over. Gia put her lips to the blue glass straw and sucked.

'So I said I just wanted to apologize for my behaviour at the Brasserie.'

'But I thought that's what you didn't have to do. I thought that's what he was fixing for you.'

'Maria, I'll kill you. The cop had a fucking heart attack. What else did you want him to do? He was sweet.'

'I know he's *sweet* . . .'

'Christ, I don't think you can imagine this. I was so frightened, I would have said anything. I'm sure you would have been digni- fied, but I wasn't. I would have said anything. It just poured out of me.'

Maria squeezed her hand. 'Poor Gia.'

'Then he *interrupted* my grovelling. That was *really* humiliating. He just cut across me and said, give me your number – I'll have to ring you back. By then I was back in at the office and I didn't want him to know I worked for the Taxation Office but I didn't have any choice. And then I just sat by the phone for an entire hour. I won't tell you all the things I thought, but it was like torture. Ken tried to ring me up to have a chat, and I really fancy him, and I had to say, Ken I can't talk to you, and he got really offended. Then Fischer finally rang back and said yes he would accept my apology. He made me promise I wouldn't ever say anything like that again, and I did. It was so pathetic.'

'God, it's so creepy. It's as though you had to talk to something with scales. It's like some slimy thing you think is mythical. You think it doesn't really exist and then there it is and you're touching it. You talked to him about your execution while he was just sitting in his car. It makes me hate this city.'

'Don't hate Sydney, Maria. It makes me really anxious when you hate Sydney.'

'It's Sydney I hate, not you.'

'All cities are like this. Where could you go that would be different?'

'This city is really special.'

'When you say that I think you're going to go away. But where could you go that would be any different?'

'This is the only big city in the world that was established by convicts on the one side and bent soldiers on the other. I'm sorry. I'll shut up. You must be feeling terrible.'

Gia's straw made a loud sucking noise at the bottom of her glass.

'Only when you talk like that.'

'I've stopped. I didn't know it made you anxious.'

Gia picked the maraschino cherry from her drink and ate it. 'Maria, I feel great. I'm alive and no one wants to kill me. I'm going to take a week off and just go to the theatre and the art galleries and have lunch with my friends.' She picked up the orange-slice umbrella and ate the flesh from it. She looked around for a waiter but they were all – Peter too – eating. 'You saved my life,' she said.

Maria shook her head: 'No.'

'But you did.'

'They weren't really going to kill you,' Maria said.

Gia narrowed her eyes.

'Oh Gia, I'm sorry. I didn't mean that.'

'I know that's what you think.' Gia drained her glass for the second time and waved her hand.

'I think it's horrible. I think it's really frightening.' Maria said. She held her friend's forearm and stroked its pale soft underside. 'Who can ever know if they would have or not?'

'I'm sure you would have behaved quite differently.'

'No. I think you were amazing. I wouldn't have known what to do. You were very brave.'

'What's your fellow's name?'

Maria Takis bit her lip and raised her eyebrow and coloured. She dabbed her wide mouth with a paper napkin. 'Which fellow?'

'Maria!'

'What?'

'Stop blushing.'

'Jack Catchprice? He's actually a classic investigation target.'

'Is he nice looking?'

Maria smiled, a tight pleased smile that made her cheekbones look even more remarkable.

'Is he married?'

Maria looked up and saw Jack Catchprice walk into the Brasserie. He was ten minutes early. Jack was talking to Peter. Peter was pointing out towards the garden. Maria shook her head at Gia.

'Is this what I think it is? Maria what have you been *doing*?'

'Shush. Don't look. I've been trying to tell you. Don't look, but he's here.'

It was not a good idea to say 'Don't look' to Gia. She turned immediately, and looked straight back, grinning.

'Maria,' she said in that same whisper that had started the trouble with Wally Fischer, 'he's a doll.'

42

Jack had asked her out while they stood in the kitchen of his mother's apartment. Rain fell from the overhang above the rusting little steel-framed window behind the sink. The rain was loud and heavy. It fell from the corrugated roof like strings of glass beads. Water trickled through the plaster-sheeted ceiling and fell in fat discoloured drops on to a bed of soggy toast and dirty dishes. A red setter tried to mount Jack's leg.

'Listen,' she said, 'I can't go out with clients.'

'I'm not your client.'

'But you have an interest, you know.'

'I have *no* interest, I swear.' He looked around and screwed his face up. 'I got out of this family a long, long time ago. Their problems are their problems.'

'Really?'

'Really,' he said. 'Cross my heart. Check the share register.'

'Well,' she said, but the truth was that she had already clearly communicated, through a series of well-placed 'I's', her single status, and she would like to be taken out to dinner more than anything else she could think of. 'I leave Franklin at three. It's a little too early for dinner.'

'God, no, not Franklin. I didn't mean Franklin.'

'I have drinks with a friend at the Blue Moon Brasserie at six.' She did not say it was the attractive friend Jack had already talked to.

'The Blue Moon Brasserie?' he asked. 'In Macleay Street? I could meet you there. We could eat there. Or we could walk over to Chez Oz. I was thinking of Chez Oz. It's round the corner.' And when she hesitated, 'It doesn't matter. We can decide later.'

'Oh, I can't . . .' Maria's face betrayed herself – she would dearly love to be taken to Chez Oz.

'Jack,' Mrs Catchprice was calling him from the other room. 'I hope you're behaving yourself.'

'I have to drop in on my father at half-past seven. He's certainly not round the corner. Nowhere near Chez Oz.'

'Then I can meet you at the Brasserie and we could have a drink and then I could drive you to your father's. You like Wagner? You could put your feet up. I could play you some nice Wagner. It doesn't have to be Wagner. I have the Brahms Double Concerto that is very appropriate to this weather. I have a nice car. I would wait for you while you visited your father. I won't be bored.'

She did not prickle at the 'nice car' although she knew he had a Jaguar from John Sewell's. She had sat in John Sewell's herself, two years before, copying down the names of Jaguar owners as starting points for tax investigations.

'I'll be driving my own car to the Brasserie.'

'I'll drive you back to it after dinner.'

'My father lives in Newtown.'

'That's O.K., I can find Newtown.'

'I mean it's not a very exciting place to sit in a parked car for half an hour.'

'Oh,' he smiled. His whole face crinkled. She liked the way he did that. He had nice lines around his mouth and eyes and his face, tilted a little, had a very intent, listening sort of quality which she found immensely attractive. 'I think I can manage half an hour in Newtown.'

She was in the middle of an investigation of his family business. She might be the one who made his mother homeless, but he was flirting with her, more than flirting and she was reciprocating. He was the first man to treat her as a sexual being since she began to 'show'.

'Listen,' she said. 'It is an odd situation in Newtown. I have to sneak into Newtown sort of incognito. I might have to ask you not to park outside the house.'

He pursed his lips and raised his eyebrows comically.

'It's ridiculous,' she said, 'I know.'

'I used to go out with a Jewish woman called Layla. She was twenty-four and I was nearly thirty but I could never take her home. I had to sit outside in the car.'

'Yes, but you're not "going out" with me,' Maria smiled.

'No, of course not.' He coloured.

What was weird was that this embarrassment was pleasing. Indeed, the prospect of this 'date' gave everything that happened for the rest of the day – including her second serious chat with Mrs Catchprice about the company books, and her unpleasant phone conversation with her section leader where she requested one more day on the job – a pleasant secret corner, this thing to look forward to.

She had never planned to introduce him to her father, or have him sit in that little kitchen drinking brandy. That only happened because they were a little late and because, even after two circuits, the only parking spot in Ann Street was right in front of George Takis's house where he was – in spite of all the rain – hosing down the green concrete of his small front garden. It was the mark of his widowed state – it was the woman who normally hosed the concrete.

Maria got out of the Jaguar in front of him but he was so taken by the car he did not recognize her.

'Ba-Ba.'

'Maria?'

Maria started to walk towards the house but George was drawn towards the Jaguar. When she called to him he did not even turn but patted the air by his thigh, as though he was bouncing a ball.

'Ba-Ba, please.'

But he knew there was a man in that sleek, rain-jewelled car and he became very still and concentrated, a little hunched and poke-necked, as he stalked round the front of it, not like a poor man in braces and wet carpet slippers who is shamed in the face of wealth, but like a man coming to open a present.

George Takis opened the door of Jack Catchprice's Jaguar and solemnly invited him out into the street.

It was not yet dark in Ann Street. You could still see the flaking paint sign of the 'Perfect Chocolate' factory which made the cul de sac. You could see the expressions on the neighbours' faces. They were out enjoying the break from the rain, sitting on the verandas of the narrow cottages which gave the street its chequered individuality — white weather-board, pale blue aluminium cladding, red brick with white-painted mortar, etc., etc. The Katakises and the Papandreous were sitting out, and the Lebanese family were in their front-room sitting down to dinner in the bright light of a monster television. Stanley Dargour, who had married Daphne Katakis's tall daughter, was redoing the brake linings on his Holden Kingswood but he was watching what was happening in front of George Takis's house, they all were, and George Takis not only did not seem to care, but seemed to revel in it.

It was not yet dark, only gloomy, but the street lights came on. George Takis left his daughter alone on the street next to the mail box with the silhouetted palm tree stencilled on it. The light was really weak and still rather orange but Maria suffered a terrible and unexpected feeling of abandonment. There was nothing to protect her from the judgement of the street. She could not run back into the house, she could not come forward, and yet she had to. Stanley Dargour had put down his tools – she heard them clink – and was standing so that he could get a better view of her over the top of the Jaguar.

Jack Catchprice had stayed in the car with the door shut even while the Tax Inspector's father had come directly towards him. He had blackened windows and thought he knew what Maria Takis wanted of him, but then the door was opened and he had no choice but to turn the music off and get out.

They shook hands under the gaze of the street.

Then George Takis put his hand up on Jack's shoulder and guided him into the house. Sissy Katakis called out something to Ortansia Papandreou but Maria did not catch it properly.

In the painfully tidy neon-lit kitchen George Takis made Maria and Jack Catchprice sit on chromium chairs while he fussed around in cupboards finding preserves to put out in little flat glass dishes and then he poured brandy into little tumblers which bore sandblasted images of vine leaves – the Easter glasses. He watched the stranger all the time, casting him shy looks. He was small and shrunken as an olive, his eyebrows angrily black and his hair grey and his whiskers too, in the pits and folds of his shrunken, fierce face.

'So,' he said at last. 'You got a British car, Mr Catchprice.'

'Yes.'

'I used to make them cars,' said George Takis. 'When the British Motor Corporation became Leyland, we made some of these in Sydney. They are a good motor car, eh? They got a smell to them? That leather?'

'Yes.'

'No rattles. Tight as a drum. You could float it on the harbour, it wouldn't sink.'

Maria frowned. She knew they had made a grand total of ten Jaguars in Australia and that the men had been mortified to be told that the production was ceasing because the production quality was too low.

'She don't like them,' George said. 'You have one of them cars, you're a real crook. That's what she told me, mate. Now she's changed her mind, eh, mori?'

'Ba-Ba, lay off.'

'Ha-ha,' said George, so eager to make a pact with the new 'intended' that he could not worry about the feelings of the daughter he was so afraid of alienating. 'I always tell her, there are nice people have these cars. Some bastards, but not all. You know what? You know the trouble? You never met one, mori. You never had a chance to discover the truth.'

Maria said, 'That is about half true.'

'No, no,' George said, waving his finger at her in an imitation of a patriarch, topping up his glass with brandy and then Jack's. 'Completely true.'

'Half true,' said Maria. 'We never did like people with money in this house. We mostly grew up thinking they were crooks, or smart people.'

Jack smiled and nodded, but Maria thought there were strain marks on his face.

'We didn't like Athens Greeks, did we Ba-Ba? That was about the worst thing to be in our view.' She was irritated with her father.

'You've got to be careful with this brandy,' George said, adding a little to Jack's glass. 'You ever drink Greek brandy before?'

'Once or twice.'

'You've been to Greece?'

'Ba-Ba, we've got to go. I just came round to see you were O.K.'
Her father ignored her. 'So,' he asked Jack Catchprice, 'you
single? Would you like to marry my daughter?'

'Ba-Ba!'

'She looks after me real good,' George Takis said. 'Here.' He
tugged on Jack's lapel and led him to where his dinner stood, in
the brown casserole dish on the bare stove. 'Keftethes,' George
said. He lifted the lid. Jack looked in. 'Meat balls. You want to
taste? She can cook.'

'Ba-Ba,' Maria said. She was trying to laugh. She knew she was
blushing. 'Mr Catchprice is a client of mine. There's nothing going
on here, Ba-Ba. He just gave me a lift, O.K.' She rearranged the
knife and fork and place mat he had set for himself at the table.
She could not even look at Jack. She felt him sit down again at the
table. She heard him scrape the preserves from his little glass
plate.

George was spooning cold keftethes on to a dish. 'Every night
she comes, or if she can't come, she calls.' He fossicked in the
cutlery drawer and found a knife and fork. 'I know people have to
pay some service so if they get a heart attack there is someone will
know. I said to the fellow, mate, I don't need one. I'm a Greek.'

He placed the cold keftethes in front of Jack who sat looking
back at him with an odd, shining, smiling face.

'You interested?' George asked.

Jack picked up the fork. Maria put her hand out and took it from
him.

'Sige apo ti zoemou,' she said.

She stood up. Her ears were hot. She carried the fork, not the
knife, back to the cutlery drawer. She picked up her handbag and
put it over her shoulder. Her father – standing alone in the middle
of the lonely neat kitchen where her mother's eyes had once
burned so brightly – she was sorry, already, for what she had said:
keep out of my life.

In English she said: 'You're very naughty, Ba-Ba.'

'She works too hard,' George said.

She should not have said it. It was wrong to see him take this
from a daughter. She was shocked to see his eyes, not angry at all,

a grate with the fire gone out. 'I'll be back tomorrow,' she said. 'O.K., Ba-Ba?'

Jack was standing, buttoning his suit jacket, tucking in his tie.

'You come again,' George said to him. 'We'll drink brandy together.'

Jack smiled this shining, bright smile. You could not guess what it might mean.

George detained them a fraction too long in the harsh light of the front door and then again, at the open door of the Jaguar he made a fuss of retracting the seat belt and making some suggestions about the best seat position. Jack Catchprice watched tolerantly while George Takis adjusted and readjusted the rake of the seat while the street looked on.

'O.K.,' he said, crouching by the window when they were leaving. 'Now just relax, O.K.?'

He stepped back, still crouching, with his hand held palm upwards in a wave. *Sige apo ti zoemou.* She should never have said it.

The Jaguar window slid up silkily without Maria touching the handle. The car slowly rolled out of Ann Street.

'Oh God,' said Maria. 'I'm sorry.'

'Don't be sorry. I liked him. It was fine.'

Jack braked at the corner beside the cut glass and gilt jumble of fittings of PLAKA LIGHTING and nosed the car into the eight o'clock congestion of King Street. He pressed a button and the Brahms Double Concerto engulfed her in a deep and satisfying melancholy so alien to Ann Street in Newtown.

'Greeks!' she said.

'It must be hard for him.'

'Yes, it's hard for him,' Maria said.

'But he doesn't have to have the baby, right?'

She laughed.

'There's a sleeping bag down there,' Jack said. 'You might like to rest your legs on it.'

She accepted gratefully. She shifted her legs up on to the top of the feather-soft cylinder and kicked her shoes off. The seat was absolutely perfect. She shut her eyes. The music in his car sounded better than the music in her house. The smell of leather engulfed her.

She said: 'I hope you weren't too embarrassed.'

He turned the music down a little in order to hear her better.

'He is so obviously smitten with you. It was very touching. It's impossible to be embarrassed by that.'

'I would have thought we were at our most embarrassing when we were smitten.'

'Oh no,' said Jack, turning right into Broadway. He turned to her and smiled. 'Never,' he said. 'How are the legs?'

Maria was silent for a moment. 'Do you entertain a lot of pregnant women?' she asked.

'Sorry?' he asked, discomforted.

He passed his hand over his mouth as if hiding his expression and she had the sense that she had touched an 'issue'. He was too good-looking, too solicitous. His interest in her legs suddenly seemed so unnatural as to be almost creepy.

'Not a lot of men would think about the legs.'

'My partner's wife is due next week. I just drove her home before I picked up you.'

It was not the last time Maria would judge herself to be too tense, too critical with Jack Catchprice, to feel herself too full of prejudices and preconceptions that would not let her accept what was pleasant and generous in his character. She sought somehow to make recompense for her negativity.

She said: 'It's a lovely car. Do you get a lot of pleasure from it?'

'Well it's a sort of addiction.'

'A pleasant addiction?'

'I never had one you could say was pleasant. It's an addiction – it's something I think I can't do without, but every now and then I "feel" it – just like you're feeling it now. Not often.'

'I don't think I'd ever get used to it.'

'Oh you would.'

'And it wouldn't make me any happier?'

'No. Make you worse. Make you a *bad* person, an Athens Greek.'

'Oh,' Maria said. 'I thought my father made me seem like a vindictive person, full of envy. I'm sure that it all fitted so neatly together – how I would obviously end up being a Tax Officer.'

'He didn't make you seem like that at all.'

'No?'

'Not at all. You came out of it very well – calling every night, cooking his meals. A little moralistic perhaps,' he raised his eyebrows, 'but that's no bad thing,' he smiled. 'It's actually attractive.'

He was coming on to her, and she was excited, and suspicious.

'I do have a moralistic streak, but I do like this car. I'm surprised how much I like being in it.' She didn't say how surprised she was to be having dinner with a property developer.

'You shouldn't be surprised. None of these addictive things would be addictive if they didn't make you feel wonderful. Do you think crack is unpleasant?'

'I bet it's wonderful.'

'How about Chez Oz?'

'I bet that's wonderful too.'

'Have you ever been there?'

'Hey,' Maria said, 'I'm a Tax Officer. I'm doing very well on $36,000 a year. You work it out. How am I going to get to Chez Oz? I don't know anyone who could afford Chez Oz. I was thinking about this last night, and you know – almost everyone I know works for the Australian Tax Office, or did. That's how it is in the Tax Office. We divide the world up into the people who work there and the people who don't. Tax Office people socialize with Tax Office people. They marry each other. They have affairs with each other. When I was younger I used to be critical of that, but now I sympathize with them. Now I usually lie about what I do, because I can't bear the thought of the jokes. You know?'

'I can imagine. It must be horrible.'

'It's rotten. And people, mostly, are not well informed about tax. So I live in a ghetto. Something like Chez Oz I read about in the paper and I see on American Express bills when I audit.'

'What does that do?'

'Well, let's say it makes me pay attention.'

'Good,' said Jack. 'That's perfect. I want you to pay attention.'

43

Maria dressed well. On the one hand, she knew she dressed well, but on the other she feared she did not understand things about clothes that other women knew instinctively. She had invented her own appearance, part of which was based in a romantic, 'artistic' idea about herself, part in defiance of her mother (an embrace of

'Turkishness'), part in the Afghan-hippy look of the early seventies which had never ceased to influence her choices. She collected red, black, gold, chunky silver jewellery with such a particular taste that she was, as Gia said, beyond fashion. She had herself so firmly into a look that she could not choose anything that did not, in some way, fit within its eccentric borders. She did not know how to dress differently, and whenever she tried – her black suit, for instance – she felt inauthentic. She was as inextricably linked with her wardrobe as men often were with their motor car.

In her parents' house there had been no money for female fashion. Her mother wore black as she had in Letkos and fashion was something you made over a noisy sewing machine in Surry Hills. Maria had grown up in a house without clothes just as someone would grow up in a house without books or music. It had affected her sister Helen in the way you could see – she bought clothes at Grace Bros at sale times, and so even though she and Con now owned five electrical discount stores Helen still dressed like a piece-goods worker from Surry Hills.

As Maria entered the very small foyer at Chez Oz, pressed in behind the bare tanned shoulders of women with blonde coifed hair and little black dresses, she suddenly felt herself to be vulgar and inelegant, and not in the right place.

'Am I dressed well enough?' she asked her partner who, although she had not even thought about it in Franklin, so obviously was. Now she saw the insouciant crumpled look was 100 per cent silk.

'Perfectly.'

She was thirty-four years old and thought herself at ease with herself, but now she was self-conscious, and on edge. Through a gap between the bodies in front of her she saw a famous crumpled face – Daniel Makeveitch – a celebrated artist whose work she much admired. She was shocked, not merely to see him in the flesh for the first time, but by the juxtaposition of this old Cassandra with these black-dressed women with expensive hair. *He comes here?* He was their enemy, surely?

They were guided through the restaurant. Maria hardly saw anything. She felt herself being stared at. They sat beside the glass brick wall she had seen glowing from the street.

'The clones are looking at you,' Jack said, breaking his bread roll immediately and spilling crumbs across the cloth. Maria saw she was indeed being looked at.

'They're anxious,' Jack said. 'They're thinking – what if this is the new look? How will I know?'

'Is it too extreme?' said Maria who realized slowly she was the only person, of either sex, whose clothes were not predominantly black or grey. Many of the men, like Jack, wore black shirts. 'I suppose I look like a circus to them.'

'You expose them as the bores they are.'

'You know them?'

'A few. Now,' he picked up the wine list, 'I take it we have to throw this away.'

'I'm permitted one glass.'

'Then we'll both limit ourselves to one glass of something wonderful.'

Alistair would never have done that, not even Alistair at his charming best. He would have confidently gone on doing exactly what he wanted to do and assume that this was why you would like him, which was mostly true. He was gentle and loyal but he also had a will of iron, and when she felt Jack Catchprice bend his will to hers she felt a gooeyness at her centre which surprised her.

He guided her through the menu and she was amused to find herself enjoying the experience of being pampered until he said: 'You should have protein, am I right?'

'Yes,' she said, 'you're right.' But it made her distrust him and he saw this, she thought, because his smile faltered a second and his mouth seemed momentarily weak and vulnerable. She was immediately sorry.

'This restaurant is perfect for protein,' he said, looking at his menu. 'It is famous for protein.'

If she had known him better she would have laid her hand on his arm and said, 'sorry'. Instead she did something she had never done in her life – encouraged him to order for her. He chose oysters from Nelson Bay and, for their main course, duck breast with a half bottle of 1966 Haut Brion. It was, admittedly, a little more than one glass each.

Maria sipped the Haut Brion and smiled. 'I can't believe this.'

'The wine?'

'You,' she said.

'What about me?'

'From Catchprice Motors in Franklin.'

'From that terrible place, you mean?'

'I didn't mean that at all. Although,' she paused, not quite sure if she should smile or even if she should continue, 'you seem so totally unconnected with them. You're Cathy McPherson's brother. It seems impossible.'

'I'm like my mother, physically.'

'But you're not *like* any of them.'

'Well they got stuck there. They didn't want to be stuck there, but by the time they realized it they had no other choices. The environment affects you. If I'm different it was because I had to get out. If I hadn't got out, I would have been just like them, different of course, but the same too.'

'But you got out. That makes you different.'

'You know why I am sitting here tonight?' Jack said, wiping the corners of his very nice mouth with the crisp white napkin. 'It wasn't discontent. It was because I couldn't sing.'

She laughed expectantly.

'If I was musical, I'd still be there. Mort and me, side by side.'

'But you love music. You have great taste in music.'

'I love it, but I listen to it like an animal,' he said. 'If you want to picture how I listen, think of the dog on the HMV label. Intelligent, attentive, and ultimately – puzzled.'

'Oh dear.'

'Oh dear, exactly. No matter how many times I listen to that Wagner, I never know what's going to happen next. Every second is a surprise to me.'

'Well I guess we're all the product of little tragedies,' Maria said. 'This wine is amazing. I have never tasted wine like this in my life.'

'Mort and Cathy have really very good voices,' he said. 'Our father loved music, so he loved them. He had them up in the middle of the night to sing, not rubbish – opera. He had them singing Mozart to drunken farmers. He couldn't help himself. He'd come into the room and shake them and shake them until they were awake. He was like me though – he couldn't sing. No one ever knew this, but I found him once, in the back paddock, trying to sing. I watched him for an hour. He had sheet music. It was really terrible. One of the worst things I ever saw, like an animal trying to talk. You could not believe all the effort in the face and the terrible noise.'

'The poor man.'

'Well it's worse than what I'm saying, obviously.'

'I hear lots of bad things,' she said.

'You'll tell me your bad things, too?'

She thought: surely he doesn't want to go to bed with me. 'Yes,' she said, 'if you want.'

He cut a piece of perfect white potato and joined it to a piece of duck which he had already neatly dissected. 'He messed around with them,' he said.

'Oh.'

He tore his bread and mopped up a little gravy.

She drank from her water glass. 'How horrible.'

'He was always at them in the night. I don't really know what happened. Sometimes I think I invented it, or dreamed it. I stood beside Mort in church last Christmas and he was miming the words. He wouldn't sing out loud.'

'He told me your father was a wonderful man.'

Jack shrugged.

'And your mother?'

'Who would have any idea what goes on in that head? Who would guess what she knew or understood? But it was definitely my father who decided there was no room for me in the business. I was very hurt, at the time. Can you believe it – I cried. I really wept. All the things I'm lucky about, they hurt me at the time.' He hid his eyes in the depths of his wine glass. 'Your turn.'

'I sort of lived with a man for a long time and he had a wife and I wanted a baby and I made a choice and this is it.'

'You were happy with him?'

'Yes,' Maria said, then: 'No.' She smiled. 'I think I was rather depressed for rather a long time. I'm just noticing it. I think I must have got used to it.'

'Now?'

'Well, yes, now.'

'Now you're what?'

'I'm not depressed right now,' she laughed, and then looked down, unable to hold his eyes, aware of the movement of his knee an inch or two away from hers.

'Do you know who Daniel Makeveitch is?' she asked.

'A painter sitting two tables to your right.'

'You know him?'

'You mustn't seem so surprised,' he said. 'I know I'm a property developer and I even used to be a second-hand car salesman . . .'

He was smiling, but his eyes were hurt and Maria was embarrassed at what she had said.

'I'm sorry. I thought you would have mentioned it.' She put out her hand and touched his sleeve. 'When we sat down.'

'Oh,' he said, 'I used to spend a lot of time being offended, but I'm not any more.' None the less his face had closed over and showed, in the candlelight, a waxy sort of imperviousness. 'When I was a car salesman in the Paramatta Road – I worked for Janus Binder and I started buying paintings because he collected them. People were always amazed – gallery owners, people who should have known better. It was as if there was something ludicrous about car dealers having any sensitivity or feeling. But once I was a property developer, no one was surprised at all. They expect it of me. There's a great relief, socially, in not being a car dealer.'

'Like being a Tax Officer.'

'You don't even half-believe that, Maria.'

She blushed. 'In its social isolation, I meant.'

He paused and looked at her and she felt herself seen as dishonest. She blushed.

'Do you like Daniel Makeveitch's work?'

He allowed enough space to register the change of subject, but when he spoke his eyes were soft again and his manner as charming as before. 'Would I seem too *nouveau* to you if I said I owned one?'

'Oh please, Jack, do I really seem that bad? Which one?'

' "Daisy's Place",' he said.

'I'm impressed,' she said.

His lower lip made an almost prim little 'v' as he tried not to smile. 'It's only tiny.'

'What I hate,' she told him, 'is how impressed I am.' She laughed and shook her head in a way she knew, had known, since she was sixteen, made her curling black hair look wonderful. 'I hate being happy here with all these people.'

'With me too?' he smiled.

'With you too,' she said and allowed him to hold her hand a moment before she reached towards her glass of water.

44

At half-past ten on Tuesday night, Maria Takis left Chez Oz to see the Daniel Makeveitch painting at Jack Catchprice's beach house.

As Chez Oz was on Craigend Street, and as the Brahmachari ashram was around the corner, it was not astonishing that they should, in hurrying out into the night, bump into Vishnabarnu on the pavement, but Maria was astonished none the less.

'Hi,' she said, with an exuberance and a familiarity totally new in her relationship with Vish. 'Small world.'

'Not really,' said Vish, and nodded at Jack.

He was with another Hare Krishna, a soft, olive-skinned man of forty or so who had noticeably crooked teeth and a scholarly stoop.

'The ashram is here,' Vishnabarnu pointed to the grey stucco block of flats. 'The temple is round the corner from the fire station. I walk past here six times a day.'

'That's an ashram?' Maria smiled. She was excited and happy. 'I always imagined something more exotic.'

The other Hare Krishna took a step away and stared off into the night.

'I could have given you a lift to town,' she said.

'Yes.'

'Well, I guess I'll see you tomorrow?'

Vishnabarnu looked at his friend. Something passed between them. When Vish looked back to Maria he was almost laughing.

'No,' he said.

The older Hare Krishna began to walk towards the ashram.

'This is goodbye.' Vish shook Maria's hand. 'Excuse me.'

And then, without saying a word to his uncle, he followed his friend, who was already in the dark, arched doorway of the grey stuccoed building.

'He thinks I'm the devil,' Jack said as he let her into the Jaguar.

'I don't like them generally,' Maria said. 'The way they treat their women . . .'

'It's about what you'd expect from people trying to duplicate life in a sixteenth-century Indian village . . .'

'But they do feed the street kids in the Cross and also when your sister was trying to have your mother committed. Yes, that happened on Monday. He was very good then. You get the feeling he's capable of doing what's needed.'

'What was needed?'

'Well not much as it turned out. But you get the feeling from him that he is timid but that he would go to the wall with you. That's a very impressive quality.' She paused. 'Even if he does think you're the devil.'

They drove down past the lighted car showrooms in William Street with their back-lit, bunny-suited, teenage prostitutes and the long, slow line of cruising traffic in the kerbside lane. They turned right down into Woolloomooloo beneath the Eastern Suburbs railway bridge and up beside the art gallery and on to the Cahill Expressway which cut like a prison wall across the tiny mouth of Port Jackson.

'If you look at the Cahill Expressway,' Jack said, 'you can understand almost all of this city. I had an investor here from Strasbourg last week. It was his observation. That you can see how corrupt the city is from looking at it.'

'Because of the Expressway?'

'Things like the Expressway.'

'Was this a good thing or a bad thing, from an investor's point of view?'

He looked at her, bristling a little. 'A disappointing thing,' he said at last. He was silent for a minute as they came up the rock cutting and on to Sydney Harbour Bridge, but then he went on more softly. 'You can read a city. You can see who's winning and who's losing. In this city,' he said, 'the angels are not winning.'

'I'm sorry,' she said. 'Did I sound offensive?'

'No,' he said, but she was sure he was sulking and she had, as they drove beneath the high, bright windows of insurance companies and advertising agencies in North Sydney, one of those brief periods of estrangement that marked her feelings for Jack Catchprice.

'It's true I go to work in the swamp each day,' he said, 'but I do try to wipe my boots when I come into decent people's homes.'

'Oh relax,' Maria said. 'Please.'

'I am relaxed,' he smiled. 'Well, no, I'm not relaxed. I probably want you to like me too much.'

'I like you,' she said uneasily.

At the top of the hill above The Spit, he took the long, lonely road which cuts across the back of French's Forest.

'I never came this way,' she said.

'You normally go through Dee. Why? This is much nicer.'

Maria did not like the countryside particularly. She did not like the lonely gravel roads she saw disappearing into the bush on either side of the road. The signposts to places like Oxford Falls did not sound romantic to her, but reminded her how foolish she was being taking this drive with a single man who kept special pillows for pregnant women's legs.

He was a Catchprice, for Chrissakes. He came from a disturbed and difficult home. Anything could have happened to him. It was stupid to place herself in this situation to see a painting she had already seen in the Makeveitch retrospective at the art gallery of New South Wales.

He began to play Miles Davis, 'Kind of Blue'. She imagined his father holding his sheet music, roaring like a beast in a fairy tale. She loved this music, but now she knew he was tone deaf it suggested a sort of inauthenticity and forced an unfavourable comparison with Alistair, who was musically gifted and whom she saw, in the soft green glow of the Jaguar's instrument lights, Jack Catchprice rather resembled.

'It's farther than I remembered,' she said, a little later as they emerged from the bush into the brightly lit coastal strip at Narrabeen.

'Are you tired?'

'A little, I guess.'

'You could sleep there if you wanted. There's a guest room.'

'Oh no,' she said.

'Or I could take you back.'

'I'll just stay a moment and look at the painting.'

But it was not the painting but the house that captivated her, and when she was standing there at last, she could not fear a man who lived in a house whose main living-room had an arched roof which opened like an eyelid to the night sky, whose side walls were of pleated canvas, a house whose strong, rammed-earth back wall promised all the solidity of a castle but whose substance then evaporated before her eyes as Jack, clambering first on to the roof, and then round the walls, opened the house to the cabbage tree palms which filled the garden and in whose rustling hearts one could hear brush-tailed possums.

It was a night of clouds and moon, of dark and light, and as Maria sat in a rocking-chair in the middle of the teak-floored living-room she felt as she had previously felt one late summer afternoon in the Duomo in Milan, a feeling of such serendipitous peace that she felt she could, if she would let herself, just weep. She sat there rocking gently, looking up at the moon-edged clouds scudding across the belt of Orion and all the dense bright dust of the Milky Way while Jack Catchprice made camomile in a small raku teapot.

'You should develop Sydney like this,' she said when he came back, kneeling beside her in a sarong and bare feet. She rocked back and forth. 'I didn't know that places like this even existed on the earth.' A moment later she asked: 'Is the architect famous?'

'Only with architects. Watch the tea. I'm putting it just here. When you've finished it, we can look at the painting.'

He was standing at the back of the rocking-chair and she stood, to be able to talk to him properly.

'Look,' he said, 'there goes the possum family.'

She turned. Along the top of the wall, at the place where the eyelid of roof opened to the sky, she could make out a brush-tailed possum.

'See,' he said, 'the baby is on her back.'

He was standing behind her, with his two hands holding her swollen belly and nuzzling her neck. 'It's very beautiful,' he said.

In another situation the sentimentality of this observation might have made her hostile, but now it actually touched her. She began to do exactly what she had planned she would not do and as she, now, turned and kissed him, she felt not the weight of her pregnancy but the quite overwhelming ache of desire.

'Oh,' she said. 'Aren't you a surprise.'

He had a very beautiful mouth. Up close he smelt of apples. She kissed him hungrily but insistently, hanging on his neck and feeling him take her whole weight in his shoulders and in his arms. She was not willing to be parted, made a small humming sound of pleasure in the back of her throat while mosquitoes drew blood from her shoulder and the back of his hands.

He noticed first. He held up his thumb and forefinger to show her a crumpled wing and bent proboscis, a smear of blood.

'Normally I light coils,' he said, 'but I think they may be too toxic . . . for this fellow.'

'Oh yes,' she said. He made her feel negligent.

'I have mosquito netting,' he said. And before she understood what he meant he had led her along the galley-like kitchen and down into a bedroom which was hung with a cobalt blue silk net.

'Hey, hey,' she said when she realized his intention. 'Whoa, Jack, stop now.'

But he was already inside the net. He sat cross-legged, smiling at her.

'There are no mosquitoes in here.'

'I'm not going in there,' she said.

'Just a cuddle,' he said.

She laughed. There were mosquitoes in the air around her hair. She could feel them more than hear them.

He grinned. He flicked on a switch at the bed head. A light illuminated the cabbage tree palms in the garden. Then he lit three fat yellow candles above the bed head. Their flames were reflected in the pool immediately outside the bedroom window.

'Jack, I'm too old for this bachelor pad stuff.'

'I never bring strangers here,' he said.

'I bet,' she said, but then she thought, what the hell. She got in under the net but now she was there the spell was broken. She had been so happy kissing him but now she was inside the net she was lumpy and graceless. She was too big. There was nowhere to put her feet.

'Look, Jack,' she said. 'Look at me.' She snapped at the support stockings which had hitherto been hidden under her long dress. 'Do you really wish to seduce this? You're a nice man. Why don't we wait a few months?'

'You look beautiful.'

'My back hurts. I can't even see my feet when I stand up. Even while I'm kissing you I've got this thing inside me kicking and nudging me for attention. I can't concentrate.'

'We could try. We could just lie here.'

'I don't know you.' She put her arm around him, but she felt the wrong shape to kiss sitting down. 'You don't know me. It's not smart for people to just jump into bed any more.'

'Is this a discussion about the Unmentionable?'

'I don't want to offend you.'

'You don't offend me at all. We could play it safe.'

'Safer, not actually safe,' she smiled. While still involved in her monogamous adulterous relationship with Alistair, she had complacently pitied those who must go through this. She had never thought that the tone of the conversation might be quite so tender.

He touched her on the forehead between her eyes and ran his finger down the line of her nose. 'I'll make love to you 100 per cent safe.'

She had never imagined you could say these words and still feel tender, but now she was lying on her side and he was lying on his and he had those clear blue Catchprice eyes and such sweet crease marks around his eyes. She touched them. These were what women called 'crow's feet'. They were beautiful.

'Is there 100 per cent?' she asked.

'Is this safe?'

'Mmm?'

'Does this feel safe?'

'Jack, don't.'

'Don't worry. I'll keep my word. Is this safe?'

'Of course.'

She let him undress her and caress her swollen body. God, she thought – this is how people die.

'Is this beautiful to you?'

'Oh yes,' he said. 'You glisten.'

He cradled her stomach in his hands and kissed her back and then he turned her and kissed her stomach, not once but slowly, as if he was following the points on a star map that only he could see.

Maria unbuttoned his shirt.

'Oh,' she said, 'you're very beautiful.' He had a tanned chest covered with tight curled golden hairs. He was already releasing his sarong. She began to kiss him, to kiss his chest, to nuzzle her face among the soft apple-sweet hairs, discovering as she did so a hunger for the scents and textures of male skin.

'Get the condom,' she heard herself say.

'You sure?'

'Mmm.'

'I've got it.'

'I'm crazy,' she said.

It was the second night she had stayed up late with members of the Catchprice family.

45

'Why would you ruin your life?' Benny said, smiling, holding the sawn-off shot gun an inch or two above his expensively tailored knees.

Sarkis took down his velvet jacket from the wire coat hanger with arms that trembled and twitched so much he could not fully control them. His legs were not as unreliable, but they hurt more and the pains in the legs were deeper, hotter, more specific – the left ankle would turn out to be gashed like a knife wound.

He looked at the ugly jagged cut across the barrels of the gun. 'I don't care about my life,' he said.

He had thought of all the things he would do to this juvenile delinquent for all the time he was held captive on that humiliating board. He had thought it through the terror of the dark, through the drum-beat of his headache. In just eight hours he had turned into someone no decent person could understand. He was the Vietnamese man who had gone crazy with the meat cleaver. He was the Turk who had thrown petrol over the children in the day care centre. He did not care what he did or what happened to him because of it. He looked at the sawn-off end of the gun. It was cut so badly that there was a sliver of metal bent over like a fish hook.

The pale and pretty Benny took a plastic shopping bag and laid it across his knees so he could rest the oil-slick gun there for a moment. He had pale blue cat's eyes, as full of odd lights as an opal.

'You're my F&I man,' he said.

'I'm going to kill you,' Sarkis said, rubbing his wrists and opening and closing his hands which were still very white and puffy, like things left too long in water. They did not have the strength to squeeze an orange.

'You're my F&I man.'

Benny held the shot gun up with the right hand and pulled something out from under the couch with his left. He threw it out towards Sarkis so that it fell half on the wooden planks and half in the iridescent water beneath them – a bright blue collapsible umbrella. 'You'll need your suit dry in the morning.'

Sarkis stooped and picked up the umbrella. It was cheap and flimsy and was useless as a weapon.

'You're going to jail, you silly prick.'

'I'm going to jail – you're going to kill me – make up your mind,' Benny smiled. If he was afraid or nervous about the consequences of what he had done, the only thing that showed it was his lack of colour, his pale, clammy glow. 'You've got a job,' he said. 'You think about that for a moment, Sam. You're off the street. You're going to be an F&I man. Do you understand that? Your life has just changed completely.'

Sarkis bit his pale forefinger to make it feel something. 'You're going to have to carry that gun a long time, junior.'

'Oh come on, give it up. It's *over*.'

'It's not over,' said Sarkis. 'You don't understand me. You don't have the brains to know who I am.'

'Hey . . .'

'You do this to me, it can't just be "over". You think this is "over", you're retarded.'

'Hey,' the boy said and did something with the gun which made it click-clack. 'My stupid teachers told me I was stupid. My stupid father thinks I'm stupid. But I'll tell you two things you can rely on. Number one: I'm going to run this business. Number two: you're going to be my F&I man.' Maybe he saw what he had done. His voice rose, it changed its tone, although you could not say it was anything as strong as pleading. 'You'll be able to drive a car,' Benny said, 'eat at restaurants, order any fucking thing you want.'

Sarkis tried to spit but his mouth was dry and all that came out were a few white bits. 'I'm going to kill you,' he said. 'I won't need a gun.'

'You're going to kill two hundred thou a year?' Benny stood, and smiled. 'Jesus, Sam, if I'd known you were going to get this upset . . .'

'You'd what?' he said.

Benny frowned. 'You don't get it, do you? I'm going to transform your life.' He looked very young and not very bright. There was perspiration on his upper lip and forehead.

Sarkis groaned.

Benny's brow contracted further: 'I could have chosen anyone . . .'

Sarkis did not bother to remind him it was Mrs Catchprice who had chosen him. The gun was so close. The thought he could grab it and twist it away was very tempting, but also stupid.

'All you need to remember,' Benny was saying, 'you just learned – I'm the boss, and you never contradict me on the job.'

'How can you be the boss?' Sarkis said. 'How old are you? Sixteen? I bet you don't even have a driving licence.'

Benny held the gun out with his right hand while he moved a step towards the wall. Sarkis thought, he's an actor: if he fires that now he'll break his wrist. With his left hand (smiling all the time) Benny unscrewed the wide-necked jar where a fat brown king snake lay coiled on itself in a sea of tea-coloured liquid. He took a black plastic cap from an aerosol can and dipped it into the liquid which he then raised to his red, perfect lips, and drank.

'That's my licence,' Benny said, 'I live and breathe it. Comprendo?'

Sarkis comprendoed nothing. He watched Benny smirk and wipe his lips and walk towards the cellar door, backwards, across the planks, never once seeming to look down. When he was at the door he transferred the gun to both hands and held it hard against his shoulder.

'Say you're my F&I man,' he said.

Sarkis looked at his eyes and saw his brows contract and knew: he's going to murder me.

'Say it,' Benny's chin trembled.

'I'm your F&I man.'

'We start fresh tomorrow. O.K. You understand me? Eight-thirty.'

'I'll be here,' Sarkis said. 'I promise.'

Benny unlocked the bolts on the rusty metal door and swung it open. Sarkis felt the cool, clear chill of the normal world. He limped up the steps towards the rain, but all the time he felt the dull heat of the gun across his shoulder blades and not until he was finally through the labyrinth of the Spare Parts Department, in the dark lane-way leading to the workshop, did he realize he was too badly hurt to run. He limped slowly home through the orange-lighted rain, ashamed.

Wednesday

46

Jack Catchprice woke with his prize beside him in the bed, her mouth open, her chin a little slack, her leg around the spare pillow he had fetched for her just before dawn. He put his hand out to touch her belly, and then withdrew it.

He knew then he was going to keep her, and the child too, of course, the child particularly – another man's child did not create an obstacle – it had almost the opposite effect. She had arrived complete. She was as he would have dreamed her to be – with a child that was not, in any way, a reproduction of himself.

It was all he could do not to touch her, wake her, talk to her and he slid sideways out of the bed as if fleeing his own selfish happiness. He lifted the veil of mosquito netting and put his feet on the floor.

The walls were open to the garden and he could almost have touched the cabbage tree palms dripping dry after the night of rain. The new pattern of wet summers had depressed him, but now he found in the rotting smells of his jungle garden such deep calm, such intimations of life and death, of fecundity and purpose that he knew he could, had it been necessary, have extracted happiness from hailstones.

The sun was shining, at least for now. He could roll back the roof and wear his faded silk Javanese sarong and pad across the teak floor in bare feet and watch the tiny skinks slither across the floor in front of him and see the red-tailed cockatoos and listen to the high chatter of the lorikeets as they pursued their neurotic, fluttering, complaining lives in the higher branches of his neighbour's eucalyptus.

He made coffee, he looked at the garden, he let the Tax Inspector sleep past seven, eight, nine o'clock. When it came to nine, he phoned his office.

The woman's voice which answered his office phone was deep and rather dry.

'Bea,' he said, 'we're going to have to cancel Lend Lease this morning.'

A long silence.

'Bea . . .'

'I hear you,' she said.

'So could you please tell the others . . .'

'What do you want me to tell them? That they worked two months for nothing?'

'Sure,' Jack smiled. 'That's perfect. Also, if you could call Michael McGorgan at Lend Lease.'

'I suppose I tell him you've fallen in love?'

Jack's lips pressed into the same almost prim little 'v' they had made last night, when he told her about Makeveitch's painting. How could he tell Bea – he had been given the impossible thing.

'All I hope,' Bea said, 'is this one doesn't have a PhD.'

Jack finished his call with his face and eyes creased up from smiling. He walked barefoot through the garden to borrow bacon and eggs from the peevish widow of the famous broadcaster who lived next door.

When the bacon was almost done and the eggs were sitting, broken, each one in its own white china cup, he went to the Tax Inspector and kissed her on her splendid lips, and wrapped her shining body in a kimono and brought her, half-webbed in sleep, to wait for her breakfast in the garden. She smelled of almond oil and apricots.

'You know what time it is?' she said as he brought her the bacon and eggs.

'Yes,' he said. 'I hope you like your eggs like this.'

'You really should have woken me.'

He sat opposite her and passed her salt and pepper. 'Pregnant women need their sleep.'

She looked at him a long time, and he felt himself not necessarily loved, but rather weighed up, as if she knew his secrets and did not care for them.

'Are you sorry?' he asked her.

'Of course not,' she said, but drank from her orange juice immediately, and he saw it was all less certain between them than he had hoped or believed and he had a premonition of a loss he felt he could not bear.

'Should I have woken you early?'

'Oh,' she smiled. 'Probably not. These are lovely eggs.'

He watched her eat. 'Today I'll get a blood test,' he said, a little experimentally. 'I don't know how long they take but I'll send the results to you by courier the moment they are in. I don't want you to worry about last night.'

'Oh,' she said, but her tone was positive. 'O.K., I'll do the same for you.'

'You don't need to. They've been running HIV tests on you since you were pregnant.'

'Can they do that?'

'No, but they do.'

He had no idea if what he said was true or not. He was not worried about HIV. He was concerned only with somehow establishing the presence of those qualities – scrupulousness, integrity – the lack of which he was sure went so much against him.

She leaned across and rubbed some dried shaving cream from behind his ear. 'And what else will you do?'

He took her hand and held it in both of his. 'What else are you worried by? Let me fix it for you. It's what I like most about business. Everyone is always brought down by all the obstacles and difficulties, but there's almost nothing you can't fix.'

'Not the money?'

'Not the money what?'

'Not the money you like about business. I would have thought that was very attractive?'

'Well money is important of course, in so far as it can provide.' He used this word carefully, suggesting, he hoped, ever so tangentially, accidentally almost, his credentials as *provider*. 'But after a certain stage, it's not why people work. Do you doubt that?'

'Uh-uh,' Maria said, her mouth full of bacon. 'But there's nothing you can fix for me. I tried to fix mine myself.'

'Maybe I could succeed where you've failed.'

'This is very specialized.'

'Just the same . . .'

'Jack, this is my *work*.'

'I'm a generalist,' he smiled. 'Tell me your problem.'

He could see her deciding whether to be offended by him or not. She hesitated, frowned.

'Will you tell me the truth if I ask you a direct question?'

'Yes,' he said.

215

'Did your family call you up to somehow "nobble" me?'

'My mother called me, yes. But I came to calm her down, not to nobble you.'

'Would you believe me if I told you I had already actually tried to stop their audit myself, and that my problem is I couldn't – can't?'

'Sure . . . yes, of course, if you said so.'

'Jack, this is a big secret I'm telling you . . .'

'I'm very good with secrets.'

'I'm telling you something I could be sent to jail for. I tried to stop it.'

'Why would you do that for Catchprice Motors? I wouldn't.'

'It's nothing to do with your family. It's between me and the Tax Office.'

'You don't seem a very Tax Office sort of person.'

'Well I am,' Maria reddened. 'I'm a very Tax Office sort of person. I hate all this criminal wealth. This state is full of it. It makes me sick. I see all these skunks with their car phones and champagne and I see all this homelessness and poverty. Do you know that one child in three in Australia grows up under the poverty line? You know how much tax is evaded every year? You don't need socialism to fix that, you just need a good Taxation Office and a Treasury with guts. And for a while we had both. For five years. I didn't join to piddle around rotten inefficient businesses like your family's. I never did anything so insignificant in my life. I won't do that sort of work. It fixes nothing. I'm crazy enough to think the world can change, but not like that.'

Without taking her eyes off him she put three spoons of sugar in her tea and stirred it.

'Maria,' Jack said, 'I'm on your side.'

'I'm sorry . . .'

'I know I have a car phone . . .'

'I'm sorry . . . I was offensive . . .'

'No, no, I know you don't know me very well, but I would do anything to help you.'

'Jack, you're very sweet. You were sweet last night.' She touched his face again, and traced the shape of his lips with her forefinger.

'You need someone to come and pick up your laundry in hospital . . . do you have someone who will do that for you?'

'Jack,' she started laughing, 'please . . .'

'No, really. Who's going to do that for you?'

'Jack, you are sweet. You were very sweet last night and today, I'm sorry, I was irritable with you when you didn't wake me. You wanted me to rest and I read it as a control thing. I was wrong. I'm sorry.'

'Will you have dinner with me again?' he asked her.

He could see in her eyes that it was by no means certain. She took his hand and stroked it as if to diminish the pain she was about to cause him.

'It could be early,' he said, 'I love to eat early.'

'Jack, I really do need to sleep. I'm thirty-two weeks pregnant.'

'Sure. How about tomorrow night then?'

She frowned. 'You really want to see me so soon?'

'I think the world can change too,' he said, and Maria Takis knew he was in love with her and if she was going to be honest with herself she must admit it: she was relieved to have him present in her life.

47

Sarkis could not know that he was limping back and forth across the Catchprice family history. He did not connect the names of the streets he walked along on Wednesday morning – Frieda Crescent, Mortimer Street, Cathleen Drive. He carried Benny's broken blue umbrella along their footpaths, not to reach anywhere – they did not go anywhere, they were criss-crosses on the map of an old poultry farm – but to save his pride by wasting time.

He was going back to Catchprice Motors to stop his mother going crazy, but he was damned if he would get there at eight-thirty. The air was soupy. His fresh shirt was already sticky on his skin. He walked in squares and rectangles. He passed along the line of the hall-way in the old yellow Catchprice house which was bulldozed flat after Frieda and Cacka's poultry farm was sub-divided. He crossed the fence line where Cathy had set up noose-traps for foxes. He passed over the spot – once the base of a peppercorn tree, now a concrete culvert on Cathleen Drive – where Cacka, following doctor's orders, first began to stretch the skin of his son's foreskin.

He walked diagonally across the floor of the yellow-brick shed where Frieda and Cathy used to cool the sick hens down in heat waves, trod on two of the three graves in the cats' cemetery, and, at the top of the hill where Mortimer Street met Boundary Road, walked clean through the ghost of the bright silver ten-thousand-gallon water tank in whose shadow Frieda Catchprice let Squadron Leader Everette put his weeping face between her legs.

Sarkis had pressed his suit trousers three times but they were still damp with last night's rain. His jacket was pulled very slightly out of shape by the weight of the Swiss army knife.

His mother had always been smiling, optimistic. Even in the worst of the time when his father disappeared, she never cried or despaired. When she lost her job she did not cry. She began a vegetable garden. Through the summer she fed them on pumpkin, zucchini, eggplant. She triumphed in the face of difficulties. She made friends with the stony-faced clerks in the dole office. When the car was repossessed, she spent twenty dollars on a feast to celebrate the savings they would make because of it. When Sarkis was on television, she pretended she had never seen the programme.

But on the night he was captured and tortured by Benny Catchprice, she had cooked him a special lamb dinner on the strength of a pay cheque he had no intention of receiving. She had been waiting for him six hours. He came in the door without thinking about her, only of himself – the wound in his leg, his fear, his humiliation and when he spoke, it was – he saw this later – insensitive, unimaginative.

He should have had room in his heart to imagine the pressure she lived under. It did not even occur to him.

He should also have spoken clearly about what had happened. He should have said, 'I was captured and tortured.' So she would know, immediately.

Instead he said, 'I'm not going back there.'

She began sobbing.

He tried to tell her what had happened to him, but he had said things in the wrong order and she could no longer hear anything. He tried to embrace her. She slapped his face.

He behaved like a child, he saw that later. He was not like a man, he was a baby, full of his own hurt, his own rights, his own needs. And when she slapped his face he was full of self-righteousness and anger.

He shouted at her. He said he would go away and leave her to be a whore for taxi-drivers.

The neighbours complained about the shouting as they complained about her Beatles records – by throwing potatoes on the roof. Who they were to waste food like this, who could say – they were Italians. The potatoes rolled down the tiles and bounced off the guttering.

In response she fetched a plastic basin and gave it to him.

'Here,' she said. Her eyes were loveless. 'Get food.'

He saw that she meant pick up the potatoes — that they should eat them.

'Mum. Don't be ridiculous.'

'You're embarrassed!'

'I am not embarrassed.'

'You coward,' she said. 'All you care about is your suit and your hair. You coward, you leave me starving. Zorig, Zorig.' Tears began running down her face. She had never cried for her husband like this. Sarkis had watched her comforting weeping neighbours who hardly knew Zorig Alaverdian, but she herself had not wept for him.

Sarkis could not bear it. 'Don't, please.'

He followed her to the back porch where she began struggling with her gum boots. 'If he was here we would not have to pick up potatoes,' she said. 'We would be eating beef, lamb, whatever I wrote on the shopping list I would buy. Fish, a whole schnapper, anything I wanted . . . where is the flashlight?'

'We don't need to pick up potatoes. Never. Mum, I promise, you won't go hungry.'

'Promise!' she said. She found the flashlight. He struggled to take it from her. 'You promised me a job,' she said.

He took the basin and followed her out into the rain with the flashlight and umbrella. He said nothing about the wound in his leg. He helped her pick up potatoes.

Then she sat at the table under the portrait of Mesrop Mushdotz. He helped her clean up the damaged potatoes. They peeled them, cut out the gashes, and sliced them thin to be cooked in milk.

'What is the matter with this job, Sar?' she said, more gently, but with her eyes still removed from him. 'What is not perfect?'

'It is not a question of "perfect" . . .'

'What do you think – a man to come home to his wife with no food because the job was not perfect. You think it was ever perfect for any of us? You think it is perfect for your father, right now?'

Sarkis Alaverdian left for work at ten past eight next morning. He could not bring himself to arrive at Catchprice Motors at the hour Benny had instructed him to. He walked up Frieda Crescent, Mortimer Street, Cathleen Drive. It was not until half-past ten that he finally carried the blue umbrella across the gravel car yard towards Benny Catchprice.

Even as he walked towards him he was not certain of what he would do. The smallest trace of triumph on Benny's pretty face would probably have set him off, but there was none. In fact, when Benny put out his hand to shake he seemed shy. His hand was delicate, something you could snap with thumb and finger.

'Hey,' the blond boy said, 'relax.'

Sarkis could only nod.

There was a young apprentice fitting a car radio to a Bedford van. He was squatting on the wet gravel, frowning over the instruction sheet. Benny and Sarkis stood side by side and stared at him.

Then Benny said, 'You were a hairdresser.'

Sarkis thought: he saw me on television.

'My Gran says you were a hairdresser,' Benny said.

'You got a problem with that?'

'No,' Benny said, 'no problem.' He took a few steps towards the fire escape and then turned back. 'You coming or what?'

'Depends where it is.' When he saw how Benny's gaze slid away from his, Sarkis wondered if he might actually be ashamed of what he'd done.

'Look,' Benny said, 'all that stuff is over. It's O.K.' He nodded to the fire escape. 'It's my Gran's apartment.'

'I'm not cutting your hair,' Sarkis said, 'if that's what you think.'

'No, no,' Benny said. 'My Gran wants to see you, that's all. O.K.?'

'O.K.' Sarkis put his hand into his jacket pocket and clasped the Swiss army knife and transferred it, hidden in his fist, to his trouser pocket.

48

The first thing Sarkis saw was the dolls lined up in a way you might expect, in an Australian house, to find the sporting trophies. They occupied the entire back wall of the apartment, in a deep windowless dining alcove. They were lit like in a shop.

Only when Benny turned the neon light on, did Sarkis notice Mrs Catchprice sitting, rather formally, in the dining chair in front of them. She looked like an old woman ready for bed or for the asylum. Her long grey hair was undone and spread across the shoulders of a rather severe and slightly old-fashioned black suit. An ornate silver brooch was pinned to her artificial bosom. The skirt was a little too big for her. Her slip showed.

Sarkis clasped his knife in his fist. The air was close.

'You like my dolls?' she said.

He smiled politely.

'I never cared for them,' she said. 'Someone gives you one because they do not know you. Someone else gives you a second one because you have the first. It's so like life, don't you think?'

'I hope not.'

'I do too,' she said, and winked at him. 'That's why I like to have young people working for me.'

'It's Granny needs a hair-do,' Benny said.

Sarkis tightened his jaw.

'Not me,' Benny said. 'I said it wasn't me.'

When Sarkis lived in Chatswood, his mother's friends would sit around beneath the picture of Mesrop Mushdotz and pat their hair a certain way and curl their fringe around their fingers. When they asked outright, he said to them what he now said to Mrs Catchprice.

'I don't have my scissors.'

'She's got to have a hair-do,' Benny said. 'It's an occasion.'

'All my gear's at home,' Sarkis said. 'You should go to a salon. They have the basins and sprays and all the treatments.'

'But you're a hairdresser,' Mrs Catchprice said, 'and you work for me.'

'I thought I was going to be a salesman.'

'You will be,' said Mrs Catchprice. 'When you've cut my hair.'

No one offered to drive him – Sarkis walked, first to his home for his plastic case, then to Franklin Mall to buy the Redken Hot Oil Treatment. The air was hot and heavy, and the low grey clouds gave the low red-brick houses a closed, depressed look.

When he returned to Catchprice Motors he washed the disgusting dishes in Mrs Catchprice's kitchen sink and scrubbed the draining board and set up basins and saucepans for the water. He could see Benny Catchprice in the car yard below him. Benny stood in the front of the exact centre of the yard and he never shifted his position from the time Sarkis began to wash Mrs Catchprice's hair until he'd done the eye-shadow.

There were people, old people particularly, so hungry for touch they would press their head into the washer's fingers like a cat will rub past your legs. Mrs Catchprice revealed herself to be one of them. You could feel her loneliness in another way too, in her concentration as you ran the comb through her wet hair, her intense stillness while you cut.

Sarkis stripped the yellow colour from her grey hair with L'Oréal Spontanée 832. When he applied the Hot Oil and wrapped her in a towel she made a little moan of pleasure, a private noise she seemed unaware of having made, one he was embarrassed to have heard.

He did not ask her how she wanted her hair done. He styled it with a part and a french bun set a little to one side. It did nothing to soften the set of her jaw or the effects of age, but it gave her, in this refusal to hide or apologize, a look of pride and confidence. It was the same approach as you might take with a kid with ear-rings in her nose – you gave her a close shave up one side of her head, declared her ugly ears, did nothing to soften the features, and therefore made her sexy on the street.

He softened Mrs Catchprice a little with her make-up – some very pale blue eye-shadow and, from among all the grubby, ground-down Cutex reds she brought him, one Petal Pink.

'How's that?' he asked, but only because he had finished and she had said nothing.

'I look like a tough old bird,' she said.

He was offended.

'It's just what the doctor ordered,' she said. She opened her handbag and uncrumpled a $20 bill which she pushed into his hand.

'Thank you,' he said, although it was not enough to cover the cost of the Redken and the Spontanée 832. He brushed off her shoulders and swept up the floor and swept her hair on to a sheet of newspaper and put it in the rubbish. He folded the sheet he had used for a cape and placed it on top of the yellow newspapers on top of the washing machine. Then he let the dog out of the bathroom.

He came back into the living-room with the dog skeltering and slipping around his feet and found a pregnant woman with a briefcase, Benny Catchprice and Cathy McPherson all pushing their way into the living-room.

'It is true?' Cathy's voice was tremulous. 'Just tell me?'

Haircuts can alter people and this one seemed to have altered Mrs Catchprice. She led the way to the dining-room table and sat with her back to the row of brightly illuminated dolls. She looked almost presidential.

'What are you dressed up for?' Cathy asked.

The pregnant woman with the briefcase sat next to Mrs Catchprice. Benny sat opposite the pregnant woman.

Cathy took the big chair facing the dolls' case, but would not sit in it. She grasped its back.

'What are you dressed up for? Is it true?' she asked her mother. 'Because if it is, you really should tell me.'

'The investigation,' Mrs Catchprice said, 'has been stopped.'

Sarkis did not know what investigation she was talking about but when he saw her speak he saw her power and thought he had created it.

'Mrs Catchprice . . .' the pregnant woman said.

'How come you're dressed up?' Cathy asked. 'How come you know?'

'She doesn't know,' the pregnant woman said. 'There's nothing to know. Mrs Catchprice, Mrs McPherson, you can all calm down. The investigation has not been stopped. Once a Tax Office investigation starts, it has to go on until the end. Not even I could stop it.'

'It's been stopped all right,' said Benny in a thin nasal voice that cut across the others' like steel wire. He was trying to smile at the pregnant woman. 'I'm sorry,' he said. He used her first name, 'Maria.'

Maria was pushing at the pressure points beside her eyes.

'We like you,' Benny said. He used her first name again. 'We don't blame you for what you did . . .'

'Maria' coloured and tapped on the table with her pencil.

Mrs Catchprice held the edge of the table with her hands. She seemed to spread herself physically. Sarkis thought of Bali, of Rangda the Witch. She had that sort of power. The whole room gave it to her and she threw it back at them. It was not the haircut. It was her.

'Can I remind you all,' Maria said, 'that I'm the one who's from the Tax Office.'

Mrs Catchprice gave her a smile so large you could think that all her teeth were made from carved and painted wood. 'You'd better phone your office,' she said. 'Use the extension in the kitchen. It's more private.'

The Tax Inspector hesitated, smiled wanly, then left the room. Mrs Catchprice turned to her daughter.

'So now you can go, Cathy,' Mrs Catchprice said. 'You want to go square dancing, you go. I'm taking the business back for safe-keeping.'

'It's not yours to take back.'

'That's irrelevant, Cathy,' said Benny. 'You get what you want. We get what we want.'

'The business isn't hers. It's not her decision. She's a minority shareholder.'

But Mrs Catchprice did not look like a minority of anything. Her jaw was set firmly. Her face was blotched with liver spots and one large red mark along her high forehead below her hairline. She looked scary.

The Tax Inspector, by contrast, looked white and waxy and depressed. She had not come all the way back into the room, but stood leaning against the door jamb with her hand held across her ballooning belly. Her hands were puffed up, ringless, naked.

'I've been called back to the office,' she said.

'How lovely,' said Mrs Catchprice. 'You'll be closer to the hospital. What hospital was it? I forget.'

'George V,' said Maria Takis. All the colour had gone from her wide mouth.

'It's a lovely hospital.'

'My mother died there.' The Tax Inspector clicked shut her briefcase.

'Let me,' Benny said. He took the briefcase from her, smiling charmingly. 'I'd like to walk you to your car.'

49

At the bottom of the fire escape, Benny took the car keys from the Tax Inspector's hand. She let him take her briefcase, imagining he would carry it to her car, but he immediately set off across the gravel towards the back of the yard where a faded red sign read LUBRITORIUM.

'Wrong way,' she said.

He turned, and his lower lip, in trying not to smile, made a little 'v' that was disturbingly familiar. 'You can't go,' he said. He threw her car keys in the air and caught them. 'It isn't over yet.'

'It's over. Believe me.' She did not know how the audit could possibly be over, and she was confused, and mostly bad-tempered that it was. It was not logical that she should feel this, but she felt it. She held out her hand for the keys.

Benny grinned, then frowned and held the keys behind his back. 'I've got stuff I want to show you.'

'Come on, I've got work to do.' She was going to the Tax Office to shout at Sally Ho. That was her 'work'.

Benny pouted and dangled the keys between his thumb and forefinger. She snatched them from him, irritated. The minute she had done it and she saw the hurt in his face, she was sorry.

'You should be happy,' she said. 'Isn't this what you wanted when you came to my house? Isn't this exactly what you wanted to achieve?'

'Yes,' he said. 'Sort of.'

She began to walk slowly, purposefully, towards her car. 'So?' she said.

He was close beside her – a little ahead. She could feel his eyes demanding a contact she did not have the energy to give him.

He said, 'I thought we might be, sort of, friends.'

She began to laugh, and stopped herself, but when she looked up she saw it was not in time to stop her hurting him. By the time they reached the car he had a small red spot on each of his cheeks.

'I don't see why not,' he said. He held out his hand for the keys and she gave them to him, in compensation for her laughter. He unlocked her door and held it open for her. She squeezed herself in behind the wheel. He passed her the briefcase. She held out her hand for the keys. He wagged his finger and danced round the minefield of puddles to the passenger side. She watched him, wearily, as he unlocked the passenger side door and got in. He locked the door behind him.

'O.K.,' she said. 'But now I've got to go.'

She held out her hand for the keys. He placed them in her open palm. She inserted the keys in the ignition switch then turned it far enough to make the instrument lights, the three of them, shine red.

'I came to talk to you last night,' he said. 'I thought we could, you know . . . I came by myself.'

'Why?'

'Why not?'

She moved the gear stick into neutral.

'I got the company books for you,' he said. 'I brought them to your house. I was going to leave them on the veranda, but you didn't come home all night.'

She felt her hair prickle on the nape of her neck. 'I was at my father's,' she said.

'That's who you had dinner with?'

'Yes. It is absolutely who I had dinner with.'

'But you went out to dinner with Uncle Jack.'

She turned to look at him. He was smirking.

'You don't want to waste your time with him,' he said. 'He's a creep.'

'Benny, what do you want from me? What is it?'

Benny shrugged and looked out of the window at a pair of men at A.S.P. Building Supplies loading roofing iron on to the roof-rack of an old Ford Falcon. 'How old are you?' he asked, still not looking at her.

Maria started the engine.

'How *old* are you?'

He turned. He looked as if he was going to cry.

'I'm thirty-four.'

'I like you,' he said. 'I never liked anyone like that before.'

'Benny, that's enough.'

'This is serious,' he said.

'Enough.'

But he was unbuttoning his shirt.

Maria opened her door. 'I'm going to get your father.'

'My father is a joke,' said Benny. He pulled down his jacket and his shirt to show her his upper arm. 'Just look, that's all. Please don't turn away from me.'

Maria Takis looked. She saw a smooth white scar the size of a two-cent piece surrounded by a soft blue stain.

Benny looked at her with large tear-lensed eyes. 'My mother did this to me. Can you imagine that? My own mother tried to kill me.'

'Benny,' Maria said. 'Please don't do this to me. I am an auditor from the Australian Taxation Office.'

'I was three years old.'

'What is this serving?'

'For Chrissake.' Benny kicked out and smashed the glove box. It flipped off and fell on to the floor. 'I'm trying to show you my fucking life.' He looked at her. His eyes were big and filled with tears. 'You wouldn't come with me. I wanted you to come with me. I can't *stand* that.'

'Benny, what can I do? I'm a stranger to your family.'

'You're kind,' he said. He rubbed his nose with the back of his hand. He picked up the glove box lid and tried to fit it back on. 'I know you're kind.'

'Benny,' she gave him a tissue from her bag, 'just take my word for it – I'm very selfish.'

He wiped his eyes and blew his nose. 'You care about other people, I know you do. You live all by yourself and you're having this baby. That's not selfish.'

Maria looked forward out the window, not wanting to hurt him, fearing his anger, wishing it would end.

'You could have had an abortion.' He persisted with the glove box lid. Every time he closed it, it dropped to the floor.

'I often wish I had.'

'No, you don't.'

'You want to know the truth? I wanted to hurt the baby's father. That's why I'm having a baby – to make him feel sorry for the rest of his life.'

Benny took the glove box lid and squinted at it, as if trying to read a part number.

'You're kind,' he said. 'You can't put me off by lying to me. I can replace this glove box,' he said. 'If you come back tomorrow I'll replace it free.'

'Benny I'm not coming back. I'm sorry.'

'You come out here, you try to screw my life. I'm interested in you. I'm interested in your baby, everything. I like you, but you don't even take the trouble to see how I live. You know how I live? I live in a fucking hole in the ground. You wouldn't even use it for a toilet. Come and look at it. I'll show you now.'

The Tax Inspector shook her head. She looked down at her skirt and saw it rucked above her knees. They looked like someone else's knees – old, puffy, filled with retained fluid. In the middle of the anxiety about Benny she had time to register that she had developed œdema.

'You can't just dump me. You think you can go away and leave me to rot in my cellar, just let me rot in hell, and nothing will ever happen to you because of it.' He was folding his jacket. He was opening the car door. He was leaving her life.

Maria Takis waited for the door to slam. It did not seem smart to start the engine until it did.

50

Granny Catchprice had made her life, invented it. When it was not what she wanted, she changed it. In Dorrigo, she called them maggots and walked away. She had gelignite in her handbag and Cacka was nervous, stumbling, too shy to even touch her breasts with his chest.

There was no poultry farm, she made one. There was no car business, she gave it to him, out of her head, where there had been nothing previously. She freed him from his mother. She gave him a yard which he paved with concrete so he could hose it down each morning like a publican, a big man in his apron and gum boots. He was Mr Catchprice. She was Mrs Catchprice. She hired boys and girls in trouble and showed them how they could invent themselves. Little Harry Van Der Hoose – she tore up his birth certificate in front of him. He watched her with his mouth so wide open you could pop a tennis ball inside.

'Now,' she said. 'What are you?'

Years later he wrote a letter from Broome where he had a drive-in liquor store. He said: 'Before I had the good fortune to be employed by yours truly, I was what you would call a dead-end kid. Whatever life I enjoy here today, I have you to thank for.'

Mrs Catchprice stood in the annexe on Wednesday afternoon and watched them bring the horrid-looking 'Big Mack' tour truck right into the yard. It belonged to Steven Putzel, the pianist – a nasty little effort with sideburns and a tartan shirt. They had to move the Holdens and that black foreign car to one side. They made a mess of the gravel doing it.

Her daughter ran out from under the LUBRITORIUM sign, carrying guitar cases.

'That's a joke,' Frieda said. She lit a Salem and folded her arms across her prosthetic chest. It was a bumpy, silly thing and she was sorry she had put it on.

'What is?'

She looked and saw Mort was standing next to her. This sort of thing happened more and more. She damn well could not remember if she had known he was there or if he had sneaked up on her. She said nothing, gave nothing away. She held out the Salem pack to him. He shook his head.

'What's a joke?' he said. She remembered then – he gave up smoking when he married Sophie.

She looked out of the window at her daughter who was now struggling out into the sunlight carrying a big amplifier.

'Where's she think she's going?' she said.

'You know exactly what she's doing,' Mort said.

She guessed she did know. 'She can't sing.'

'Jesus, Mum. Give up, will you?' Mort grinned. She was a tough old thing, that's who she was.

'She *used* to sing as well as you. She used to sing the "Jewel Song" for your father. People would pay to hear that.'

'Come on, lay off – you know she's popular.'

'Is she?' said Granny Catchprice. 'Truthfully?'

Mort folded his arms across his chest and looked down at her with a thin, wry grin on his face. 'You're not going to get a rise out of me.'

She was not sure if she was taking a rise out of him or not. She knew, of course, that Cathy sang in halls. She was popular enough to sing at a dance in a hall. She could sing for shearers, plumbers, that sort of thing.

'She'd do anything to get herself written up,' she said.

THE TAX INSPECTOR

'Our Cath always did like attention,' he said. 'It's true.'

'And you were always so bashful.' Cathy was trying to climb into the truck and Frieda felt nervous that she had somehow allowed this thing to get this far. 'She could be a bit more bashful with that backside.'

At ten years old, you should have seen her – a prodigy. She never knew what Country & Western was. She knew *Don Giovanni, Isolde, Madame Butterfly*. Her teacher was Sister Stoughton at the Catholic School. She sang 'Kyrie Eleison' at St John's at Christmas before an audience which included the Governor General. There was no 'Hound Dogs' or 'Blue Suede Shoes'. The nearest she came to Hill-Billy or Rock-a-Billy, she had a checked shirt and jeans with rolled-up cuffs to go and learn square dancing at the Mechanics' Institute. She did not know anyone with duck-tailed hair or Canadian jackets. She did not like square dancing either, said it was like going fencing with a wireless playing. She was nine years old when she said that.

Frieda said: 'I suppose she's got our money entered in her bank book.'

She was trying to enlist him, but he took her shoulder and made her turn towards him.

'Look at me,' he said. He held her too hard. It hurt but she did not tell him. 'Listen to what I'm saying – whatever Cathy is, she's not a criminal. Now come on, be a good stick, eh? You've pushed her this far. You let her go ahead and jump.'

'I'm not any sort of stick.'

'Let her do what she wants to do.'

'I'm going down to talk to her.'

'You've already talked to her.' He stood in front of her and for a moment she thought he was going to block her way. He was frightening – big, and emotional, like a horse that might do anything.

'Come with me, Morty.'

He shook his head, but he stepped aside and held the door open. 'You told her you didn't need her. That was the message you gave her. If you want my opinion, you are incorrect . . .'

'If I'm incorrect, then help me talk to her.'

'No, Mum.' He shook his head with those big teary eyes, like his father.

230

'You don't know anything about Cathy and me. You never did understand.'

'You've got her like a monkey on a stick.'

'Rot and rubbish.'

'You're very cruel, Mum.'

That hurt her, hurt her more than she could imagine being hurt but she did not show it.

'You always panic,' she said. 'You're like your father.'

That made him sniff and put his mouth into a slit. 'You're the one who should be panicking,' he said.

She let that pass.

'Walk me down the stairs?'

'No,' he shook his head.

So she walked by herself and left him sulking.

She met her daughter in the old lube bay, carrying a big cardboard box of papers. Cathy brushed past, saying nothing. She passed the box to Steven Putzel and then hurried back across the cracked, oil-stained lube bay floor where Benny had painted the skull and cross bones and the Day-glo no admittance sign. Frieda remembered when that concrete floor was wet and new. You could have written anything in it. Cathy began to go up the metal stairs to the flat. Frieda followed her.

Half way up, Cathleen stopped and turned.

'Just leave me alone,' she said.

'I'm not stopping you,' Frieda said, but she saw then – in the way Cathy was standing – that it was not too late to stop her. She started feeling better than she had.

'You'll fall and break your hip.'

'I've every right to see my house.'

'It is not your house any more.'

But she had invented it. There had been nothing there before she started. She had chosen that red marbled Laminex, that lemon wall paint. The floors were strewn with newspaper, record covers, sheet music. In the middle of the room was the yellow vinyl chair she had covered for Cacka. He used to sit in that to listen to his records. She loved to watch him listen. His big eyes would fill with moisture – glistening like in the movies when people were in love. Now it was his daughter who stood before her, red faced, her hands on her hips, her lips parted.

'You know I won't live too much longer,' Frieda said.

'Don't start that . . .'

'We got through this far . . .'

'Just don't, O.K.?'

Howie came into the living-room. He stood back in the corner as if none of this was to do with him.

'You never had children, Cathy,' Frieda said. This was not exactly aimed at Howie. She did not mean it this way, but she glared at him when she said it. 'Unless you've been through labour you couldn't understand.'

Cathy began to give that nervous laugh and shake her head like she had water in her ear. 'Listen, Ma – it's not going to work . . .'

She got that 'Ma' from Howie. It was common. Frieda hated it. 'You're going to be alive a long time yet, Cathy. You're the one that'll have to live with the guilty conscience.'

'Mrs Catchprice,' Howie said. He was leaning against the door frame with his arms folded. 'You've got no right to say these things to her.'

He was a no one. She had made him, invented him. He came into her shop with his greasy hair and brothel creepers and a note from the police sergeant.

'I'm her mother, Howie.'

Cathy said: 'You never did what a mother should have done.'

'You mean that business with Mr Heywood's cat?'

'You know I don't mean that. Don't make me say it. Just don't make it hard for me to go.'

Howie spoke out of the shadow near the bedroom door frame. It was so dull there you could not even see his eyes. 'He used to rub her tits,' he said.

Frieda felt she had missed something.

She looked up. Steven Putzel was there at the doorway next to Howie, listening.

'How dare you speak to me like that,' she said, but she was confused by the circumstances and did not speak with her full force.

'He used to rub her tits.'

'You little filth.' She could not believe the *language*.

'He's not a filth,' Cathy said. 'He's a decent man.'

Decent?

'He is a filth, all right,' she said. 'I knew he was a filth when I saw him. I thought I could change him but look how wrong I was.'

'He used to lie on top of me so I could not breathe.'

'You were the one who wanted to marry him.'

'Your husband. My father. He used to lie on top of me so I could not breathe.'

'He loved to tease you,' Frieda said.

'For Christ's sake, Mother, our father was a creep. He used to touch my tits. He used to lie on top of me. You saw him do it. You used to watch him do it.'

'I did not.'

'You did, you old fool. You used to sit there, in the same room. He used to do things to me while you were *knitting*.'

Cathy had her by the arm, squeezing her, pulling at her, shouting about ten hours of labour, but Frieda had already slipped away. She was running through the ring-barked trees, down the wet clay road. Walking towards her was Cacka, smiling, in his Magpies jacket.

She had the gelignite in her handbag when she met him. She had it in the butcher's. The detonators clinking around her neck. She had it there from the beginning.

51

Ghopal's was hot and busy when Govinda-dasa took the call. When he heard the old woman's voice he had a mental picture of a demon with tusks, one of the servants of Yamaraja, the lord of death, who came to claim the soul of Ajamila.

'O.K.,' he said to Vishnabarnu. 'It's her.'

Vish picked up the phone and cradled it between his big smooth chin and yellow cotton shoulder.

'Hi, Gran.' He continued to ladle out the Sweet and Sour tofu. He passed the plate to Ramesvara and then began to fill a blender with banana and milk, yoghurt, cinnamon, honey.

'Vish,' Gran Catchprice said, 'I need you out here.'

'Oh no, Gran,' Vish said. 'I'm sorry. One sec.' He turned on the blender and mouthed to Govinda-dasa: 'It's O.K.'

'I don't think there's too much I can do about Benny any more,

Gran,' he said as he poured the smoothies into their tall green glasses. 'I think he needs to see a doctor.'

'I'm the doctor,' Gran said.

'Good luck, Gran.' He smiled. He handed the glasses to Govinda-dasa who added the mint sprig and placed them on the counter top for Ramesvara.

'You're the doctor,' she corrected.

'No way, José.'

'But I'm going to follow your prescription – let the business go to hell, wasn't that it?'

'Gran I can't come back now. I've gone now. I've gone for ever. I'm sorry.'

Govinda-dasa turned his back and began to dish some stuffed eggplant. But if Govinda-dasa understood Vish perfectly, Granny Catchprice would not.

'Isn't that what you told me?' she said. 'Let the business go to hell?'

'It is hell,' Vish said. 'That's the truth.'

'I think so too,' she said.

Vish shut his eyes, puffed up his cheeks, blew out air.

Govinda-dasa made a sign with his finger, like a record going round. He meant: don't enter into argument or discussion, just keep repeating it – I – AM – NOT – COMING – BACK.

'Gran, I'm not coming back.'

'Not even to get your brother out of his hole?'

'I'm not coming back.'

'You don't care what happens to your brother?'

'Gran,' Vish turned back towards the wall and the painting of Lord Nara Sinha, 'he's sawn off Grand-dad's shot gun. He's suffering from delusions. The best thing you can do is keep away from him. Don't go down there.'

'I'm not going to go down there. I'm not going to even talk to him.'

'Well, I'm not either. Gran, there's nothing anyone can do.'

'Oh yes there is.'

'What?'

'I can't say on the phone.'

Vish grinned and turned back to look at Govinda-dasa who was making the record sign – I – AM – NOT – COMING – BACK. 'This is not Dorrigo,' he said. 'There's no operator listening to the call.'

'I know it's not Dorrigo,' she said. 'Do you really think I don't know that? I'm going to wind this business up. It makes me sick myself.'

He said nothing.

'It makes me ill in my stomach just looking out of the window. I feel like such a fool . . .'

He did not ask her what she felt a fool about. He smiled at Govinda-dasa and played the record: 'Just the same, Gran – I can't come.'

'You never want to see it again?' She was persistent, like a salesman. 'As long as you live?'

'Gran. I can't come.'

'You don't want to see it, but it's always there. It won't go away. It just goes on and on like some bad dream . . .'

He did not answer her. He nodded.

'If you could wave a magic wand and make it go . . .'

'A magic wand . . .' he laughed. 'Sure, Gran.'

'Well, yes or no?'

Govinda-dasa was all the way over at table 14 but he saw what was happening. He walked rapidly back towards the counter, making circular motions with his index finger.

'Did you hear me?' she said.

'Yes I heard.'

There was a long silence on the phone while Vishnabarnu felt the cool dry wall against his cheek.

'I'm not talking to my father,' he said.

52

Jack Catchprice was scared and amazed by what he had brought off. The thing happened so fast. Really, he was just enquiring – could he do it? He was testing his strength – did he know the guy who knew the guy? Did he have the clout with the first guy to get him to use his clout with the second guy? Did he have enough in the favour bank to get this investigation stopped? The truth was – he was flirting with it. But then he was in the deep end and suddenly he was in a very dark place and it was, like, you want it or not, yes or no, shit or get off the can. 'Sure,' he said. What the fuck else could he say?

Thirty minutes after she left the Bilgola house, without her knowing anything had changed, Catchprice Motors was no longer a part of Maria Takis's professional life.

Jack had not been able to achieve it in two steps, but in three, and the steps were dirty and the connections dangerous. He was now joined to things he would rather not be joined to.

He wanted to ring Maria, straightaway, and tell her what he had done. But it was like ringing to check that a dozen long-stemmed roses had arrived – you could not do it. You had to wait to be thanked.

For Jack who had made his impatience into something like a professional virtue, waiting was difficult. But he did it. He had no choice. He told Bea he would take any calls from Maria Takis, and any call from any female who did not seem inclined to give a name.

He had a meeting with the dopey architect who had wilfully ignored his brief and now wanted to give the Circular Quay land to the city for a park in return for the right to put two towers in the water where the ferries came in. It was like a giant π, a gateway to the city with a ballroom, a fucking *ballroom*, across the top. It was wrong to call him dopey. The guy was right in everything he said. He was trying to make a proper gateway for the city. He said the Cahill Expressway was like the Berlin Wall. He was a fucking genius, but he did not see that Jack could not *sell* a ballroom, and he did not have the resources to fight ten years to build in the water at Circular Quay. But he could not bear a gifted man like this to dislike him – he asked him to take his drawings to another stage.

After that, he called all the troops in for the Lend Lease meeting – three hours later than scheduled but Lend Lease still bought the whole Woolloomooloo package and when they went out of the door he opened a couple of magnums of Moët for the staff to celebrate.

There was still no call. He started to worry the connection had fucked up, that the case had not been stopped. He went back into his office. He picked up the phone, put it down, picked it up, put it down again.

Then he buzzed Bea and had her book a table for two at Darcy's for that evening, just in case.

'You're not going to Darcy's,' Bea said. 'You've got dinner at Corky Missenden's.'

'Then I'll cancel Corky. Get me Corky.'

'Good luck,' Bea said.

But of course there was no way Corky was going to excuse him.

'All right,' Jack said. 'Well, if I have to come, I'm going to have to bring someone.'

'Jack, don't do this to me.'

'Corky, I don't want to. I have to.'

'You're a shit, Jack. This dinner has been planned for weeks. You don't know what a tricky placement this is. Who is this person? Is she anyone I know? Does she *do* anything?'

Jack thought it best not to reveal her occupation. 'You'll like her,' he said, 'she's a friend of Daniel Makeveitch. You'll love her.'

But there was still no call from Maria.

Jack was tight and twitchy in the legs and at the back of his fingers. He had lunch at Beppi's with Larry Auerbach and took his cellular phone to the table like some nerd from the Parramatta Road. When Larry went for a piss, he rang Catchprice Motors, but the phone wasn't even answered.

At three he got the Taxation Office but her number did not answer either, and the switchboard said she was unavailable.

At four, now in his office, he telephoned Maria's home and got the answerphone.

'Hey, Maria. You there? It's Jack . . . Catchprice . . . I just had a crazy idea,' he said. 'It might be fun.'

She picked up.

He stood up and pulled the phone off his desk. 'You're there.'

'If it's fun, I'm up for it.'

'Are you O.K.? I worried you had gone into labour.'

'My fingers look like sausages,' she said, 'and I've had my worst day all year . . .'

'Nothing good happen at all? All day?'

'Not a thing.'

'Are you absolutely sure?'

'Did my legs look sort of funny last night? Were my knees puffy?'

'No!'

'Are you sure? Because if they looked like they do right now, I'm going to die of embarrassment.'

'Maria, you've got great legs. What happened that was so bad?'

'Something very shitty. I don't want to even think about it.'

'But your investigation stopped, right?' *He had done the fucking impossible. He had fixed what she had failed to fix.* 'You got called back to your office? Catchprice Motors is out of your life?' *Remember me? The generalist?*

There was a pause. 'Jack, how do you know this?'

'How do you think?' he said. *I did the fucking impossible for you. I crawled down sewers. I shook hands with rats.* 'How would you reckon?'

'Oh, your mother told you.'

He made a silent face.

'Well,' Maria said. 'She's pleased.'

'Sure,' he said, 'you can rely on that, but I'm sorry you're not happier.'

'Oh, I want to have fun *now*.'

He felt anxious that now she would not like him, angry that she did not appreciate what he had done for her, indignant at what he suspected were her double standards, relieved she would probably come out to dinner with him, even if it was at Corky Missenden's.

'You might say no when you hear – but there's a dinner party at Rose Bay I thought you could have a good laugh at.'

'I like the laugh part.'

'You know this fellow Terry Digby – Lord Digby – who just paid $23 million for the de Kooning? He's in Sydney, and there's a dinner. It's Corky Missenden – she's good at this sort of thing. There'll be money and art, mostly, but the Attorney General will be there so that might be amusing. In any case, the food should be very good and we could leave early if you were bored – you'd be a perfect excuse for me to leave.'

'What would I wear?' she said.

He persuaded her she could wear exactly what she wore the night before, that it would be perfect. He said it because he figured that was who she was, but also because he was not going to lose her because she had nothing suitable to wear, and when they arrived out at Rose Bay, it made Corky Missenden raise a questioning eyebrow in his direction.

He had too much on his mind to be offended by Corky's eyebrow. He had seen that she was setting up her dinner party with two tables in two rooms, and, as he and Maria passed through the house, even as he pointed out the less embarrassing choices in Corky's erratic art collection, Jack's mind was racing, thinking what he could offer Corky, what he could trade her, how he could *make* her have Maria Takis sit at his table. He had Maria drink champagne. He looked at the harbour and pointed out a school of leather-jackets swimming up against the sea wall, but he had none of the lightness of heart his creased-up eyes and loose curly hair suggested – he knew that he would be sent, in a moment, to be charming to the Attorney General and Maria would be bumped into the second room with the rich and reactionary George Grissenden and the snobbish Betty Finch. He had fucked up. It was the wrong way for her to see his life.

53

At four o'clock Maria Takis had been in her one-bedroom cottage in Balmain with her puffy feet elevated, staring at the discolouration on her freshly painted ceiling. At eight-fifteen she was standing beside Sydney Harbour with a long glass flute from which very small bubbles rose slowly through straw-coloured Dom Perignon. At four o'clock she had had red eyes and a headache. At eight-fifteen waiters with black shirts and pony tails brought hors d'oeuvres to the sea wall where she sat with a man with curly blond hair and a tanned face. The light was mellow, the water of the harbour pearly, touched with pink and blue and green. It was like nothing so much as a television commercial.

That she should like the too-good-looking man, that the setting itself – terra-cotta tiled terrace, flapping striped awnings, elegant men and women in black dresses – should be actually *pleasant* was disturbing for her.

She had been in homes like this before, often, professionally, but she had never allowed herself to think of wealth as attractive, was so accustomed to seeing it as a form of theft that it was shocking for her to feel herself responding to it at all, as if she were allowing herself to be sexually excited by a criminal.

The harbour licked and lapped against the wall she sat on. It slapped against the sandstone and smelt of sea-weed. She wondered if people in these houses bothered to fish. If ever she had a house like this, she would fish. She saw her mother on the sea wall casting out towards where the water boiled with tailor.

'I thought about you all day,' he said.

But she was suddenly so uncomfortable with his attractiveness, his straight, perfect teeth – he was a 'type' she would once have labelled superficial or yuppy – that she could not bring herself to say she had thought of him – although she had, often – or even that she was pleased and excited to be here.

'Should we be mingling?'

'We don't have to do anything we don't want to do,' he said.

But then it turned out that they must sit, not merely apart, not merely at separate tables, but at tables in rooms separated by french doors.

'Surely we can sit together?' she said.

'I'll fix it,' Jack said, and disappeared into the house.

She stayed alone on the wall, looking out at the harbour where a long, low, wooden boat slowly putted past, no more than five metres away. A little girl, no more than ten, sat alone at the tiller. The girl waved. Maria waved back. She thought: I could handle this. That's the truth. I would actually love to live in a house like this.

When Jack came back to admit he could not change the seating she was disappointed, but not greatly.

'I've decided to enjoy myself,' she said. She held his hand.

'Are you sure? I'm sorry. We can leave straight after the pudding.'

When he put his hand against her stomach, she did not mind – the opposite.

'I like it here.' She kissed him softly on his expensive-smelling cheek and went to sit at the long dining-table in the room closest to the harbour. She found her name card, seated herself, permitted herself to take pleasure from the white linen, the Lalique bowl – she peered around the base and found the signature – even the heavy chandeliers above their heads. She was here to enjoy, not cross-examine.

A tall blond Englishman on her left introduced himself as 'Terry'. His hair fell over his forehead in a stiff lick. He had a black cotton shirt with overlapping double collars which she noticed straightaway. Later she intended to ask him where he bought it.

'Are you the de Kooning man?' she asked.

'Well, not the de Kooning woman,' he said, smiling.

'Well, I'm grateful for that,' Maria said, also smiling.

'Oh,' he said, pushing his lick of hair away, 'you're not fond of them?'

'He's such an extraordinary painter,' she said. She was pleased to be here. Tax Department people never talked about painting. Alistair was an educated man, but he would barely have known who de Kooning was. 'I love his work, but the women always frighten me.'

This made the man smile at the edges of his mouth. His eyes became thoughtful.

'Seen the butter?' he asked.

Maria looked for the butter, but could see none. 'He's so lyrical and beautiful,' she said. 'I mean, it's like I'm giving my heart to him and then I walk into the next room and feel I'm in the power of a serial killer. I mean, is he Ted Bundy?'

The man turned towards a puffy-faced dark-haired woman on the other side of the table. Maria imagined he was going to ask for butter. Instead he said: 'Janice, I was very impressed by your piece on our mutual friend, although I really do think you could have taken the matter even further.'

Maria saw she had been cut. She thought: how could you be so unkind to someone who was a stranger and not at home?

She looked across the table towards a man and woman engaged in conversation. The table was very wide. The conversation seemed too far away to enter. The woman was in her early fifties with large eyes and a way of listening that must have been most flattering to the man, who was short and smooth and shaved so close his red cheeks shone like soup bones.

'The thing I object to,' the man said, 'is to pay my taxes, fine, but not to subsidize some bored housewife so she can be pleasured by a doctor.'

It was a moment before she understood his use of 'pleasured'. He meant a vaginal examination. Maria looked at his listener who was studiously brushing toast crumbs off the table cloth. *You hate him surely. You are nodding your head while you despise him.*

'I agree, I agree,' she said. 'I like the American system.'

'No one ever goes to the doctor in the States just because they're bored.'

'My God, no.'

'But these women are bored,' the man with glistening cheeks said. 'Probably hubby is ignoring them. So they go along to good old Doctor-of-your-choice with their little green and yellow Medicare card.'

When Alistair was running the department it had been flexible enough to accommodate the passions Maria Takis now felt. (You wrote down a Rolls-Royce number plate and checked it out. You saw a lot of marble on a building site, it was enough.) She would have taken pleasure wringing the tax out of the complacent little gynophobe. Indeed, she might yet do it, or have someone do it for her. She looked across the table trying to read his place card upside down.

'I think you're absolutely correct about the de Kooning women,' the man on her right said. 'I never knew how to take them either.'

He introduced himself, but she already knew who he was. She knew his paintings and admired them. She responded to their spareness, their austerity, their refusal ever to be pretty. They did not mesh with the face, which was rather pudgy, and pasty, but rather with the flinty light in his small grey eyes. The colour clung to the canvas like crushed gravel, and it was through them that Maria had learned to love the Australian landscape which she still saw, everywhere, in their terms. It was exhilarating to be in agreement with Phillip Passos about de Kooning.

'Did he buy a "Woman"?' she whispered. 'I feel such a fool. I've insulted him.'

'Him? He's not Digby.' Passos was breaking his bread roll with his shockingly small white hands.

'Then who is it?'

'No one to worry about. Digby's in there, at the Big Table. He bought a rather nice abstract piece from the early fifties. Not "pivotal",' he smiled, 'but "major". He paid $23 million for it.'

'I heard.'

'Well, he thought he had a bargain, because the market is so soft, but now he's in a panic because maybe the market is still falling and he's got to decide whether he has to bid for the next de Kooning. And that's a "pivotal" one. Sotheby's auction it in New York next week. He'll have to be over there to prop up his own investment.'

'I wonder what de Kooning thinks of all this.'

'Not much. He has Alzheimer's, I believe.'

'Well he should be benefiting somehow.'

'Mmmm,' said Passos, looking a little vague.

'Doesn't France have something like this? A Droit de Suite? Don't French artists now get a cut on all future sales of their work?'

Passos cut his smoked salmon carefully. 'What do you do?' he asked.

'Oh, just a public servant,' she said, and was disappointed and relieved to see she had satisfied his curiosity.

'You know what this dinner party is about, do you?'

'The de Kooning man.'

'Nah,' said Passos. 'He's just a bowl of fruit on the table. He's a *nature morte*. He's a thing you arrange other things around. The hidden agenda is Droit de Suite.'

'Oh, you're lobbying? Now?'

'The Attorney General wants artists to love him, and so he introduced this Droit de Suite legislation. Now he's hurt because we don't want it.'

'I would have thought it was great for artists.'

'So did he. So did I. But if it's going to work the art galleries have to keep honest records on how much people paid for paintings.'

Maria was already acting like a spy. 'Oh,' she said, 'so is that a problem?'

'Not if you pay tax. But they don't. They pay cash. Over half of it is funny money. So what the commercial galleries are saying to the government is Droit de Suite is too complicated to administer, and what they're saying to their artists is that over half our collectors will just stop collecting once the Tax Department can check on what is really going on. I can see I've disappointed you.'

'No, really. It's fascinating. Really.'

'Well, you know, we took dirty money from the Medicis, so I guess we'll take it from Jack Catchprice too.'

The smoked salmon on Maria's plate was subtle and flavoursome, and it became, as she separated it from itself on her plate, not like a fish, but something at once alive and abstract, which had been bred for the pleasure of the connoisseur and about whose death she would be wise not to enquire too closely.

54

Frieda's son was now a big man with whorls of tight hair across his chest like a black man. He had soft, teary eyes and his father's lips. 'What did he do to you?' she asked him.

Mort had his big male hand around her arm, above the elbow. He had found her walking up the street towards the highway. He was propelling her back across a gravel car lot in Franklin. She lost one shoe. She kicked off the other. It fell between the treads down on to the gravel.

The annexe smelled like her father's bedroom in Dorrigo.

In her living-room, he pulled out her chair for her and she sat in it. Her stockinged feet were wet. She looked at the room, surprised by its disrepair. He pulled out a dining chair and did not seem to know what to do with it.

'Don't panic, Mort,' she said.

He said: 'I'm really sorry you had to hear this smut.'

'What did he do?'

'He was a good man,' Mort said, holding the back of the chair and lowering his big square stubborn head, his father's head. 'You can rely on that.'

'She says he touched her bosom.'

He sat on the chair. He leaned across and took her hand. 'He was widely liked. I could draw a map for you Mum, and show you where he was liked, all the way over to Warrakup, right over as far as Kiama even,' he smiled. 'I find old codgers who remember him. They hear my name and they say, "You Cacka's son?" I met one old man last week in the Railway Hotel at Warrakup, a Mr Gross.'

'Hector,' she said, but she was not thinking about Hector.

'His wife is called Maisie.'

'Minnie. She had bandy legs.'

'He said, "Your old man sold me a Holden and when I complained about the rattle he bought it back from me, cash, in the pub." He said, "I respected him for that."'

'He always had cash. We did a lot of cash business at the

auctions.'

'Probably not a good idea to mention this with the Tax Office snooping around.'

'What did he do to you?'

'He didn't do anything.'

'He touched her bosom.'

'So she says.'

'He did something to you too. That's what she was suggesting.'

'Did WHAT?' he bellowed. It made her jump, the sheer noise of it. That was like him – the father – great rushes of rage coming out of nowhere, not always, not even often, but when you got close to things he wouldn't let you touch.

'Don't panic,' she said.

He had his arms bent around his chest and his forehead lowered and his brows down and his eyes were brimming with enough hate – no other word for it – to burn you.

A moment later he put his hands on his knees and said, 'Sorry.'

A moment more: 'You like me to make a cup of tea?'

Frieda said, 'She's quite correct when she said I knew it was happening.'

'Don't say that.'

'I didn't believe a man would do that, but I knew. I *knew* but I didn't believe.'

'He loved us,' Mort said. 'Whatever he was, he loved us. I know that. I rely on that, to look at him and know he loved us.'

'It's why she hates me, isn't it?'

'It's not for us to judge him. What would they have done to him if it had all come out? How could they understand he loved us?'

'It's why you won't sell cars.'

'What?' Mort screwed up his eyes and pushed his head at her. 'What are you saying?'

'Is that why you won't sell cars . . . because you won't do that for him? You're angry with him still.'

'For Chrissakes, he's dead.'

'But it's what he always wanted for you. He always wanted you to be a salesman.'

'You silly old woman . . .' Mort yelled. 'Someone takes that fucking workshop off my hands, someone hires a service manager and a foreman, I'll sell cars like you never saw them sold.'

'Do you think it's going to rain?' said Mrs Catchprice, looking up towards the ceiling.

'Just lay off,' he said.

'I really think it's going to rain.'

'Get off my back, Frieda. I've got enough problems without this.'

'Good for the gardens,' she said.

They were both silent for a while then, although she could hear him breathing through his mouth. After a while she leaned over and patted his knee. 'There's a boy,' she said.

Mort looked up at her. 'I'm sorry,' he said.

She took his hand and stroked it. 'You know I never wanted this business for myself?'

'Yes, I knew that.'

'You knew?'

'Jesus, Mum,' he took his hand back, 'you told me a hundred times. You wanted a flower farm.' He stood up.

'You think I'm a silly old woman.'

'No I don't.' He sat down. He took her hand in his. 'You know I don't. It would have been a very profitable business. You would have been well situated here.'

'But he still would have been who he was . . .'

'By the railway,' Mort said. 'Right on the railway.'

'He wanted the motor cars so much, I made sure he had them. He loved that first Holden as much as Dame Nellie herself. I must have loved him, don't you think?'

'Of course you did.'

'I don't know I did.' She paused. 'I thought he wasn't very interested in s-e-x. I thought it was the music he had, instead. I couldn't have loved a man who was doing that to my children. I never worried about him playing around. I saw his face listening to the opera. I can't explain the feeling, but I thought – he isn't going to play around. What did he actually do?'

'It's too late now, Mum.' He took his hands back and held them on his knees and rocked a little.

'I'm not dead yet,' she said. 'I have a right to know.'

Mort laughed and shook his head.

'What's so funny?'

He rubbed his hand across his face. 'You're incredible.'

'I said I have a right.'

'Oh no, you have no right.' She had set him off again. He had his arms wrapped around his chest. His eyes were staring at her – hate again – a different person. 'You have no damn right to anything. You are lucky I am still here. You are lucky I don't hate you. You're lucky to have anyone left who'll tolerate you, so don't say you didn't love him, because that would just be . . . I couldn't stand it.'

'Tell me,' Mrs Catchprice said. 'I'm not a child.'

'Jack pisses off. He doesn't care. Cathy pisses off. She doesn't care. I'm the one who's stayed to look after you. So listen to me: don't say you didn't love him, because I couldn't bear it.'

He was breathing hard. She was frightened of him.

'You want to know what he did?' he said at last.

Frieda thought it best to stay quiet.

'DO YOU WANT TO KNOW WHAT HE DID?'

He stood up. He had 'Mort Catchprice' embroidered in blue on his overall pocket.

'I'll tell you. I'm going to tell you. You're old enough to know,' he laughed, an ugly loose-mouthed laugh. 'He had a book, a dictionary of angels, with pictures. Did he ever show it to you? Of course he bloody didn't. He made me dress up like an angel and sing the "Jewel Song". Is that enough?'

It was enough. She nodded.

'You wouldn't want to know what else he did. You wouldn't want to even imagine it.' He was crying. He was ruined, wrecked, a human being with nothing.

She had made this, invented it. She knew she was 100 per cent responsible.

'What would that have done to you?' he said. 'What sort of person would you have become?' He had tears running down his big squashed nose. He was all crumpled up like rubbish in the bin.

Frieda went to the kitchen to phone the Hare Krishna temple.

55

'What's that film?' the Attorney General said. 'I forget its name . . .'

'*Jean d'Aboire*,' Jack said.

'That's the one,' the Attorney General said. 'It was pure Louis Quatorze. Most of them stuff it up, you know, the Yanks all the time, but the Frogs too – they put Empire and even Chippendale in with Louis Quatorze, but this *Jean d'Aboire* was spot on. They got the clothes right, everything. They got the little bodices,' he made small pinching gestures with his big fingers, holding them up near his tailored lapels. 'Just right,' the Attorney General said, before returning to his smoked salmon. 'They got everything right, it was just immaculate.'

Jack was worried about Maria. His view of her was obscured by the return wall with the doubtful Tiepolo on it. All he could see was her shoulder and George Grissenden. Grissenden could be very funny, if he wanted to be.

Across the table Digby was complaining loudly about Sotheby's who were offering to finance his bid on the New York de Kooning. To his left, Betty Finch had her eyes glued on the Attorney General and Jack had, occasionally, to head off her graceless attempts to bring the conversation directly to the matter of Droit de Suite. Nobody had bothered to brief her on the manners of lobbying.

He saw Maria stand and leave the room. He smiled in her direction, but she did not seem to see him. Then, through the open archway to his right, he saw her use the hall phone.

'So when you see a movie,' Jack said to the Attorney General, 'you're really more interested in the spoons than the drama.'

It was intended as a joke, but the Attorney General took it seriously. 'Absolutely,' he said. 'This *Jean d'Aboire* got it spot on.'

Jack looked towards the hall. Maria had gone. He looked towards her place – George Grissenden was removing smoked salmon from the plate in front of her empty chair.

From the street he heard electronic beeps and a hissing, high-pitched Holden water pump. *Maria.* He excused himself and walked out on to the street still carrying his damask napkin. The taxi's tail lights were speeding away in the direction of the cul de sac. He was so confident it was Maria, that he stood in the middle of the road, waving the taxi down with his napkin.

He shaded his eyes, moving round the car towards a window which was already rolling down.

'Enjoy your dinner,' Maria said. 'We can talk tomorrow.'

'What happened?'

'Nothing happened.'

'It was George Grissenden. He's such a fascist. What happened?'

'Jack, I'm eight months pregnant. I'm very tired.'

'I'm driving you home.' He opened the door.

'Please, no, *please*.'

But he coaxed her from the cab, paid off the driver, escorted her to his car, and ran back into the house with his white napkin. He was back at the Jaguar in a moment.

'I told them you were going into labour.'

She did not smile.

He started the engine. 'I told them your family all had short labours.'

He could see her in the corner of his eye with her hands across her belly and the high fine nose and curly hair silhouetted against the window. He felt the silence like a screw turning in his throat. He drove quickly, but with excessive care, as if there was some fragile thing in the trunk he was fearful of breaking.

He turned right and headed down the hill towards Double Bay where Maria had left her car parked in front of his house.

'They're creeps, I guess,' he said at last.

'Yes,' she said.

He was frightened by the bluntness of her answer. He waited for her to say something else but nothing else was forthcoming.

'Were they terrible creeps?' he asked at last.

'Oh no,' Maria sighed. 'Probably not,' but there was a weariness in her voice that suggested to him that he had already lost her. 'I've admired Phillip Passos for years. It was great to meet him.'

'What happened then?'

'Oh, it's nothing new.'

'Were they rude to you?'

'I'm always shocked to hear wealthy people complaining about tax. I should be used to it. I should be very thick-skinned. In fact, I thought I was thick-skinned, but I watch them eating with their Georg Jensen cutlery and I want to stand up and shout and make speeches about poverty and homelessness.'

They had to stop for a red light at O'Sullivan Road. Across the road there were yachts bobbing at their moorings in the moonlight.

'I knew this was a bad idea,' Jack said. 'But I wanted to see you so badly and I was impatient. I was being expedient again.'

'Is expediency a problem with you?'

She had that edge in her voice, the same as when she asked him about working for money.

'Not normally,' he said curtly.

He did not need her to tell him – expediency ruled his life and made it shallow and unsatisfying. He could analyse all this a hundred times better than she could, more harshly too. He was a Catchprice – damaged, compromised, expedient – full of it.

'Know a man's friends and you know the man,' he said, bitterly.

'You are different?'

'Don't I seem different?'

'Yes, you do seem different.' It was the first time her voice had softened. When he looked across she was, finally, looking at him.

'Have you heard me complain about taxes?'

'Jack, tonight I listened to a very distinguished artist argue against Droit de Suite. In fact, I discovered, that's what we were there to do.'

'No,' he said. 'We were there because I've fallen in love with you and I had to go to dinner.'

She gave no sign of what this declaration meant to her.

'He was against it,' she said, 'because he believed the "funny money" would not go into art if investors had to pay tax on that money first.'

'You mean I'm taking bread out of the mouths of children.'

He was embarrassed and humiliated. He turned right into Cross Street, swinging the wheel and accelerating so that the Michelins screamed and smoked.

'I'm *pregnant*. Slow down.'

He slowed down, until the car was barely moving and then slid into the kerb.

'That was *stupid*.'

He turned off the engine and turned in his seat.

'I'm sorry,' he said. 'That was reckless. I love you both.'

He felt it himself – it was a false note, but God damn it, it was true. 'So now,' he said, 'you don't like me.'

'I don't doubt you have these feelings,' she put her hand on his. 'I just feel odd about you. Jack, I've only just met you and I'm very tired.'

'I want to look after you, and the baby too. It's all I want.'

She did not answer him. When he looked across he was shocked to see that she had begun to cry. She said: 'Do you want a baby? Is that it?' He tried to hold her but she pulled away from him, her face distorted.

'Maria, please . . .'

'I wish you could have it, Jack. I really do.' She looked like a Francis Bacon smeared with neon light. 'I don't want the fucking thing. I don't want to give birth to anything.'

'It'll be O.K.,' he said, shocked by her language.

'Don't you dare say it's O.K. *Christ.*'

'I'm with you.' He gave her tissues from the glove box.

'No, Jack, I'm sorry.' She blew her nose.

'What if I let you audit me?'

She looked at him with her mouth open, her cheeks wet. Then she started laughing and shaking her head. She blew her nose again, loudly.

'Is that so funny?'

'Yes, it's very funny.'

'Why?'

'Oh Jack . . .'

'Why?'

'Jack, please, if you care for me, just drive me to my car so I can go home and sleep.'

'You can sleep at my house, not the Bilgola house, the one here. You could be in bed in five minutes.'

'Jack, I'm tired, I'm not interested.'

'Maria, please, I'm not talking about sex.'

'No,' she said. 'I'm not coming to your house.'

He put his hands on the wheel and his head on his hands. 'I'm getting angry because I feel I'm ruining something very important in my life. We are just getting to know each other and I'm ruining it.'

'Jack,' she said. She unclasped a hand from the steering wheel and held it. 'You're very sweet and gentle, but you belong to an alien culture.'

He took his other hand from the steering wheel and put both his hands around hers. 'I can change. Don't roll your eyes.'

'I'm sorry. I'm tired.'

'If no one can change,' he said, 'what point is there in anything? If we cannot affect each other's lives, we might as well call it a day.

The world is just going to slide further and further into the sewer.'

She turned away from him. He saw her staring into the brightly lit shop where they advertised Comme des Garçons and Issey Miyake at 50 per cent off.

'You don't believe that we can change?' he asked. 'We can.'

'You should have said these things to me when I was twenty. How would you change, Jack? What would you do?'

'I could become a person you could trust, whom you could rely on totally.'

'Are you that now?'

'Not totally, not at all really.'

'Why me? Why am I so important to the Catchprices?'

He hit the steering wheel with his fist. He did not know his nephew had done a similar thing with a glove box lid. 'I'll drive you to the hospital when you go into labour. I'll come round and do the laundry for you. I'll make the formula. O.K., you'll probably be breast feeding, but I'll do what you need. I've got money. I'll hire help. Maria, please, I've done some rotten things, but the only reason I'm sitting here with you is that I'm not going to be like that any more.'

'You're going to be transformed through love?'

'Yes I am.'

She shook her head.

'Parents die to save their babies through love,' he said. 'There's nothing romantic about it. It's a mechanism. It's built into us whether we like it or not. It's how the species saves itself.'

She was listening to him. She was frowning, but her lips were parted, had in fact been parted so long that now she moistened them.

'If we can't change,' he said, 'we're dead.'

He leaned forward to kiss her. The Tax Inspector took his lips in hers and found herself, to her surprise, feeding on them.

56

At half-past eleven, standing in her kitchen, Maria Takis drank the bitter infusion of raspberry leaf tea and worried, as usual, if she had made it strong enough, if it would really work, if the muscles of her uterus were being really aided by this unpleasant treatment, or if it was some hippy mumbo jumbo that would – if it was too strong – give her liver cancer instead.

She removed her make-up, put on her moisturiser in the bathroom and then lay on the living-room floor to do her pelvic floor exercises. In bed she massaged her perineum, swallowed three 200 mg calcium tablets and a multi-vitamin pill. By the time she could begin her 'Visualizing, Actualizing' exercise it was already half-past twelve. She turned off the overhead light and flicked on the reading light. She propped herself up on two pillows and closed her eyes.

She descended the blue staircase (its treads shimmering like oil on water, its bannisters clear, clean, stainless steel).

At the bottom of the blue staircase she found the yellow staircase.

At the bottom of the yellow staircase, the pink.

At the bottom of the pink, the ebony.

And the end of the ebony, the Golden Door.

Beyond the Golden Door was the Circular Room of Black Marble.

In the centre of the Circular Room of Black Marble, she visualized a Sony Trinitron.

She had found a picture of the Sony. She could visualize it exactly, right down to the three small dots beneath the screen: one red, one blue, one yellow.

She imagined turning on the Sony Trinitron. She imagined the picture emerging: Maria and her baby, sitting up in bed. She had done this almost every night for three months now, but still she could not get the mental picture clear. It was a little girl she tried to visualize. She made her pink. This was corny, but achievable. She could visualize the colour but not her face. The face shifted, dissolved, shivered, like an image on a bed of mercury. She held the shawl against her. She held it to her breast. She pressed her eyes tight, trying to stop thinking about Jack Catchprice. The picture of her baby would not come clearly. It never would. The baby cried and pushed at her. She could feel anxiety and impatience, but not the things she wanted to. Love was not visual. It did not work.

At twenty-past eleven, Cathy McPherson was still celebrating with the band. It was her last night inside the enclosure at Catchprice Motors. She poured a Resch's Pilsener for Mickey Wright. On stage he would wear the glittery black shirt Cathy had chosen for him, but now he was his own man and he wore blue stubby shorts, a 'Rip Curl' T-shirt, and rubber thongs. He had sturdy white legs and heavy muscled forearms. As she poured the beer he tapped the glass with a ballpoint pen. He was a drummer. He couldn't stop drumming. As the beer rose, the pitch changed. It was not a joke, not an anything. He could not help himself. With his right hand he paddled a table tennis bat upon his knee. He was the drummer. Drrrrrrrrrr. He was the one who had to take the drummer jokes. *Q: What do you call someone who hangs around with a band? A: A drummer. Q: Why should Mickey go to the Baltic States? A: He might get independence too.*

The truth was: Mickey was the best musician of the lot of them, and as for independence (the ability to keep different rhythms going simultaneously) he had it in bags. There were drummers making records, famous drummers on hit records, who could barely keep two patterns going. Buddy Rich could do two. Mickey could do four.

He was the ambitious one. The others would settle for a living, but Mickey was always pushing towards places it was bad luck even to dream about.

'I'll tell you what you want to do, Cathy, you want to get "Drunk as a Lord" to Emmylou Harris. No, no, not her agent.' He had a squashed-up Irish face, a boxer's nose. His whole manner was dry, dead-pan. 'Not her agent. Agents never know. You get it to her, direct.'

'The truth is,' said Howie, who was playing poker with Stevie Putzel, 'Emmylou Harris wouldn't do it half as well, you want to know the truth.'

'Sure,' said Mickey. He made a paradiddle with the tennis ball against the table: drrrrrrrrr. 'We'd all get rich listening to her fuck it up.' He looked up at Howie, blank-faced. Who could say if he would be trouble or not.

Howie was playing poker with Steve Putzel. The two of them were standing up, using the ping-pong table for the deck. Howie was watching Cathy more than his cards and was losing badly because of it. Cathy was mad at Mickey for calling in the lawyers.

'Come on, come on,' Steve said to Howie. 'You chucking out or what?'

'We're going to make it, Cath,' said Mickey. He drummed the bat, table, knee: Drrrrrrrrrrrrrrrr. Mickey could talk about success like other guys could talk about sex. He was never sick of it.

Cathy smiled. The apartment did not feel like a home any more, but like a clean-up room in a country motel. There were peanut husks and empty beer cans on the floor. It had never looked so good to her.

'This time, no shit,' Mickey said. Drrrrrrrrr. 'We're the right age for it. You read your history books. We're the right age to make the break, believe me.'

'You're a fucking megalomaniac,' said Johnno Renvoise.

The lead guitarist was stretched out to his entire six foot three inches beneath the ping-pong table with his hand-tooled boots folded underneath his head.

'You know what a gentleman is, Johnno?' Mickey asked.

'Ha-ha.'

'A gentleman is someone who can play the accordion and doesn't.'

'Ha-ha,' Johnno Renvoise was happy. He kept *saying* he was happy. Everyone knew he had lost his wife and kids but he was happy because Big Mack were on the road. He held out his empty beer glass with one hand; with the other he threw crackers against the bottom of the table top and tried to catch the fragments in his mouth.

'Christ, Howie,' said Steve, 'you're so fucking impulsive.'

'Never rush,' Howie smiled and lowered his heavy lids.

Howie laid down his hand on the table where he had filled in the PA forms for each and every one of Cathy's songs and copyrighted them at $10 U.S. a time with the Library of Congress. He had made her use Albert's for her demos. Sometimes they paid two thousand bucks just for a demo. It was investment. He did not want to count the dollars. Now she had 'Drunk as a Lord' on the Country charts but even now – while everyone celebrated – he knew he would have to deal with some new tactic from Frieda. She would not let her daughter go so easily.

Mort Catchprice walked round the edge of the Big Mack truck feeling its chalky duco. It was a shitty vehicle for a Catchprice to have, an offence to anyone who cared about how a car yard should be laid out – its wheels were crooked, it dropped oil on the gravel, its front tyres were half scrubbed, and it was parked bang smack beneath the rear spotlight.

Mort's shoulders were rounded and his hands hung by his sides. He walked round the side of the old lube into the dark alleyway which led to his empty house.

Sarkis Alaverdian lay on his back in his bedroom with his arm flung out and an open copy of *Guide to Vehicle Sales at Auction This Week* on his broad bare chest. His mother tried to remove the book but he began to wake. She turned off the overhead light and knelt at the foot of the bed. Dalida Alaverdian prayed that Zorig might still be alive. She prayed that she would get a job. She prayed for Mrs Catchprice and the prosperity of Catchprice Motors.

A little after midnight Vish let himself into the Spare Parts Department, cut off the burglar alarm, and walked through the tall racks of spare parts through the car yard and up the stairs to his grandmother's apartment. She was waiting for him in the annexe, dressed formally in the suit she had worn to her husband's funeral.

'Are you game?' she asked him.

'I'm game,' he said, but he was frightened, by the suit, by the manner, but more by the realization that she had probably been standing alone in the dark here for an hour or more.

'I don't want your life ruined by this,' she said. He did not ask what 'this' was. He followed her across the creaking floors to her bedroom. 'You can go back on the milk train when it's done.'

In the half-dark bedroom she knelt in front of her old mirrored armoire.

'Gran what are we doing?' he said.

From the armoire floor she produced shoes, slippers and a pair of men's pyjamas.

'Do I have to explain it to you?' Granny Catchprice asked. Her mood was odd, more hostile than her words suggested. She threw the slippers and pyjamas into the corner. She pulled out a roll of something like electrical wire, striped red and white.

'Well yes,' he said, 'I think you do.'

The dog took the slippers and brought them back. It jumped up on Vish's back. He slapped its snout. The dog snarled and then retreated under the bed with the striped pyjamas. When Vish looked up he found his Granny looking at him. Her mouth was sort of slack.

'It's Vish,' he said.

'For God's sake,' she said. 'I do know who you are.'

'You said you were closing down the business if I came.'

'I know I'm just a stupid old woman, but why don't you look in front of your nose.' She nodded her head towards the open armoire door. Vish could smell camphor but all he could see inside the armoire was some item of pink underwear. 'It's at the end of your nose,' she said. She gave him an odd triumphant smirk that did not sit well with her cloudy eyes. It was the first time he ever thought her senile.

She winked at him. It felt lewd, somehow related to the ancient underwear which she now – smiling at him all the time – lifted. Underneath was a beautiful wooden crate with dovetail joints.

'I'm just a silly old woman,' she said. 'I know.'

If he had been able to pretend he did not know what he was up to, that time had passed. The word was on the box: Nobel.

'Well,' she grunted and stood, indicating that he should lift it out.

Vish had always imagined gelignite would be heavy, but when he picked up the box its lightness took him by surprise. Sawdust leaked from it like sand and gathered in the folds of his kurta.

They opened the box on Granny Catchprice's unmade bed. Its contents smelt like over-ripe papaya.

At half-past two Maria, who had dozed off in the middle of her Visualizations exercise, opened her eyes and saw Benny Catchprice standing at the foot of her bed.

At two-thirty-three, Vishnabarnu and Granny Catchprice began to lay the first charges in the structural walls of the showroom beneath her apartment. They had the main overhead lights turned off, but the lights in the yard cast a bright blue glow over their work. Granny Catchprice was on her knees at the east wall. She had a chisel and a hammer and she was looking for the place where the electrician had brought through the power cable thirty years before. Later there was a rat hole there – she remembered it.

'How are we going to get them out?' Vish said. 'I don't want to murder anyone.'

'There'll be no trouble getting them out. By jove,' she laughed. 'You'll see them running. Here give me that stick.'

The rat hole had been plugged with mortar and paper. A bodgey job, but now it made a perfect place to pack the gelly.

'You'll get the blame,' he said. 'They'll know it's you.'

Of course – he looked like Cacka. She always knew that. It struck her in a different way tonight – when he repeated back to her things she had already told him. That was Cacka all over.

'Blame me,' she said. She cleared the mess from the hole with the chisel and jammed the gelignite without any concern for the ancient material's stability. 'Blame me. It's mine, that's what they forget. It was my idea. It's mine to do with what I like.'

'Gran, I think you sold your shares.'

'One thing I learnt in life, you'll always find people to tell you you can't do what you want to do.' She wiped her sticky hands on her suit jacket. 'Help me up. My knees hurt.'

She found another hole against the skirting board but it was not substantial. The gelly would have done nothing more than blow the skirting board off.

'You're going to have to go down under the floor,' she told him. He had that square head and those lips. 'The bricks are old hand-made ones, so they're soft,' she said.

'Gran, do you really mean to be this drastic?'

'It's not hard, you can knock a brick out with a hammer. What you've got to do is pack it tight.'

'How do you know they won't get hurt?'

'They won't be there,' his Gran said. 'We'll tell them and they'll leave.'

'They'll call the police,' Vish said.

'Police!' she said, and clipped him around the ears.

She was thinking of Cacka.

'Please, no,' Vish said. 'Maybe this is not such a great idea.'

'You coward,' she said, hitting him again. She shocked herself with the strength of her blow, the pleasure of it. She pulled up the trap door beside the salesman's office. She gave him the flashlight. 'You leave the police to me. I never have a problem with police,' she said. 'You get down there, filth. I want a stick every three feet, and when you've done that you come back to me and I'll teach you how to use the crimping pliers.'

She sat down then in the swivel chair behind the Commodore brochures. She lit a Salem and drew a long rasping line of smoke down deep into her lungs. She closed her eyes and opened her mouth and let the smoke just waft away. *The dragon lady.* She grinned. Perhaps she was too angry to be actually happy and yet a certain amount of anger or irritation had never been incompatible with Frieda McClusky's happiness. Revenge, retribution – these were pepper, curry. She smoked her Salem in long deep drafts and enjoyed the slow abrasive feeling. *I'm not dead yet*. She had been duped, yes, but she was alive and he was dead. She had a plan. She was always the one with the plan.

I know I'm just a stupid old lady . . .

To call it a 'plan' was to diminish it. Once she would have done that. *I'm just a silly woman*. This was not a plan. It was a vision, the same one, the only one – a flower farm on the site of Catchprice Motors. *Do you think that it's impractical?* Irises, roses, petunias, long rows running parallel to the railway line and right across to Loftus Street. Propane trucks and concrete trucks bounced beside them, but in the centre of the farm there was just the smell of humus, of roses and the rich over-ripe smell of blood and bone.

In this garden Cacka did not exist. Her children had not been born.

57

As Maria Takis entered the cellar, Benny Catchprice remained behind her with his shot gun pushing into the base of her spine. He had already cut her cheek with it, and it did not even occur to her to plead with him.

It was like a subway tunnel in here. She could smell her death in the stink of the water. Even while she had fought to stop his grandmother being committed, all this – the innards of Catchprice Motors – had been here, underneath her feet. She did not see her name written on the wall, but in any case she did not understand the parts or what they did – the snakes in bottles, the cords tied with plastic, the writing on the wall, the ugly white fibreglass board with its straps and buckles. How could you ever understand it? It was like some creature run over on the road. The rough-sawn barrel grabbed and tore at her dress.

Benny saw the thing he had made: belts, buckles, trusses. He knew already that it was wrong. He had built it for her but he had not thought of how she was. He said he was going to fuck her. He did not want to fuck her, not at all. On the other hand: this was his course. He had visualized it, committed to it. He was going down this road at 200Ks. No way could he turn around.

Maria felt the beginning of another period pain. It was only now she realized these must be contractions. They were coming every five minutes or so. The pain tightened in her gut – this one made it hard to breathe. Through the pain she heard Benny Catchprice: 'This is where I come from,' he said. 'This is where I live.' He was whining. When he whined, he seemed softer, blond and pink-cheeked, baby-skinned, but he was not softer. The whining was joined to the anger, the anger was joined to the gas-jet eyes that threatened her and tore at her with the barbed steel of the shot gun barrel. 'I know you wouldn't ask a human being to live here. But you just walked away and left me here.'

The pain in her womb was like a great fist clenching. If it had been within her power she would have squashed him like a cockroach.

As the pain began to leave her, he moved round her and sat in front of her on the sofa. He balanced the gun on his knee while he began to take his shoes off.

'I like you,' Benny said, looking up from unlacing. He was taking one step at a time. He should tell her get her clothes off, but he did not want to. He did not have a fucking hard-on yet. He took his shoes off slowly, as slowly as he could manage it. 'You tried to run away from me, but I still like you.'

Maria thought he had pretty, slippery lips and dangerous, senti-mental eyes. She saw a teenage boy beset with lust and shyness – they were squashed in together like buckshot into chewing gum. He probably did not even know himself what cruelty he was ca-pable of.

'I won't run away,' she said.

'Bullshit,' he shouted. He liked to shout. He liked to feel his voice fill up the room. He scared himself at the thought of what crazy thing he might next do. When he shouted at Cathy she always, finally, collapsed before him. Her face would turn from hard to sorry.

Maria flinched when he shouted, but then the face just hardened. You could see it set into place. He saw her eyes becoming dark and hostile. He could not let her stay like this.

'You don't like me,' he said. He wanted to be friends with her. He wanted her to stroke his hair, maybe, kiss him on his eyes, that sort of thing. Not fuck, not unless she made him. Most of all he wanted her to smile at him. He was trying to find a way back to the place where that might just be possible.

She watched him pout. She watched in chilly fascination as he pulled off his thin black socks, and rolled them up one-handed.

'It's dirty here,' he said. 'I'm sorry about that part of it.' She noticed that his hands were trembling. He rubbed his heels and soles with his hands. He gave the impression of being fine and pretty, but his feet were big, netted with the red chain-mail imprint of his socks. 'I didn't want it to be dirty.'

Her mouth was dry. She thought of all the 'useful tips' in birth class, how you should take a spray pack of Evian water and a sponge to suck.

'I wanted it to be clean.'

Now he was removing the trousers, with one hand, holding the shot gun with the other. He had shiny hairless legs like a girl.

'This isn't what you want,' she said. 'You don't do this to someone you like.'

'Shut *up*,' he said. 'You don't even know what I'm going to do to you.'

'This isn't what you want,' she repeated.

'Shut up,' he screamed. 'I'm the one in charge.'

Her eyes just seemed to narrow. When he saw her go like this, he knew he would have to make her cry.

'Don't tell me what I want,' he said. 'I know what I want.'

He would have to make her soft.

She said it again: 'This isn't what you want.'

'You don't get it,' he said. 'I *visualized* what is happening now. I *committed*. With a witness. Everything I commit to, I do. This is why I am a success.'

'You committed? You made an affirmation, is that what you mean? You sent away for the tape?' She stepped towards him. He pushed back at her with the gun. 'You paid five hundred dollars?' she said.

'You think I can't afford it?'

Oh dear God, I am part of Benny Catchprice's affirmation.

'Benny, am I your objective?'

'Mind your own business. How do you know about this stuff?'

'What was your Desire?'

'You bitch. Don't you do this. Don't you steal my stuff.'

'I was your Desire?'

'I am an angel. I'm a fucking angel now.' He was standing and shouting. She had all her clothes on. He was almost fucking starkers. 'I am an angel.' He screamed at her. It was his mad act. He was a demon. He made himself dribble. 'Ask me what angel I am.' He had the gun up, pointed at her head.

Maria Takis knew she would have to die. Another contraction was here already, so soon. She felt the pain coming into the dark cloud of her present terror.

Benny Catchprice was still yelling: 'Ask me! Ask me!'

She managed to say: 'What angel are you?'

'Angel of lust,' he said. He licked his lips. 'Angel of fire.'

'You're going to have to kill me,' she said. 'You know that. If you think you're going to put me on that thing, you're going to have to kill me. That means you'll kill my baby too.'

'No.' He exploded. He was a spider, a lethal creature with his long shapely hairless legs protruding from a black silk carapace. He shoved his gun forward at her face. She screwed up her face against the darkness of the barrel, but then she saw him change his mind. He lowered the gun, and slapped her face. Her head jolted sideways and she felt a searing pain down her side. He did it again, so lights exploded against the screen of her retina. She stumbled and fell. 'Don't you ever, don't you *ever* even think of it.'

On the floor, she scraped her arm across a board and found her hand in tepid water. It touched something – a bar, a rod. She grasped it. He took a step back and she clambered to her feet, holding out her weapon: a tyre lever, slimy with rust. She hardly recognized the voice that came from her throat. 'You come near me,' she shouted, 'I'll break your arm.'

She was breathing hard. The pain came again. It was a tight hard pain, so hard she could not have talked if she had wanted to.

'You don't like me,' he said. 'I like you but you don't like me. What's the matter? What's the matter?'

The matter was the pain. 'Shut up.'

'I am my word,' Benny said. 'You've got to understand that – I committed.'

Behind her she heard the door handle rattle, a light tap on the cellar door.

Thank God. Dear God please save me.

'It's me, Vish,' a voice said. 'Can I come in?'

'Piss off.'

'Benny, you got to get out.'

'I'm not getting out.'

Maria screamed through the middle of her contraction. Benny lifted the gun towards her and she swung the bar hard at him. She missed.

'You got to get out. This place is going to go sky-high.'

Maria screamed again. 'Help me!'

Benny waved the sawn-off gun at Maria Takis while he shouted at the door. 'I don't need you, you fucking sell-out, you Jesus creep.'

'I'm coming in,' said Vish.

There was no warning: the shot gun exploded and blew a splintered hole in the wooden door. Shot rattled and ricocheted around the cellar. Maria felt a hot stinging in her upper arm, her waist, her thigh, her calf.

She looked at Benny Catchprice as he walked towards the door, bleeding from the cheek. He opened the door, but there was no one there. He turned back to her.

'What do you think I am?' he said.

She did not understand the question.

'I don't want to hurt the baby,' he said.

'Shut up.' She panted. She did not want to pant. She did not want to let him know what was happening to her. But now the pain was so bad she had no choice but to pant through it. She had the iron bar. He took the gun into his right hand, but then he put it back.

'You think I'm an animal, because I live here. I wouldn't hurt your baby.'

The pain was going.

'You're doing it now,' she said. She saw it frightened him. 'You're hurting the baby right now, this minute. You're killing it.'

'No,' he shouted.

'I'm having the baby now,' she said. 'It's coming.'

She saw his face. He was a child again, undecided. His mouth opened.

'This is very serious,' she said.

'Shut up, I know.'

Maria lowered the iron bar. 'You get me out of here right now,' she said. 'You can save this baby if you want to.'

Thursday

58

Vish's arm was like a run-over cat. It did not hurt. He could see pieces of white among the red. He thought: bone. The red ran through the yellow robe like paint on unsized canvas. He felt the blood drip on to his foot. It felt warm, oddly pleasant.

He walked up the steps from Benny's cellar, crossed the old lube bay and went straight on up the stairs to Cathy's flat. He banged on the door and walked right on in. He was hollering even going across the kitchen. 'Get out,' he said. 'She's going to do it.'

He turned on the lights in their bedroom. They had no air-conditioning on account of Howie's asthma. They were lying on top of the sheets. Howie was bright purple across his chest. He had a fat ugly penis with a ragged uncircumcised foreskin. Cathy was wearing an outsize T-shirt with 'Cotton Country' written on it.

'Come on,' he said. 'Sorry.' He meant there was blood dripping on their shag pile carpet.

'What's happened?' Howie asked. He was fishing in the drawer for his underpants. His back was white. He had no arse to talk of.

'Hurry,' Vish said.

He shepherded them through their kitchen. There were big splashes from his arm across the floor. 'She's crazy. She's blowing us all up.'

'What did she do to you?' Cathy said. She was looking at his arm. She thought Gran had hurt his arm. She wanted to tie a bandage but he pushed her away with his good arm.

'Run,' he said. 'The fuses are burning.'

This was not true.

Howie had underpants on. Cathy's shirt came to her knees. They came down the stairs to the lube bay and hippety hopped across the bright-lit gravel like people walking barefoot from their car to a beach.

Granny was at the bottom of her fire escape still holding the roll of safety fuse.

'There she is,' he shouted.

He shouted not for them, but for her. He was trying to signal

Granny Catchprice that the plan had got to change now. Howie and Cathy ran towards her. Then Howie was holding Gran. He was taking the safety fuse from her. Cathy and Howie had already stepped over a two-metre length of it at the bottom of their stairs without noticing. It was bright red and white and striped like a barber's pole but they did not see it. There were other pieces, one, two, three metres, sticking out from the air vents at the base of the workshop and the showroom walls. Each one ran into the cob-webbed underfloor, where it was crimped tight inside a detonator. Each detonator, in turn, was jammed into a clammy half stick of gelignite. The gelignite was wedged in among the crumbling brick piers which supported the building.

While Cathy and Howie shouted at Granny Catchprice, Vish stooped to light a fuse. He had not been able to get gelignite below the ground at the old lube bay. There was no sub-floor – only cellar. He had to pack it into the drainpipes which ran beneath the con-crete slab. He lit the fuse the way his Grandma had taught him, holding the match tight against the fuse and scraping the box across it. He chanted as he scraped. Hare Krishna, Hare Krishna. The fuse did not sparkle like a fuse in a cartoon. You could hardly see a flame at all. The fire slipped down into the tunnel of fuse casing. It made an occasional spark, a fart of blue smoke, a tiny heat bubble. It sneaked off like a spy, travelling 30 centimeters every ten seconds.

Vish thought he might die. He thought about God. Hare Krishna, Hare Krishna, running through this gravel-floored hell of bright painted things.

Howie and Cathy were pushing Granny back towards the fire escape. He hollered to them, 'No, she lit them off already,' and then he remembered he was not thinking of God, he must think of God, that all that was necessary was to think of God.

He prayed Benny would be safe. He was in the cellar with some woman. He did not know he would be safe. How could he know?

Cathy and Howie were now walking towards him. They had left Granny Catchprice standing alone at the bottom of the fire escape. Cathy had seen the plume of blue smoke coming from a fuse. She was pointing at it, stamping at it.

'It was her,' he pointed back at Granny Catchprice. Hare Krishna, Hare Krishna. 'She's crazy.'

Behind Cathy and Howie's shouting faces he could see his grandmother in her severe black suit. She had walked across the car yard to the workshop wall. She was working her way along the side of the wall, stooping, like a gardener weeding. She was lighting fuses. She had damp matches from her kitchen. Sometimes, he could see, these slowed her down.

Howie was panting and shouting at him. It was a moment before he saw what he wanted – the matches.

He pointed across the yard at Granny Catchprice. 'It's her,' he said. He handed Howie the matches. 'I took them off her, the crazy bitch. There she goes again.'

Hare Krishna, Hare Krishna. Not die. Not go to jail.

'Where's Benny?' Cathy yelled.

'You can't go down there,' he said. 'You'll get blown up.'

She tried to. She ran for the steps.

Howie grabbed Cathy. She had no underpants. He picked her up and carried her bare-arsed across the yard. She struggled and hit his head.

'Mort,' she called. 'What about Mort?'

'He's O.K.,' Vish said. He did not know he was O.K. He had fucked it up. He had changed the plan. It was Benny's fault. He had tried to murder him. It was Krishna who came to punish the people who hurt the followers of Krishna.

Vish walked slowly across the yard. He felt heat like a furnace in his wounded arm. He did not hurry. The Lord would decide when it ignited.

He had reached the front gate when the first explosion came. It spat out bricks and showered them over the cars. They rained down, bang, bang, bang.

He turned and saw a hole, like a tunnel, in the wall of Spare Parts. Nothing more. Granny Catchprice was fumbling with her matches at the Front Office. Then the next one went. It made a deeper 'crump' you could feel in your feet, in the earth. When Vish turned to look, he found the wall of the workshop was missing. The yard lights shone into the dusty rafters. A brush-tailed possum stood on the great iron beam above Mort's desk. Its eyes shone bright yellow through the mortar dust.

Then many things happened at once. Vish lay down on the ground and felt it move beneath him. He put his head under the Audi radiator. There was some fire, flame. He felt the heat in his bare legs and saw the orange light across the gravel. There was a 'Whoomf' noise.

It was then he thought about the petrol tanks beneath the cracked concrete at the front of the front office.

He stood up and started running towards the street.

59

Howie raised himself from the ground beside his wife. The yard was filled with lime dust and petrol fumes. The lights stood on their tall poles, sloping, twisted on their stems like Iceland poppies. Granny Catchprice, dressed in a tattered black, white and red clown's suit, moved into their beam, dust still swirling all round her.

The old chook could walk through hell.

As she turned, she looked as though she came from hell: she had put on a mask, like a witch with long, carved, wooden teeth. She stopped to pick a lump of brick from the bonnet of the Commodore. It was too heavy for her. She pushed it off, scraped it across the duco, down the slope of the bonnet and on to the ground.

Cathy was sitting on the gravel beside him. She said: 'I got no pants.'

Howie helped her to her feet. She tugged down on her T-shirt, more worried about her arse than everything around her. He put his arm round her shoulders and felt she was shaking like a leaf.

'Come on, honey,' he said. 'Come on baby, it's O.K.' He walked her towards the street, towards Granny Catchprice who was now pushing at a clump of bricks which had fallen on the Audi's sleek black hood.

'I need a dress,' Cathy said. 'Where are my shoes?'

'I'll get the truck out,' he said. 'All the gear is in the truck. Once we get the truck out we're O.K.'

It was then he saw the flowers on the gravel, a line of them from the crumpled Spare Parts Department wall to the buckled Cyclone gates, splashes the size of carnations. They fell from Granny Catchprice's face – fat drops of bright blood.

There was a noise like a calf bellowing. Howie turned to see a black track-suited figure running over the rubble of what had been their apartment. The noise was Mort. A figure in yellow robes was also stumbling towards them. The noise was Vish. They were both the noise, coming towards Granny Catchprice. She recognized the noise and turned. It was then Howie saw how badly hurt she was – the gelignite had ripped her face back to the bone, up from the gums and teeth to the nose. In the middle of this destruction, her eyes looked out like frightened things buried beneath a muddy field.

'He touched her breasts,' she said.

Howie put his hand around beneath her ribs to steady her. There was nothing to her – rag and bone. As he lay her down upon the gravel, she trembled and whimpered. It seemed too cruel to lay her head upon the gravel. He placed his hand beneath her for a pillow and squatted down beside her.

'It's O.K., Frieda,' he said.

'Rot!' she said.

Howie felt himself pushed aside. It was Cathy, Mort, Vish – the Catchprices. They pushed him out like foreign matter. Cathy took her mother's head and cradled it. Mort held her hand. They made a clump, a mass, they clung to her, like piglets at an old sow.

'Come on, honey,' he pulled at his wife's shoulder. 'Come on.' But they made a heap of bodies which left no room for him.

Howie walked back to the Big Mack truck alone. The engine was new and tight, but it started first off. He threw the long stick back into reverse, and edged the truck back until he felt resistance. Then he squeezed it forward, manoeuvring between the dust silver Statesman with black leather upholstery and the Commodore S.S. with the alloy wheels. It was a tight fit. He edged slowly past the red Barina Benny nearly sold to Gino Massaro.

But when he came to the Audi, he knew there was no longer room. He felt the resistance as the truck tray caught the Audi's right-hand rear guard, nothing definite, but soft, like a sweater snagged in a barbed wire fence. He increased the pressure on the accelerator just a little. There was a drag, a soft ripping sensation. He knew he was cutting it like a can opener.

'Sweet Jesus,' he said. It felt as good as shitting.

It only made a small noise, a screee. The diff caught momentarily on a pile of bricks but the old Dodge lifted, lurched and rolled on like a tank, out across the crumpled Cyclone fence and arrived, its front tyre hissing, out on to the street.

60

There was this noise in the dark: huh-huh-huh. It came and went. She would do it for a minute. She would stop for a minute. Huh-huh-huh. Benny had Cacka's hurricane lamp. He had that almost from the moment the lights went, but the problem was the matches. He found cigarettes but no matches and he had spent half an hour standing on tip-toe slowly working his way up and down the low rafters of the ceiling looking for the book of porno matches Mort had brought from the bar in Bangkok.

When he came close she struck out at him with the iron bar. It was pitch black. She could have killed him. He never found the porno matches. They were probably in her corner. He found instead an old box of Redheads still above the door frame. He struck the match, raised the sooty glass, and lit the wick. Maria Takis was standing by the work bench, her hands pushed against the wall making a noise like a dog.

'Vishna-fucking-barnu,' he said. 'The fucking turd.'

She stared at him. She made this noise: Huh-huh-huh-huh.

'Don't think you're getting out of this,' he said. 'This alters nothing.'

He came towards her. She held up the iron bar. She had muscled legs like a tennis player. She had them tensed, apart, her back against the wall. Her face was red, veins standing out. She looked so ugly he could not believe it was the same person. Huh-huh-huh, she said. A witch.

Then she stopped making the noise. She stood straighter and tried to lick her lips. 'Get me something clean,' she said.

'There's nothing clean,' he said. 'This is where I live.'

'That.'

First he thought she meant him. She wanted him. She had her hand out towards his cock, his belly. He stepped back. She was pointing at his shirt. He could not believe it. He could not fucking *believe* it.

'Get fucked,' he said.

'Please.'

'It's my shirt.'

'It's clean.'

'You shouldn't get me mad,' he said. 'Not now. You understand?'

he shouted at her. 'You see what has happened? The jealous cunt blew up my *career*. He didn't want it, so he killed it for me.'

She reached out her hand to grab at the shirt. He grabbed at her wrist but she brought the iron bar down with her other hand. The bar crashed down on to the work bench.

He saw then that she was crazy. Her eyes were so hard and dark, he could not look at them.

'Come on,' he said. 'This is my *shirt*.'

'Huh-huh-huh.' Her face was going red again. Tendons stretched down her neck. She started hunching up her shoulder and putting her arm inside her dress, and then she stayed there: 'Huh-huh-huh.'

He went back to the doorway and looked at the rubble. He pulled out a brick, but it was hopeless. There was concrete and steel reinforcing rod twisted in together. When he turned back he saw she had stepped out of the dress, and lifted it up high as if it might get soiled just touching anything that belonged here. She had an industrial strength bra with white straps. He was shocked by how her stomach stretched, by the ragged brown line down her middle, by the size of everything, the muscles in her legs, the redness of her face. She had buckshot wounds in her arms and thighs. She was trying to spread her dress across his couch with one hand, but the dress was too small and would not stay still. She held it out to him.

'Cut it,' she said.

'Fuck you,' he said.

'Just do it,' she screamed. 'Cut the fucking dress down the side.'

'Fuck you,' he said, 'I'm not your servant.'

'You want this baby to die,' she said. 'You want to kill this baby too.'

She knew he could not stand her saying that. 'Don't you say that,' he said. 'You don't know a thing about me. You think I'm some creep because I live down here.'

'If you're not a creep, what are you?'

'Angel,' he yelled. 'I told you.'

She stared at him, her eyes wide.

'I am a fucking angel.'

They were looking at each other, a metre apart. She had the iron bar in her hand, dressed in pale blue knickers and a white bra.

'Huh-huh-huh.' She hunkered down. She held the bar up. There was a vein on her forehead like a great blue worm.

'This baby needs a hospital, and doctors,' she gasped. 'If we keep it here it'll choke on its cord. It'll be your fault.'

'Why would I kill a baby? I am an angel.'

'Sure,' she said.

'I changed myself,' he said. 'It's possible.'

'See,' she said. She looked him in the eye. 'Now you're going to shoot it.'

'Don't *say* that, I'm warning you. Don't *say* that.'

'Huh-huh-huh-huh-huh-huh.' She held the bar in both hands. She stepped back, leaned against the wall. 'Huh-huh-huh.'

Water and blood gushed out from between her legs, passed through her blue knickers as if they were not even there.

'Shit,' he said.

'Huh-huh-huh.'

He went to the door again, but it was useless. He dirtied his shirt.

Behind him, the Tax Inspector was hollering.

'Huh-huh-huh.'

Up in the street he thought he could hear sirens, he was not sure.

'Huh-huh-huh.'

She was backed against the wall, all her pants soaked with blood and water, dripping.

He turned back to the bricks. You could see pale daylight but the stairs were jammed with a mass of masonry and steel.

'I didn't do this,' he said. 'This is not my fault. All it was: I liked you. You never listened to me. I never wanted to do nothing *wrong.*'

Then she started hollering again. He could not bear it. She was shrieking like he was murdering her.

'What do I do?' he said. 'I'll help you. Tell me what to do.'

She did not talk. Her eyes were so wide in her head he thought they were going to pop out. Then she calmed down.

'Cut up my dress. We need a clean surface.' He had razor blades in the old coke stash. He had gaffer tape on the bench. He sliced open her dress and stuck it to the couch with gaffer tape.

'Now – your shirt.'

'No.'

'We don't need to cut it.'

'Forget it.'

'It's coming. It's too soon. It's coming. Help me down.'

He helped her. He put his arm around her. It was the second time he touched her, ever. She was dead heavy, a sack of spuds. He helped her towards the couch.

'Oh Jesus,' she said, 'oh fuck, oh shit, oh Christ, oh no.'

'Are you O.K.?'

'Oh no,' she screamed. 'Oh noooo . . .'

This time he knew she was dying. It was terrible. It was worse than anything he could imagine.

'Here,' he said. 'It's O.K.' He took off his coat. He put it under her. It was terrible there, in her private parts. He was frightened to look at the hole. It was like an animal. It was opening. Something was pushing.

'I won't hurt you,' he said. 'I never meant to hurt you.'

'Shut up,' she screamed again. 'No.'

He could see the actual head, the actual baby's head. It was black and matted, pushing out from between her legs. He did not know what to do. From the noises that came out of her throat he knew she was going to die. You could see in her face she was going to die. He knelt beside her to stop her rolling off the couch.

She screamed.

He looked. The head was out. Oh Christ. It looked like it would break off, or snap. It turned.

'Cord.'

He did not know what she meant. He was kneeling on rough bricks on his bare knees. It hurt.

She said, 'See the cord.'

He could not see anything.

'The umbilical cord,' she said, her hands scrabbling down in the bloody, slippery mess between her legs. 'Christ, check my baby's neck?'

Then he saw it. There was a white slippery thing, the cord, felt like warm squid. He touched it. It was alive. He pulled it gingerly, frightened he would rip it out or break it. He could feel a life in it, like the life in a fresh caught fish, but warm, hot even, like a piece of rabbit gut. He looped it back over the baby's head. Then, it was as if he had untied a string – just as the cord went back, the child came out, covered in white cheese, splashed with blood. Its face squashed up like a little boxer's. It was ugly and alone. Its legs were up to its stomach and its face was screwed up. Then it cried: something so thin, such a metallic wail it cut right through to Benny's heart.

'Oh Christ,' he said.

He took off his cotton shirt. He threw his bloodied suit jacket on the floor and wrapped up the frightened baby in the shirt.

'Give him to me,' Maria said. 'Give me my baby.'

'Little Benny,' he whispered to it.

'Give me my baby.'

She was shouting now, but there had been so much shouting in his life. He knew how not to hear her. Tears were streaming down Benny's face. He did not know where they were coming from. 'He's mine,' he said.

He closed his heart against the noise. He hunched down over the baby.

'Don't worry,' he said. 'Nothing's going to hurt you.'

61

Maria felt already that she knew every part of her tormentor intimately: his thin wrists, his lumpy-knuckled fingers, his long, straight-sided, pearl-pink nails, his shiny hair with its iridescent, spiky, platinum points, his peculiar opal eyes, his red lips, real red, too red, like a boy-thief caught with plums.

He sat on the edge of the sofa, by her hip. He had one bare leg up, one out on the floor, not easily, or comfortably, but with his foot arched, like a dancer's almost, so that it was just the ball of the foot that made contact with the floor, not the floor exactly, but with a house brick balancing on the floor. He hunched his bare torso around the child and talked to it.

'Give me my baby,' Maria said again.

'Benny,' he said. 'Little Benny.'

He talked to the child, intently, tenderly, with his pretty red lips making wry knowing smiles which might, in almost any other circumstances, have been charming. He cupped and curved himself so much around her baby that she could barely see him – a crumpled blood-stained shirt, an arm, blue and cheesey, and small perfect fingers clenching. She would do anything to hold him.

She asked him once more: 'Please,' she said. 'Give him to me.

He's getting cold now. He needs me.'

But it was she who felt the coldness, the cold hurting emptiness. She stretched her arms out towards him. In the yellow smoke-streaked light of the hurricane lamp, Benny Catchprice's naked skin was the colour of old paper. When her fingers touched him, he flinched, and moved so far down the sofa that the umbilical cord stretched up tight towards him.

'Please. He's cold. Give him to me.'

But he was like a man deaf to women, a sorcerer laying spells. He was murmuring to the baby.

'Give him to me,' she said. 'I'll do what you want.'

He looked up at her and grinned. It was then, as he twisted slightly in his seat, Maria finally saw her baby's face. She thought: *of course*. There were her mother's eyes, bright, dark, curious, undisappointed.

'My baby.' She sobbed, just once, something from the stomach. She held out her empty, cold arms towards the little olive-skinned boy.

Her captor turned away and the baby's bright round face was hidden once again. She could not bear it. She reached out and touched Benny's forearm. 'You want to do it to me, do it to me.'

'Come *on*,' he said incredulously.

He pulled away. It hurt her.

'Please,' she said. The tug on the cord either triggered or coincided with a contraction. She knew the placenta would be delivered and soon, any minute, there would be nothing to join her to the child.

'They lose body heat so fast, Benny, please.' That caught him. He actually looked at her. 'Give him to me.' She held out her arms. 'I'll find you a really nice place to live. Would you like that? I'll get you out of here.'

He began to smile, a bully's smile she thought.

'Just give him to me, I'll pay you,' she said. 'I'll give you money.' She felt close to panic. She must not panic. She must be clear. She tried to think what she might offer him.

'Two thousand dollars,' she said.

'Shush,' he said. 'Don't be stupid.'

'Don't shush me,' she snapped.

He laughed, and kept on laughing until there were tears in his eyes. She had no idea that he was as near as he had ever been to love. She saw only some pretty, blond-haired, Aussie surfer boy. 'Oh, shush.'

On the floor beside his foot, next to his shoes, she could see the shot gun. He had placed it on a garbage bag on top of a plank. It was only as she thought how she might edge towards the ugly thing that she realized she still had the rusty iron bar beside her on the couch, had had it there all the time.

'Shushy shush,' he said to the baby. 'Oh shush-shush-shush.' All her baby's brain was filled with Benny Catchprice's face.

Maria lifted the iron bar like a tennis racket above her head. She saw herself do this from a distance, from somewhere among the cobweb rafters. She saw her ringless hands, the rusty bar.

'Give him to me,' she said. Her voice, scratchy with fear, was almost unrecognizable.

Benny looked up at her and smiled and shook his head.

How could this be me?

She brought down the bar towards his shoulder blade. She brought it down strong enough to break it, but he ducked. He ducked in under and she got him full across the front of the skull. It was a dull soft sound it made. The force jolted him forward. All she felt was *still, be still*, and yet when he turned to look at her, nothing seemed different afterwards from before.

I have to hit him again.

Benny held the baby on his left side, against his hip. He did not have the head held properly. He lifted his right hand up to his own head and when he brought it away it was marked with a small red spot of blood. He actually smiled at her.

'Abortion!' He shook his head. His eyes wandered for a moment, then regained their focus. 'You're such a bullshitter, Maria.'

Maria's legs were trembling uncontrollably. 'I'll kill you,' she said. She picked up the iron bar high again. Her arms were like jelly.

'You're the real thing,' he said. 'I knew that when I saw you.' A dribble of bright blood ran from his hairline down on to his nose. He nodded his head with emphasis. Then slowly, like a boy clowning at a swimming pool, he began to tilt forward. His eyes rolled backwards in his head. He held out the child towards her.

'Take,' he said.

As Benny Catchprice fell, the child was passed between them – Maria slid her arms in under the slippery little body and brought it to her, pressing it against her, shuddering. Benny hit the floor. He made a noise like timber falling in a stack. Maria put her hand behind the damp warm head. She could feel lips sucking at her neck. She brought her arms, her bones, her skin, between her baby and her victim.

It was then, as Benny lay amid the planks and bricks with his bare arm half submerged in puddled seepage, she saw his tattooed back for the first time. At first she thought it was a serpent – red, blue, green, scales, something creepy living in a broken bottle or underneath a rock. Then she saw it was not a serpent but an angel, or half an angel – a single wing tattooed on his smooth, boy's skin – it was long and delicate and it ran from his shoulder to his buttock – an angel wing. It was red, blue, green, luminous, trembling, like a dragon fly, like something smashed against the windscreen of a speeding car.

She took her little boy, warm, squirming, still slippery as a fish, and unfastened her bra, and tucked him in against her skin.